Compelled

Inge-Lise Goss

Olivebranch Press

Dedicated to my daughter, Nicole

ACKNOWLEDGMENTS

My gratitude goes out to my outstanding editors, Jeff LaFerney and Nancy Buford. Their comments and edits greatly improved my story and helped me become a better writer. I also want to thank my early readers—Nicole Varela and Marsha Coons, who read very rough drafts and never complained. I am especially grateful to my husband, Peter, for always giving me encouraging words. I wish to extend a thank you to Ernest Walwyn and Debbie Prince, members of the Rainbow Writers Group, for their professional critiques of my work. I want to give a special thanks to C. Michelle McCarty who generously gave suggestions and edits to help enhance the story. Last, but not least, I'd like to thank Lee Helfrich for so freely giving her time to answer my legal questions and Ashley Fontainne for designing the book's stunning cover.

PROLOGUE

April 20th
San Diego, California

After spreading rose petals from the patio door to the hot tub, Mara slipped out of her black silk robe and eased her naked body into the warm water. She gazed around the dimly lit, secluded yard, surrounded by an eight-foot cedar fence covered with lush green vines. Her eyes dropped to the bottle of Champagne that tilted in the ice bucket next to a tray filled with sausage-stuffed mushrooms, Aden's favorite appetizer. She caught a glimpse of the MP-3 player and quickly climbed out of the hot tub to switch on soft, romantic music.

Stepping back into the water, she smiled to herself, thinking everything looked perfect for her husband, Aden, whom she hadn't seen for almost two months. She anticipated hearing his taxi stop out front any minute and envisioned him going through the house and out the patio door into her waiting arms. Then they could make up for lost time. Mara had left their two children with her parents in Los Angeles, the place they had planned he'd join them the next day to celebrate her grandfather's ninetieth birthday. She had been there all week, helping with the arrangements. Not wanting to wait one more day to see Aden, she had driven home to spend a night alone with him without any interruptions.

She leaned back and closed her eyes, thinking about all the harsh words she had thrown at him when he told her about his infidelity with Kate, one of his co-workers. He claimed it happened only once. Whatever that relationship was, he swore he had ended it. Mara cringed, recalling the way she had carried on after learning about the affair—charging into his office to confront Kate, yelling and screaming. She'd never forget the shocked expression on Aden's face. Apparently, he had expected tears when he confessed, not the rage that consumed her. Right before Aden left for his work assignment in Brazil, Kate moved out of state. Mara had a hard time shaking the vision of Kate in Aden's arms, yet she was determined not to let it spoil their first night together after such a long separation.

The creaking sound of the side gate opening startled Mara. She sat straight up, wondering why Aden hadn't gone into the house. She sighed, thinking he had probably lost his key again and felt disappointed he would miss the trail of roses leading to her and the scrumptious aroma of prime rib, garlic potatoes, and crescent rolls keeping warm in the oven.

Excitement began building up inside her as she waited breathlessly for him to emerge through the dark shadows at the side of the house.

"Oh, it's you," she said, pursing her lips, disappointed the man walking toward her wasn't her husband. "Aden's not home yet."

"Wasn't Aden picking you up tomorrow at your folks' place?"

"I came home early to surprise him." Mara reached for her robe and wrapped it around her, allowing the bottom of it to float in the water as she climbed out of the hot tub. "Whatever you need to talk to him about, can it wait until tomorrow?"

"No," the familiar intruder replied with a stern expression.

Mara noticed gloves on his hands and something shiny clutched in his fist. Aden's co-worker seemed edgy. As her eyes fixed on the tightly held object, he slid his hand behind his back. "What's wrong?" she asked, feeling an uneasy sensation churning in her stomach.

The sound of a car engine and tires crunching on the driveway filtered into the backyard.

The visitor briefly glanced over his shoulder, and then his eyes returned to Mara. With a trembling hand, he raised the pistol and pulled the trigger. "You weren't supposed to be here," he whispered.

The bullet struck her in the chest before she could scream. Blood oozed from the wound. Her last thoughts were about Aden, the man she would love forever.

Chapter 1

Pain shot into Sidney's chest. Gritting her teeth, she sucked in air, clenched her arms over her body, and felt every muscle in her chest tightening. She moaned as the pain intensified.

Chas flipped on the light. Seeing his wife's face contorted in agony, his eyes pinched with worry as he caressed her arm. "What's wrong?"

Beads of sweat lined her forehead. Gasping for air, she guessed, "A heart attack."

Chas grabbed the phone and punched 9-1-1.

As soon as a woman answered, Chas blurted out, "My wife's having a heart attack! Hurry, send an ambulance." Then he gave the address.

"Get her to swallow an aspirin," the woman said. "An ambulance has been dispatched. It'll be there within five minutes."

Chas disconnected, looked at Sidney doubled over in pain with tears streaming down her face, and leapt out of bed. He rushed to the bathroom, pulled the aspirin bottle from the medicine cabinet, and snatched the bottle of water sitting on the counter.

"Honey, take this," he said, gently raising her chin.

Her lips trembled as she pushed the pill into her mouth and forced it down with a gulp of water.

Perspiration poured down Sidney's sides, and her nightgown clung to her body as Chas carefully laid her head back onto the pillow. She briefly closed her eyes and pressed her lips together while the pain continued wracking through her chest.

Brushing sweat-soaked strands of hair from her face, he said, "The ambulance is on its way." He took a handful of tissues and dabbed her cheeks as he silently prayed she'd be okay.

Shortly after midnight, Chas held Sidney's hand while the paramedics wheeled her into the emergency room. He felt relieved that the sedative drip had suppressed the pain, but it had also left her only semi-conscious. The paramedics had told him in the ambulance all of her vital signs—heart rate, blood pressure, temperature, respiration—seemed normal. From the way his wife's body twitched in pain, he couldn't understand how that was possible and suspected one or both paramedics didn't know what they were doing. As a New York Assistant DA, he was suspicious of everything that didn't seem right.

A heavyset man with thinning, disheveled gray hair and wearing heavy, black-rimmed glasses and a white lab coat approached the gurney. He stuck out his hand. "Mr. Langston, I'm Dr. Nielsen," he said, shaking Chas's hand. "I'll be taking care of your wife. While the paramedics transported her here, they filled me in on her condition. We're going to start by running a series of tests to determine what is causing the pain." He turned toward a short, auburn-haired younger man also wearing a white lab coat. "We need to take her to the lab on the second floor."

The man nodded, and with the help of a nurse began pushing the gurney toward the elevator.

"May I go with her?" Chas asked, not wanting to let Sidney out of his sight.

"I'm afraid that won't be possible. We'll bring her back to the emergency room when we've completed the tests." Dr. Nielsen gestured toward a draped-off area.

Chas watched as Dr. Nielsen followed the gurney into the elevator. He sat down in a chair next to the nurse's station, stared at the floor, and gripped his hands together until he was instructed to go to the waiting room.

At 1:15 a.m., he stepped into a large, pale-gray waiting room with windows covering the far wall, giving all the visitors a view of a well-lit parking lot. That wasn't anything he wanted to see, nor did he want to interact with the six people leaning back in their chairs with their eyes glued to the television screen hanging on the wall next to him. Chas eased down into the chair farthest away from the other people and picked up a magazine. He thumbed through it and attempted to read an article about endangered species, but visions of Sidney wrenching in pain kept churning in his mind.

Laying the magazine down, his eyes drifted to the emergency room's doors, hoping whatever was wrong with Sidney wasn't serious. He placed an elbow on the chair's armrest and scratched his forehead as he tried to recall the last time Sidney had been sick, but all that popped into his head was a cold several years before.

When a nurse walked into the waiting room with her face drawn and creased with concern, he assumed she was coming for him. Figuring she wasn't going to deliver good news, he held his breath, sat up straight, and swallowed hard. He inhaled deeply as she stopped in front of an elderly couple. Chas watched her escort them through the doors leading to the emergency room. Twenty minutes later, the door opened again, and the couple trudged out. With the man's arm around the woman and her head buried in his shoulder, they went toward the hospital exit.

Chas's brow wrinkled and his palms became moist. He thought about Sidney's daily exercise routine and her last physical which had been only a few months before. His eyes dropped to the tile floor. *Why didn't the doctor catch anything then?*

"Mr. Langston?" asked a nurse standing next to him.

His mind had been so preoccupied with Sidney that he hadn't even heard the nurse's footsteps approaching him.

She went on. "Dr. Nielsen would like to talk to you."

"My wife?" he asked in an anxious tone.

"She's resting comfortably."

Chas sighed with relief and rose to his feet. He followed the nurse down the hall, through a set of double doors, and into Dr. Nielsen's office. The doctor was leaning over a large, light oak desk and writing on a notepad.

Glancing up, Nielsen motioned Chas to take a seat in a dark green, padded chair that faced the desk. "I'll be just a minute," he said as he continued scribbling.

Chas sat and scanned the comfortably furnished office. He

noticed the diplomas and licenses adorning one wall. His eyes fixed on them. He discovered Dr. Nielsen was a heart surgeon. He was surprised that a doctor with those credentials would have ER duty.

Dr. Nielsen laid down his pen and looked up. "Mr. Langston, based on all the test results currently, we haven't been able to determine the reason for your wife's discomfort."

"Discomfort?" Chas repeated tersely. "She was in severe pain, and you're calling it *discomfort?*"

"I'm sorry. It's been a long day. Let me rephrase that. At this point, none of the tests I have put your wife through indicate a physical problem."

"What's that supposed to mean?" Chas said through gritted teeth.

"Mr. Langston, because of your wife's painful cries and her twitching body, she has been kept sedated since she arrived at the hospital. I've compared the test results from her physical three months ago to our results. Nothing has changed. I'm having some additional blood work done so we don't overlook anything. Right now, she's sleeping soundly and will probably stay that way until mid-morning. I've had her admitted to the hospital, and my colleague, Dr. Harris, will be handling her case."

Chas nervously tapped his fingertips together. He felt relieved that Sidney hadn't suffered a heart attack, but at the same time, he couldn't swallow the notion that his beautiful, physically fit wife— who had only sucked in air when a stupid repairman accidentally shot a nail into her foot last summer—could groan and whimper in pain if nothing were wrong with her. "So before all the results are in, you're just turning my wife over to someone else?" he asked in a cold and irritated tone as he narrowed his eyes.

"I happened to be in the hospital when the call came in that a woman with a heart problem was on her way here," Nielsen explained. "I can assure you now, nothing is wrong with your wife's heart. Dr. Harris is an excellent doctor and one of the hospital's residents. He'll take good care of your wife."

Chas's shoulders sagged and his chin dropped as his mind searched for other possibilities for Sidney's condition. He suddenly recalled how upset Sidney had been over the loss of her partner, a detective she had worked with for over five years. "You mentioned something about Sidney not having a physical problem. Do you think she's having a mental breakdown?"

"Because your wife was sedated, I wasn't able to talk to her. From her file, I learned she's a detective with the Nassau County Police Department, and I'm sure that's a very stressful job. I'm not a psychiatrist, and I don't have the expertise to assess mental states." Nielson glanced at the clock—4:38 a.m. He rose to his feet. "Mr. Langston, if you have any additional questions, Dr. Harris can answer them for you. I'm sorry, but I have to leave now and try to get some shut-eye before my ten o'clock surgery."

Chas jumped up, hurried to the door, and blocked the man from being able to leave. "Dr. Nielsen, my wife—will she be in pain when she wakes up?"

"Like I mentioned earlier, we haven't been able to determine the origin of your wife's pain. It doesn't appear to be a physical problem. Given that scenario, there is a possibility she could wake up pain free." Nielsen began moving around Chas. "Now, if you'll excuse me."

Chas leaned over Sidney's bed railing, gently stroked her pale cheek, and kissed her forehead. As he sank into the chair next to the window, he felt relieved it was Saturday so he could watch over her all day. Leaning back and stretching his legs in front of him, he thought about her therapy sessions with Judy Lavin, the police department's shrink, after Matt, her partner, had been killed two months earlier right before Sidney's eyes. She'd been sitting with Matt outside a fast-food stand eating hamburgers when the thug drove up, shouted something about cops, and started shooting. Sidney had ducked under the table, yanked out her pistol, and returned the gunfire. Matt wasn't as lucky. A bullet struck him in the head before he'd had a chance to react. Neither Matt nor Sidney wore uniforms, and they drove an unmarked vehicle. How the culprit knew they were cops was still being investigated.

He pulled out his cell phone and checked for messages. One came from his boss, District Attorney Morrison. He moved into the hallway and returned the call.

"Hey, it's Chas."

"Right before seven this morning, I got a call from Fregman's attorney. Now the boy wants to plea bargain."

"Closing arguments are Monday, and he had a chance for that

earlier. What did you say?"

"Too late. Any possibility we could lose this one?"

"I doubt it. Even though the eyewitness has a blemished reputation, there're fingerprints on the murder weapon, threats, and a strong motive. What more could the jury want? But we've had other cases that I thought were going to be a slam dunk until the verdict was delivered." Chas peeked in at Sidney and saw she was still sleeping peacefully. "Tyler, Sidney's in the hospital," he began. Then he proceeded to fill him in about her condition.

Chapter 2

Bernice rested her head against the back of a pink floral, cushioned chair and meditated as she prepared for her three o'clock client. She felt worn out after being awakened in the middle of every night for the past week by a female voice screaming a man's name in her head. Being a medium, she had experienced restless nights before. All those spirits had been familiar to her from prior readings, but not this woman who wouldn't allow her a peaceful night's rest. She didn't have a clue what message this woman was trying to deliver and to whom.

A soft knock came from the side door, the door used by her clients. Bernice stood and shuttled down the hall toward it.

After her client, a gray-haired woman in her early sixties, was settled on the sofa across from her, Bernice flipped on the recorder and immediately connected with some of the woman's relations who were no longer on the earth plane. With only five minutes left in the hour session, the woman's voice that had caused the sleepless nights popped into Bernice's mind. The name Aden bounced back and forth inside her head. Closing her eyes, she focused more deeply as she tried to tune into the spirit. A hazy form of a slender woman with long, brown hair appeared in her mind. Bernice opened her eyes. "I'm picking up the name Aden. It might be a woman with that name."

"Aden?" Her client shook her head. "None of my relatives who

9

have passed in the last century have that name. And I don't know any Adens. Does the person have a message?"

The spirit kept repeating that name. Trying to shake the voice, Bernice briefly closed her eyes again, but instead of going away, the voice became louder and sounded agitated. With her temples pounding, Bernice glanced at the clock and discovered it was four o'clock. As she ended the session, she turned off the recorder and ejected the tape. She slipped it into a pre-labeled container, handed it to the gray-haired woman, and escorted her to the door.

"You're great," the woman said. "Can I have an appointment the first part of July?"

"Let me check my schedule," Bernice said, eager to close the door so she could be alone, "and give you a call."

"Thanks," the client said and then headed toward the sidewalk.

With her fingertips pressed against her temples, Bernice strolled into her bathroom. She retrieved two aspirin, pushed them into her mouth, and chased them down her throat with a swig of water. She went to her bedroom and flopped onto the bed. Just as she started to drift off, her phone rang. Not wanting to talk to anyone, she turned over and waited for the answering machine to start.

"Bernice, pick up," came the voice of Trudy, her best friend and a psychic. "I've got this sense that you need me. Is something…"

Bernice grabbed the receiver and interrupted the caller. "Hey, Trudy. I was planning to call you later. Do you have any more clients today?"

"I'm finished and walking toward my car."

"Can you stop by on your way home?"

"Sure. See you in a few," Trudy said and then clicked off.

Bernice knew from personal experience that Trudy was exceptionally gifted. She had diagnosed Bernice's medical condition before the doctor did. She had warned Bernice to immediately get out of a grocery store. Right after she left, it was robbed and two customers were shot. She had alerted her to poisonous gas spreading through her house before the carbon monoxide detector beeped. She had also given Bernice clues that something was going on with Frank, Bernice's husband. It didn't take Bernice long to discover the affair.

Twenty minutes later, Trudy was sitting in Bernice's living room, enjoying a glass of red wine. "What's going on?"

"A woman keeps shouting the name Aden in my head. I haven't

been able to sleep through the night once this week. Any ideas?" The voice in Bernice's mind faded away, and she felt the presence of the brown-haired woman in spirit hovering over her. "Wait," Bernice said as her hand dropped into her lap and everything around her became a murky blur of blacks and grays. Her eyes flicked and closed. Her head swung to the side and landed on the armrest. "Sidney…get Sidney," she stuttered in a sweet voice, an octave higher than Bernice's usual tone. "He's innocent."

"Who's innocent?" Trudy asked, sensing the spirit's energy floating through the room.

"Aden…my…husband."

Trudy's psychic intuition kicked in, and the spirit's name leapt into her head. "Mara. Mara, who's Sidney?"

"Need…Sidney." Bernice's arms folded over her chest, tears ran down her cheeks, and she made a painful moan before her eyes sprang open. Feeling disoriented and groggy, she gazed at Trudy with a puzzled expression. "Did I pass out?" she asked, cocking her eyebrows.

Trudy studied Bernice for a few seconds before she responded. "Bernice, the spirit that won't let you sleep just used you as her vessel."

Bernice grabbed a tissue and wiped her face. "I hate it when that happens."

"How was it?"

"Right after I told you about her, a soft breeze floated over my shoulder, and then I felt her presence. So, what did she have to say for herself?"

Trudy relayed everything the spirit had said along with the spirit's name. "Also, your hands were grasping your chest."

"Mara must have died from something to do with her heart or lungs," Bernice said. "Aden is probably in jail."

Trudy's right hand twitched, a sign she received for *yes*. "He's behind bars someplace."

"Sidney—a son, friend, or maybe the guilty person?"

Trudy's left hand twitched, her intuitive *no* sign. "No, that's not it." She tapped her fingertips together. "There must be some reason this woman picked you." She put her psychic gift to work by focusing on Bernice's energy and then smiled. "When were you in jail?"

Bernice bit her lower lip. "You know, sometimes it's hard to be your friend," she huffed.

"So?" Trudy asked, prying for information.

One of Bernice's eyebrows lifted and her forehead creased as her lips thinned into a hard line. She knew it was impossible to hide anything from Trudy no matter how hard she tried. "Okay," she spit out. "I was only eighteen. I never even mentioned being there to my ex-husband, that jerk."

"Bernice, I'm not judging you. I'm trying to help you figure this thing out."

Bernice inhaled deeply. "It's just that's part of my past I've tried hard to forget. When I was in high school, I really liked this guy, and he was a member of a gang. I began hanging out with the rough kids. A couple of days before graduation, he picked me up in this new, bright, shiny red Porsche. I knew he didn't have the money to buy anything like that, but he had a rich uncle, so I figured he'd borrowed the car."

She picked up the wine bottle, filled Trudy's glass and hers, and then took a big swig. Bernice licked her lips and continued. "Phil, my boyfriend, asked me if I wanted to have a turn driving the gorgeous car. After I said yes, he stopped in front of a drug store, and we both got out. I climbed in behind the wheel. Before he got back in, he said he was going inside to buy cigarettes. A few minutes later, he came running out, holding a gun, and leaped into the car. The store owner charged after him, hollering for him to stop. Then the guy raised a rifle and shot at the car, shattering the back window. All this time, Phil was yelling at me to take off. Feeling panicky and hearing bullets striking metal, I pushed down the pedal and plowed out." Bernice raised her glass with trembling hands and drained her wine.

She went on. "Since the dumb shit had stolen a high profile car to use in his robbery, we didn't even get a few miles before the cops stopped us and hauled us to jail."

"You were only behind bars for a weekend," Trudy remarked as her intuition tuned in to her friend. "Phil got five years."

Bernice's head bobbed up and down. "My folks couldn't afford to bail me out, so I had to stay the whole weekend. I watched hookers, shoplifters, and those brought in for DUIs come and go until I saw a judge on Monday. He appointed a public defender for me. I got off on probation, but since I was eighteen, I have a record."

"New York, right?"

Bernice nodded. "Baldwin. That's where my family used to live. Now, Mom and Dad live in Panama on social security, and my kid brother is in the Marines."

"The Baldwin police station might be the connection. Let's order pizza and then see what we can find on your computer. Sidney and Aden aren't common names."

After finishing the pizza and spending two hours on the Internet, they discovered a detective with the first name of Sidney worked for the Nassau County Police Department located in Baldwin, the same place Bernice had been incarcerated for a couple days. Yet they weren't able to find anyone in a New York prison or jail with the name Aden.

"I'm going to call Detective Sidney Langston tomorrow and just ask him if he knows someone named Mara or Aden," Bernice said. "He might not tell me, but I can't think of anything else to do."

"Let me call him. Maybe my intuition will pick up something."

Before her nine o'clock appointment, Trudy placed the call. "May I speak to Detective Sidney Langston?"

"Detective Langston's calls are being taken by Sergeant Altman. Would you like to speak to him?"

"No. I'd rather speak to Detective Langston. Can I leave a message to have him return my call?"

"Detective Langston is on leave, and I'm not sure when *she'll* be back," the receptionist said. "Sergeant Altman will be happy to assist you."

"My call is of a personal nature, so he can't help me." Trudy pushed the end button on her phone. Then she speed-dialed Bernice's number.

Bernice glanced at caller ID as she answered. "Did you get anything?"

"Sidney is a woman, and she's on leave. While I was on the phone with the receptionist, my intuition buzzed, and I learned Sidney is on medical leave. It has something to do with chest pains."

"Chest pains?" Bernice said, squinting and scratching her forehead as she recalled sensing Mara's death had something to do with that part of the body.

Chapter 3

June 15th
Baldwin, New York

Sidney stared at the ceiling, wondering if she was ever going to be able to manage walking around the house without being drugged. Often she had tried to wean herself from the medication, for it only dulled the pain; it didn't eliminate it. With each attempt, the pain came back worse and monopolized her every move. It had been almost two months since it had begun. Every test known to medical science had been performed without finding out what was wrong with her. She refused to accept the explanation that it was mental, not physical. Sure, she felt badly that her former partner had been shot and died, but deep down she never liked the guy. She thought he was arrogant, and he always treated her like an underling. She really liked her new partner, Kent, and felt disappointed that he was assigned to work with someone else on their cases.

But what was *really* gnawing at her the most was Chas. He was still the attentive, loving man she had married, though she was beginning to see doubt behind his deep, blue eyes each time they had a meeting with one of the three doctors assigned to her case. She wasn't sure if the doubt was because he was beginning to think her condition was mental or because he feared she'd never be cured.

The phone rang, startling her out of her self-pity. She reached over to the nightstand and picked up the receiver. "Hello."

"Ms. Langston, please don't hang up on me again."

Sidney recognized Bernice's voice, the woman who had repeatedly called her claiming some dead person was trying to reach her. *If I fell for that nonsense, then I would* need *a shrink.* "Bernice, don't call me anymore. If you persist, I'll report you to the authorities." Ready to hang up, she removed the receiver from her ear.

"Mara needs you!" Bernice shouted, and then suddenly, Sidney's pain stopped.

Sidney sat up in bed, raised the receiver again, and painlessly ran her fingers over her chest. "What did you say?"

Bernice sighed, thinking maybe Sidney would finally listen to her. "I said Mara needs you."

"Who's Mara?"

"I'm still working on that," Bernice said.

"How do you expect me to help someone if I don't know who she is?"

"Well, that is a problem," Bernice admitted. "I've been working with a psychic and another medium trying to figure it out."

"What makes you think I'm the right person for the job?"

"Well…every night for the past two weeks, Mara, a woman in spirit, has woken me up and told me she needs Sidney's help. Her husband Aden is in jail, and he's innocent."

"How do you know you've got the right Sidney?"

"That's a long story. To sum it up, Mara had to have a reason to reach me. Once I was in Nassau County Jail, so that's how I tracked you down. Then we learned you were on leave due to some kind of chest problem, and Mara died from either a heart or lung condition."

"You're telling me because I work for the Nassau County Police Department, my name is Sidney, and I've got a medical condition in my chest area, I'm the right person? No last name or anything else to go on? That's all you've got?" Sidney asked, drumming her fingers on her thighs and growing more irritated by the minute.

"Pretty much," Bernice confessed.

"Bernice, feel free to give me a call when you figure it all out. Until then, leave me alone." Sidney slammed down the receiver. Simultaneously, pain rippled through her body. Her heart hammered away, and her breathing came in wild gasps. Tears streamed down her cheeks, and a horrible cry escaped her throat.

Jean, a robust, middle-aged nurse Chas had hired, charged into the room. Seeing Sidney's face twisted in pain, she filled a syringe and pushed the tip into Sidney's arm. Within a few seconds, Sidney's body went limp, and her eyes flickered and then closed. Jean adjusted Sidney's pillows and tucked the blankets over her.

Hearing voices in the hallway, Sidney stirred and briefly opened her eyes.

"How's she doing?" Chas asked.

"The same. She's resting peacefully now," Jean said.

"Oh, Jean, I don't know how much more she can take. All the shots and pills only put her to sleep, nothing is really helping her. If the doctors don't come up with a cure soon...I'm so afraid I'm losing her."

"I'm praying for her, Mr. Langston." Jean headed down the stairs and left for the day.

Sidney raised her eyelids when Chas eased down on the bed beside her and stroked her cheek. Enduring the pain, she forced a smile, and he wrapped his strong arms around her. She lifted her chin and gazed at him, wishing for a romantic evening. They had tried a few times, but the pain always got in the way.

"How're ya doin, Babe?" he asked tenderly as he brushed her hair away from her face.

"For a few minutes today, I didn't have any pain," she said, recalling the time she spent on the telephone.

Chas cocked his eyebrows. "Really? Had you taken a new pill or something?"

"No, I was on the phone." She suffered through the dull pain in her chest as she filled him in on Bernice's call.

A brief flash of dismay crossed his face. "The pain started again as soon as you hung up?"

"Uh-huh."

"Do you think it was just a coincidence?"

Sidney shrugged.

"Maybe you should try calling this Bernice. Just as an experiment. See if the pain ends again."

"Chas, I think it was a fluke that the pain left when I talked to her. I can't imagine she has any magical powers or anything like that. She claims to be a medium, not a healer."

"Strange things sometimes happen, even if that means dealing with a wacko. Just call her. Please?"

Sidney scanned her husband's face. She saw his drawn, sad eyes and the deep lines forming in his forehead and suspected he had aged five years since she had become ill. "Okay, I'll give it a try," she said, reaching for the phone. She checked caller ID and dialed Bernice's number.

"Sidney, I'm so happy you called, and hopefully, Mara will be too," Bernice answered in an uplifted tone.

Sidney's pain vanished again. Her eyes opened wider, and they darted to her husband's face. "It's gone."

"What's gone?" Bernice asked.

"Can I call you right back?" Sidney said, wanting to test the pain theory.

"Sure."

Sidney disconnected. Immediately her chest ached, and she briefly closed her eyes while trying to understand what talking to Bernice meant.

With compassion in his eyes, Chas caressed her cheek. "Babe, you okay?"

"It's back," she murmured, biting her lower lip as her eyes became moist.

"I'm calling her." Chas grabbed the phone and pushed the redial and speaker buttons.

"Hello," Bernice answered.

"Bernice, this is Chas Langston, Sidney's husband," he said, looking at his wife.

Sidney sat up straight, smiled, and mouthed, "Gone."

Chas gently touched Sidney's cheek. "Can you tell me what's going on?" he asked Bernice.

"Huh?" Bernice said, sounding bewildered. "I only called your wife because a woman in spirit wants her help. That's all."

"If that's all, then how do you explain the pain my wife has been experiencing? I don't believe in spells, but I've seen some weird stuff."

Chad's words invoked memories within Sidney about some bizarre incidents he had shared, specifically one about a victim being pronounced dead at the scene. An hour later, he came back to life in the morgue with a hole in his chest. Prosecuting the assailant became a challenge for the DA's office since the perpetrator obviously meant to kill the man, but through some miracle the intended victim didn't die. Murder one had to be taken off the table. The trial became a joke with all the eyewitnesses mumbling on the stand, not one able to spit out a coherent sentence.

Chas continued. "What kind of a hold do you have on Sidney?"

"Hold? What are you talking about?"

"My wife has been suffering from severe chest pains since April twentieth," he began. "And then while she's talking to you on the phone, lo and behold, the pain stops. You can't expect me to believe that you had nothing to do with her suffering," he snapped. "Now whatever witchcraft, voodoo thing, or trick you're using, I want it stopped, or I'll make sure you suffer some consequences. Do you understand?" Chas's eyes were dark with rage, and the muscles in his jaw flinched.

"Mr. Langston," Bernice stifled, "I swear to you I have nothing to do with your wife's pain. I swear. Check the website, Bernice Dixon, or Google me. I've written books on mediumship. I'm not a quack. I don't do any witchcraft thing. Check…please."

Breathing easily without the throbbing pain in her chest, Sidney sensed Bernice was telling the truth. She stroked Chas's arms. "Let's check."

"Yes…Yes…check," Bernice pleaded.

Chas gazed into Sidney's glowing eyes, eyes he hadn't seen glow for almost two months. "We'll check," he said and ended the call. Suddenly, his eyes shot open wider and fear gripped his features. "The pain…you still okay?"

Sidney nodded. "I don't ache anywhere."

"Good." He sighed and then gave Sidney a warm smile, raised her chin, and lightly kissed her lips. "Do you want me to get the laptop, or do you want to go to the den?"

"Let's go to the den." Sidney scooted to the edge of the bed, dropped her feet to the floor, and, as she stood, Chas clutched her arm. Seeing the concerned look on his face, she said, "Stop worrying. I'm not in any pain."

After going through all the information on Bernice's website, reading some testimonials, and following all the links, Sidney and Chas believed Bernice had told them the truth about herself. However, they both voiced doubt that anyone could get messages from a dead person.

On that thought, Sidney felt a slight tingling sensation in her upper body and swallowed hard, fearing the pain was beginning to emerge again. She briefly closed her eyes, wondering if her skepticism about afterlife communication could play a role in her condition. She pondered over all of her visits with numerous doctors. Not one had a clue about what was wrong with her. It seemed like Bernice held some kind of a key to her well-being. Sidney figured she had no choice but to help the dead woman Bernice claimed had requested her assistance—at least until medical science found a remedy for her medical situation. With that decision, the tingling in her chest ended and fresh air flowed into her lungs. Breathing deeply, her chest expanded without the slightest hint of any pain.

"Chas, I know every word Bernice has said about this dead woman wanting my help seems farfetched, yet right now when I'm thinking about helping her, I'm pain-free. Tomorrow I'm going to do some research to see if a guy named Aden is in prison somewhere."

"How can you do that without a last name?"

"I'll talk to Maxine, the department's computer wizard. Maybe she can come up with some way."

He leaned toward her and trailed his index finger across her bottom lip.

Her pulse quickened with his touch, and it aroused an excitement in Sidney she hadn't felt since that dreadful day in April. She wrapped her arms around her husband and smothered his lips with a passionate kiss.

"Have I missed that," he said softly and then kissed her neck. "Let's go to the bedroom."

"No," she said as his lips against her bare arm added fuel to the burning desire roaring inside her. "The sofa is closer."

Chapter 4

Chas picked up his briefcase and said, "Jean won't be here until noon. Call me if you have the slightest pain."

"Honey, I'll be fine," Sidney said as she stood next to the front door.

His deep-blue eyes sparkled as he pulled her close to him. "You certainly were fine last night. Maybe making love only once every two months might be the way to go."

She gazed at the smirk on his face. "Not on your life."

"I'll try to be home early. We need to make up for lost time."

"Good."

Chas kissed his wife goodbye.

After closing the door behind him, Sidney went back to the kitchen and poured another cup of coffee. She carried it into the den, placed it on the desk, and then sat down. With her elbows on the arms of the chair, she clasped her hands together and rested her chin on them. Staring at the computer screen, an idea flashed into her head.

She punched in *Newsday* website—the Long Island and New York City news source—on her keyboard and went to the obituaries. There she searched for a person with the first name of Mara who had died during the past year. No one with that name appeared. Then she logged into the police department site and searched through the data base for a person with the name Aden. Again, no leads.

Sidney drank her coffee as she wondered if Aden could be in prison in another state, another country, or if he even existed. She picked up the phone and dialed her precinct. After chatting with two of her fellow officers about her health, she was connected to her favorite computer technician.

"Hi, Sid," Maxine said in her high-pitched voice. "When you comin' back to work?"

"Don't know. I need to be released by my doctor first. Department rules. Hey, I'm trying to find someone who might be in jail or prison somewhere, and all I have is a first name. Is there some way I can locate him without any more info?"

"Does this person have something to do with a case?"

"No."

"Then why do you want to find him or her?"

"You'd think I'd cracked up if I told you."

"Try me."

"A medium. Do you know what a medium is?"

"Sure. My sister is big into that—messages from beyond the grave," Maxine said in a mocking tone.

"A medium called me and said a spirit wanted my help."

"You're kidding, right?"

"'Fraid not."

"She just called you out of the blue?"

"Yeah. And she keeps calling me, so to get her off my back," Sidney said, not wanting to reveal any more of the story than necessary to solicit Maxine's knowledge, "I'm doing a little research."

That bit of information sparked Maxine's curiosity. "What's the person's name?"

"Aden."

"Aden? You're kidding, right?"

"No. Why?"

"A guy by that name is sitting in a California jail for the murder of his wife. Boy is he dreamy—olive-skinned, jet-black hair, and dark, seductive eyes. Poor fellow can't even get out on bail since the prosecutor convinced the judge he's a flight risk because he's a pilot and owns a plane."

"Last name?"

"It's weird...Uzzz something. Let me pull up the article," Maxine said and flipped through several computer pages. "Here it is. Uzelac. Aden Uzelac."

"Wife's name?"

"Mara."

Stunned, Sidney's mouth flew wide open. Then a thought popped into her head: *Had Bernice also read about Aden?* She inhaled deeply and slowly exhaled. "Thanks for the info."

"Hey, let me know if the medium tells you anything else. My sister would love to hear about it."

"Will do," Sidney said and then hung up.

Sidney called Bernice. After five rings, she left a message requesting a call. Next, she searched Google for Aden Uzelac.

Numerous newspaper sites appeared with articles about the murder. Reading through the first one, she gasped and stared at the date of the crime—April 20, the same day she was rushed to the hospital with chest pains. The day she believed she was having a heart attack. Her eyes scanned further down the article, and she discovered Mara had been shot in the heart. *That doesn't mean anything*, she thought. *Other murder victims are shot in the heart.* As she read on, she learned that Aden claimed his wife was dead when he arrived home from a business trip. He had found her in the backyard lying next to their hot tub in a blood soaked robe.

Another article mentioned Aden had been involved with another woman, and he had a heated argument with his wife before flying to Brazil. He had been there for two months, and during that time, he had not seen his wife.

Sidney jumped when the phone rang. Glancing at the caller ID, she answered it. "Bernice, exactly why do you want my help?" Her voice held an undertow of anger.

"Didn't you check out my website?" Bernice asked, assuming that was the reason for Sidney's irate tone.

"Aden and Mara's names have been plastered all over California newspapers and news reports. You'd heard about them before you called me. Do you know the guy? And you're hoping a detective from another state will step up to the bat and throw a wrench into the investigation? Is that what this is all about?"

"Sidney, I swear to you I hadn't heard about a person named Aden or a woman named Mara until her spirit kept waking me up at night. The past two nights, after I finally talked to you, I've been able to sleep soundly again." Bernice paused, and Sidney suspected she was searching for another lie that might convince her to work for Aden. "I can't come up with anything else to say that might sway you into believing me."

"Well, ask your spirit gal to tell you something that isn't in the newspapers. Until then, don't call me," Sidney snapped and then slammed down the receiver. She stood up and headed toward the kitchen to fill her coffee mug. As she stepped into the hall, a throbbing pain sprang through her entire body. Clutching her chest, she buckled over, landing with a thud on the hardwood floor and sending her mug tumbling against the baseboard. She gripped a door frame and tried to get up, but with each attempt, the pain intensified. Moaning, she stayed curled up into a ball on the cold, hard surface and shivered as perspiration drenched every inch of her body.

Chapter 5

An hour later, Jean entered the house, strolled toward the kitchen, and gasped when she saw Sidney, lying on the floor trembling. She bent down, brushed her patient's damp hair away from her face, and stroked her arm. "You shouldn't be out of bed."

Gasping for air and reeling in pain, Sidney muttered, "I felt okay earlier. Can you help me back to bed?"

Jean managed to get her patient upstairs, sat her on the edge of the bed, and quickly wiped the moisture from her skin with a dry towel as she removed Sidney's wet clothing. She slipped a nightgown over Sidney's head, tugged it over her arms, and pulled it down her body until it draped over her knees. After she had Sidney settled in bed, she gave her a shot to ease the pain and a sleeping pill. Following Chas's instructions to let him know if anything out of the ordinary happened, Jean called him.

"She was doing so well when I left," Chas said, his voice heavy with despair. "How long will she be out?"

"About three hours."

"I can't leave that early. When she wakes up, tell her I'll be home as soon as I can."

After he hung up, Chas leaned back in his chair and rubbed his chin with his knuckles in quiet deliberation as he thought about his wife. Except for being ten pounds lighter, Sidney had seemed so healthy without any pain the night before and in the morning. Chas recalled that she planned to do research over the internet for Aden and Mara. *Did Sidney's relapse have anything to do with that? Could it be she couldn't find anything about them which would make it impossible for her to help free Aden?* He pushed a button on his phone that went to Susan, a paralegal in his office. She was exceptionally skilled in research, and he relied on her expertise often.

Susan's voice, sounding hurried, came over the intercom. "Hey, Chas, I'll have the Monson case on your desk before two."

"When you finish with that, can you check the obituaries for a woman with the first name Mara?"

"Last name?"

"Sorry, all I have is a first name."

"Do you know where she died?"

"Haven't got a clue."

"I'll see what I can do," Susan said.

At 3:30 p.m., Susan walked into Chas's office. "I found two Maras who died in the U.S. this past year. Only one had an obituary, but I suspect that's the woman you're looking for. There wasn't a cause of death listed, so I searched through the homicide data base. Sure enough, this Mara had been murdered." Susan handed a sheet of paper to Chas. "Let me know if she's not the right one, and I'll continue the research."

"Thanks," Chas said as Susan turned to leave his office. He looked down at the document and saw the image of a pretty woman with long, brown hair and full, perfectly-shaped lips that reminded him of Sidney's. His eyes stopped cold on the dates right underneath the woman's name—she was born on the same day as Sidney, and she died on the day Sidney's pain started. Feeling a lump in his throat, he thought, *What a bizarre coincidence, or did the dates mean more than that?*

Chas returned to his current case and tried to focus on the file again, but he found it impossible to concentrate. If it weren't for his four o'clock appointment, he would have been out the door and hurrying home to show Sidney the obituary. As he continued mulling over what he had read about Mara, his phone buzzed announcing Lois Thornton had arrived for the appointment her brother insisted she needed. Chas held down a button on his telephone. "Send them in," he said, knowing she wouldn't show up alone.

Mrs. Thornton's fifteen-year-old daughter had been raped, stabbed, and her face so badly slashed that her mother couldn't recognize her only child. Mrs. Thornton's husband had also died at the hands of the assailant when he attempted to rescue the teenager. The first case Chas had ever tried was against a man who had brutally raped and slain three young girls. The jury had found the perpetrator innocent, and he walked. Three months later, the freed man had left two more victims in his wake before he was apprehended again. Chas had blamed himself for lacking enough evidence to have gotten a guilty verdict, and he vowed that would never happen again.

His eyes dropped to Ted Monson's picture. Chas had the DNA results, two eyewitnesses seeing Monson fleeing the victims' house, the man's blood-stained clothes, and the murder weapon. Even though Chas had managed to obtain a ninety-two percent conviction rate on the cases he tried, he knew never to take anything for granted. He suspected Mrs. Thornton's visit was for the same reason she had met with him three times earlier—to get assurance that Monson would get the verdict he deserved, an assurance Chas couldn't give.

As his door opened, Chas rose to his feet and saw the frail-looking woman with puffy eyes and red, blotchy face clinging onto the arm of her brother. He walked around his desk and shook the hand of Ralph Shelton, a tall, pudgy man. When Mrs. Thornton didn't extend her hand, he patted her arm. "What can I help you with today?" he said, gesturing for them to take the two chairs facing his desk.

"W…well…" she stammered.

Taking charge, Shelton said, "We're here because Lois needs to know that bastard is going to die for what he did."

"Mr. Shelton and Mrs. Thornton, we're working hard preparing for the trial, and I can assure you, we're doing everything possible to make sure justice is served. However, we can never guarantee the outcome of any trial."

"So the asshole might walk?" Shelton asked, raising his voice.

"He won't walk. He admitted to the rape. As a minimum, he'll be sentenced for that crime."

"That's not enough," Shelton said, gritting his teeth while Lois wiped her eyes.

"I know that, and it certainly isn't what we're working toward," Chas said and then proceeded to explain the trial process again to Shelton and Mrs. Thornton.

Forty-five minutes later, Shelton and his sister left Chas's office. Chas sank down in his chair, stuck all the Monson documents back into their folders, and sighed, impatient for the trial to begin. He was prepared and confident that he could get a conviction, yet he'd never share his optimism with Lois Thornton or her brother just in case something unexpected popped up during the trial. *It's better if they're not led to expect a certain verdict. Then they can be happy if it goes the right way but maybe not completely devastated if it doesn't.* Of course, he knew they'd still blame him if Monson wasn't found guilty of first degree murder.

Finally at 5:15 p.m., Chas tucked Mara's obituary into his briefcase and strode out of the building.

Chapter 6

"How was she after you called?" Chas asked Jean as he bumped into her in the upstairs hallway.

"She's only been awake for an hour. The pain seems to be consistent with how it's been for the past two months. I've given her a couple of pills, and she managed to get down some chicken broth. Do you want me to stay longer today?"

"No. I'll be home the rest of the evening."

"Then I'll be back tomorrow at nine." Jean headed toward the stairwell.

Seeing Chas in the doorway, Sidney leaned on her elbow and raised her head above the pillow. In a weak, soft voice, she said, "Oh, Chas, it was all a lie."

He hurried to his wife's side and stroked her cheek. "What was a lie?"

Sidney's lips quivered, and she bit the lower one. "Everything...everything Bernice said. I was actually starting to think a ghost had called to her for my help. Maybe I was grasping for straws. Since the pain vanished when I talked to her, I went along with her scheme. I so wanted to find a reason for my pain." Tears trickled down Sidney's cheeks. "I thought maybe someone on the other side had caused my pain just to get my attention. How could I be that stupid?" she sniffled. "Instead of someone calling from the great beyond, it was someone calling from California."

Chas furrowed his brow. "Huh?"

"Probably Aden's girlfriend."

He sat down on the edge of the bed and tucked Sidney's hair behind her ears. He pulled out several tissues from the box on the nightstand, dabbed her face with one of them, and handed the rest to Sidney. "Babe, you've lost me. What does California have to do with it?"

Sidney wiped her eyes and blew her nose. "Aden is in jail there. He's been arrested for the murder of his wife…who happens to be Mara. It's in all the California papers. No dead person contacted Bernice."

A confused expression splashed across Chas's face, and the corners of his eyes were pinched.

"Don't you see?" Sidney asked. "Someone wanted another person, a cop, snooping around just to stir things up. I've read the newspaper articles. This guy, Aden, was having an affair. He'd been fighting with his wife. Everything points to him. The only thing missing is the gun. He obviously ditched it before he called the police."

"If Bernice was trying to help out a friend, how do you think she happened to pick you?"

"I've been mulling that over." Sidney ran her hand over her chest, trying to soothe the lingering pain. "She mentioned once she was in the Nassau county jail. Maybe she made friends with one of the officers, and she thought a woman would be more gullible. I'm the only female detective there."

"You could be right, but let me show you what I found before we jump to any conclusions." Chas stood, retrieved his briefcase, and took out the page Susan had given him. "My paralegal did a little research this afternoon for obituaries with the first name of Mara. She ran across this one," he said, easing down on the bed next to Sidney and giving her the sheet. "You and Mara are exactly the same age. She died the day you went to the hospital."

"The newspaper articles said she was shot in the heart, and I thought I was having a heart attack." Sidney squinted, her mind churning as she rubbed her forehead. "How is that possible? How did Bernice know I was born on that day? Of all the people with that same birthday, how in the world did she know that? And the hospital? Medical privacy? Without consent, they'd never release my medical information."

Chas took Sidney's hand. "Babe, I have to admit when I read that obituary, something clicked. This can't be just a slew of coincidences, especially since your pain disappears when you're thinking about helping."

"So you think someone from the beyond is responsible for my pain? And I need to help Mara to get rid of it?"

Shrugging his shoulders, Chas said, "Don't know. I'm having a hard time believing that, but it does seem to play a role in your well-being." He wrapped his arms around her, held her head against his chest, and took a deep breath. "All I know is that I want you healthy again. I want your suffering to end. I want to hold you close to me and not fear that I'm causing you more pain."

She touched his cheek. "I love you, and I want what we had last night back. My last conversation with Bernice was pretty nasty. Let me give her a call. Maybe if I tell her about the dates, she might know what it means. You know, like does that make some kind of connection in her work?" Sidney slowly exhaled and a faint smile creased her lips.

His eyes opened wider and fixed on her. "What?"

"The pain. It's gone again."

Chas kissed her forehead. "There has to be something here. Something I don't understand and probably never will."

Feeling tired of being cooped up in the bedroom, Sidney slipped on a robe while Chas changed into sweatpants and a t-shirt. Then they headed downstairs to the den. She called Bernice and pushed the speaker button. After apologizing for the way she ended the prior call, Sidney filled Bernice in on the newspaper articles and the obituary. "Mara and I were born on the same day, and my chest pains began the day she died. Does that mean anything to you?"

"I suspect there is some kind of a bond between you and Mara. Maybe you knew each other in another life. Maybe you were related. I don't do past life regressions, but there are some mediums who are very gifted in that area. Would you like me to give you some names?"

"Do you think I need that to help Mara?"

"No."

Sidney's eyes flashed to Chas, and she mouthed, "Now what?"

He shrugged, leaned over the desk, and caressed Sidney's hand.

"Okay, then I won't go down that road. Have you had any more messages from Mara?" Sidney rolled her eyes and shook her head, not believing she was buying into the messages from the beyond.

"Well, now that you mention it, she did make her presence known during one of my readings, but she seems to be having difficulty communicating. It might be because she only recently crossed over."

"What does that mean?" Sidney asked as she exchanged a look of bewilderment with Chas.

"Normally, when someone leaves the earthly plane, it takes six months, if not longer, to be able to communicate through a medium. All I got from her today were the words 'short, brown hair.' Are you short, and do you have brown hair?"

"No. I'm five-foot-nine and have blonde hair."

"Well, then she wasn't describing you. But since Mara is working so hard to send messages, I know she desperately wants you to help her husband. Have you decided to help?"

"Yes," Sidney said, fearing the pain would return if she didn't. "Let me know if she contacts you again."

"I will."

Sidney clicked off and stared at the ceiling, thinking about how to begin. "I guess I better pack a suitcase and head to California."

Chas's blue eyes brimmed with worry. "Do you think you're well enough to travel?"

"Remember, upstairs, you thought there was something to what Bernice had said. I can't help clear an innocent man in California if I'm in New York. I need to investigate."

"Sidney, you haven't been able to work out for almost two months."

"Not like I used to. But even with the pain, I did some exercises almost every day. You think my body has become flabby? I'm in bad shape?"

"No. No. That's not what I meant." He cocked his brow, gave her a warm smile, and squeezed her arm. "You'd still have every guy in town crawling all over themselves just to get a glimpse of you in a bikini. Boy, do I remember the first time I saw you strolling toward the witness box. Your gleaming hazel eyes, full scrumptious lips, long legs, and fantastic curves made me stop and take a deep breath before I could start asking you questions. I had a hard time waiting for the trial to end, so I could ask you out—didn't want to be accused of witness tampering."

Sidney blushed as a crooked smile flickered across her lips. "Are you working up to having your lustful desires fulfilled tonight?"

He kissed her hand. "Am I that transparent?"

Sidney nodded. "Yeah. So I'm physically fit for a night of passion, but you're not sure if I'm up to traveling?"

"That's not what I said. It's just that you haven't been able to do any endurance training for a while, and if Aden didn't kill his wife, you're going to be dealing with someone who did."

She stared into his eyes brimming with concern. "Honey, think about my job. I'm a detective. This won't be the first murder I've investigated, but it *will* be the first where I lack authority."

Chas stood up, moved around the desk, and knelt next to her. He held both of her hands in his and kissed them. "Think about the time before you went to work for the Nassau County Police Department. The time you were shot when you worked for the CIA. *Here*, you can send for backup. You investigate in teams."

Sidney lowered her eyes as she recalled the mission that went so smoothly only to have three of her colleagues killed while they tried to escape Beirut. The officer-in-command had neglected to inform the CIA patrol group they were heading to the secured area. A fusillade of gunfire riveted their vehicle in the small passage to what they believed was their safe haven. Friendly fire was the verdict. Sidney no longer had any physical scars, but the mental scars would never completely heal. She couldn't look at her boss without rage and disgust, so she left the CIA and went to work for the Nassau County Police Department where she could put the guilty behind bars. Since Sidney had taken an oath working for the CIA, all Chas knew about her CIA experience was that she had been shot on foreign soil. She wouldn't have even divulged that much except the wound left her with only a slight chance she could ever bear a child.

Sidney placed a hand on Chas's cheek. "I know what I'm doing."

His eyes fixed on her face. "Once you've made up your mind, getting you to change it is like getting the sun to rise in the west. At least, hire a private investigator to do some of the leg work." He stroked her arm. "I wish I could go with you, but I'm tied up with two murder trials. Since you've been laid up, you can't go alone. How about taking Jean with you?"

"Jean? She's a nurse. How do you expect her to help me?"

"Just in case we have this wrong and the message from beyond had nothing to do with your health condition, I want someone looking out for you."

Sidney saw the worried expression etched on Chas's face. "Do you think she'll go?"

"Let me give her a call."

"And I better call the Chief," she said, referring to her boss. "I can't travel to California while I'm on sick leave. I'll make up some excuse that I need to visit a friend, so I'll take vacation leave or time without pay."

"He'll ask about your health."

"Yeah. He knows I haven't been cleared to return to work yet." Sidney tapped her index finger on her lower lip. "Maybe I should mention I'm searching out an alternative treatment or something like that. Hopefully, he won't ask too many questions."

Chapter 7

The following evening, Sidney, with Jean in tow, boarded a plane for San Diego. During the six-hour flight, Sidney spent her time reading all the articles about the murder again and scribbling notes. Jean took a long nap.

Stepping into a two-bedroom Grand Hyatt Hotel suite that Chas had reserved, Sidney's eyes drifted over the living area decorated like an upscale New York apartment with modern furniture and a large, open-floor plan. Doors on opposite walls led to bedrooms and floor-to-ceiling windows lined the exterior wall. She walked to the windows with Jean.

"Oh, what a magnificent view of the city," Jean said. "I've never stayed in this fancy a place."

Shortly after 9:30 the next morning, Sidney drove out of the hotel's parking garage and headed for the county jail, her first stop. There, it took her almost half an hour to get clearance to see Aden Uzelac. She was escorted into a large room divided into stalls for visitors with a glass-and-wood panel that separated them from the prisoners. Her footfalls echoed through the room as she moved toward the second stall while she scanned the space and didn't see any other visitors. She sat down at the counter attached to the panel, folded her arms across her chest, and waited for Aden to appear.

A door behind the transparent panel opened. An officer escorted a tall man with jet-black hair through the doorway. He wore an

34

orange jumpsuit, and his head was bent down as if he was watching his feet shuffling across the linoleum. As the man came closer to the partition, he raised his chin, and then his eyes locked on Sidney. With a sad, droopy face, he took the chair facing her and continued staring.

Sidney's breathing became uneven. Her pulse quickened. A tingling sensation swam through her body. The panel between them was the only thing that prevented her from leaping out of her seat and running into his arms. *Why do I have this yearning for this stranger? I love Chas.* Yet there was something so familiar about this man. She knew his touch. The way he felt when he made love. His smell, his walk, the size of clothing he wore—everything about him flashed into her mind. Even the birthmark on his upper thigh wasn't hidden from her. Beyond any doubt, she knew Aden hadn't killed Mara, the woman he loved. *How is it possible that I know intimate details about him? What's wrong with me?*

Neither one of them spoke while they studied each other's features. Finally, Aden broke the silence. "Have we ever met?"

Sidney cleared her throat and tried to shake the desire running through her body for the stranger sitting on the other side of the partition. "No."

"You remind me of my wife. You have her same hazel eyes, her lips. I know all her relatives, and you look more like her than any of them. Who are you?"

Sidney adjusted herself in her seat and held her hands firmly in her lap as she forced herself to maintain a professional demeanor in front of this man whom she knew intimately, though they had never touched. "Sidney Langston. I'm a detective with the Nassau County Police Department."

Aden squinted, lightly shook his head, and sighed. "Don't tell me someone thinks I'm guilty of something there, too?"

She gave him a warm smile as the urge to comfort him darted through her mind. "No. I'm not here in an official capacity. I'm here to help you."

Aden arched an eyebrow. "Who sent you?"

"Someone close to you. That's all I can tell you," Sidney said, fearing if she told the truth he might think she was a nut case.

His dark eyes focused on her face. "Ms. Langston, I certainly could use your help. If you've read about my case, you know things do not look good for me, but I'm afraid I can't accept your assistance if I don't know who has employed you."

"No one has employed me."

Aden furrowed his brow, and his jaw became rigid while he continued staring at Sidney. "Let me make sure I have this straight." He rubbed his chin with his knuckles. "Because someone asked you to help me, you traveled here from New York on your own time without anticipating any form of compensation. Have I got that right?"

Sidney nodded.

He pressed his lips together and shook his head. "Don't tell me...you're a friend of Kate. One night—that was it. Tell her I don't want her help."

While Sidney continued hiding the feelings that were churning inside her, she swallowed hard and said, "Aden. Is it okay if I call you Aden?"

He nodded.

"I don't know Kate." Sidney frowned and pushed her hair behind her ears, realizing she'd have to tell him the truth if she expected any cooperation from him. And without that, she was dead in the water. "Okay, I'll tell you who sent me, but I doubt you'll believe it."

"Try me."

"Mara."

A gasp escaped his mouth, his nostrils flared, and his jaw muscle tightened. "Mara?" Veins in his throat twitched and he snapped, "How dare you play games with me?"

Sidney raised her hand. "Please, calm down. I knew you wouldn't believe it, but it's the truth. She contacted a medium. Do you know what a medium is?"

Aden inhaled deeply and slowly exhaled as he gazed at the floor. "Yes. A co-worker visits one all the time—swears by her." He rubbed his temples, raised his chin and stared at her. "So you're into mediums?"

"No. Quite the contrary. The medium tracked me down."

"How?"

Sidney filled him in on all the points that brought her to the San Diego County Jail on the visitors' side of the panel.

"Chest pains?"

Sidney bobbed her head up and down. "Yes. They wouldn't stop until I agreed to help you."

"Amazing." His eyes dropped to the counter. "Every night, I sense Mara in my cell, lying right next to me. I inhale her sweet, fresh smell. I can feel my hair move as she touches it. Oh, God, I miss her," he said with a trembling voice.

As he raised his head, Sidney gazed at his blurry eyes filled with unshed tears. She had no idea how to respond to the pain she saw on his face. "Well, Mara wants me to help prove you're an innocent man, and that's what I'm going to do. So let's begin." Sidney reached down into the briefcase that sat by her feet and pulled out a notepad and a pen. "Your lawyer is Gregory Fowler?"

Aden straightened his shoulders. "Yes. Greg. I've known him for years."

"Has he hired an investigator?"

"He had a guy, Sam, trying to track down the taxi driver. He might be an investigator. I'm just not sure."

"Taxi driver? Nothing I read in the newspapers mentioned a taxi driver. Tell me about it."

"The night Mara died," he said in jerky breaths, "I had just gotten home from a work project in Brazil. When the taxi driver dropped me off, a loud gunshot rang out. We both heard it. It sounded like it came from behind the house, but since I thought no one was home, I assumed the noise had come from the neighbors' house. It's about two hundred feet from the back fence, but sound carries. I'd planned on calling that neighbor once I got inside."

"Neighbors' names?"

"Lamar and Vicky Midgley."

"Do you have other neighbors?"

"Yes, across the street. The houses on our side of the street have bigger lots, and they're set farther apart. Our house is on a double lot, and it's surrounded by trees that give us a lot of privacy. The neighbors can't see the front door."

"Do you know if any of the neighbors heard the gunshot?"

"Yeah, some of them did, but they weren't outside. A couple of them gave the police the time they heard it. Since it happened about the same time as I got home, they can't say if it was before or after I got out of the taxi."

Sidney jotted the information down. "What did you do after the taxi left?"

"I went to unlock the door and found it wasn't locked. Because

I'd heard a gunshot, I crouched down and cautiously opened the door. I can remember smiling to myself when I smelled a roast cooking and saw rose petals scattered on the floor leading down the hall. I dropped my luggage, followed the trail, and went out the patio door, expecting to see my beautiful wife in the hot tub." His voice cracked and his eyes filled with water again. A few tears drizzled down his cheeks.

Seeing the agony and despair on Aden's face, Sidney felt a lump in her throat. She wanted to wrap him in her arms and take away his pain. "I'm so sorry for your loss," she said tenderly, and then she sat silently and waited for him to regain his composure. Five minutes later, she resumed questioning him. "Did Sam locate the taxi driver?"

Aden shook his head. "No. He checked with the taxi company and found the taxi that picked me up at the airport, but the heavyset, white taxi driver who claimed he drove me home wasn't the thin, Hispanic guy that dropped me off. He was lying."

Sidney scribbled more notes. "Aden, according to the newspaper, no one knew your wife would be home. Is that right?"

He nodded. "She hadn't even told me. I was going to drive to L.A. the following morning. She'd been there with the kids, helping plan her grandfather's ninetieth birthday party. We hadn't seen each other for two months." He hung his head. "I guess she wanted to surprise me."

"Where were the kids?"

"L.A., with her parents."

"There's no need for you to answer any more questions if I can get the information from your attorney's files. Can you call him, tell him to let me see them, and let him know that I'll be working on your case?"

"Sure. No problem."

"Good." Sidney put her notepad back in her briefcase and stood up. "After I've read over your files, I'll be back if I need additional information."

"When?" Aden said, sounding anxious.

"Maybe tomorrow," Sidney said as she felt a surge of regret that she had to leave him.

After Sidney climbed into her car, she stared out the windshield and contemplated calling Chas. She had spoken to him before she left the hotel, and they planned on talking to each other later that evening, but she had a strong urge to tell him everything she had experienced when she saw Aden. For some reason she couldn't understand, she felt guilty for having been with Aden, even though a partition had separated them.

She rubbed her temples. *Confession. Do I need to confess the desires that ran through my body for Aden?* She briefly closed her eyes and envisioned Chas, knowing he was the only man she had ever loved, and she would never do anything to hurt him. Somehow, Mara was controlling her—not only her physical well-being but also her emotions. Sidney sensed she'd never be herself again until Aden was set free. She retrieved her cell phone from her purse, brought up a picture of Chas, gazed at his handsome face for a few minutes, and then reluctantly placed the call.

Chapter 8

Sidney entered the foyer of a modern, forty-story building that housed the law office of Gregory Fowler. After checking the directory attached to a granite pedestal in the center of the foyer for his office number, she stepped into the elevator and pushed the button next to 34.

The law firm of Fowler, Maxwell, and Johnson occupied most of that floor. The reception area was impeccably decorated with sleek black and red leather furnishings and a curvy, black slate top information counter. Sunlight streamed in through lightly-tinted windows that covered an entire wall, giving the space an open, airy feeling.

Sidney explained to the receptionist that she was there on Aden Uzelac's behalf and would like to talk to Gregory Fowler about his case, but she didn't have an appointment. The receptionist called his office. Sidney remained by the counter and waited patiently.

"If you'll have a seat, he'll be with you shortly," the receptionist said, placing the phone down on its cradle.

Sidney wandered over to a red leather chair and sat down. She scanned the room and saw six men huddled together in the corner, talking in low voices. Outside that group, she was the only other person waiting.

A few minutes later, a round-faced, bald man with heavy black-rimmed glasses perched on a prominent nose stepped into the reception area from a side hallway. His eyes darted around and then stopped on Sidney. He strolled over to her, moving briskly for one so elderly.

"You must be Sidney Langston," he said, stretching out his hand toward her.

"Yes, and you must be Mr. Fowler." She shook his hand.

"Please call me Greg."

"And call me Sidney."

Fowler led Sidney past the counter, down the hall, and through a door where a woman sat in a small office in front of a set of open double doors. He introduced Sidney to Phyllis, his secretary, and then they proceeded through the doorway.

A massive oak desk dominated the well-appointed room. Like the reception area, windows covered one of his walls, which gave Fowler a terrific view of the cityscape.

As Fowler moved to his high-backed office chair, he gestured Sidney toward the chair facing the desk. When they were both seated, he said, "According to Aden, you're in San Diego to help free him. He was a little sketchy about the details that brought you here. Could you fill me in?"

Sidney hesitated while she pondered how to answer his question. "It's a weird story," she began and then relayed the sequence of events from her being rushed to the hospital, the undiagnosed pain, Bernice, Mara's obituary, and the news articles. "To sum it up, if I don't help free Aden, I might suffer with chest pains forever."

With his elbows resting on the arms of the chair, Fowler tented his fingers and pursed his lips, looking at her intently. "You say that you and Mara were born on the same day, and you experienced chest pains the same day she was shot?"

"Yes." Sidney pulled her wallet out of her hand bag, flipped it open, and showed Fowler her driver's license. "See, I was born the same day as Mara. I don't have any proof with me that I was hospitalized the day Mara died, but I could have something faxed to you supporting that statement if you want confirmation."

Fowler took a folder from behind him and thumbed through it. His eyes moved from a page in it to Sidney's license. "Same birthday. Interesting. Do you have anything with you proving you work for the Nassau County Police Department?"

She reached into her briefcase and yanked out her police badge. "Here," she said, placing it on the top of his desk.

Fowler examined it. "Does your department know you're here

volunteering your services?"

"No. I'm on vacation leave, and I'm not here in any official capacity."

"Aden certainly can use all the help he can get. I've had an investigator searching for the taxi driver. He keeps running into stumbling blocks. Maybe you'll have better luck."

"Before I start searching for the taxi driver, I'd like to look through all the files."

"Certainly. My secretary will set you up in the conference room and bring them in."

"Thank you," Sidney said, standing up. "Do you know if the police looked for or had other suspects?"

"I doubt it. They questioned Aden's neighbors, co-workers, Mara's family, a few of her friends, but it appears they were just gathering evidence to convict him. I don't think anyone in the police department ever considered anyone else could have been the culprit; they had their man and didn't look further. They still haven't been able to locate the weapon. I had a team search around Aden's house, the nearby stream, and dumpsters for the gun. Unless a Good Samaritan finds it and turns it over to the police, I doubt that gun will ever show up. We've interviewed the same people the police questioned. We haven't been able to locate anyone who didn't like Mara. No enemies."

"How about Kate Morrison, the woman Aden once slept with?"

"When Aden didn't want anything more to do with her, she moved to Colorado. She has an ironclad alibi. An investigator thoroughly checked every detail she gave about her whereabouts. It's all in the files. The trial is in five weeks. So you'll be working against the clock to come up with something that might shed a light on his innocence." He gave her a pleasant smile. "I'm glad you're on Aden's team."

Sidney returned the smile. "So am I."

As soon as Sidney was settled in the conference room, Fowler had Kristie, one of the law firm's paralegals, check and verify Sidney's credentials. The paralegal confirmed Sidney Langston was a detective for the Nassau County Police Department. She had been out on sick leave, which recently changed to vacation leave. Kristie wasn't able to tap into any of Sidney's medical records, but she did learn Sidney had been rushed to the hospital on April 20. She also discovered that prior to working for Nassau County, Sidney had been employed by the CIA. Kristie couldn't find out in what capacity. In the process of doing the research, the paralegal stumbled upon Sidney's husband, Charles Langston, Assistant DA for the state of New York.

After Kristie delivered the information to Fowler, he studied it. Twenty minutes later, he leaned back in his chair and locked his fingers behind his head as he thought about what he had read. Sidney never attended a police academy. She went straight from working for the CIA to the police department, and they didn't send her to any training school, yet she passed all the required tests. Fowler assumed that meant Sidney had been trained by the CIA. Since she had worked there for seven years, he suspected she had been one of their agents. He had known several police officers who went to work for the CIA, but he had never heard of anyone going the opposite direction. He mulled over the various possibilities as to why she left the CIA and then decided he was wasting his time dwelling on it and sat up straight. He smiled to himself, feeling convinced a former CIA agent was now working on the Aden case.

At 4:45 p.m., Sidney closed the last file, picked up her notes and skimmed over them. Based on all the documents she had scrutinized, she saw numerous holes in the case against Aden. She didn't share Fowler's opinion that it was as solid as he had led her to believe. At the same time, she knew juries could be swayed if the evidence was well presented, especially when there wasn't anything to indicate another potential shooter. She had to find something that would cast doubt in the jurors' minds even if she couldn't determine the guilty party.

The door to the conference room opened, and Fowler stepped in. "How's it going?" he asked.

"I've been looking over their witness list. Lester Zisk, the taxi driver, is prominently listed on it. There's a letter in the files that says he won't be able to attend the trial due to a scheduled surgical procedure that he can't move to another date." Sidney glanced at her notes. "His sworn statement supported by a taxi log shows he picked up Aden at the airport at 7:39 p.m. and dropped him off at 8:27 p.m.

I also saw his picture. According to Aden, the heavyset man is not the taxi driver who drove him home."

Fowler sat down in a chair opposite Sidney. "As I mentioned earlier, we've been searching for the right guy. Until we find him, we can't prove Zisk wasn't driving that cab. It was checked out to him. My investigator, Sam Jordan, spoke to Zisk about that before we received the witness list. I suspect that's why Libby Martin is on the list."

"I read about her. She's in charge of checking out the cabs and dispatching them. Since Zisk won't be at the trial, is the DA's office planning to depose him?"

"Yes, but they haven't set up a time yet." He looked at his notepad. "This morning I was told that Deidre Carlson, Mara's best friend, might have to leave town before the trial. She has an aunt in Australia who is dying, and Deidre is her only living relative. The DA's office is making arrangements to have her deposed. I'll have an opportunity to cross-examine her and Zisk at their depositions."

"Do you intend to take any depositions?"

"In California, we can't depose any witnesses in criminal cases unless there's a strong likelihood they won't be able to attend the trial, and then it's handled the same way as if the witness were in court. However, we can interview prosecution witnesses, even though their statements won't be under oath or recorded.

"In three weeks Kate Morrison will be visiting a friend in San Diego. I've made arrangements to interview her when she's in town. After that, she won't be back until the day before the trial." Fowler laid his hand, palm up, on the table. "Hand me the witness list."

Sidney opened the top folder and pushed it across the table.

"Sam talked to most of these people before they showed up on the list, so we already know what they'll be testifying about." His eyes scanned the names. "Besides the police lab folks, a few officers who were first on the scene, and the four we've already talked about, there's Lamar and Vicky Midgley, Aden's neighbors. They'll testify they heard a gunshot around 8:30 p.m. Aden's co-workers, Victor Grenshaw and Molly Heller, will be testifying about the argument Aden had with Mara before he left for Brazil."

"Do you know if anyone else in the office heard that argument?"

"Our witness, Payton Russen, heard it."

Sidney thumbed through her notes. "He'll be testifying about how much Aden loved his wife, and he's Aden's character witness, right?"

Fowler nodded. "Along with Mara's parents, Thomas and Eva Irvine."

"Do you mind if I talk to your witnesses?"

Fowler sat forward in his chair and shook his head. "If any of the witnesses are reluctant to talk to you, tell them you work for me and we're just making sure we have everything covered."

Since there was a murderer at large, Sidney knew it wouldn't be wise to talk to any of them alone. "Can I have your investigator, Sam Jordan, come with me?"

"No problem. I think you and Sam will make a great team. I'll have him give you a call."

While Sidney ate dinner with Jean in the hotel restaurant, her cell phone vibrated. She plucked it out of her pocket and glanced at the unfamiliar number on the monitor. She apologized to Jean and then answered it, suspecting it might be Fowler's investigator.

"This is Sam Jordan," the caller said in a deep, raspy voice. "Greg Fowler wants me to work with you on the Aden case. He mentioned something about going to chat with our witnesses again."

"Yes. That's where I'd like to start. Can you go with me tomorrow morning?"

"Sure. What time?"

"Nine. I'll drive. Where can I pick you up?"

Sam proceeded to give her his office address and then said, "I'll meet you out front."

Chapter 9

Sidney climbed into her rented Lexus, set the GPS for Sam's address, and then drove out of the parking structure. Within twenty minutes, she found herself entering a slum neighborhood with its dilapidated buildings, rusty old cars, and shabbily dressed people sitting on apartment stoops while they smoked and chatted. Sidney took several deep breaths as she thought about Sam Jordan. Since Fowler had spoken highly of him, she had assumed his office would be in the high-rent district.

The GPS indicated she had reached her destination. Sidney cut to the curb and spotted a tall man in his mid-forties with sandy-colored hair wearing a navy-blue suit. He stood next to a two-story building that was badly in need of a paint job. Her eyes caught a glimpse of the sign next to the door that read: "S. Jordan and Company, Private Investigators." She wondered if Sam had other employees or if he had added "and Company" just for advertising.

As the man strolled toward the car, Sidney noticed his thick neck and broad shoulders. He appeared to have a muscular build, and from the way he moved, to be in great shape. When he was close to the passenger door, Sidney pushed a button, sending the electric window gliding down.

"Sidney Langston?" he asked.

"Yes. Sam Jordan?"

"Yep."

"Please get in."

He opened the door and scooted into the passenger seat. He eyed her up and down as he shut the door. "You're a cop from New York and a friend of Aden's?"

"Yes," she said, nodding and thinking being called "a friend of Aden's" was simpler than the truth. Sidney pushed on the accelerator and eased into the traffic. "I made an appointment with Mara's parents before I left the hotel."

"Nice folks. They didn't have one thing bad to say about Aden."

Sidney's hands remained on the steering wheel and her eyes on the road as she sensed Sam still scrutinizing her appearance. "Do they know about Aden's affair?"

"Yes. They also know it was only a one-night stand. Apparently, Mara was very close to her folks and didn't keep anything from them."

While they continued their two-hour trek to Los Angeles, Sam brought Sidney up to speed about the taxi driver. He had discovered Zisk worked part-time for a loan shark.

"He collects, or should I say swipes, cars, jewelry, electronics, and cell phones— anything portable of value from those who don't make timely payments. One source I tracked down said Zisk was working for Ladler, the loan shark, that night."

"Can't Fowler subpoena that source?"

"The source has a record as long as your arm. The prosecutors would have a field day with him. His testimony wouldn't stand up under the scrutiny."

"Were you able to find out anything at all about who might have driven the taxi that night?"

"No one wants to talk. There are a lot of illegal aliens in Zisk's neighborhood. I suspect it was one of them trying to make a few bucks."

"Did you mention that to Fowler?"

"Yeah. He says if I can find the guy, he'll work something out with the DA's office about the immunity issue before he puts the guy on the stand. But it's hard to get an illegal to trust that testifying won't get him shipped back across the border."

"I doubt a notarized statement or a video of the guy telling his story would work."

"You're right. The DA would never go for that. No cross-examination. They'd want to question the guy." Sam lifted a package of cigarettes out of his breast shirt pocket. "Mind if I smoke?"

"Yes. Also, the rental car company wouldn't like it," Sidney said, although she wasn't aware of a stipulation on the rental agreement about smoking in the vehicle.

Sam slipped the package back in his pocket. "I can wait."

"Is Zisk a family man?"

"Hell no. He's pretty rough around the edges. I can't imagine any woman would put up with him full time."

"Full time? So he has girlfriends?"

"If you want to call the girls he picks up in sleazy bars 'girlfriends.' I guess he's got some."

Sidney decided to redirect the conversation to Aden's witnesses. "Anything about Payton Russen that might be a problem?"

"He's Aden's best friend. He was the best man at Aden's wedding. They're like brothers. Payton's an upstanding citizen. He's never had any trouble with the law."

"Was he in Brazil with Aden?"

"Part of the time. He flew back and forth so he could deal with another project Brimwell Engineering has on the table."

"It's a small company, right?"

Sam nodded. "Yeah. Only nineteen full-time employees. When they get a project going, they hire subcontractors."

"Have you ever talked to the president, Marcus Brimwell?"

"Yep. He's a sixty-seven-year-old man who travels all over the world—anywhere a bridge might be built. He only occasionally socializes with the employees. Every year there's a summer and a Christmas party at his house. He did mention that his wife, Angelica, was very fond of Mara. Mara would visit her sometimes when he was out of town, and she brought her flowers each time Angelica came home from the hospital. He didn't disclose Angelica's health problems, but I got the impression they were continuous—maybe a heart condition or something like that. To him, Aden and Mara were the perfect couple. He can't understand what could've gone wrong. Right now, he's out of town. He left for Brazil last week to check out the site that Aden selected as the best location for the bridge."

"Were there several places they could build the bridge?" Sidney probed for additional knowledge about Aden's work.

"Three potential sites. One was immediately dropped because of the sandy soil. The other two were viable. Brimwell told me the construction costs would be cheaper for the site Aden picked. Aden also drew up the preliminary sketches. Brimwell said it all in engineering jargon, but that's what I got out of it in layman's terms."

Sam rubbed his chin. "Brimwell thought Aden was the best engineer he had. He didn't know about Aden's affair with Kate until he read about it in the paper. When Kate quit, she told him it was because she had a relative in Colorado she needed to look after. All his employees who weren't out of the country knew about the affair, but obviously, no one mentioned it to the boss. Not even his secretary, Molly."

"Molly Heller, the prosecutor's witness?"

"That's her. I only talked to her once, but the way she chatted about everyone—nothing in that office escapes her. I was surprised she had the ability to restrain from telling Brimwell all the details about the affair."

"It was just a one-night stand."

"Not according to Molly. Aden and Kate had been lusting for each other for months before they finally gave in to their desires."

"I wonder what Kate will say about it when Fowler interviews her," Sidney said, thinking out loud, while she continued following the GPS instructions and exited the freeway.

Suddenly, a car cut in front of her almost clipping her front bumper. In order to avoid a collision, she swerved to the right shoulder of the pavement, sending Sam's arm smashing into the passenger door. "Sorry about that. Are you okay?"

"Yeah, and that wasn't your fault. It was that jerk driving a dark gray Suburban. He probably doesn't have the faintest idea he almost caused an accident." Sam's eyes fixated on an emblem in the Suburban's back window. "On the other hand, that might have been an intended maneuver."

"What are you talking about?" Sidney asked as she stopped for a red light right behind the Suburban.

"Fowler isn't my only client," Sam explained.

"That Suburban is following you?"

"Probably. See the emblem that resembles a mountain range in the back window with SLI in the center. That emblem belongs to a company I'm investigating."

"You think they followed us all the way from your office?"

"Not that car. I've been watching. They must be using more than one vehicle."

"Why are they following you?"

"They're trying to figure out the name of my client."

"Then the guy driving that Suburban is pretty stupid. When you follow someone, you should stay behind that person's car and try to remain invisible, not alert them to your presence. Dumb."

Sam shook his head. "Whoever it is at SLI who wants to know didn't hire the swiftest group to get the info. A listening device they attached to my landline peeped when I picked up the receiver," he said, chuckling.

"You're kidding, right?"

"No," he said, still chuckling.

"You sure it was them?"

"Yep. Caught the car on a surveillance camera the night before."

"You don't have a security system?"

"Got one, all right. Had a rush job. No time to set it."

"So they're not professionals. Amateurs can be dangerous too."

"This group...doubt it. They like to show some muscle, like forcing you onto the shoulder of the road. Maybe if they ran into me in a dark alley, they might throw a few punches. Outside that, they're harmless."

Sidney didn't believe that. She had been in too many situations where amateurs started nervously shooting because they couldn't figure out an alternative. Pressing her lips together, she had to remind herself she was in L.A. for one reason—to prove Aden was innocent, nothing more. "If they continue keeping track of you all the way to the Irvines' house, they might hassle the Irvines after we leave. We can't let that happen. Let's lose them."

"I know this area. The guy is still in front of us. Turn right at the next intersection without signaling. Then make a sharp left. Go a block and make another sharp left. Forget your GPS. I'll get us to the Irvines'."

Within thirty minutes they stopped in front of the Irvines' house, a large two-story brick bungalow with a well-manicured lawn and trimmed bushes that surrounded the concrete porch running the width of the house. They climbed out of the Lexus and surveyed the road for the Suburban. Satisfied, Sidney and Sam headed to the front door flanked with stained glass windows on each side.

Before Sidney could push the doorbell, the door opened. A white-haired, attractive, slender woman in her early sixties greeted them.

"Hello, Sam." Her eyes moved to Sidney, and she gasped. "Oh, my dear, you resemble my beautiful Mara," she said with misty eyes as her voice quivered. She held open the door while she pulled a tissue out of her pocket and dabbed her eyes. "Please come in." She gestured toward the living room. "Take a seat, and I'll get Thomas."

Stepping into the room, Sidney admired the stone fireplace with a built-in dark oak bookcase on each side. A painting of Mara and two small children hung above the mantel. Sidney eased down into an upholstered armchair next to the one Sam had taken. The two chairs faced a coffee table. A couch stood on the other side of it.

Sidney watched as Thomas and Eva Irvine entered the room and sat down on the couch. After brief introductions, she began. "As I explained on the phone, I'm working for Gregory Fowler to help him prepare for the trial. He wants to make sure he hasn't missed anything." From her briefcase, Sidney took out a manila folder and a notebook with a pen attached. She noticed Sam pulling a small notepad out of his suit jacket inside pocket.

"I've read over the information you provided to Sam the last time he was here, so I'll begin by summarizing that. Stop me if I've got something wrong or if something is missing." She opened the folder. "Aden and Mara were married for nine years."

"Before that," Eva said, "they lived together for three years."

Sidney scribbled that down. "Aden was a loving husband and during that time, you never witnessed any harsh words between them."

"That's right," Thomas said.

Sidney continued. "As far as you both knew, Mara had no enemies."

"I just don't understand how anyone could shoot my baby," Eva said with trembling lips.

Thomas put his arm around his wife's shoulder. "Eva, she's gone to a better place. We'll see her again."

Eva wiped the tears from her cheeks. "I'm sorry. Mara's death and Aden in jail has been very hard on us. The children losing both parents. They might end up just like their dad. Aden was orphaned when he was twelve and raised by his grandparents. Now, we're the only family he has. I can't figure out why anyone would lock up Aden for murder. He loved our daughter."

Sidney flipped through her notes. "On April twentieth, Mara left the children with you so she could go home and surprise Aden."

"Yes," Thomas said, nodding his head.

"Besides you two and the children, did she tell anyone else she was going home?"

"No one," Eva said. "Not even Deidre, her best friend. She didn't want to take a chance that anyone would disturb them. Mara even planned on disconnecting their landline when she got there." Eva's lips began trembling again, and she ran her fingertips over them. "She was so excited to see him when she left here." Tears filled her eyes, and she buried her face in Thomas's shoulder.

"Sweetheart," Thomas said to his wife as he gently wiped her eyes.

While Sidney waited for Eva to regain her composure, she looked at Sam and saw he was busy scribbling in his notepad. "Just one more question. I hate to ask this, but we're working on trying to free your son-in-law. Mara told you about Aden's infidelity?" Sidney watched as Mara's parents both nodded. "How do you think that affected their relationship?"

"According to what Aden told Mara, it only happened once," Thomas said.

"Do you believe that?"

"Yes. Aden is a good man. He couldn't keep secrets from her. He was away on an overnight business trip with that woman. For some reason, he got extremely lonely, and that's when it happened. Why he got that lonely or what was going through his mind, only Aden can answer those questions. After Aden told Mara about it, she went to his office and yelled at the woman, and then she came here and cried on our shoulders. Aden came after her with a large bouquet of roses and begged her to come home."

"Mara was pretty embarrassed about causing a scene at his office," Eva said. "From what she said, I guess she also yelled at Aden there. But he didn't yell back at her. He never raised his voice toward her."

"He's gone on a lot of business trips, and he never got involved with another woman before that or since. We trust him," Thomas said. "Aden loved Mara. He called her every day from Brazil. They talked a long time. Mara visited us often when Aden was there. All she talked about was him. Her face glowed, and she sang as she helped put up decorations for her grandfather's ninetieth birthday. She couldn't wait for him to come home. Does that sound like a woman who wasn't getting along with her husband?"

"Why didn't she visit him in Brazil?"

"She planned to," Eva said. "Had airline tickets and everything. A couple of days before she was going to leave, Leon, her six-year-old son, came down with tonsillitis. She cancelled her trip and stayed home to take care for him. Leon ended up going to the hospital and having his tonsils out."

Sidney closed the folder and put it along with the notebook in her briefcase. "Thank you for your time," she said, easing out of the chair.

"Grandma," a boy yelled at the top of the stairs. "Sharie woke up from her nap."

"It's okay," Eva said. "You can both come down now." She turned to Sidney. "Sharie is our two-year-old granddaughter."

Sidney stood in the shadows next to the door as the children bounced down the stairs. She noticed the little girl with a cute, round face and short, curly hair looking in her direction. Suddenly Sidney felt a tingling sensation through her body as the child rushed toward her.

Sharie wrapped her arms around Sidney's legs. "Mommy, Mommy, pick me up."

Without a second thought, Sidney scooped the little girl into her arms and held her tight against her chest as if Sharie belonged to her.

Eva hurried over to them. She put her hands on Sharie's waist. "Sharie, honey, this nice lady isn't your momma," Eva said, attempting to lift Sharie from Sidney's arms.

Sharie leaned back and gazed at Eva's face. "Momma's smell." The little girl clung to Sidney while Eva tried to pull her away. "No, Granny," Sharie cried. "Stay here."

Sidney felt her eyes getting moist. "Sharie, I'm not your momma," she said and forced herself to help Eva take the child from her.

When the crying child was securely in her grandmother's arms, Eva moved away from Sidney.

Sam took Sidney's arm. "We'll call if we have any more questions," he said to Eva while he hurried out the door with Sidney.

Leon ran out of the house after them. "Will you give me a hug?" he asked Sidney as a tear drizzled down his cheek.

"Of course," she replied, bending down. She wrapped Leon in her arms and held him close.

"Leon," Thomas said, standing in the doorway. "Come into the house."

Sidney reluctantly released her hold on Leon. "Sweetie, go to your grandfather." She watched as Leon slowly made his way to the door while he looked over his shoulder at her.

When the door closed behind Leon, Sidney turned, went to the car with Sam, and got into the driver's seat as her eyes watered. She pulled a small tissue container from her purse and took out a handful. She wiped her face and blew her nose. Out of the corner of her eye, she saw Sam staring at her with raised brows and a perplexed expression on his face.

"Do you want me to drive?" Sam asked.

"If you don't mind."

Sidney and Sam switched places. After she snapped on her seatbelt, her eyes fixed on the Irvines' house while Sam turned the key, pushed the accelerator, and drove away from the curb. She couldn't make sense out of what had caused the children to act that way, or for that matter, why she didn't want to let them go. She wondered if subconsciously she was yearning for children, but as that thought swirled in her head, she knew that wasn't it. While the children were in her arms, their lives had flashed through her mind— from when they were born to the present. *How is that possible?* It reminded her of the time she saw Aden. She knew things about him, things she shouldn't know. *What is wrong with me?*

"It's tough on kids to lose a parent," Sam commented. "I've seen it too many times."

"So have I, but there was something different about those two," Sidney said, immediately wishing she could take the words back. She didn't want Sam to know anything about her conversations with Bernice.

"Maybe they've heard from their grandparents you're trying to help their dad."

"Yeah, that's probably it," she said, though she doubted that was the reason.

"Where to?"

"Let's stop for lunch and then head to Brimwell Engineering. I want to talk to Payton Russen."

"He might not be there," Sam said hastily.

"Why?"

"Sometimes he's not there. He goes out a lot. You should

probably make an appointment with him first."

Glancing at Sam, Sidney wondered about his response. It seemed he wanted the meeting postponed. *But why? Was something going on between them?* She studied his face for any signs of being edgy. She spotted his jaw muscle slightly tightening, nothing else. "If he's not there, we can chat with one of the other employees, maybe Molly or Grenshaw, the prosecutor's witnesses."

Chapter 10

"I need a smoke before we go in," Sam said, stopping in front of the Brimwell Engineering building.

As Sam stood next to the car enjoying his cigarette, Sidney looked at the large, gray metal structure and noticed no distinguishing features. The windows in the front were twelve-by-twelve-inch square panels, not big enough for anyone to climb through. The door was painted bright yellow. Along the side of the building were high windows and a set of garage doors.

When Sidney and Sam entered the building, they were greeted by a perky, middle-aged woman with short, gray-streaked, red hair. Light brown eyes sparkled in her round face.

"Hello, Molly," Sam said, and then he proceeded to introduce the two women.

"Did you see the game last night?" Molly asked Sam with excitement rising in her tone.

"Sure. Wouldn't have missed it," Sam replied. "What an ending with…"

While Sam and Molly chatted about the game, Sidney's eyes darted around. Behind Molly's desk was a door. She suspected that lead to Brimwell's office. Next to it was a line of offices, each with a nameplate on the door. The first one read: Aden S. Uzelac. Something clicked in her mind, and she knew the S stood for Spencer. Two doors down from Aden's was the office of Payton T. Russen. Opposite the offices was a large, open space with huge tables scattered throughout. Drawings and maps covered the surfaces. Two men and a woman were huddled around one of the tables. Posters of bridges hung on the walls.

"Is Payton Russen in?" Sidney asked, interrupting Sam and Molly's conversation.

"Yes. Let me buzz him." Molly pushed a button on her phone. "Sam and…" Her eyes shot up to Sidney. "Sam and a woman are here to see you."

Sidney rolled her eyes, deducing that Molly had already forgotten her name.

"Send them in." A male voice came through the speaker.

Sam tilted his head toward Payton's office. "This way."

Sidney walked a few feet behind him and noticed out of the corner of her eye that the two men working at a table were looking her way.

When Sam opened the door, Sidney heard Payton say, "I told you I didn't want to talk about it here." She caught a glimpse of Sam raising his hand in a stop position toward Payton.

Stepping into Payton's office, she wondered what was going on between the two of them and hoped whatever it was didn't have any bearing on Aden's case. *Could Sam be so unethical that he would work both sides of the fence?* Yet she knew Payton was a witness for the defense and was reported to be Aden's best friend.

Payton rose from his chair when he saw her and came around his desk. He was a short man with ash-brown hair and an attractive, square jaw. His green eyes were amplified by his wire-rimmed glasses.

"This is Sidney Langston. She's working for Fowler on Aden's case," Sam said.

Sidney shook Payton's hand. "Nice to meet you, Mr. Russen."

"Call me Payton."

Sidney gave him a pleasant smile. "Payton, I'm here to go over the information you provided Mr. Fowler…and to make sure we've covered everything."

"I'll say whatever you want me to say to get Aden off the hook," Payton said.

Sidney squinted as that statement caught her off guard. "Payton, we're not here to plant words in your mouth. We want you to tell the truth. Nothing else."

"Okay. Got it. Have a seat," he said, pointing toward a chair by the round table in the corner.

Sidney sat down while Payton snatched two chairs by his desk and brought them to the table. Sam carried one of them to the other side of Sidney.

When they were settled and Sidney had her folder and notepad on the table in front of her, she began. "Let's start with the argument you heard between Aden and his wife."

"It wasn't any big deal. It's been completely blown out of proportion," Payton said, raising his hands and swinging them out to his side, mimicking an explosion. "So they had a little fight. What married couple doesn't?"

"Apparently, it's a big deal to the prosecutors," she said with her pen in her hand, ready to write. "Tell me about it."

"It was right after Aden came back from a business trip with Kate…Kate Morrison. She used to work here." Payton pushed back his chair. "Hey, do you guys want some water or a soda? I sure am thirsty."

"I'm fine," Sidney said.

"So am I," Sam said.

"Be back in a minute," Payton said as he hurried out the door.

"Where to after we finish with Payton?" Sam asked.

She fished her cell phone out of her purse. "It depends on whether Payton has anything new to offer. I want to quickly check my voice mail." She held her phone next to her ear and listened. The first message was from Chas. He was just checking up on her. The day before, he had called four times, and she expected no less today. The second and final one came from Fowler. His message said, "Sidney. Deidre Carlson is leaving for Australia soon. The DA's office has set up her deposition for tomorrow at 9:30 a.m. Since they're having some remodeling done in their offices, I've told them they could use my conference room."

Sidney turned off her cell phone and slipped it back into her purse.

"Anything important?"

"A deposition…"

"Who's being deposed?" Payton asked as he entered the room, holding a soda pop can.

"A witness in the case," Sidney answered, giving no more details.

Payton sank down in his chair and swigged a big gulp of Coke. He placed the can on the table and then wiped his lips with the back of his hand. "Where were we?"

"You were telling us about the argument between Aden and his wife."

"Aaah. Right. Right after that trip, Mara stormed into the office. She could be pretty feisty. She approached problems head on...never held back anything." Payton took another sip of Coke.

Sidney felt her left shoulder being pushed forward, like someone had poked her. She glanced behind her but saw no one. As the poking sensation continued, she raised her hand and pressed her fingers into her shoulder blade to try to stop the sensation. When Payton put down his drink, Sidney picked up her pen and prepared to start writing again.

Fiddling with the pencil container in the center of the table, Payton went on. "She yelled Kate's name. Kate used to occupy the office next to mine. Anyway, Kate heard her and came out. Mara started screaming at her, saying something like 'Aden's a married man with two children.' Boy, the look in Mara's eyes. For a minute there, I thought we might see two women wrestling it out. Then, Aden walked in, took Mara's arm, and tried to calm her down. She didn't stop, but instead of continuing to scream at Kate, she started screaming at Aden. Aden pulled her out the door. Several of us looked through the windows and saw Mara jump into her car. Aden tried to open the passenger door. It must've been locked because he started pounding on the window. Mara drove off. Aden rushed to his car and followed her."

Sidney was having a difficult time concentrating on what Payton was saying since the feeling of being poked in her shoulder became more rapid. She laid down her pen, wrapped her hand around her shoulder, and asked, "Payton, when Mara was screaming at Aden, what did she say?"

"I don't remember the exact words, but something like, 'How could you? You're a family man...if this is the woman you want, go for it.'"

"Then he left for Brazil, right?"

"Yeah. The office was in an uproar. Kate quit the next day. Aden left a couple of days after that." Payton drained the rest of his Coke and then tossed the can in the waste basket next to his desk.

Sidney picked up her pen and scribbled in her notebook as she endured the unrelenting poking. Assuming it might have been caused by a twitching muscle from her early morning workout, she rolled her shoulder. "Let's go on. You were with Aden in Brazil?"

Payton nodded. "Most of the time, but I didn't leave with him."

"Aden's and Mara's cell phone usage summaries show they talked to each other almost every day. Some were long conversations. Did Aden ever mention any problems his wife was having at home?"

"One of the kids had tonsillitis. Had to go to the hospital. Stuff like that?"

"No. Problems with an adult."

Payton shook his head. "I can't think of anything."

"Did Aden talk often about his wife?"

"Oh, God, always! He was crazy about her. That's why I was shocked at the Kate situation."

"Is there anything that comes to your mind that might help Aden's defense?"

Payton scratched his forehead and pressed his lips together. A minute later, he said, "Nope. I know Aden didn't do it. He'd never hurt Mara. He's told me about the taxi driver. Any luck in finding the right guy?"

"We're still looking," Sam said, slipping his notepad in his suit coat pocket.

Sidney tucked her notebook, folder, and pen away. "Thank you for your time, Payton," she said and shook his hand. Her left arm ached as she picked up her briefcase in her right hand.

When Sam and Sidney were seated in the car, he asked, "Is something wrong with your shoulder?"

"I think I overdid it lifting weights earlier."

"That's easy to do."

"What's going on with you and Payton?"

"Going on?" he asked, drumming his fingers on his thigh.

Sidney arched an eyebrow. "Sam, I'm not here to play games. I expect an honest answer. When I was right outside Payton's office, he said he didn't want to talk to you there. Tell me what's going on?"

"I'm working on something for Payton. It has absolutely nothing to do with the Aden case."

Sidney gritted her teeth and snapped, "It better not."

"Hey, Sidney, I have two ex-wives to support and four kids. I can't afford to lose my license. I'm not about to get involved with anything that's a conflict of interest."

She didn't detect anything in his voice to indicate he was lying. At the same time, she wasn't convinced he was telling the truth. She wondered if Payton knew something that could be detrimental to Aden's case, and Sam was working on sorting it out. *If that's it, why wouldn't Sam share that with Fowler?* Sidney knew she couldn't let it go, and she doubted Sam would tell her anything more about it. Since she didn't want to take a chance that something ugly might be revealed during the trial, she was determined to find out exactly what Sam was working on for Payton through other means.

Sidney glanced at her watch—4:15 p.m. "One more stop. I want to check the crime scene."

Chapter 11

After following Sam's driving directions for thirty minutes, Sidney entered an area of tree-lined streets and made several sharp turns until he instructed her to pull into the next driveway. She drove through an opening between oak and pine trees and bushes that shielded the two-story, white brick house from the street. "This is secluded. I read the description and saw the photos, but there wasn't one taken from the road," she commented. "Now I understand why it took the police department so long to search the property for the weapon."

"Fowler hired a group to do the same thing. Wherever that gun is, it's nowhere around here."

Sidney strolled around the front yard while Sam leaned against a tree and puffed on a cigarette. Her eyes scanned the bushes and shrubs that lined the parameter of the property. A bush in the front corner caught her attention. She moved closer and saw part of it was mangled with broken twigs lying next to it. She paused and wondered if that had occurred when the yard was being searched or if that had been caused by the perpetrator. Standing next to it, she turned toward the house and knew it would be easy to reach the gate leading to the back yard without being noticed at night from that location. The shadows created by the bushes could keep any intruder well hidden.

Edging her way toward the gate, Sidney carefully surveyed the ground in front of her. A long indentation ran between the grass and the bushes. Sidney knelt down to check it out. She ran her hand over the stretched footprint that appeared to have been caused by a person running toward the road. She brushed some fallen leaves away from the dirt, but she couldn't find another print. One of her eyebrows lifted and her mouth thinned into a flat line. This wasn't a clean crime scene. *It's been over two months since Mara was murdered. The crime scene has been completely contaminated by people trudging around searching for the weapon and whoever provides lawn care. My chances of finding any evidence here is probably nil, but I'm not giving up.* At the rim of the footprint, she noticed a brownish-orange substance. Even though she suspected it might not have come from the perpetrator's shoes, she yanked on a pair of latex gloves and scooped up the substance into a plastic container.

"What did you find?" Sam asked, walking toward her.

"Some orange stuff around a footprint. Since a lot of people have wandered around this front yard, it probably has nothing to do with the crime, but I don't want to leave any stone unturned. Do you know which lab Fowler uses?" asked Sidney, putting the container in her bag.

"No. When I'm dealing with one of his cases, I give him whatever I find, and he takes care of it. But you're probably right. I doubt if there's any evidence left to find around here. It's either been hauled away or destroyed."

Sam stood behind Sidney as she examined the latch on the backyard gate. "There's a place here," she said, pointing to the spot, "for a lock. I don't see any signs that a padlock was ever inserted in that hole. Can you confirm that?"

"I asked one of the officers about it. He said the police report stated there wasn't a lock on the gate at the time they arrived. He also mentioned if the gate had been locked when Mrs. Uzelac was shot, Mr. Uzelac probably removed the lock when he ditched the gun."

"There aren't any scrapes or indications of wear around the hole. I'm going to call Mara's folks and ask them about it."

Sam closed the gate behind them and then followed Sidney to the hot tub.

"Part of the outline of where Mara's body was found is still visible," Sidney said, gazing at the marking.

"According to the forensic tests, the shooter was only ten feet away."

Sidney turned her head as her eyes darted around the back yard.

"The hot tub is approximately fifty feet from the patio door, and seventy-five feet from the gate," she said, thinking out loud while she studied the place where the victim had been shot. "Mara had a bottle of Champagne in a cooler next to the hot tub along with two glasses and a tray of hors d'oeuvres. She was wearing a robe, so she hadn't been caught off guard soaking in the water with the noise of the jets drowning out footsteps. For the perpetrator to get that close to her without her attempting to run, knocking something over, or grabbing an object to protect herself, she had to have known her shooter."

"That's the same conclusion the cops came to," Sam said. "I don't mean to play the devil's advocate, but no one else besides her family knew she was home."

Sidney crossed her arms across her chest and stared at him. "You're working for Fowler," she said with a sharp edge in her voice. "And you don't have the slightest doubt Aden is guilty?"

Sam held up his hand with his palm facing her. "Hey...hey. That isn't what I meant," he said, trying to soften the rage he saw in Sidney's eyes. "It's just that there aren't any other suspects. If someone had been stalking Mara, watched her drive into their driveway, and waited for nightfall, he wouldn't have charged into the back yard and shot her without at least attempting to have his way with her first. Come on, there weren't any signs of a struggle." He took a deep breath. "Like you said, it had to be someone she knew."

"That's the premise I'm currently working on," Sidney said, lowering her arms to her sides. "Even if we don't find the guilty party, we have to find something that will help establish doubt in the minds of the jurors—like the taxi driver." She headed toward the back door. "I want to check out the inside of the house."

"It's locked, and there's an alarm."

She slightly smiled. "I can take care of that." She guessed Sam could too. Within five minutes they were in the house and the alarm had been disabled. Sam had been in the house often, so he decided he'd stay in the kitchen and wait for her.

Sidney strode into the spotless, cream-colored living room. She gazed at the happy faces of Aden, Mara, and their two children in the portrait hanging above the sofa. Pictures covered a tall, narrow table that stood next to a large window at the front of the house. She picked up the one with Aden dressed in a tuxedo and Mara in her bridal gown.

After she set it back down, Sidney moved into the hallway and envisioned a trail of rose petals lying on the tile floor. She went into the family room off the kitchen and saw a row of pictures of the children from babies to the present. They reminded Sidney of the images that had flashed through her mind when she hugged the children.

She peeked into the den, and then she quickly swept through the upstairs bedrooms. Sidney doubted the perpetrator entered the house, and if by chance he had, any trace of him would be gone by now. When she stepped into the kitchen, Sam was nowhere in sight. Glancing out the window above the sink, she saw him standing with his back to the house and cigarette smoke rising above his head.

After briefly scanning the kitchen, Sidney moved to the patio door, looked out, and had a long moment of reflection. She knew trying to prove Aden was innocent would be an uphill battle. The crime scene had been destroyed, the trial was quickly approaching, and the taxi driver the police rounded up was willing to commit perjury. Sam was right; there wasn't another likely suspect, so she'd have to find an unlikely one. With that in mind, she enabled the alarm system, and marched out of the house, locking the door behind her.

Climbing into the car, Sam asked, "Where to now?"

"Let's call it a day."

While she drove Sam back to his office, she spotted the dark gray Suburban a few cars behind them. She took her eyes off the road and glanced at Sam. He was busy checking messages on his cell phone. He appeared completely oblivious to the tail. *Oh, well. That's not my case.*

Chapter 12

Sidney strolled into Fowler's office at 8:45 a.m., their agreed upon meeting time. Fowler motioned for her to take a seat while he finished his phone call. Hanging up the receiver, he said, "The court recorder will be here at 9:15. John Baxter from the DA's office will be coming with Deidre Carlson. If you don't mind, I thought I'd introduce you as my assistant."

"That's fine. Also, could you refer to me as Sidney Malaney? That's my maiden name."

"I can do that. During my cross-exam, I'm going to ask Deidre Carlson what she was doing the evening of April twentieth, unless that was already addressed in her direct examination." He regarded Sidney intently with steely blue eyes. "Is there anything specific you would like me to question her about?"

Sidney thought about the bruise on her shoulder in the same spot where she had the sensation of being poked the day before at Brimwell Engineering and wondered if Mara was responsible for it. *Could the killer be associated with that company?* "Ask her how many of Aden's co-workers she knows." The corner of her mouth curved up into a half smile. "And if any of them were extra friendly." She paused. "Your witnesses yesterday didn't give me the slightest inkling or point me in any direction as to who might be a suspect. So this is a fishing expedition, nothing more. Is it okay if I pass you notes in case she mentions something in her testimony that might be interesting to pursue?"

"That's why I want you in the room." Fowler stood and grabbed a couple of folders from the top of his credenza. "They'll be here soon."

When Fowler and Sidney entered the conference room, the court reporter was busy setting up her equipment. "Hello, Patricia," Fowler said.

"Hello, Mr. Fowler," Patricia said. "Bart from the DA's office has already finished hooking up the videotaping equipment." She held up a square remote. "I just need to push this when we get started."

Sidney glanced at the video camera and monitor at the far end of the room.

Fowler moved to the other side of the long, light oak, oval table. Behind it stood a tall narrow table that held an assortment of bottled beverages and glasses. After he introduced Patricia and Sidney, he gestured toward the beverages and said, "Help yourselves." Then he reached over and took a bottle of apple juice and an empty glass.

Sidney had just filled a glass with water when a stout man with auburn hair and an attractive, petite, brown-haired woman entered the conference room.

"Hello, John," Fowler said, shaking the man's hand.

Within five minutes, the introductions were over, and Patricia was checking the spelling of everyone's name.

Sidney sensed Baxter eyeing her. She knew she had seen him before and guessed it was at one of the conventions she had attended with Chas.

"Ms. Malaney, you look familiar. Have we met before?" Baxter asked.

"Possibly. Do you surf?" she asked, though she doubted it looking at the overweight man.

"No," he said with a smile.

"Let's get started," Fowler said, and Sidney felt relieved that Baxter couldn't speculate about where he had seen her any longer.

John Baxter and Deidre Carlson took seats at the head of the table in marked spots where they could be seen by the video recording camera.

Baxter waited for the court reporter to swear Deidre in, and then he began. "Ms. Carlson, how long did you know Mara Uzelac?"

"Since ninth grade."

"How would you describe your relationship with Mrs. Uzelac?"

"We were best friends," Deidre said as she nervously fidgeted with her fingers in her lap. "I was maid-of-honor at her wedding. We talked on the phone at least two or three times a week. We hung out a lot, went shopping, went to the gym. I sometimes babysat her kids. They call me Aunt Deidre." She inhaled deeply and gripped her hands together. "Mara was always there for me whenever I needed her. She helped me through some rough times," she said with moist eyes.

"As far as you know, did Mrs. Uzelac have any enemies—anyone she didn't get along with?"

"I keep thinking about that. Everyone loved Mara."

Sidney noticed a slight flinch under Deidre's left eye, and from her years with the CIA and Nassau county police department, she had developed expertise at subtle body language to detect lies. She sensed Deidre was not being truthful. Yet, based on everything she had been told, she doubted Deidre and Mara weren't getting along at the time of the crime. *Who was this witness trying to protect?*

Deidre went on. "I can't think of one person who didn't like her except for Kate Morrison. Now, Aden, that's a whole other thing."

"What did you mean about Aden?"

Deidre bit her lower lip. "Well, I think he might have had enemies…or at least one."

"Why do you think that?"

"I heard him almost shouting on the phone a couple of times when I was there."

"Do you know what it was about?"

"Work stuff. Bridge construction materials…where a new one should go…something like that."

"Do you know who he was talking to?"

She shook her head. "No."

"You said you heard Mr. Uzelac on the phone twice talking in an angry tone."

"Objection," Fowler interrupted. "She said he was almost shouting. She never mentioned an angry tone."

"Let me rephrase that," Baxter said. "Ms. Carlson, you said you heard Mr. Uzelac on the phone twice almost shouting. Did those conversations occur recently or over a period of several years?"

Deidre wrinkled her nose and squinted.

After a minute, Baxter said, "Ms. Carlson?"

"This year, before Aden left for Brazil," Deidre answered.

"Did you talk to Mrs. Uzelac on April twentieth?"

Nodding, Deidre said, "Yes. Just for a few minutes. She was busy getting stuff ready for her grandfather's birthday party. Over two hundred guests were invited. I planned to go."

"During that conversation, were you aware that Mrs. Uzelac wasn't staying at her home?"

"Yeah."

"Did she mention she would be going to her house that day?"

"No."

"That's all the questions I have for Ms. Carlson. Mr. Fowler, would you like to cross-examine her."

"Yes," Fowler said, and then changed seats with Baxter.

Fowler began, "Ms. Carlson, do you know any of Aden's co-workers?"

"A few—Payton, Victor, and Molly."

"Do you know them well or just casually?"

"I've gone with Mara a few times to Aden's office. I chatted with Molly while I waited for her. Payton is Aden's best friend. I ran into him often at their house—whenever there was a party. And I'm dating Vic."

That's interesting, Sidney thought. Victor was going to be testifying about Mara screaming and yelling, and Deidre was testifying about how everyone loved her.

"Ms. Carlson, what were you doing the evening of April twentieth?" Fowler asked.

"I went to dinner with Vic, but he had some business stuff he needed to take care of, so he brought me home and left around eight. Then I watched television."

"So you were home alone at eight-thirty?"

Deidre's eyes sprang wide open. She leaned forward and clasped the edge of the table. "You think I shot Mara?"

"Ms. Carlson, I'm just trying to establish your whereabouts when the shooting occurred. That's all."

Deidre inhaled deeply and straightened her back. "Okay. I was home alone." She lifted her glass and took a sip of water.

Fowler scrawled a note in the border of a printed page. "Did you ever witness any arguments between Mr. and Mrs. Uzelac?"

Deidre shook her head. "No. They were always loving and considerate about each other when I was there."

"Did Mrs. Uzelac ever complain to you about Mr. Uzelac?"

"Only once."

"What was that about?"

"Kate Morrison. After Aden told Mara about the affair."

"Did Mrs. Uzelac refer to Mr. Uzelac's relationship with Ms. Morrison as an affair?"

"No. She called it a one-night stand, but she was still pretty mad about it."

"To the best of your knowledge, was she mad at Mr. Uzelac all the time he was in Brazil?"

"No. They made up before he left." Deidre's eyes dropped to the table. "She really loved him."

"I don't have any more questions," Fowler said. "Mr. Baxter, do you have any re-direct?"

"Yes," Baxter said, and switched chairs with Fowler again. "Ms. Carlson, you said Mr. and Mrs. Uzelac made up before he left for Brazil."

She nodded. "Yes."

"How do you know that?"

"Mara told me."

"Did you see them together after Mr. Uzelac told Mrs. Uzelac about his infidelity?"

Deidre shook her head.

"Please answer verbally for the recorder," Baxter said.

"No."

"So you have no personal knowledge that their relationship had mended after Mr. Uzelac disclosed his affair to Mrs. Uzelac."

"Objection," Fowler said. "The word 'affair' implies a longer relationship than one night. The length of that relationship has not been established in this proceeding."

"Let me rephrase," Baxter said. "Ms. Carlson, do you have any personal knowledge that Mr. and Mrs. Uzelac's relationship had mended after Mr. Uzelac's disclosure of infidelity?"

Deidre's eyebrows rose. "But Mara wouldn't lie to me."

"I'm asking about what you personally saw," Mr. Baxter said. "Did you see them displaying affection toward each other after Mr. Uzelac's infidelity disclosure?"

Deidre spun around her charm bracelet. "No."

"Thank you, Ms. Carlson. I have no more questions."

Back in Fowler's office, Sidney said, "That made it pretty clear that the prosecutors are going after the infidelity angle."

"And they've got witnesses supporting that scenario. In fact, my witnesses don't have any personal knowledge things were okay between the two. Aden came after Mara at her parents' house. She agreed to go home with him. He hugged and kissed her, but even the Irvines will say Mara hadn't completely forgiven him when they left the Irvines' house. Aden took a taxi to the airport because their son would be home from school before Mara could drop him off and return home."

"So no adult saw them together as a loving couple after the incident at Aden's place of employment?"

"That's right. Everything is hearsay."

"Any idea what reason the prosecutors might give to the jury as to why he didn't just divorce her instead of kill her?"

Fowler shook his head.

"There's Aden's cell phone summaries," Sidney said. "Most of the calls I saw went to either Mara's cell phone or their landline. Do any of the other phone numbers belong to Kate Morrison?"

"We've traced all of them. Not one was placed to Ms. Morrison. However, Aden received a number of calls from her. They were short, but they're there. The prosecutors could make the argument that Aden used a pay phone to call her so it couldn't be traced."

"Then the prosecutors should submit her telephone summary to prove she received calls from Brazil."

"I asked for everything like that in discovery. It wasn't among the documents I received. I intend to address that during Ms. Morrison's interview."

"If—and that's a big if—I were able to locate the taxi driver, can you give him any kind of guarantee he won't be deported?" Sidney asked, thinking she could call in a favor and get the guy a green card, but that could be construed as paying him for his testimony. She could envision how the prosecutors would use that against Aden—a witness lying under oath to get legal status.

"If you can deliver the guy, I'll work something out so he doesn't need to fear testifying for that reason."

"Has the DA's office set up a time to depose Lester Zisk?"

"Yes. Ten o'clock Thursday morning. It'll also be in my conference room."

"That gives me two days to do a little snooping into his life."

Chapter 13

As Sidney parked next to the county jail to visit Aden again, she recalled the gate lock and placed a call to the Irvines. Thomas answered on the first ring. After they greeted each other, she asked, "Did the gate leading to the back yard at the Uzelacs's house ever have a lock on it?"

"No. Mara didn't want to look for a key whenever she went from the back to the front yard. The kids are well trained to stay in the backyard when the gate is shut."

"Thanks. That's all I needed to know."

"I hope you can find something that will prove Aden is an innocent man. The kids sure do miss their dad."

"I'm working on it." Sidney disconnected and then called Sam.

Sam picked up after two rings and asked, "We going someplace today?"

"Can you shadow Lester Zisk?"

"Sure. Anything special I should be looking for?"

"No, unless he talks to a Hispanic guy that meets the description Aden gave. Outside that, I just want to know where he'll be later tonight."

"Got it," Sam said and clicked off.

Sidney got out of her car and strode toward the county jail visitors' entrance. This time it didn't take her very long to get cleared through security. Within fifteen minutes, she was seated in a stall in the visitors' room and flipping through her notebook as she waited for Aden.

Ten minutes later, he walked through the door behind the panel with an officer. A sudden excitement flared in her as their eyes riveted on each other. Her breath came in wild gasps. She felt her heart hammering in her chest and her legs trembling. Forcing her body to relax, she closed her eyes and thought about Chas. When her legs no longer vibrated and her heartbeat slowed down, she opened her eyes and saw Aden sitting at the counter opposite her.

"Are you okay?" he asked in his deep voice.

Sidney cleared her throat. "Yes. I was just running some things over in my mind."

His forehead creased, and his lips quivered slightly. "I still can't get over how much you look like my wife."

Sidney didn't want him to speculate too long about that, so she dug right in to asking questions. "Aden, I need some answers. Last time you told me you only had a one-night stand with Kate. Some of your co-workers believe it was more than that. Can you tell me how they could've gotten that impression?"

"Kate started at Brimwell Engineering a couple of years ago, right after she graduated from college. I think she viewed all of us as her mentors, except for old man Brimwell. She bounced around from office to office asking questions. Last year, after I worked with her on a project, she stopped making rounds to all the offices and started coming into only mine. From the way she looked at me, I suspected she had a little crush. I tried to brush her off by telling her I was too busy whenever she showed up next to my desk. I told her one of the other engineers could help her. She left me alone for a while, spending more time in Payton's office. He loved it."

"Did Payton ever date her?"

"They went out for beers sometimes after work, but nothing more than that. Payton went on a business trip, and then Kate began asking me questions again."

"What about the other engineers?"

"They were tired of being bothered by her, so they all used the 'too busy' excuse. Some of my co-workers started with the company right out of college, but none of them were as needy as Kate. I decided to talk to Brimwell about it after the holidays, but then the contractor Brimwell had hired for a bridge in France had an accident. He flew over there. When he came back, his wife was having some medical problems, so I put it off again." Aden hung his head, rubbed his forehead, and stared at the floor. "Boy, do I regret that."

Sidney squinted and pursed her lips in confusion. "If Kate was that big of a problem, why did you sleep with her?"

"You have no idea how many times I've mulled over that same question." He ran his fingers through his hair. "She went with Vic and me to a seminar in Denver. After dinner and listening to the keynote speaker, the three of us went to the hotel bar. We started chatting about Brazil. I'd already been dreading the trip since Mara and the kids weren't going with me." He fidgeted with his hands. "They've always gone with me on business trips that last longer than a month, but now Leon's in school. Mara and I talked about leaving the kids with her folks, but we agreed that would be too hard on her parents—running around after two kids that always seem to be on the move." A sad expression crept across his face. "Now look what's happened. Her parents will probably end up raising them."

Sidney feared he might be right if she didn't succeed in discovering the real culprit. "Aden, I'm going to find a way to prove you're innocent." Her stomach churned. "You're going to get out of here."

He gave her a smile, but she saw doubt in his dark brown eyes.

"You're in the hotel bar having drinks and talking about Brazil. What happened next?"

"I started to feel the booze, but that didn't stop me from ordering another drink. Vic excused himself and went to his room. Kate moved to my side of the booth and started stroking my thigh as I wallowed in self-pity, thinking about how I'd soon be alone in a foreign country without my family and how much I was going to miss Mara. After that, all I remember is waking up in Kate's room with my arms around her." Aden squeezed his eyes shut and shook his head as though he was trying to wipe the vision out of his mind.

Sidney sat quietly for a minute while she absorbed what he had said, and then she scrawled a few notes. "Do you recall the name of the hotel and the date?"

"Almost the worst night of my life. I'll never forget the Denver Hilton or February twenty-first."

Sidney wrote down the information. "Did you ever call Kate while you were in Brazil?"

"Hell, no! After that night I couldn't stand being around her. It was difficult for me to board the plane with her. She kept clinging to my arm, and I kept brushing her away. I'm sure Vic suspected something might have gone on between Kate and me after he went to his room."

"Did she call you?"

"Yes. The first time she called, I didn't recognize the number. Like a fool, I answered it, and then I told her to get lost. The next time she called, I was with Payton. He wanted to talk to her, so I handed him my cell phone."

"Did Payton have access to your phone to make calls?"

"No. I keep it in my pocket, but I wouldn't be surprised if he called Kate when we were there. Is someone saying I called her?"

"On your cell phone summary, it shows she called you a few times. There aren't any outgoing calls to her." Sidney didn't want to tell him Fowler's theory that the prosecutors might claim he called from another phone, which, she knew now, could be a real possibility since Payton might have called her from Brazil.

"Before you left for Brazil and after you made up with Mara, did any of your friends or other adults see you two together?"

Aden ran his fingers through his hair again. "Oh, come on," he said in a frustrated tone. "Are they saying Mara and I weren't getting along when I left?"

"It's a potential scenario, so I want to make sure we have it covered. Did someone see you two together?"

He shook his head. "No. We wanted to spend those couple of days alone. The kids were there, but we still managed private time," he said with a slight smile and sad eyes.

"In February when Deidre was at your house, she heard you yelling at someone on the phone. Do you remember that conversation?"

"Yeah," he said, nodding. "It was over a location for a bridge in Brazil."

Sidney cocked her head to the side, trying to figure out why they'd be discussing it before they checked it out. "The same bridge you went to Brazil about?"

Aden's head bobbed up and down. "The same one. There were three potential sites. Payton had gone there a few months earlier to do an initial assessment. He came back claiming only one site would be suitable but only brought soil samples back for that site—no pictures, nothing else." He tapped his fingertips together, and his brow furrowed in irritation. "We do more than just sample the soil to make that determination. We were already scheduled to do a complete analysis of the three sites—that was the trip I took with Payton. We hired some locals to help us when we got there."

"So why were you yelling on the phone?"

"He thought we didn't need to do any more analysis. He knew the best site, so we should cancel the trip. Payton knew it wasn't my call—only Brimwell makes that kind of decision. He wanted me to talk to Brimwell."

"Why didn't *he* want to do that?"

"He had already mentioned it to Brimwell, and Brimwell still wanted us to go. Payton thought if I supported him, Brimwell might reconsider. Anyway, I told Payton I wouldn't talk to Brimwell about it since I didn't believe the sites had been adequately evaluated. Payton can be a real hothead, so that's when the yelling started. He yelled, and I yelled back. That wasn't the first and I'm sure it won't be the last time we yell at each other."

"Why did he care that much about the sites?"

"It wasn't the sites. It was his ego. Brimwell always wants a second opinion on Payton's choices."

"Only Payton's?"

"No. Some of the other engineers get the same scrutiny, but they haven't been with the company as long as Payton."

"And you?"

"Brimwell checks all my documents, but he never requests a second opinion." He paused, and then he briefly closed his eyes and his jaw tightened. "Don't tell me because I yelled on the phone they're going to claim I have a bad temper?"

"I don't know how the prosecutors are going to portray you. The yelling came up in this morning's deposition of Deidre Carlson when she was asked if Mara had enemies."

"Everyone liked Mara."

"That's what Deidre said, but she thought you might have enemies because she heard you yelling on the phone." Another question popped into Sidney's head. "When you were in Brazil, did you select the same site Payton had chosen earlier?"

"No. One of the other sites was geologically better, and the cost to build the bridge there would be significantly less. Payton was pissed off about my recommendation, but the final decision was made by Brimwell."

"The site you picked?"

Aden nodded.

Sidney wondered if Payton would make more out of the relationship between Kate and Aden than existed because he was mad about Aden not going along with his decision on the bridge location. "Aren't you and Payton best friends?"

"Yeah. He comes here to see me almost every other day." He raised his hand and waved it sideways. "Hey, just because Payton and I don't agree over something at work, that doesn't affect our friendship. He got over it. He's not harboring any resentment. If he was, he wouldn't keep visiting me."

Sidney turned the page in her notebook. "Is there anyone in your life you don't get along with—enemies?"

His eyes fixed on the counter as he rubbed his chin with his knuckles and held his lips tightly together.

Sidney read over some of her notes while she patiently waited for his response.

Finally, he spoke. "There have been a few people I didn't get along with, but the ones that stand out I haven't seen for years. In recent times, the only person that comes to mind is Kate. And I'm not sure if she hates me as much as I hate her." His eyes met Sidney's. "You're not thinking someone killed Mara to get even with me over something, are you?"

"Aden, someone killed her, and I'm looking at every potential motive, even if it seems farfetched. Right now, I'm not ruling anything out."

Aden's shoulders slumped, and his face lined with stress. "All this time I've been thinking it was a stalker, a stranger, someone who didn't know her. I never imagined it could be someone I knew."

"Visiting time is over," the guard said, looking at the clock on the wall.

"Aden, I never said it was someone you knew, but I want to cover all the bases. Everyone is a suspect until I can narrow it down."

Sidney gathered up her things and watched Aden trudge through the side door with the guard. A sense of grief and sadness flooded her mind. She wanted to be near him and hated seeing him leave. Yet, she loved Chas and missed him terribly. Sidney recalled the conversation she had with her husband the first time she saw Aden.

She hadn't held anything back. She had even told him about the way she felt when she saw Aden. Sidney smiled as she thought about Chas's comment. "I sure am damn glad he's locked up. Otherwise, I'd have to arrange for a duel with swords." Chas excelled in fencing, and it was his favorite sport. She suspected Aden had never even held a sword, so he'd be no match against her husband.

She inhaled deeply, picked up her briefcase, and headed toward the exit.

Chapter 14

Getting ready to meet Zisk, Sidney fixed her hair in a mass of flowing curls, tucked one side of it behind her ear, and secured it in place with a red bow. Next, she covered her face in a heavy coat of makeup and highlighted her eyes with long false eyelashes. Then she slipped on black fishnet tights; a tight, short, red leather skirt; a low cut, white peasant blouse; long, dangly black-and-red earrings; and five inch platform heels. She attached a sheath to her thigh and inserted a two-edged knife. She dropped her Beretta in her newly acquired, oversized, black patent leather purse. Sidney shouldered the handbag and gazed at her image in the mirror. She felt pleased with her new appearance and figured she'd easily pass as a hooker.

Jean's mouth flew wide open and her eyebrows rose when she saw Sidney. "You're going out like that?"

"Jean, it's a costume. I'm not planning on making a career change. Relax," Sidney said, turning the doorknob that lead to the hotel hallway.

After climbing into her car, she called Sam. "Where is he?"

"At Fernan's, a bar close to where he lives."

"He's not driving a taxi tonight?" Sidney said, feeling disappointment. She wanted to be his next customer.

"No. He hasn't even checked one out today. Maybe Tuesdays are his day off."

Sidney thought for a minute. After all the time she spent prepping for her meeting with Zisk, she wasn't about ready to give up and not get information from him. "Okay, where's the bar?" She punched it into her GPS as Sam gave her the address. "Meet me out front."

Twenty-five minutes later, she saw the sign that read "Fernan's." It was a plain one story structure with an artificial, brick façade sandwiched between tall apartment buildings. Two small, round tables stood in front of it. Sidney drove around the building until she found a parking spot. She swung her hips, sauntering to the entrance. Sitting at one of the outside tables was Sam, puffing on a cigarette. Trying out her new role, she moseyed over and sank down in a chair near him. "Hey, Mista, ya got a smoke for me?" she said in a slow drawl.

Sam eyed her up-and-down. "I sure do." He took a cigarette out of his package.

Sidney touched his hand. "No thanks, Sam," she said in her normal voice.

Sam's forehead creased as his eyes opened wider. "Holy shit! Sidney, you need to warn me. I was just starting to think I might get lucky tonight."

She smiled. "Who knows? Maybe someone else will come by. How's Zisk doing inside? Has he already picked up a new girlfriend?"

"He's been talking to the woman sitting next to him at the bar. I think he might've bought her a drink. But if you're going to make moves on him in that outfit, he'll dump her quick."

"That's exactly my plan, but I need to get him talking about driving a taxi. That isn't something a guy would normally spit out to impress a gal. So when you see me close to him at the bar, come in and say something like, 'Zisk, can I talk to you about your taxi?'"

"He'll recognize me."

"I'm hoping he does. That will help me to get him to talk."

"Anything you want me to do after that?"

"Hang around out here in case I have trouble losing him when I leave." She cocked an eyebrow. "I hate beating up grown men. They always get so angry when a woman takes them down. Besides, I don't want to ruin my outfit in case I need it for the right taxi driver."

Feeling doubtful that slender Sidney could handle a man as big as Fisk, Sam rolled his eyes. "I'll stick around."

Sidney entered the dimly-lit building. The bar ran half the length of the room. Above it, a mirror hung glimmering in the gloom that made the establishment look twice as large. She spotted the man in the photo sitting on a barstool next to a bleached blonde, average-sized woman with enormous boobs. On the other side of Zisk was an empty barstool. She strolled toward him and slowly inched her way onto the stool "accidentally" bumping Zisk in the process.

"Sorry, Mista," she said in her soft drawl as he turned her direction.

"That's quite all right, little lady," he said, sizing her up-and-down. He swiveled his chair toward her. "You been in here before?"

"Just moved inta town."

The woman on the other side of him grabbed his arm. "Hey, Lester, you ready to go now?"

He looked over his shoulder at her. "Changed my mind, Betty. See if Hank wants to go." He nodded toward the guy at the end of the bar.

Zisk swung his face around and smiled at Sidney. "Little lady, can I buy you a drink?"

"Sure." Heavy footsteps pounded on the hardwood floor behind her. Sidney assumed it was Sam and resisted the urge to look as she continued giving the heavyset man all her attention.

"Zisk," Sam said, "I want to talk to you about your taxi."

Zisk twirled on his barstool. "Get lost, Sam. According to the attorney, I don't have to talk to you." He flipped his hand, motioning toward the door. "Get outta here!"

"Tell the truth to the District Attorney. Until then, I'll be watching you." Sam turned on his heels and trudged out of the building.

"You in trouble or somethin'?" Sidney asked.

"No. That jerk's an investigator for a killer."

Sidney blinked. "A killer? Whatcha talkin' about?"

"It's all over the news—the guy that offed his wife in their backyard."

"By a hot tub?"

"Yep."

"Saw somethin' bout it on TV. Why he wantta talk to you? You the guy's buddy or somethin'?"

"No, I drive a cab. Dropped off the killer that night."

"He a rich dude...live in a fancy place?"

"Let me get you a drink first and tell you all about it. Whatcha gonna have?"

"You pick."

"Something sweet?"

"Uh-huh."

"Daiquiri?"

Sidney nodded.

Zisk placed the drink order, and then he laid his rough, oversized hand on Sidney's thigh, but not the one carrying the sheathed knife. "Yeah, that guy's rich. Big house, almost a mansion."

"Really? What's it look like?" Sidney asked, leaning a little closer to him.

"Lots of tall windows. Sits right on top of a hill. Curved driveway. Triple car garage. The front yard has a little patch of grass. The rest is covered with flowers. A Mercedes and a Jaguar were parked in front of the garage. The guy's loaded. Tipped me fifty bucks."

Sidney didn't detect Zisk was lying when he described the house, so she assumed it was a house where he had actually dropped off a customer. "Rich guys don't go to jail. Fancy lawyers. Won't serve no time." She took a sip of her drink and then nodded toward the door. "Why that guy mad at ya?"

"He's after me to say I wasn't driving my taxi."

"He wan ya to lie for the rich guy?"

His eyes glanced at Sidney's glass. "Hey, little lady, drink up." He turned to the bartender. "Brad, get me another one."

The bartender poured a shot of scotch in a tumbler filled with ice, set it down in front of Zisk, and picked up the empty glass.

"After I finish this drink," Zisk said. "What you say we go to my place and order Chinese?"

She offered him a coy smile. "Sure. I just need to go to the little girls' room first." Sidney slid off the barstool, grabbed her purse, and strolled toward the restroom while she occasionally glanced over her shoulder and smiled at Zisk.

When she no longer could be seen by Zisk, she hurried out the back door, jumped into her car, and drove to the front of the building. Sidney spotted Sam leaning on the edge of a table and chatting with a blonde dressed in a tight skirt and tank top. "Sam!" she yelled.

He looked over his shoulder at her.

"Meet me at your office."

"Be right there," he said, and then she sped away.

Sidney stopped in front of Sam's place and scanned the neighborhood while she waited for him. She caught a glimpse of a Suburban parked around the corner from his building. She reached under the seat and took out a bag containing her night goggles. She held them against her eyes and saw two men sitting in the front seat of the vehicle.

Sidney wondered if Sam slept in his office since she couldn't imagine any surveillance group hanging around all night for him to show up to work the following day. Then, she remembered they seemed like amateurs. *Would even amateurs be dumb enough to wait that long for their subject?*

The glare of headlights behind her made the night goggles useless. She lowered them and saw a ten-year-old blue Chevy truck with a dent in the hood cut to the curb behind her. She watched Sam climb out.

After putting her goggles away, Sidney stepped out onto the deserted sidewalk and dug a cell phone out of her purse. "Here," she said, handing it to Sam. "This belongs to Zisk."

"You snatched his phone?"

She nodded. "Somewhere in his contact list is the number of the guy who drove his taxi. I'm assuming you have contacts that can trace the names and supply addresses if they're not listed."

"I can get the information. Are you going to tell Fowler you pilfered Zisk's cell phone?"

She shook her head. "It's better if he doesn't know. By the way, I think the goon who tried running us off the road and a buddy are sitting in that Suburban around the corner, probably waiting for you to show up. Do you live here?"

"Upstairs. Second floor is an apartment."

"Are you sure they're harmless?"

He nodded his head. "Yep."

"Okay, call when you get the addresses, and then we'll drive around until we find him. Sure hope Zisk doesn't have a lot of numbers in his cell phone."

"So do I," Sam said and went into his office.

After Sidney settled into the driver's seat, she gazed at Sam's building and saw the lights flip on inside. She pulled away from the curb, swung around the corner, and then backtracked to see if the guys in the Suburban would make a move since Sam was home. With traffic on the light side, she assumed they had noticed her Lexus parked in front of Sam's office. Not wanting to raise any suspicion, she parked in a spot several buildings away and turned off her headlights. Two men emerged from the Suburban and headed around the corner toward Sam's office. From her location, she couldn't see the front façade of the building. Sidney flipped on her headlights, made a u-ey, and quickly drove around the block and stopped by the edge of the road when she had the two men in her sight.

The men stood by Sam's office door, and it appeared they were having a heavy discussion about something with their arms swinging in various directions. Sidney decided to warn Sam and punched his number in her cell phone.

"Sidney," Sam answered. "What's up?"

"Those two guys from the Suburban are next to your front door. You could be getting company soon."

"Got it covered. Don't worry about me. Go home and get some sleep."

"Okay. We'll talk tomorrow," she said and then disconnected and dropped the cell phone into her purse. She was curious about how Sam had "it covered," so she stayed and kept her eyes on the potential intruders.

The shorter one took a small shiny object out of his pocket, bent down, and stuck it in the door lock. Immediately, he leapt backwards and landed on his bottom. Sidney smiled as she figured the guy had been shocked from a booby-trapped lock.

The man rose to his feet and hit his accomplice in the shoulder. The men began shoving each other, and from her vantage point, it looked like they were arguing. Then the taller one knocked the other guy out of the way, raised his leg, and kicked the door.

Suddenly, red-and-white strobe lights illuminated Sam's office entrance, and loud, blaring beeps rang out. The would-be intruders dashed to their car. A few seconds later, tires squealed, and then they were gone. Sidney smirked while she started the engine and pushed down on the accelerator.

Chapter 15

Sidney woke to the ringing of her cell phone. Feeling disoriented, she turned on the nightstand lamp. Slowly, the fog began to lift as she glanced at her alarm clock—6:00 a.m. Without looking at the caller I.D., she picked up the phone and pushed a button. "Hello," she answered, sounding groggy.

"I'm sorry to call you this early." Bernice's voice came over the airwaves, and she sounded anxious. "It's Mara. She kept me up most of the night. Every time I started drifting off, she made her presence known again. My first client is due in a half an hour, and I suspect Mara will keep interrupting my reading if I don't talk to you first."

"What does she want?"

"I wish I knew. All I'm getting is a few words, short phrases— nothing I can piece together and put into a sentence."

Sidney couldn't shake the uncomfortable way she felt about a ghost contacting her. Yet, she was starting to come to grips with the emotions that invaded her body when she was around Mara's family. She knew the departed Mara somehow had control over her, and if she didn't comply with Mara's wishes, she'd never get her life back on track. "What exactly did she say?"

"She kept repeating, 'Tell Sidney, pres house, blond hair, short.' Mara mentioned 'blond hair and short' before. Does any of that make sense to you?"

"Not right now, but it might when I get further into the investigation. Was that press house?"

"Possibly, but I don't think so. It sounded like it only had one s—

pres house."

"Bernice, have you ever known of a spirit's transference—like letting their feelings flow into a living person?"

"Yes. It often occurs in séances." Bernice paused. "Aaah. Are you experiencing that?"

"It seems like it happens whenever I'm around her family."

"Those feelings most likely will cease when Aden becomes a free man."

"What happens if no evidence surfaces to help prove he's innocent?" The line went silent. After a noticeable pause, Sidney asked, "Bernice, are you still there?"

"Yes. Sidney, I don't have an answer to that question. Although I doubt Mara would have sought you out if she didn't believe you were capable of helping set her husband free."

Sidney wasn't that optimistic as she thought about the crime scene, the taxi driver, and potential suspects—none of those were in her grasp. The crime scene had been destroyed. The taxi driver hadn't been located. The suspects were currently nonexistent. "Thanks for the call," she said while the words Bernice had given her swirled around in her mind.

"I hope Mara lets me sleep tonight," Bernice said. "I'll call if I hear from her again."

Sidney hung up, got a notebook, and wrote down the words. Gazing at "pres," she wondered if Mara was referring to "president." On the other hand, it might be "press"—something written in the newspaper, even if Bernice didn't think that was the word. She moved her eyes to the next words—blond hair, short. Sidney leaned back in her chair. *Both Deidre and Payton have blond hair, and they're both short. Could one of them be the shooter or know who is?* Then she mulled over the bruise on her shoulder from the poking she felt at the Brimwell Engineering office and decided she needed to pay a visit to Brimwell's wife, Angelica, and check out the company president's house.

At 10:00 a.m., Sidney picked up Sam, armed with the addresses of the male contacts on Zisk's phone. "Thank goodness Zisk doesn't have a lot of friends," Sam said, buckling his seatbelt. "On April twentieth, the day he claimed he drove Aden home, he only called three guys.

Let's start with the third one."

"Good idea," Sidney said, thinking that would be the most logical candidate. "Where to?"

Sam spit out the directions as she eased into the traffic. Fifteen minutes later, she parked in front of a three story, brown brick apartment building badly in need of maintenance. Most of the paint on the wood trim around the windows and the front door had peeled away. The cement stoop leading to the door was cracked, and corners were missing.

"This place is within a mile of Fernan's, Zisk's favorite bar. Where does he live?"

"In that building," Sam said, pointing at a seven story apartment building two structures down on the other side of the street. It appeared to be better maintained than the one closest to Sidney's car.

"Why don't you go to the guy's apartment and try to get a picture of him with your cell phone?" Sidney wanted to remain out of sight.

A confused expression flashed across Sam's face. "Any reason you don't want to go?"

"Just in case he's the right guy, he might need a little extra persuasion."

Sam grinned. "You think you might get a chance to use the outfit you wore last night, don't you?"

"Don't want to take anything off the table," she said with a smile.

"Since I didn't recognize you in that outfit, I doubt that guy would."

"Right now I'm not willing to take that chance."

"Okay. Have it your way," Sam said, opening the car door.

While Sidney waited, she studied the people walking along the sidewalk. She estimated about thirty percent were Hispanic. Within a few minutes, Sam was back. "That was quick," she said.

Sam slid into the passenger seat. "The guy only opened the door a few inches, but I got a glimpse of his beer belly."

"Yeah, that doesn't fit Aden's description of a thin guy. Do the other two fellows Zisk called on that day live close by?"

"One lives in the same apartment building as Zisk."

Sidney cocked her brow, thinking if Zisk spotted Sam knocking on his friend's door, it might lead to a problem. "Do you think Zisk is driving around in his taxi?"

"Possibly. He has an erratic schedule."

"Is Zisk's apartment on the same floor as the guy?"

"No. Zisk is on the fourth, and the guy's on the second."

"Let's save that guy to last. Where does the other one live?"

"In the apartment building right over there," Sam said, pointing to a dingy looking structure across the street. "I'll check him out." He climbed out of the Lexus and jaywalked around traffic until he made it to the other side of the road.

Even though Sidney didn't want the actual taxi driver to see her, she suspected Sam was right—he wouldn't recognize her if she decked herself out the way she did the night before. Realizing that, she grabbed her purse and slipped out of the car. When there was a break in the traffic, she rushed across the street.

She kept track of the entrance to Zisk's apartment building as she waited for Sam. A thin Hispanic man in his early forties stepped out the door and strode along the sidewalk toward her. Sidney stuck her hand in her purse, grabbed her cell phone, and held it next to her ear. When the man came closer, she lowered it, pretended she was checking messages, and snapped a picture of the thin stranger.

"Hey, Sidney," Sam said, standing behind her. "I thought you were going to stay in the car."

"It's going to take both of us if we want to get a peek at the next guy. Since we don't want Zisk alerted to anything, he can't see you snooping around. What's Zisk's apartment number?"

Sam pulled his notepad out of his breast pocket, flipped through it, and then said, "Four-eleven."

"I'll hang around on the fourth floor while you see if you can get a snapshot of Zisk's friend on the second floor. Oh, by the way, how did it go with that guy?" she said, nodding toward the apartment building Sam had just visited.

"I got his picture," he said, shaking his head. "He's Hispanic, but average-sized, not thin."

"Too bad," Sidney commented as they walked toward Zisk's apartment building.

Going through the entrance, Sidney noticed the building had an elevator and doubted Zisk would take the stairs when he had that option available.

Sam tilted his head toward the elevator. "The other two apartment buildings didn't have that luxury. This must be a high rent place."

Sidney's eyes moved around the bleak lobby with worn carpet, graffiti marked walls, and an overflowing garbage can standing next to a bank of mailboxes. The smell of stale cigarette smoke lingered in the air. Though she hadn't been inside the other two buildings, she couldn't see anything in this place that would warrant paying a higher rent.

Sam noticed Sidney eyeing the foyer. "Trust me. This is luxurious compared to the other two buildings."

The elevator squealed and jerked as it ascended. "I'll meet you out front in ten minutes," Sam said, stepping out on the second floor.

On the fourth floor, Sidney paced around the hallway as she kept glancing at Zisk's apartment door. Ten minutes later, she pushed the elevator button and then decided she'd rather take the stairs. As she moved toward them, Zisk's door opened. She charged toward the steps, sprinted down, and hurried out the front door. She saw Sam on the stoop. "Let's get out of here."

Sidney darted to the street and dodged cars with Sam only a few feet behind her. When she reached the Lexus, she pushed the unlock button on the car key, yanked the door open and slid in. Sam was already in the passenger seat as she shut the door.

"What was that all about?" he asked.

"Zisk's on the loose."

They gazed at the apartment building entrance as Zisk emerged.

Sidney waited for a truck to go past her, and then cut into the traffic. "Any luck?"

"A woman answered the door and said her husband wasn't home."

"Any kids?"

"Yeah. I heard two or three."

"While I waited out front when you were checking out the second guy, I snapped a picture of a man leaving Zisk's building that matched Aden's description of the taxi driver. Maybe it was the guy who lived on the second floor."

"You realize Zisk might not have called the taxi driver that day, don't you? He could have just knocked on the guy's door."

Sidney frowned and nodded. "I know. It would be so much easier to find the guy if we had a picture of him. Before we hunt down the other guys on the Zisk list, could you go to the county jail and show Aden the two pictures?" She wanted the information, but, at the same time, hoped to avoid seeing Aden because of the emotional upheaval she felt each time she got close to him.

"I'm at your disposal all day. Tonight I have to deal with another investigation."

"SLI?" she asked, recalling the surprise the two SLI guys received at Sam's office the night before.

"No. A client wants more pictures of his cheating wife in a compromising position. I hate that type of work, but it pays the bills." He pulled a notebook out of his pocket, opened it, and began writing. "Anything else you want me to talk to him about?"

What Bernice had told Sidney earlier—pres house, short, blond hair—bounced around in her head. "His boss. Ask him about Mara's relationship with Brimwell's wife and if Brimwell paid a lot of attention to Mara at their parties—stuff like that." Sidney wanted to continue discussing the case, but not in heavy traffic. She turned into a drug store parking lot and stopped in the first empty slot.

"Do you think something was going on between Mara and Brimwell?" he asked skeptically as he gazed at her in utter disbelief.

"No. At least not from Mara's side, but she was a gorgeous woman. Men would be attracted to her." Sidney tucked hair behind her ear and then leaned on the armrest and mulled over everything she had learned or suspected about the crime. "There must be a connection between Mara's death and Brimwell Engineering. I might be out in left field, but that's where I'm focusing. There isn't much time before the trial. Have you got any other hunches?"

He shook his head. "Not a one."

"If neither man in the pictures looks familiar to Aden, ask him if he recalls any of the taxi driver's features—anything that might help us locate the guy."

Sam nodded.

"Have you got Brimwell's home phone number?"

He lifted up his cell phone. "Yeah," he said and gave it to her. "Are you planning to talk to his wife?"

"Yes. I'm hoping to set up an appointment with her today."

Chapter 16

Sidney dropped Sam off, and then she placed a call to Angelica Brimwell. After introducing herself, she said, "I'm working for Gregory Fowler on Aden Uzelac's case, and I have a few questions I'd like to ask you."

"Is Mr. Fowler with the DA's office?" Angelica asked.

"No. He's Mr. Uzelac's attorney."

"Well, then, I'd be happy to talk to you," she said, sounding pleased to help Aden.

They agreed upon a three o'clock appointment. Angelica gave Sidney the address along with the driving directions to her home and claimed GPS was worthless to use in that part of the city.

At 2:30 p.m., Sidney headed to Brimwell's home. It was located in a plush part of town with most of the homes well hidden behind high, solid walls and locked gates. The few Sidney could spot through wrought iron entrance gates were huge, probably over ten thousand square feet. Reaching Brimwell's gate, she pushed an intercom button mounted on a post abutting the driveway. A baritone voice answered, "May I help you?"

Sidney wanted to talk to Angelica alone and hoped that Brimwell hadn't come home from his business trip early and it was his voice coming through the speaker. Though, she thought the voice sounded too young to belong to a sixty-something-year-old man. "This is Sidney Langston. I have an appointment with Mrs. Brimwell."

"She's expecting you," the voice said. The gate swung open.

As Sidney followed the curve of driveway between large bushes and trees, she saw a magnificently manicured lawn with a center fountain and flower beds scattered in arcs framing the water. When she got closer to the two story, white stucco mansion, the lawn ended and terra cotta decorative rocks lined the cement driveway. The brownish-orange substance she had gathered from a footprint in front of Aden's house sprang into her mind. *Could this be its source?* She was tempted to call Fowler for the test results of the substance but didn't want to keep Angelica waiting.

When the front door opened, Sidney's brows rose as she found herself gazing at a handsome man around forty years old with curly, dark auburn hair, dressed in a black suit and white shirt topped by a bowtie. She had never seen a butler who looked more like a bodyguard, muscles straining against the taut fabric covering his arms. He led her through the foyer, past an ornate, carved stairwell, to a rock patio that surrounded a large, rectangular swimming pool in the backyard.

Angelica Brimwell soaked up the sun, sitting at a round table with a glass of iced tea in front of her. She was a striking, elegant looking woman with shimmering aqua blue eyes. Her chestnut brown, blonde streaked hair was twisted into a French knot. She wore a sleeveless, long, flowing, sandy-colored dress; a diamond pendant hung from a gold chain around her neck. Sidney was surprised that Angelica appeared to be in her early forties, appreciably younger than Brimwell. Angelica gave Sidney a warm smile as she approached behind the butler.

"Hello, Mrs. Brimwell," Sidney said, shaking Angelica's delicate hand.

"I'm so glad to meet you, Ms. Langston," she said in a dignified voice. "Please take a seat. Would you care for some tea?"

Sidney eased down in the chair across from Angelica. "Yes, thank you. Iced tea."

Angelica glanced at the butler. "Lewis, also bring some of those nice cakes Thelma made this morning."

He nodded and then turned on his heels and walked toward the house.

"I hope you don't mind meeting outside, but this is such a pleasant day," Angelica said.

"No. It's lovely out here." Sidney's eyes swept over the patio, pool, and a small white building that she thought might be a guest house or possibly a pool house. Still, she was disappointed she wouldn't be able to look around the inside of the main house. Gazing at the mansion with two one-story wings, she speculated about how Brimwell could afford the place. Admittedly, she didn't have a clue as to how much civil engineers could make designing and building bridges, but since he owned the company, it must be substantial.

Angelica sipped her tea and then placed the glass on the table. "I've been so worried about Aden. How is he doing?"

"Not well. He's having a hard time coping with the loss of his wife. With the approaching trial, life is getting even more difficult for him."

"I was so hoping by now the police would have found the one responsible. I don't believe Aden would ever harm Mara. She was such a wonderful person. A day doesn't go by that I don't think about her. I used to always travel with Marcus on his business trips, but lately I've had some health issues. Mara was so generous with her time. She often came for a visit when Marcus was out of town. If the weather was nice like it is today, she'd bring her two sweet children, and we'd sit right here and watch them play in the pool."

Lewis came with a large tray containing a pitcher of iced tea, a platter covered with multi-colored cake squares, plates, and silverware. After placing the items on the table, he asked, "Is there anything else I can get you, Mrs. Brimwell?"

"A shawl for my shoulders."

He smiled, gave her a slight nod, and headed into the house.

"Since my surgery, I sometimes get a little chilled even on warm days," Angelica explained while she handed Sidney a silver cake knife. "Please help yourself."

Sidney scooped up a cake square and took a bite. The creamy chocolate frosting melted in her mouth as she tasted the white cake. "This is delicious."

"Thelma is a wonderful cook. Marcus and I enjoy everything she puts on the table."

Lewis returned with a shawl and laid it over Angelica's shoulders. As he began tucking it around her, she leaned away from him. "Lewis, I can do that myself."

"Sorry, Mrs. Brimwell." He straightened his back and broad shoulders. "Will there be anything else?"

"No, thank you, Lewis," Angelica said, and then he headed back to the house.

Between bites, Sidney said, "Mrs. Brimwell, I understand you have a couple of company parties here each year."

"That's right—a summer party and a Christmas party. But this year, because of Aden, we're not planning on having the summer party."

"During those parties, have you ever noticed any friction between any of your guests?"

She inhaled deeply and then slowly released her breath. "There was a small problem at our Christmas party, but it wasn't that significant."

Sidney laid down her fork. "What was it?"

"I can't imagine it could have a bearing on the crime."

"We're looking at every possible scenario."

Angelica folded her hands in her lap. "Well then, I certainly want to help Aden any way I can, even though I doubt the incident means anything." She adjusted herself in her seat. "Victor came to the party with a date, a young attractive brunette. Mara became upset. From what I gathered, Victor had been dating one of her friends but not the woman who was accompanying him. Victor and Mara went outside and talked. When they came back in, I noticed an irritated expression on Mara's face. She avoided Victor the rest of the evening. We all still had a very nice time, and everyone seemed to be enjoying themselves. I'm sure Mara was just concerned about her friend."

"Was Victor's date anyone associated with Brimwell Engineering?"

"No," she said, shaking her head. "I had never seen her before, and I can't remember her name."

"Do you know if Victor stopped dating Mara's friend?" Sidney asked, though she already knew the answer.

"Marcus never discusses anything that goes on at work between his employees." The corners of her mouth curved up. "He probably doesn't even know. He just focuses on the projects they're working on. Shortly after Aden left for Brazil, Mara came to see me. She mentioned that Victor was still dating her friend." She lifted up the iced tea pitcher and filled their glasses. She put two teaspoons of sugar in her tea, stirred it, and took a sip.

"Besides that incident, have you noticed any others?"

Angelica's hand trembled slightly as she placed her glass back on the table. She briefly pressed her lips together. "No. I can't recall another one."

Sidney heard a tinge of anxiety in the woman's voice, knew she was holding something back, and wondered if Angelica's reluctance had anything to do with her husband. *Was Brimwell involved in the problem?* Sidney picked up her napkin from her lap and laid it next to her plate. "Thank you for your time and the refreshments." She pushed her chair away from the table and rose to her feet.

Angelica pressed a button on the arm of her chair. "I wish I could have been more helpful." Lewis strode across the patio and stopped by her side. "If you have any additional questions for me, please feel free to visit again," she said with a smile.

Lewis escorted Sidney through the house and out the front door. After the door closed behind her, she bent down and picked up a decorative terra cotta rock.

A mile from Brimwell's house, Sidney stopped on the edge of the road and pulled out her cell phone. She had three new messages but wanted to reach Fowler before he left the office. After his secretary answered, it took five minutes before he came on the line.

"Find anything?" he asked.

"I'm working on a few potential leads," she said without giving him more information. "The brownish-orange substance I dropped off at your office—have you gotten the results back from the lab?"

"It's granulated decorative rock. There are thousands of various compositions of that stuff. Most quarries are slightly different."

"If I brought in a piece of rock," she said, looking at it, "could you have the lab determine if it's a match?"

"Sure. Where did you run into it?"

"Brimwell's house. Even if it's a match, I doubt it'll get us where we need to go. But who knows at this point? It could work into something."

"Bring it in."

"I'll have it with me tomorrow morning. What time do you want me there for Zisk's deposition?"

"Nine-thirty."

"See you then." Sidney disconnected, and then she listened to her messages. Sam wanted her to give him a call. Chas didn't want her to call him until after eight Pacific time since he would be tied up until then. The last message was from Fowler, asking her to be in his office a half an hour before the scheduled 10:00 a.m. deposition. She tapped on Sam's number.

Five rings later, he answered. "Hi, Sid. I think Aden was disappointed that I was the one asking him questions and not you."

"What did you find out?"

"The taxi driver. My guy was a no go. He studied the picture of your man for a while. Some of the features were the same as the taxi driver, but Aden remembered the guy as being younger—mid-thirties."

"Brother?"

"That's exactly what I was thinking, or a cousin. Something like that. I thought I'd hang out around Zisk's apartment building tomorrow, watch for the guy in the photo, and try to get some info from him. I won't go there until Zisk's deposition. Don't want him to spot me before that. What time is he scheduled for?"

"Ten."

"Good. I'll be able to be there most of the day unless you have something else in mind."

Sidney filled him in about the confrontation Angelica mentioned between Mara and Victor.

"Are Victor and Deidre still dating?" Sam asked.

"According to Deidre's deposition, she's dating him, and he took off shortly after they ate dinner on April twentieth. Victor left her condo around eight. He might be a long shot, but right now he's the only person I've heard who exchanged angry words with Mara. The gun is still missing. I thought we'd look around his place tomorrow afternoon while he's at work."

"You talkin' about an illegal search?" he said in an amused tone.

"What do you think?"

"I think there's a rebel cop working this case."

Sidney smiled as she looked over her notes. "Getting back to your meeting with Aden, what did he say about Mara's and Angelica's relationship?"

"They were friends. Mara really liked Angelica and, at the same time, she felt sorry for her because of her heart condition, and…" Sam said, his words trailing off. He had seen too many marriages ruined over unfounded suspicions.

"And what?"

"Angelica always travelled with Marcus, but the past two years she hasn't been well enough to go with him. Mara thought he might be messing around."

"Why?"

"There was a little incident last summer at Brimwell's party. Mara was in their pool house—showering and changing, and Brimwell walked in on her. Since Brimwell changes in and out of his clothes in the house, it wasn't by accident that he strolled in there. Something happened, but Aden wouldn't give me any details. I suspect Brimwell made a pass at her or gawked while she changed. Whatever it was, Mara didn't make a big deal out of it, probably because Brimwell's Aden's boss, but she thought Angelica knew about it."

"Did he tell you what made her think that?" Sidney asked, wondering what Brimwell had done.

"The way Angelica looked at Brimwell when Mara stepped out of the pool house. Later, Mara spotted Brimwell on his cell phone strolling at the back of the yard and noticed Angelica intensely watching his every move."

"That's pretty flimsy to draw a conclusion that he's being disloyal," Sidney said.

"That's exactly what I said, but I'm missing part of the story. Aden just didn't want to spill it. Maybe for the same reason Mara didn't do anything about it—Brimwell is his boss."

"That was the summer party. Did Aden mention anything about the Christmas party?"

"Mara and Victor had a few heated words over Mara's friend, Deidre. He showed up at the party with another gal." Sam paused, and Sidney heard shuffling of papers. "That pretty much covers everything he told me."

Chapter 17

While Sidney drove to Fowler's office, her mind swirled with all the possible scenarios she had formulated the night before about the various potential perpetrators. She knew the motives she had conjured up in her head were pretty flimsy. At the same time, she thought the prosecutors had a weak case but knew it could be enough to convict Aden if she couldn't come up with something that could be used to throw reasonable doubt into the jurors' minds.

"How's it going?" Fowler asked as Sidney sat down in the chair on the opposite side of his desk.

"Slow. We might have a lead on the taxi driver."

"Aden certainly needs him," he said, gathering up some papers that were spread out on his credenza.

"That's for sure." Sidney tapped her fingertips on the arms of the chair. "Is it possible that I could stay in here and listen to the deposition over the speaker phone?"

"I can arrange that," Fowler said, assuming Sidney didn't want to be seen by John Baxter from the DA's office again. "Assistant District Attorney Sheila Ostler will be accompanying Lester Zisk today, not John Baxter."

"That isn't the reason. I told you I was going to do a little snooping around, and I don't want Zisk to recognize me."

Fowler smiled. "Find anything?"

"When you're cross-examining him, ask him about Aden's house."

"Will do. Even if he gets it wrong, the DA's office could claim he drops off people at numerous houses. He shouldn't be expected to remember all of them."

"According to the taxi log, Aden was his last customer of the day. The police talked to Zisk the following morning before he checked out a cab. That's documented."

Fowler turned toward his credenza and yanked out several manila folders. "I might need to place a couple of exhibits into the record today if Sheila Ostler doesn't," he said, thumbing through a folder. He found the documents he wanted and moved them to a brown accordion file. "I'll have my secretary stay in here with you. If you can think of other questions as we go, she can bring me a note."

Sidney nodded as she studied his telephone.

"Make sure the mute button is on," he said, standing up. "The DA's office might not like having anyone listening, so I don't intend to ask their permission. Since the phone will be off to the side and not in front of Zisk, there won't be much I can do if you can't hear something said."

"I understand."

As Fowler left the room with his accordion folder, Sidney turned the phone around and waited for it to ring. After she answered it, she switched on the speaker, and pushed the mute button so her end of the line would be silent.

The first voice that came through the speaker belonged to Fowler. He was talking to the court recorder. A few minutes later, feet shuffled and the participants chatted, and then introductions were made.

Fowler's secretary, Phyllis, hurried into his office and closed the door behind her. "Sorry, I'm late. I had to make copies of the exhibits for Mr. Fowler," she said, plopping down in his chair. "Has it started?"

"No," Sidney said.

They listened to the court recorder swearing in Zisk, followed by a soft clicking sound. Sidney assumed it was the court recorder typing on her equipment.

Sheila Ostler began by asking Zisk to state his name, profession, and how long he had been driving a taxi cab. After Zisk answered those questions, Ostler moved to April twentieth. "What time did you go to work that day?"

"Four o'clock."

"Do you pick up most of your passengers at the airport?"

"No."

"On that day, how many of your fares originated at the airport?"

"Two. It's all in the log," Zisk said.

The sound of pages being flipped echoed through the speaker. Sidney and Phyllis looked at each other as they waited for someone to speak.

"Mr. Zisk, is this the log for the taxi you were driving that evening?" Ostler asked.

"Yeah. My name's right on top along with the taxi number."

"I'd like to place this in the record as Exhibit 1," Ostler said. "Mr. Zisk, this says you picked up a passenger at the airport at 7:39 p.m. and then dropped off that person at 8:27 p.m. Is that correct?"

"Yeah. It's right there in the log."

"Do you know who your passenger was?"

"Yeah, sure. Aden Uzelac. I've seen lots of pictures of the guy, and I recognize him as being my passenger."

"Did you drop him off in his driveway or on the road in front of house?"

"Driveway."

"When you were parked in his driveway, did you hear a gunshot?"

"No. It was pretty quiet."

"Did you see Mr. Uzelac enter his house?"

"No. I drove off right after he paid me."

"I don't have any more questions at this time. Mr. Fowler, would you like to cross-examine Mr. Zisk?"

"Yes," Fowler replied.

Chairs being scooted around, the swishing sound of bottles being opened, and the clanging of glasses reverberated through the phone's speaker.

"Mr. Zisk, the night you dropped off Mr. Uzelac, did you notice any people on Mr. Uzelac's street?"

"No. Not a soul."

"Did you see cars moving up or down his street?"

"No."

"Can you describe Mr. Uzelac's house?"

"Sure can," Zisk said without hesitation. "A huge, light brown stucco house. Big windows. It's on top of a hill. Front yard covered with flowers."

Sidney drummed her fingers on the edge of the desk as she

wondered about his quick response—the same description he had given her in the bar. She didn't think Zisk was the swiftest guy in town, yet, she also didn't think he was all that stupid. *Had Zisk driven in Aden's neighborhood to check out the house and stumbled onto the wrong one?*

"One or two story?" Fowler asked.

"One. It's really spread out. Big. On top of a hill."

Shuffling of papers came through the speaker.

"That description doesn't fit Aden's house," Sidney said to Phyllis.

"I'd like this placed in the record as my Exhibit 1," Fowler said. "Mr. Zisk, do you recognize this house."

"No."

"This is the house that is located at the address listed in your log," Fowler said.

"Huh?" Zisk said.

"Did you have any passengers after you dropped off Mr. Uzelac?"

"No. It's all there in the log. He was my last customer."

"What time were you questioned by the police the following day?" Fowler asked.

"Don't recall the exact time, but it was before I went to work."

"Mr. Zisk, have you ever had another person drive your taxi during your shift?"

"No, never," Zisk said, adamantly.

"I have no more questions for Mr. Zisk," Fowler said.

"Ms. Ostler, any re-direct?" a female voice said. Sidney assumed it was the court recorder.

"Yes."

The sound of high heels clicking on the floor came through the speaker."

"Mr. Zisk, was it dark outside when you dropped off Mr. Uzelac?" Ostler asked.

"Yeah."

"When you stopped at his house, was it well-lit?"

"No. There weren't any outside lights on."

"So, is it possible that you incorrectly described the house because you couldn't see it clearly?"

"Objection," Fowler said. "Leading the witness."

"Mr. Zisk, were there any lights on inside the house?"

"No. Completely dark."

"I have no more questions."

"Mr. Fowler, any re-cross-examination?" a female said.

"No."

Fifteen minutes later, Fowler stepped into his office. "I think that went well," he said as a faint smile creased his lips.

"When you asked Zisk to describe the house, he never hemmed or hawed. He just spit out the answer. I suspect he has either driven on Aden's street and checked out the wrong house or searched online, maybe transposing the numbers. Even when you showed him the right house, he didn't backpedal."

"I'll get one of the staff investigators to look into it." He cocked a brow. "It might help our case to show he's lying about driving Aden home if such a house exists if you juggle the numbers."

Chapter 18

Shortly after 1:00 p.m., Sidney stopped in front of Sam's office. She had expected to see him standing outside waiting for her. She gave him a few minutes and then climbed out of the car and headed to the door. Stepping over the threshold, she heard a soft bell and assumed it was to let him know he had company. The pleasant, well maintained interior surprised Sidney compared to the shabby exterior. In front of her was a modern, light oak desk with a stack of files sitting on top. Across the room, a seating area with a dark brown leather sofa and two matching chairs surrounded a coffee table. A leafy plant decorated the corner next to the window. Behind the desk was a closed door. Sidney knocked on it.

"Be there in a minute," Sam yelled.

Sidney heard him talking and assumed he was on the phone. She moved toward the sofa but came to an abrupt halt when Sam said, "Payton, not …"

She went back to the door and placed her ear against it, hoping to learn what Sam was working on for Payton.

"It depends," he said. "She's not there anymore…I haven't got the foggiest idea…No. Hey, I need to run…Yeah, I can do that. Your place at nine."

Footsteps sounded on the other side of the door. Sidney rushed toward the sofa, but stumbled over a waste basket standing next to the desk, barely managing to catch her balance before she reached the sofa.

The inner office door flew open. "Sorry to keep you waiting,"

Sam said. "Need to keep the clients happy."

"No problem," she said, rising from the sofa. "Ready?"

"Yep." After locking the door behind them, he followed Sidney to her car.

"Any luck tracking down the guy in the picture?" she asked, sliding into the driver's seat.

"No. Depending on the time, I might go back to Zisk's apartment building and look for the guy after we finish at Vic's place."

Victor lived in a modern six story condominium complex. His unit was on the third floor. They wandered around the structure looking for a fire escape but couldn't spot one. That left no easy way for them to get inside the building without going through either the main or back entrance, which required a key card.

"Got any ideas?" Sam asked as they stood by the door facing the street.

"Yeah, we'll use the back door."

Based on the number of balconies, Sidney estimated the building held at least seventy condos and assumed there was a good chance that all of the condo owners didn't know each other. Also, she suspected some of the units could be rented. She prepared to dismantle the key card reader when a car pulled into the parking terrace behind the building.

"Let's walk toward the parking structure and wait for this guy to get inside," Sam said. Moving at a slow pace, they headed toward the parked cars. A tall, gangly looking man in his late thirties gave them a smile as he strode past them.

As soon as the man reached the building, Sam twirled around and said in a loud tone, "I forget something." He hurried toward the condo complex door and managed to stick his foot in the doorframe just before the door closed behind the stranger. Sam entered the structure and wandered down the hallway until the man was out of sight. Then he went back to the door and held it open for Sidney.

"I could've taken care of the key pad," Sidney said, walking through the doorway.

"Yeah, but this was simpler."

They took the elevator to the third floor and found unit three-sixteen, Victor's condo. She pulled two pairs of latex gloves out of her bag. "Here," she said, handing a pair to Sam and slipping on the other pair. Within a minute they were inside, and Sidney was putting away her lock picks.

"You come prepared," he commented, tugging on the gloves.

"Yes, I do," she said, thinking no way would she leave any evidence behind that she had broken into some place. "Why don't you start in the bedroom? Look for anything that might shed some light on this investigation."

"Like the weapon?"

"Yeah, but it's doubtful we'll find it. If he's the guilty party, most likely he would've ditched it. We know Victor had words with Mara, so this is a fishing expedition. Search for anything that might be applicable to the case."

While Sam scrounged around in the bedroom, Sidney went through all the drawers in the nicely decorated living room. She noticed a picture of Deidre in the arms of a good looking man with wavy, dark brown hair in his early forties and surmised the guy was Victor. Then she moved to the den and began rummaging through desk drawers. As she opened the second drawer, she heard a soft scraping sound. She closed the drawer, opened it again, and heard the same noise. Sidney removed the drawer from the desk, ran her hand along the bottom, and felt something taped to it. She raised the drawer, looked underneath it, and saw an envelope taped to the bottom. She carefully eased the tape off just enough so she could reach the contents inside. She slid out a sheet of paper. On it was written "54, 33, 46, 8." She guessed it was a combination to something, probably a safe.

After writing the numbers down in her notebook, she put the sheet back in the envelope, secured the tape, and returned the drawer to its slot in the desk. Sidney looked behind every picture in the room for a safe with no success. She sat back down and continued searching through the desk.

In another drawer, she came across a February bank statement with the name Deidre Carlson printed along the top. Sidney's eyes grew wider as she stared at the amount of funds—over $5,000,000—in Deidre's account. The center drawer held a spiral notepad. On it was a row of numbers with dollar signs in front of each one. The second number matched the total on Deidre's bank statement. Sidney gazed at the figures and wondered if they all represented Deidre's holdings. *Could the woman be that wealthy?* Two words Bernice said that came from Mara popped into her head—short, blond. Deidre was short and blonde. *Is there a connection to Mara's death?*

Sidney snapped out of her speculation because she didn't want to linger in Victor's apartment longer than necessary. She finished searching the desk and moved to the credenza. She stopped short when she saw a folder labeled "Aden" in the first file drawer. She placed it on top of the other folders, opened it and swallowed hard as she stared at the eight-by-ten glossy picture of Aden, his eyes closed, lying in bed with an attractive woman—not Mara. A sheet hung loosely over part of his body, but Sidney had no doubt he was naked. The woman was slender with long, dark hair. Her arm was stretched across Aden's chest, and her eyes were closed. Sidney assumed the woman was Kate. Looking at the photo, a thought flitted through her mind. *Did Aden actually have a one-night stand with Kate, or was it all staged?*

Realizing she didn't have time to ponder the possibility right then, she stuck the picture into her bag, returned the folder to where she had found it in the credenza, and resumed sifting through the drawers. She discovered a manila folder tucked in the back with Payton's name on it. Taking it out, Sidney shook her head as she wondered if Victor had plans on blackmailing some of his co-workers or if he already was. Her nose wrinkled and her eyes narrowed when she opened the folder and found it empty.

Standing in the doorway, Sam asked, "Finding anything?"

"Enough to know Victor has been up to no good. Did you run across anything?"

"Yeah," he said, raising a black binder in his hand. "His appointment book, time management, whatever you want to call it. From the entries, Victor is involved with Kate. He visits her one weekend a month, or she comes here."

"I'm not surprised," Sidney said, strolling toward Sam. "He had a photo of Aden in a compromising position with a woman."

"Kate?"

"That's what I'm thinking. Have you ever seen her?"

Sam shook his head as he handed her the binder.

Sidney thumbed through it. Besides all the entries about Kate, she also noticed numerous evening time slots with the name Payton penciled in next to them. "What you're investigating for Payton...does it have anything to do with Victor?"

"Nope."

The click of a lock turning came from the direction of the front door. "Bedroom," Sidney whispered. They moved swiftly down the hall with their feet barely making a noise. Her eyes drifted around the room. The bathroom door stood ajar. She quickly peeked in and realized hiding in there was not a viable option. "Where?" she said, motioning toward the binder in her hand.

"Nightstand," he whispered.

Sidney put it back as Sam inched the louvered closet doors open. They quickly slid inside. He carefully closed the doors and crouched down behind a hamper near the far corner. Sidney scooted around one of Victor's suits hanging in a plastic bag and stood with her back flat against the wall. She inhaled deeply, knowing if Victor needed something in his closet, there was a strong likelihood that one of them would be spotted.

A door slammed shut, followed by feet pounding down the tile hallway. Through the door slats, she saw a man walk by the closet. Her pulse raced as she recalled the last time she had hidden in a closet. That time things did not end well for the man who opened the doors.

The sound of papers being shuffled and pings from a keypad brought her back to her current predicament as a male voice said, "No. That was a week ago...You're too paranoid." A male figure moved past the closet, and then footfalls thumped in the hallway. "Okay...okay, I'll get rid of the picture."

The banging of drawers echoed through the apartment. "Did you put it in a different place?...I'll look for it later...Stop with your paranoia...Kate, relax...How?...Hey, I got to go...Need to wear a tie...Tonight."

Sidney pressed her lips together, controlled her breathing, and remained motionless though she figured any second he'd be opening the closet doors to retrieve a tie—maybe a whole outfit.

Victor returned to the bedroom. Drawers opened and closed as he moved around the room. Then she saw the back of him as he stepped into the bathroom, but he didn't close the door. Next came the sound of water spraying and splashing in a shower.

Sidney ducked out from behind his clothes and whispered, "Let's go." She eased the bi-fold doors slightly open and hurried out with Sam right behind her. They quickly made their way to the condo door. She stealthily opened it. They inched into the hall and eased the door shut. "I didn't plan that well," Sidney commented. "I should've had you stand guard in the hall." She smiled. "I guess I'm getting rusty at this."

Sam's eyes slightly pinched in the corners as a bewildered expression crossed his face. "Rusty? You broke into houses before you became a cop?"

"Something like that," she said and then immediately changed the subject as she walked at a brisk pace toward the elevator. "Any thoughts about his call?"

"Kate's worried about a picture. Maybe the one you saw. Did you snatch it?" he asked, stepping into the empty elevator.

Sidney nodded. "Yep. I bet you've taken compromising pictures."

"Sure have...too many times." Sam paused and rubbed his chin. "A picture of two adults in a bed doesn't mean anything sinister is going on," he said, holding the condo building door open for Sidney. "If one of them is someone's spouse, it could lead to a divorce, but that's about it. From everything I've heard about Kate, I doubt she'd get riled up over a picture like that unless there was more to it. What do you think?"

Sidney glanced up at Victor's condo to make sure he wasn't standing out on his balcony. Satisfied, she unlocked her car. "I'm guessing that Aden destroyed Victor's and Kate's plans when he confessed the one-night stand to Mara."

"Yeah. Can't blackmail someone when the wife already knows. Given the fact that Aden has no memory of going to Kate's room, I'm starting to think he was so drunk that they set him up. Probably never had a one-night stand—can't perform if you're passed out with too much booze in your system."

"We're on the same wavelength," she said, merging into the traffic. "The way things stand right now, Kate will claim they had an affair, and Aden won't deny they slept together."

Chapter 19

After Sidney finished her nightly phone call to Chas, updating him on the progress of the investigation, she changed into a pair of form fitting black pants and a black turtleneck jersey. She tied her hair into a pony tail and stuffed it under a black stocking cap.

Jean stopped knitting and gazed at Sidney as she stepped out of her bedroom. "You thinking about doing another career change?" she asked with a smile.

"Just a night job. No permanent change," Sidney said, returning the smile before grabbing two bags sitting by the dining room table and making her way to the door.

When Sidney reached her car, she dropped the bags in the back seat and climbed behind the steering wheel. She punched an address into the GPS and followed the instructions.

A half an hour later, she drove by Payton's house, a two story rock-faced structure that was set back about fifty feet from the road. A dark green BMW was in his driveway; she assumed it belonged to Payton. She flipped a u-ey and parked three houses down on the opposite side of the street, close enough to give her a good view of any visitors arriving but far enough away where she wouldn't be easily spotted.

Sidney glanced at her watch—8:50 p.m. Keeping her eyes on Payton's house, she waited for Sam to show up for the nine o'clock meeting she'd overheard him discussing on the phone in his office. Even though Sam had told her his business with Payton had nothing to do with Aden's situation, she wasn't convinced.

Bright headlights came around the corner and shined down Payton's street. She ducked down, peering out the bottom of her windshield. As the vehicle got closer, she identified a blue Chevy truck. She watched it pull into Payton's driveway and stop behind the BMW. Sam got out, walked to the front door, and rang the doorbell.

When he was inside the house, Sidney grabbed one of the bags and her backpack, flinging it over her shoulder as she stepped out of the car. The sound of boisterous voices caught her attention. Turning, she saw a group of teenage girls coming out of a house behind her. She ducked down, out of the girls' line of sight, took a light gray blouse from the other bag, and tugged it on over her black top, so she wouldn't look like a burglar. She rose to her feet and locked the car, then walked at a normal pace down the sidewalk until the chattering of the girls faded away. There, she glanced over her shoulder. The street appeared to be deserted again. Sidney crossed the road and continued scanning the neighborhood for any sign of movement as she backtracked to Payton's house.

Reaching her destination, she darted behind a large, overgrown bush, removed her gray blouse, rolled it up, and pushed it into a pocket on her backpack.

All dressed in black, Sidney stealthily headed toward the corner of the house and stopped when she noticed terra cotta decorative rocks in beds of plants next to Payton's porch. She crept closer to the door, bent down, and picked one up. Slipping it into her backpack, she inched toward the backyard until she was hidden in the shadow cast by the six-foot fence that abutted the back edge of his house. She quickly scanned the exterior wall, looking for security cameras and motion-sensor lights. Not spotting any, she lowered her backpack, unzipped the main compartment, and lifted out an amplifying mike. After putting on the headphones, she pressed the mike against the nearby window. Soft muffled voices came through the receiver, but Sidney couldn't pick up any words. She moved the mike from one window to another along that exterior wall of the house without getting any better reception. Assuming the men were on the other side, she picked up her backpack and slowly worked her way around the front of the house.

She started the process again by placing the mike on each successive window. The voices still weren't loud enough. She went to the back fence and attempted to push down the latch on the gate. It wouldn't budge. Trying not to make a sound, she carefully climbed over the fence.

Sidney moved the mike from window to window along the back of the main floor. A tiny furrow of annoyance appeared between her eyes as she questioned whether something was wrong with her apparatus. Wondering if there was any possibility the men could be upstairs, she stepped away from the house and looked up to the second floor.

"Oh, shit," she grumbled to herself when she saw two silhouettes behind a drawn drape. It appeared the one was sitting with his back to the window and the other one was standing a few feet away. It was the only brightly lit room on that floor. Dim light illuminated the other two second-story windows and the balcony door.

She examined the back wall of Payton's house. Nothing protruded that she could use for a foothold to get to the second floor. Still determined to find out why Payton had hired an investigator, Sidney retrieved a rope and a grappling hook from her backpack, and then tied the end of the rope to the loop at the bottom of the hook. She stepped closer to the balcony and threw the hook toward the surrounding railing.

A loud clang rang out as the metal hook touched the railing and landed on the hard balcony floor.

Sidney yanked the rope tight. She ducked under the balcony and pushed her back firmly against the exterior of the house, hoping the men would ignore the sound. An upstairs window slid open. She held her breath.

"Don't see anything," Sam said with his head sticking out the window.

"Most have come from the neighbor's house," Payton said as the window closed with a creaking sound.

Sidney edged from her hiding place, checked out the well lit window, and saw the drawn drapes slightly swaying. She held onto the rope and quickly shimmied up it. She gripped the balcony door handle and was surprised to find it unlocked. Silently opening it, she ducked inside and crept along the side of the bed to the wall closest to where the two men were talking. She pushed the mike against the wall. Nothing. Lowering it, she sighed and shook her head as she stared at the mike designed to pick up sound waves everywhere within up to a 5,000 square foot structure. Payton's house was appreciably smaller than that. She felt irritated she hadn't tested it before leaving New York. Sidney put the device and headphones into her backpack. She laid the backpack near the foot of the bed at a spot where it couldn't be seen from the hallway but close enough for her to grab on her way out the balcony door.

Without fear of being shot, like prior times when she was an unwelcome guest in a house, Sidney crept into the hall, flattened her back against the wall, and glided her feet on the carpet toward the meeting room.

"… ever," Sam said.

"Yeah. Bought it at the local micro brewery. The stout's my favorite."

"Good stuff."

"You haven't found anything new?" Payton asked.

"A little, but nothing that'll get you paid." A long pause. From the soft whooshing, gulping and gurgling sounds, Sidney figured they were both drinking. "Payton," Sam said, "I don't know how many times I need to say this. No legitimate investment company hires thugs—or whatever you want to call them—to tail and harass someone just because they're looking for information about the company. What haven't you told me about them?"

Sidney pursed her lips. *So, Payton, Aden's best friend, is Sam's client involved with SLI, the company that owns the Suburban that tried to force me off the road. Interesting.*

"Nothing. You know everything."

"Did you find the rest of your contract?"

"No. I'm still looking."

Without even seeing Payton, Sidney could hear from the slight fluctuation in his voice that he was lying…and wondered why. Hoping it didn't have anything to do with Aden's case, she wanted verification. The only way she could do that was to see the contract Payton wouldn't share with Sam.

"Judy Fuller, their receptionist, has vanished," Sam said. "The guy who took her place won't give me the time of day."

"Vanished?"

"Yeah. Tracked down where she lived. Moved out lock, stock, and barrel without leaving a forwarding address, but no missing person's report has been filed."

"She probably just left town."

"Payton, I have to be honest with you. I doubt you'll ever see a dime from those guys."

"But I talked to their V.P. in the headquarters oversees. He said he sent my money to the local office. They've got it. They just need to give it to me," Payton said in a raised voice.

"Payton, were not covering new ground," Sam said, sounding frustrated. "Come on. Now that guy won't return your call. He's never going to pay you."

"Sam, I just need you to track down the person who's heading the local office so I can talk to him. I've given you the names of all the guys I've dealt with."

"Like I told you before, those guys aren't in California anymore. You need to locate your contract, hire an attorney, and file a lawsuit."

"No…aah," Payton stammered. "I can't do that. Brimwell will find out, and he doesn't want his employees to moonlight. Maybe you could get me the home address of the company money handler. Then, I could go to his house and talk to him. I'm sure I could get paid."

Sam inhaled deeply and blew out a loud breath. "If the person won't talk to you in his office, what makes you think he'll talk to you at his house?"

"I'll figure that out later. Just get me the name and the address."

After a long pause, Sam said, "Okay, but first I need to be paid for last month. Here's the invoice."

"Got it."

Muffled sounds drifted through the hallway of papers being shuffled and chairs being scooted. "I need to go to the john," Sam said.

The door next to Sidney stood ajar. She scooted through the opening and found herself standing in a bathroom as footsteps echoed in the hallway. Raising a corner of the closed shower curtain, she slipped into the bathtub, stretched out along the bottom, and took soft, shallow breaths while remaining on full alert. She thought this was a cakewalk in comparison to other experiences that she kept hidden in the deep recesses of her mind. *Bullets aren't going to go flying.* Still, she didn't want to be caught spying on Sam and Payton.

The light turned on as Sam entered. The door closed, the lock clicked, and then came the unmistakable sound of Sam emptying his bladder. He stopped and started three times. Sidney bit her lower lip to prevent a laugh from escaping as she thought about how many beers he had downed. The sound of the toilet flushing, followed by the splattering of water against the porcelain sink, let her know he was finished. A few seconds later, the door opened and the light went off.

"Want another beer?" Payton asked Sam, as Sidney climbed out of the bathtub.

"No. Got to go," Sam replied.

Footfalls descended the stairs.

Before she left, Sidney wanted a quick peek into Payton's den. Voices drifted upstairs through the hallway. While they continued, she knew Payton wouldn't be returning to his den. Sneaking into the well lit room, she felt a sharp poke on her bruised shoulder. "Not again," she said to herself as she cupped her hand on the spot. Then, she noticed a landscape photo hanging crooked on the wall behind an oversized dark wood desk that dominated the room. Sidney moved closer to the picture and raised the corner of the frame. The sensation of someone poking her shoulder continued as she gazed at the wall safe behind the photo and speculated if the combination discovered at Victor's condo could belong to it.

The slamming of a door echoed through the house.

Startled, Sidney quickly repositioned the picture, sped back to the bedroom, gathered up her backpack, and hurried out to the balcony. Not wanting to leave any signs she had been there, she released the hook from the railing and dropped it to the lawn below with the rope still draped over the railing. Holding onto both pieces of the rope, she swung over the railing and slid to the ground. There, she held onto the hook and tugged the rope free from the balcony.

After she had everything in her backpack, she went to the gate and found it secured with a padlock. Since she didn't want to take the time to pick it, she clambered over the fence and then walked at a brisk pace to the front corner of the house. Before she stepped out of the shadows that concealed her from view, she stopped and slowly scanned the neighborhood. Satisfied no one was close by, she headed to her car. As soon as she climbed in, the poking sensation in her shoulder ceased.

Chapter 20

Around 9:30 the following morning, Sidney called Fowler and filled him in on the photo found at Victor's condo. "I checked Kate's Facebook page. She's the woman in the picture. I doubt Aden even had a one-night stand with her, but I need some verification."

"How do you expect to do that?" Fowler asked.

"I'm going to see if the bartender remembers them. There's a flight leaving around two for Denver."

"Sidney, it's been almost six months."

"I know, but I have to give it a shot. In hotel bars, there aren't many customers that need help getting to their rooms. I think that might have been Aden's situation, so there's a chance the bartender could remember something. If Sam's available, is it okay if I take him with me?"

"Sure. I'll foot his expenses."

Holding their boarding passes, Sidney and Sam went through the airport security. On the way to their gate, Sam said, "Remember the Hispanic guy in the picture who Aden thought resembled the taxi driver? I located the place where he lives—two doors down from Zisk's apartment. He wasn't too crazy about talking to me, but his neighbor, a seventy-something woman, was a real chatterbox. The guy's name is Ramon Ortega. His brother lives with him."

"A wife?"

"Ramon has a wife and three kids. If the brother has one, she's not living there."

"Big apartment?"

"Three bedrooms. It's probably a little crowded."

"Did the woman describe the brother?"

"Yeah. Mid-thirties. A little shorter than Ramon. She said they looked like brothers. When we get back in town, I'll stake out the apartment building. See if I can spot him. Even if it's the right guy, any ideas how we'll get him to talk?"

Arching an eyebrow, Sidney gave him a mischievous smile. "I've got a few," she said without elaborating.

They left their luggage in the rental car, a Toyota Camry, at the Denver Hilton and ambled into the almost deserted hotel bar with only one customer at the counter. Two more were seated at a round table. Since it was 3:30 on a Friday afternoon, Sidney hadn't expected a crowd to be there yet. The sign by the door read: "Happy Hour from 5 to 7."

She headed to the counter with Sam. They sat down on barstools and ordered drinks from the bartender, a forty-year-old, average-sized woman with a round face and shoulder length, blonde hair. When the bartender placed napkins and their drinks on the marbled surface in front of them, Sidney asked, "Have you worked here long?"

"Seems like forever." The woman studied Sidney's face, and then gazed at Sam. "You guys cops?"

"No," Sidney answered.

"We're P.I.'s," Sam explained as he swirled his straw around in his cocktail. "We're just looking for a little info that might help our client out of a jam."

"What kind of a jam?"

From the way the blonde-haired woman was eyeing Sam, Sidney decided to sit quietly and let him ask the questions.

"One that could put him in the big house for a while," he said, giving the bartender a faint smile. "So, Mavis, getting back to my partner's question, how long have you worked here?"

Sidney wondered how Sam knew the woman's name was Mavis, and then she noticed a Hilton name tag by the cash register.

Mavis smiled at Sam. "A couple of years." Her eyes glowed as she looked at him.

"Do you work shifts?"

She nodded. "Yeah."

"In February?"

"Boy, I can't remember." She rested her elbows on the counter and rubbed her hands together.

Since Sidney wasn't about to flash the picture of Kate and Aden in bed, confiscated from Victor's apartment, she had printed Kate's Facebook picture and copied a photo of Aden from a recent newspaper article. She opened her briefcase, pulled out the pictures, and handed them to Sam.

He glanced at them and showed the images to Mavis. "Do you recognize either of these two?"

Mavis shook her head, but then abruptly stopped. "Oh, I just remembered. Part of February, I was out with the flu. Jimmy worked my shift. Do you know when they were supposedly here?" she asked, still gazing at Sam.

"February twenty-first."

"It took me almost two weeks to get rid of that bug. I was home in bed."

"Where can we find Jimmy? And who else would've been working another shift that day?"

Mavis glanced at her wristwatch. "Jimmy will be here in about an hour. He starts at five. Let me think." She squinted as if in deep thought. "February. Beth and Rusty were working here then. Beth's gone. She tends bar at a strip joint across town. And Rusty's moved into management. Rusty Maxwell. He might be working now. Check with the front desk."

"What's the name of the strip joint?" Sam inquired.

"Billy's."

"Hey," a heavyset man at the end of the counter said. "Can we get a drink here?"

"Gotta go." She straightened her spine.

"Thanks for your help, Mavis." Sam held his hand up in a half wave of acknowledgement.

Her face creased in a wide smile. "Anytime, sugar." She hurried to the other end of the counter.

Sidney gathered up the pictures and put them back in her briefcase on the counter. "Why don't you stay here and keep Mavis company while I go to the front desk and see what I can find out about Maxwell?

"Sure, I can handle that," Sam said, raising his glass of whiskey.

Doubting they'd be able to make the eight o'clock flight, the last one scheduled for San Diego, Sidney reserved two rooms for the evening and inquired about Rusty Maxwell. The hotel clerk picked up a phone, buzzed Maxwell's office, and told him a customer wanted to see him. Putting the phone back down on the cradle, the clerk said, "He'll be here shortly."

A tall, lanky man in his late forties, dressed in a dark blue suit, approached Sidney, the only customer standing by the front counter. "I'm Rusty Maxwell. You wanted to see me?" he asked.

"Yes," she said and then jumped into asking him questions. After he verified that he worked in the bar during February, Sidney showed him the pictures of Kate and Aden.

He studied the two images. "I'm sorry, they don't look familiar."

Sidney, feeling disappointed, thanked him, and then headed back into the bar.

"Any luck?" Sam asked.

She eased onto the barstool next to him and shook her head.

"Mavis chatted when she brought me another drink. I mentioned to her the man and woman in the photos might have been intoxicated. She said if either one of them needed help getting back to their room, there's a good chance the bartender might remember them because that seldom happens here. Only once in the past couple of months."

"I hoped that might be the case." Sidney's eyes moved around the nicely appointed bar with its polyurethane-covered dark wood counter and randomly placed round tables. Booths lined one wall. "Rarely here."

"Agreed. This isn't a rough enough place. Now Billy's, that's probably a different call. But there, they would toss drunks out the door, not into comfortable bedrooms."

Sidney watched a short, muscular man, dressed in a white shirt and black slacks, walk behind the counter and slip on a black apron. "Must be Jimmy," she said, nodding toward the man.

"I almost hope he doesn't know anything so we can visit the strip joint," Sam said, running his fingers along the edge of his glass.

Mavis said something to the short man and motioned toward Sam and Sidney. As she left, he strolled over to them. "Understand you have a couple of photos you want to show me," he said, picking up Sam's empty glass and wiping the counter.

Sidney put the pictures on the counter. "Do you recognize either of these two people? They were in here in February."

"February…a long time ago."

"One or both of them might have been pretty drunk when they left here," Sam commented.

The man's eyes focused on the pictures. "The gal looks a little familiar. She might have been in here."

Sidney had also printed the picture Victor had posted on his Facebook page. She quickly thumbed through a folder in her briefcase, yanked out the copy, and handed it to Jimmy. "Do you recognize him?"

"I'm not positive, but they might've been together. Her," he said, pointing to Kate's photo, and then his index finger moved to Victor's picture, "and him. We had some real bad snowstorms in February. I came to work early so I wouldn't get caught up in the snow. I was just putzing around, straightening things up at the bar. Around ten in the morning, the woman asked for a glass of wine. She wasn't happy when I told her the bar wouldn't be opened for a while. Then she sat at one of the tables and complained to this guy," he said, touching Victor's picture. "They were the only two people in here, so I heard everything they were saying."

"Besides complaining about no bar service that early in the day, do you recall anything else they talked about?" Sidney asked.

"Nope."

"Hey, Jimmy," a stout man said, leaning at the end of the counter, holding up an empty glass. "Give me another one."

After Jimmy filled a few drink orders, he went back to Sidney and Sam.

"Did you see the couple later?" Sidney asked.

"Not that I recall, but some days the bar fills up if there's been a conference or something like that going on here. They could've came back, and I might not've noticed."

"You were working the day shift?" Sam asked.

"I was that day."

"Do you remember who worked the later shift?" Sam asked.

"Probably Beth. She was still working here then. She likes sleeping in and seldom worked the day shift. Beth's a bartender on the other side of town now." His eyes scanned the counter. "I have a couple of customers needing refills." He left them again, made some mixed drinks, and filled several glasses with beer. After he had taken care of the customers, he said to Sam and Sidney, "You might want to check with our barmaids."

"How many work here?" Sidney asked.

He looked down, scratched his forehead, and shook his head. "Both of the gals that were working in February are gone."

"Do you know how we could find them?" Sam asked.

"Barbara's gone back to college…somewhere back east, and I don't have any idea where Ashley went. Maybe the office might have a forwarding address for her, but I doubt they'd give it to you since you're not cops."

"Can I get some service here?" a middle-aged woman said, standing next to the counter ten feet away.

"Got to get back to work," Jimmy said as a twenty-something red-haired woman hurried around the counter.

"Sorry I'm late," she said to Jimmy while she slipped on an apron.

After checking into the Hilton, Sidney and Sam climbed into the rental car and headed toward the strip club. With the heavy five o'clock traffic, it took them almost an hour to reach their destination.

Driving into the parking lot, there was no doubt in Sidney's mind that Billy's catered to a rough crowd. Motorcycles were lined up against the two-story red brick structure. No windows appeared on the main floor. Outside, tattooed bikers with straggly beards and unkempt hair were either puffing on a cigarette or had one hanging from their lips as they leaned next to the bikes. A few women in tight pants, ultra high heeled boots, low cut sweaters, and thick makeup were chatting up the men.

"Sure you want to go in with me?" Sam asked, stepping out of the car.

"Sam, I can handle myself. These guys won't be a problem."

"Okay, after you," he said, gesturing toward the door with a huge fluorescent sign over it with the bar's name, *Billy's*, flashing.

As Sidney made her way to the door, the guys outside stopped talking and all turned and stared at her. Then a few started making remarks. "Great ass...Come over here, baby. Take a little ride with me...Want a good time?...Nice tits..."

Sidney ignored them since the person she wanted to see was inside, not among the outside crowd. Sam turned and glared at them as Sidney opened the door.

"I can't take you anywhere without you causing a stir," Sam said to Sidney in a joking tone. "Maybe you should think about taking some ugly pills...or wearing baggy clothes."

She patted his arm. "Sam, don't worry about me. If a problem arises, I can handle it."

Sam rolled his eyes, doubting her optimism.

The music blared, and the place was crowded. Customers occupied all the barstools. Three women, dressed in skimpy outfits—thongs, lace bras, and spiked heels, were pole dancing on the stage.

Sidney and Sam stood at a corner of the bar. A copper-haired, heavyset woman in her late thirties or early forties tended the bar. A white sleeveless blouse revealed tattoos covering her bare arms.

"Beth," Sam yelled.

The woman twirled toward him. "Be right there, big guy."

Five minutes later, she strolled over to them. "What'll it be?"

"We'd like to ask you a couple of questions," Sam said, giving her a coy smile. "Is there someplace we could talk?"

Her eyes darted back and forth between them, stopping on Sam's face. "You those two PI's that were at the Hilton?"

"Yep," Sam said while Sidney wondered who had tipped off Beth they were coming.

Beth looked over her shoulder. "Phil, cover for me for a couple of minutes." After Phil nodded, she said, "Sure, but not long."

Beth walked around the bar. "Over here." She led them through throngs of people to a hallway with a red arrow pointing away from the crowd and a sign above it that read "Restrooms."

"Mavis let me know you were on your way," Beth explained. "I've only got a couple of minutes. Let me see the pictures."

Sidney stuck her hand in her bag and pulled out the pictures of Kate and Aden. She handed them to Beth and then patiently waited while Beth studied each one.

"Yeah, I remember these two. Another fellow was with them.

This gal," Beth said, raising Kate's photo, "wanted me to keep the drinks coming. She gave me a lame excuse about wanting to divorce the guy and thought if she got him a little loose, he might sign the papers.

"Sometime between ten and eleven, the crowd started dying down. I noticed her cuddling up to the guy after the other fellow left. I didn't know what her game was, but it sure as hell wasn't a divorce."

"Did you see them leave?"

"No. Some basketball game ended, and the bar got busy again." She cocked her head to the side and nodded toward the bar. "Got to get back."

Sidney had noticed a slight flicker in Beth's jaw, and a minute fluctuation in her voice, and from her training, she knew those were signs of someone hiding something. "If anything else crosses your mind about the couple, please give me a call," she said, hoping Beth would reconsider and divulge what she was holding back, though she suspected it was doubtful. "We'll be staying at the Hilton tonight."

"Will do," Beth said.

Feeling frustrated that she wasn't making better progress on Aden's case, Sidney watched Beth work her way through the noisy crowd to the bar. She tapped Sam on the shoulder as he faced the stage. "Sorry I wasted your time on this outing."

He swung his head around to look at her. "This is not a waste of time," he said and then stared at the entertainers on the stage again.

"Well, let's get out of here."

"Just a few more minutes."

Sidney didn't argue about it since she had insisted he accompany her on the fruitless trip to Denver. Aden had already told her that he went to the bar at the Hilton with Kate and Victor, and Victor had gone to his room, leaving him alone with Kate. Aden drank so much booze that he had no idea how he ended up in Kate's bed. Neither Jimmy, the bartender at the Hilton, or Beth had provided any new information that might help Aden. From the outset, Sidney knew it was a long shot that someone could be found to confirm what she suspected—that Aden was in no condition that night to make love to any woman. With no witnesses to the shooting, no weapon, and a destroyed crime scene, she had to work every possible angle regardless if it seemed only remotely possible. She racked up the

Denver trip as another dead end and wondered if locating the right taxi driver and getting him to testify would be enough to put doubt in the minds of the jury.

After a couple of beers, Sidney endured the entertainment for almost an hour until Sam was ready to leave. They headed out the door.

"Hey, baby," a man leaning on a motorcycle yelled. He had a huge, tattooed potbelly hanging over his grease stained jeans and wore a leather jacket with ragged edges from torn-off sleeves that only partially covered his bulging stomach. His unshaved face was framed by unruly hair. He rose to his feet and sauntered toward Sidney. He wrapped an oversized, rough hand around her upper arm and held her in place.

"Take your hands off me," she ordered, her eyes narrowing.

"How about that ride?" the stranger asked.

Sam stepped in front of the man. "You heard the lady," he hissed. "Let go of her."

The potbellied man turned and glanced at his comrades slinking toward them. "Buddy, get lost," he said to Sam. "This is between me and this bitch."

Being called a "bitch" was too much for Sidney. She gripped the man's arm, twisted it, and flipped him to the ground. "No one calls me that."

The stranger stuck out his arm, attempting to grasp Sidney's ankle. She raised her foot and pinned the man's hand down with the heel of her stilettos.

"Get the bitch," he shouted to his buddies as he gripped her ankle with his free hand and tried to push her away from him.

Feeling a surge of adrenaline, Sidney dug her heel deeper into the man's flesh and kicked him on the side of his head with her other foot, sending him slamming into the pavement. Out of the corner of her eye, she saw Sam slugging it out with a guy while another gang member charged toward her. Her movements were quick and targeted as she spun around with one leg raised and struck the man on the cheek with her heel, leaving a gash from the three-inch spike. With blood drizzling down and smearing the attacker's face, he kept coming. She feinted at his body with her left hand and then plowed her right elbow into his stomach. He reeled backwards into another predator.

A gunshot rang out, stopping everyone in their tracks.

"Hold it right there," Sam said, brandishing his pistol toward the motorcycle gang. "Sidney, get in the car."

She briefly hesitated. She hadn't been involved in a street fight for a while and thought she could use a good workout with these punks. At the same time, she figured they all had hidden knives, maybe guns, and she didn't want to get any blood on her outfit from disarming them.

"Goodbye, fellows," Sidney said with a smirk and reluctantly scooted into the Toyota.

Sam kept his weapon pointed at the attackers as he moved backward toward the other side of the vehicle. He opened the passenger door. "Start the car."

When the engine roared, he pushed the window button and waited for it to glide down. He eased into the seat, swung his weapon around the door frame, and with his finger on the trigger, held it through the opened window.

"Ready?" Sidney asked.

"Yeah."

Spinning up gravel and dust, Sidney plowed out of the parking lot and into the traffic, horns erupting around her. She skidded around a corner to check if they were being followed. She didn't spot one motorcycle on the road but did see a black Silverado behind her with a tag hanging from the rearview mirror. She recalled seeing a similar truck parked next to them in Billy's parking lot. Squinting, she tried to make out the face behind the steering wheel. With tail lights glaring on the Silverado's windshield, only the silhouette of a person with short hair came into focus. Sidney wondered if she was paranoid or if they were being followed. As a precaution, she executed a series of evasive turns.

"I guess you *can* take care of yourself," Sam remarked, holstering his weapon under his jacket.

"I didn't realize you were packing."

"That's the reason I insisted on checking a bag." He smiled. "Airport security doesn't take kindly to guns."

"What made you think we'd need it?" she asked while her eyes darted from the road to the side mirror. Three cars behind them, she noticed the bumper of a black Silverado.

"You never know. If Aden didn't plug his wife, someone did."

"You thought we'd run into that someone in Denver?"

"Maybe. That picture with Kate and Aden—since it appears it was a setup—someone at the hotel could have helped her. Remember, she lives in Denver."

Sidney swung her head toward Sam. "I was told she had an iron-clad alibi."

"She worked all day on that Friday. A couple of her friends claim she went with them to a movie that evening."

"It's about a two hour flight from here to San Diego," Sidney said, mapping out the possibility in her head, "and there's a time change. If her friends are lying, she could have caught a six o'clock flight from here and arrived in San Diego around seven. Mara was shot around eight-thirty. Were you able to check if Kate booked a ticket for that day?"

"If, and that's a big if, she did fly out, her ticket wasn't booked under her name. She would've had to use a phony ID. I never checked car rentals at the airport."

"Yeah, the timing is pretty tight. But people do hire others to do that type of work." She glanced at the side mirror. The black Silverado was nowhere in sight. "I just don't see a motive. Assuming the picture was staged and Kate didn't even have a one-night stand with Aden, why would she shoot his wife?"

Sam shrugged his shoulders. "Got me, but it seems motives in this case are hard to find. So, until we know more, I'll keep my trusted companion tucked close to my side," he said, tapping the side of his jacket that covered his pistol.

Sidney signaled to turn into Hilton's parking garage. A black Silverado with a tag hanging from the rearview mirror had stopped next to the entrance.

Chapter 21

When Sidney reached her hotel room, she sat at the desk and scribbled down the Silverado's license number. Placing her elbows on the edge of the desk and resting her chin on her hands, she considered calling Maxine, her favorite Nassau County Police department computer whiz, to find out the owner of the truck or waiting to see if the Silverado appeared again. Then she wondered if Sam had a connection for that kind of information and hoped he did since she didn't want to pique Maxine's curiosity. After all, she was supposedly on vacation leave.

A knock on her door startled her out of her contemplations.

Unlike Sam, Sidney hadn't brought a pistol to Denver. She took her pen, tucked it into her palm, and mentally prepared to use it if the situation should arise. She strolled to the door, wishing it had a peep hole. Leaning against the wall next to it, she said, "Yes?"

"I'm Teri Crane, Beth's niece," said a young woman with a sweet voice. "I want to tell you something."

Sidney slipped the chain in place, and then inched open the door. In front of her stood a twenty-year-old, muscular girl with short, spiked, red hair, dressed in a pair of jeans and a tank top. A tattoo of a barbell was on her bare shoulder.

"Just a sec." Sidney closed the door, unhooked the chain, and then opened the door. "Come in."

The girl timidly looked at Sidney as she entered.

"Have a seat." Sidney gestured toward one of the thick cushioned chairs in the corner and sat down on the edge of the bed.

"My aunt wanted to tell you about me but first needed to make sure I was okay with it. I tried to catch you at Billy's, but I just missed you."

A thought sprang into Sidney's head. "You drive a black Silverado?"

"How'd you know?"

"Just a guess."

Sidney recalled telling Beth they were staying at the Hilton. "How did you get my room number?" she asked, her eyes narrowing.

"I used to work here. A friend's on the front desk. She told me. But, but please don't tell anyone. I don't want to get her in trouble."

"I won't," Sidney assured her. "So fill me in on what you know."

"You're working on the Aden Uzelac case, aren't you?"

"How do you know his name?" Sidney asked suspiciously. She had never mentioned the names when she showed people the pictures.

"My mom lives in San Diego. I went there for Mother's Day. I saw his picture in the newspaper and on TV. I told my mom that guy had stayed here. I also told her he got drunk as a skunk in the hotel bar, and I helped him to his room."

Sidney grabbed a notepad from the top of the desk. "Who asked you to help him?"

"My aunt. You see, I used to work here as a bellhop. She got me the job. On that day, my truck was in the shop. You can check on that if you want to. It was at Spencer's, a couple of blocks from here." She adjusted herself in the chair and folded her arms across her chest. "When I got off work, I went to the bar to wait for my aunt because she was giving me a ride home. A woman was trying to help this drunk guy out of a booth. My aunt asked her if they were staying at the Hilton. When the woman said they were, my aunt wanted me to give the woman a hand, so I did.

"It wasn't easy helping him since he kept stumbling all over and wanting to go outside instead of to his room. We finally managed to get him in the elevator, and when we got out on the fifth or sixth floor, I can't remember exactly which one, another guy met us. He took one of the drunk guy's arms, and I held onto the other one. The woman led us down the hall and unlocked the door. As we dragged him inside, he mumbled something about that wasn't his room. The woman laughed and shook her head. So I figured the poor guy has no idea where he is, and I thought the woman was his wife. The guy squirmed to get away from us. When we let go of his arms, he turned toward the door. As he staggered, he grabbed the back of the desk chair, and knocked it over. The leg of the chair hit the desk and broke. I was afraid the guy was going to land on top of the broken chair, so I grabbed his arm again and the other guy took the other arm and we hauled him over to the bed."

Sidney went to her briefcase and fished out the picture of Kate and Victor. "Is this the woman and the guy that helped you take Aden to the room?"

Teri nodded. "Yeah, that's them. My mom says I have a photographic memory. I never forget a face." She pointed to the picture of Kate. "Is that the woman Aden was having an affair with?"

"Let's finish talking about that night first. Did you leave Aden on the bed?"

"Yeah. He wasn't going anywhere. He was out like a light before I left the room."

"Given his condition, do you think he was prepared for any sexual activity?"

Teri's eyes popped wide open. "You have got to be kidding."

"The broken chair—would that repair job be on someone's bill?"

"Sure. Whoever rented the room."

Sidney continued writing for a minute. "Is there any way you can get me the bill with the cost of the damaged chair on it?"

"Maybe. Why is that important?"

"The woman in the picture is the one that the prosecutors claim Aden had an affair with." Sidney tilted her head as she studied Teri. "Can you keep what I'm going to tell you confidential?"

Teri pinched her thumb and index finger together and ran them over her mouth, like zipping it up. "Mum's the word."

"Aden believes he had a one-night stand with Kate—that's the woman's name—because he woke up in her bed."

Teri rolled her eyes. "Some guys are so gullible. That night, the drunk, Aden, couldn't have gotten it up to have an affair with anyone." She nodded her head. "Now I get it. You're here to find out the truth. You working on Aden's side?"

"Yes. He was deeply in love with his wife. He mourns her terribly."

"I saw a picture of her. She was as gorgeous as you are."

Sidney's cheeks flushed.

"You think this Kate woman killed Aden's wife so she could have him?" Teri asked.

"I don't know who killed her, but I do know it wasn't Aden. We're searching for evidence to free him. He needs to be with his children," Sidney said. Her eyes became cloudy, and she looked down to breathe and gather her composure. "Teri, would you be willing to testify on Aden's behalf?"

"What do I have to do?"

"Just tell the truth about what happened that evening. Exactly what you told me."

"Going to San Diego? I don't know. I'm working up to be in a body building competition this fall. That's why I quit my job here."

"Teri, Aden is on trial for his life. We'll pay for the airline ticket and your accommodations. You'll probably only have to be there a couple of days."

Teri sat quietly with her head bowed. After a minute, she raised her chin and gazed at Sidney. "Okay, I'll do it."

"Thank you," Sidney said, reaching out and touching Teri's hand. "Can you get that invoice about the broken chair?"

Teri nodded. "What name was the room registered under?"

"Kate Morrison."

"Better do it now," Teri said and left the room.

While Teri was gone, Sidney completed her notes about the unexpected meeting and felt a little anxious to tell Aden that he hadn't cheated on Mara. Ten minutes later, Teri returned with a printout of Kate's room charges for that night with the damaged chair highlighted with a yellow marker.

At midnight, Sidney woke with a start, gasping for air, and sprang up into a sitting position. She splayed her fingers across her chest as her heartbeat rapidly pounded. Feeling dazed and disoriented, she opened her mouth and inhaled deeply when suddenly a strong sensation of relief and joy swelled inside her as her eyes filled with water and tears streamed down her face. "He never cheated on me." The words uncontrollably blurted from her mouth. "Aden never cheated on me."

Wiping her face, she swung her feet over the edge of the bed and staggered into the bathroom for tissues. "Aden never cheated on me." Sidney heard the words escaping through her lips but wasn't saying them. *What's happening to me?* Unable to stop the pouring of tears, she grabbed a towel, buried her face in it, and sank down to the cold tile floor. Sobbing, she longed to be in Aden's arms. "No. No," she mumbled. "I love Chas. I'll always love Chas."

Thinking of both men, Sidney closed her eyes and drifted off into a tormented dream.

Chapter 22

The early morning sun streaming through the open bathroom door awakened her. Gripping the rim of the bathtub, Sidney struggled to her feet. Her image in the mirror showed a woman with dark shadows under puffy eyes. She tucked her hair behind her ears and recalled her nearly sleepless night. Everything she remembered about speaking Mara's words scared her. She hoped the memory was nothing more than a bad dream but couldn't shake the feeling that part of it had to be real. A sad expression crept across her face. *Will Mara ever let me return to my life with Chas? Or will I be bound to Aden forever?* Sidney suspected her only hope to escape Mara's hold would be if she managed to clear Aden's name. Sidney wasn't sure if that would be enough. *Do I need to find Mara's murderer in order to be set free?*

After freshening up and putting on a heavy layer of makeup in an attempt to hide her swollen eyes, she grabbed her duffle bag and headed to the foyer to meet Sam.

Sam's brows creased when he saw Sidney's face. "Rough night?"

"Bad dream," she said and then proceeded to fill him in on Teri's visit.

"Unbelievable," he said as they headed toward the parking garage.

Shortly before noon, they arrived in San Diego. Sam intended to spend the rest of the day searching for the taxi driver. Sidney dropped him off at his office and drove toward the Grand Hyatt.

Stepping into the suite, Sidney's eyes beamed and a spark of adrenaline rushed through her body as the man she loved walked toward her while their song, "I Got You Babe," softly echoed through the room. The song had never struck her as being romantic, but it was the first song they had heard after she finally said "Yes" to Chas's third wedding proposal. Before that, she had thought someday she might return to the CIA, and having a husband wasn't anything she wanted to deal with. But that special night, she saw the deep love he felt for her behind his warm, shimmering brown eyes and knew she could never be happy without him. Sidney tossed her thoughts of the CIA aside and became Chas's bride. It was the best decision she'd ever made.

"Hi, Babe," Chas said, wrapping his arms around her.

She melted in his body while he held her close. "How?" she stammered, unable to comprehend how he could leave New York with his case load.

"I couldn't bear to be away from you any longer, so I caught an early morning flight to personally deliver the items you wanted," he said, tilting his head toward a box on the table.

"That was the only reason?" Sidney asked, kissing his neck.

"What do you think?" He raised her chin and smothered her mouth with his lips, putting passion into the kiss. "Unfortunately, I can only stay tonight."

Sidney kissed him again. "Then I'm not going to do anything on the investigation until you leave. I want to enjoy every minute you're here."

"Good. That's what I was hoping you'd say, Mrs. Langston," Chas said, scooping Sidney up into his arms.

"What about Jean?"

"She's staying in another room tonight." Chas strolled toward the bedroom with Sidney cradled in his arms. "Champagne's chilling, and the Jacuzzi is waiting. All we need to do is shed these clothes."

The next morning, Sidney cut to the curb at the San Diego airport, fighting the urge to go back to New York with Chas. She had spent twenty wonderful hours with her husband and had managed not to even think about the investigation. Now, Aden monopolized her mind again. She couldn't leave with him still behind bars. Also, she had the fleeting thought that Mara wouldn't allow her to go without sending the pain running through her chest again. If she didn't get Aden out of jail and back to his children, she'd never have any peace.

Chas leaned over the seat and softly kissed Sidney's lips. "I wish you were going with me."

"So do I, but I need to finish what I started here."

"I know. I don't want your pain to return," he said, caressing Sidney's cheek. "Bye, Babe." He scooted out of the car.

"Call me when you land."

"Will do."

While watching him enter the terminal, Sidney pulled out her cell phone. There were two messages from Bernice and four from Sam. She listened to the most recent one from Sam. He said he needed to talk to her as soon as possible. Since she had already called him to let him know she wouldn't be reachable until Sunday afternoon, and he still left four messages on her phone, it had to be important. She quickly punched in his number.

"What's up?" she asked.

"Several things. Can you stop by my office?"

"Sure. I'll be there in half an hour."

When she reached the freeway, she called Bernice.

"Hi, Sidney," Bernice answered, sounding relieved. "I was just about to call you again."

"I take it you've heard from Mara again?"

"Yeah. Last night. Just words, like before, but she added a new one."

"What?"

"Safe."

The safe behind a picture at Payton's house and the numbers she found hidden in Victor's den darted into her mind. "Besides safe, what were her other words?"

"Pres house, blond hair, short. I've gotten those before. She provided me with a quick flash of a picture or painting hanging on a wall. Maybe the safe is behind it. Hey, Sidney, how are you doing with all this? Getting any closer?"

"Still looking," Sidney said, not wanting to divulge anything until she had something concrete that would help free Aden. The one-night stand with Kate never happened, but she doubted that would convince the authorities that he hadn't committed the crime.

"I'll let you know if Mara contacts me again." Bernice

disconnected.

A dark gray Suburban in the far right lane three cars behind her edged closer. Lacking a clear view of the Suburban's side panel, she couldn't see if an SLI emblem was plastered on it. Based on the way it was maneuvering toward her car, she figured it was the same vehicle that had been following Sam. Exiting the interstate, her eyes moved between the rearview mirror and the windshield as she watched for the dark SUV. The Suburban stopped at the red light two cars away from her, and with the curve in the off ramp, she caught a glimpse of the SLI emblem. Sidney considered Payton's involvement with that company. From the conversation she had overheard at Payton's place, she knew Sam wasn't buying Payton's story that he had hired an investigator just because he hadn't been paid for some engineering services. She also knew there was a signed contract, and Payton had given only part of it to Sam. *Why the holdout? What was in the rest of that contract?*

Sidney parked in front of Sam's office. Stepping out of the Lexus, she saw the dark gray Suburban passing by her. The vehicle had a small sign below the back window that read: "Stellar Land Investments."

"Get hubby off okay?" Sam asked as Sidney entered the office while he thumbed through a stack of papers at the desk in the reception area.

"Yeah." She sank down on the leather couch. "What did you find out?"

"I saw Ortega's brother. He definitely resembles Ramon. The guy won't talk to me. When he wasn't looking, I snapped a picture of him, but it's too dark to make out his features. My flash must not have been working." Sam picked up the papers. "I'll be right back." He shuffled into his office and a few minutes later returned with another bunch of papers.

"The dark gray Suburban that likes hanging out by your office followed me here from the airport," Sidney said, leaning her elbow on the armrest and tapping her fingertips together.

"SLI's?"

"Yes. Stellar Land Investments—the company involved with one of your other investigations." She stared at him through narrowed eyes. "You still don't think that has anything to do with the case we're working on?"

He waffled for a few seconds and then shrugged. "Before I came back to my office yesterday, I doubted it. But after I discovered someone had rummaged through my files and the only documents that appear to be missing are those associated with that case and the Aden investigation, now I'm sure."

Sidney pursed her lips and squinted. "Documents? What documents did you have regarding Aden?" she asked, hoping it was minor stuff.

"Not much. Time logs and mileage."

"Victor's address. Ortega's?"

"Only addresses. No apartment numbers or names. Nothing we've discovered." He tapped the side of his head. "Keep that stuff in here."

Sidney sighed with relief. "How did they get past your security system?"

"If it was SLI, they've hired some new thugs. This was a sophisticated job. No sign of a break-in. The system was hooked up and functioning. File cabinets were locked." Sam pressed his lips together and shook his head. "Can't figure it out. Had it not been for the backup string I left in a cabinet drawer and found on the floor, I never would've known that I had an unwelcome visitor until I needed one of the missing files."

Sidney leaned back in the couch. Her eyes squinted, showing tiny wrinkles in the corners. "If it wasn't SLI, it would have to be someone interested in the Aden case," she said, thinking out loud. "Why would that person also be interested in the SLI investigation?" She sat up straight and confronted Sam. "Is your SLI client involved with the Aden case?" Though she already knew the answer, she wanted to hear him admit it.

"The client wants to remain anonymous."

"Was his name on any of the documents taken?"

Sam nodded reluctantly.

"Then he is no longer anonymous. At least not to the burglars."

Sam's face creased with a crooked smile. "Good point, Sid."

"Uh-huh. Okay, who is he?"

Sam lowered himself into the desk chair and rubbed his chin with his knuckles. "There could be a problem. After I discovered the break-in, I tried contacting him. He doesn't answer his cell or his front door, but his car is parked in his driveway."

"Do you think he's in danger?"

"Sid, I don't know," Sam said, running his fingers through his hair. "According to the arrangement, he hired me to check on SLI because they owed him some money. Originally, I thought he wanted to know if they were solvent. Simple investigation. But he keeps wanting more information every time I tell him I've reached a dead end. The guy has a contract. I could see him being in trouble if he owed money, but not the other way around."

"Geez, when someone doesn't get paid for their services, and they have a contract, it's time to see a lawyer not an investigator." She crossed her legs and locked her fingers together. "How much is your client owed? And exactly what were the services he performed for SLI?" Sidney felt a strange sensation like an invisible hand rubbing her shoulder, egging her to pry deeper.

Sam cocked his brow and clenched his jaw. "He claimed it was for engineering services. Engineering services—that doesn't rise to the level of getting thugs involved. Not an illegal act. On the other hand, I've had clients lie to me before. He wouldn't be the first."

"Did he provide you with a copy of the contract?"

"Only the signature page."

"Not the rest of it?"

"Nope. I had assumed it might be because he didn't want me to know how much money was at stake."

"The copy of the signature page was taken?"

Sam nodded. "All the files related to that case are gone."

"A lot of stuff?"

"Yep. Names, times, dates when I talked to everyone. Company info. Everything's been snatched."

"Names?" Sidney said, thinking Payton might not be the only one in trouble. "SLI hired someone to keep track of you and had me followed from the airport. They're probably also responsible for breaking into your office. That's a little extreme just to find out who your client is. Don't you agree?"

"Sure do. Maybe SLI is somehow connected to Aden's case. They could be trying to figure out where we're at in the investigation."

"Assuming that's the situation, they certainly aren't being low key about it with the SLI emblem on the Suburban. We've spotted them every time they've followed us. They hang out at night by your place." She leaned forward. "A pro broke into your office, but maybe whoever is calling the shots wants us to know we're being watched by SLI. Why would they do that?"

Sam shook his head. "Not a clue."

"So, who is your mysterious client?"

As Sam opened his mouth to answer, a loud siren rang out and blinking red-and-white lights streamed through the office window. A patrol car stopped behind Sidney's Lexus.

Chapter 23

"Looks like we're in for company," Sam commented, watching two policemen stroll toward the door. One was tall with a lean build and the other an average-sized man.

Stepping into Sam's office, the tall officer asked, "Sam Jordan?"

"That's me," Sam said.

The officers glanced around the room. "Mr. Jordan, has the robber left?"

Sam hadn't reported a crime. "What?" he asked, bewildered, cocking his head.

"Less than fifteen minutes ago you called nine-one-one and told the dispatcher that a robbery was in progress at this address."

Sam shook his head. "Didn't make that call."

"Mr. Jordan, is your phone number..." He then rattled off the number.

"Yes, but I never called anyone. I've been talking to Mrs. Langston."

"Officer," Sidney said, "I can assure you that Mr. Jordan has not placed any calls while I've been here, and I've been here for almost an hour."

"Where's your cell phone?" the officer asked.

"In my office," Sam said, opening the door to the inner office. "I'll get it." A second later he returned with his phone and handed it to the policeman.

The officer briefly examined it. "Mmmh. Is there anyone else in the building?"

"Nope. Just us."

The tall officer gave the phone back to Sam. "Strange. Sorry for any inconvenience." He turned on his heels and left with the other policeman.

"I wonder what that was all about," Sam said.

Sidney stretched out her hand. "Let me see your phone." After Sam handed it to her, she dismantled it and pulled out a small disk. "Someone's been listening to your calls, and with this little gadget, they can also place calls from your phone."

Sam took the device and held it in front of his eyes. "I sure could use some of these—for listening, not calling. I guess our new buddies want to know everything."

"Not any more. If they wanted to continue listening they wouldn't have called the police to alert you to the gadget in your cell phone. Have you checked for bugs in here?"

"Yeah. Did that yesterday and again today, but I didn't pick up this little thingamajig." He studied the device. "Thinking about it, my cell phone was upstairs when I scanned this area and my office."

"Maybe this was their way of sending you a warning. Letting you know they can easily get to you."

"But why?" Sam asked, tapping an index finger against his forehead in quiet deliberation.

Sidney's eyes fixed on Sam, and she tilted her head. "You must have stumbled onto something, or they think you have. This might be their form of intimidation. I'd scan your apartment upstairs for bugs." She paused as various possibilities churned in her mind. "Do you recall any of the names of the people who signed the SLI contract?"

"My client signed along with two from SLI, Randolph Smorick and A. F. Gamboa. When I first started checking on the company, their receptionist was very helpful. She said both of the guys had left the country. She even gave me their California addresses, so I could verify it."

Sidney smiled to herself, figuring Sam had flirted with the receptionist to get that much information—flashing a dazzling smile and talking in his seductive baritone voice. Sidney had observed him throwing on the charm in Denver whenever it was to his advantage. From eavesdropping on Sam's conversation with Payton, she knew the receptionist was no longer with SLI. Suddenly, she felt concerned for the woman's welfare. "Names—I'm assuming her name and what she told you was included in the missing files, right?"

"Yep, but she no longer works for SLI. I haven't been able to track her down."

"Don't tell me she didn't give you her phone number?"

Sam raised an eyebrow. "She did, but the number isn't working, and she's moved out of her apartment."

"Personal relationship?"

"No. Not my type." He flashed a mischievous smile. "But she sure was helpful."

"I wonder if she discovered something was going on at SLI and decided to clear out."

Sam rested his elbows on the desk, tented his hands, and tapped his fingertips together. "That possibility did enter my mind when I found the files were missing. Judy, the receptionist, struck me as pretty savvy. Granted, she probably shouldn't have told me everything she did, but she didn't say anything negative about the company. Telling me that Smorick and Gamboa had left the country and giving me the addresses of where they used to live—that isn't exactly real confidential information. Addresses aren't tough to get."

"Are Smorick and Gamboa still with SLI, but at another location?"

"The headquarters is in Spain. I had assumed that's where they went. After SLI people started following me—and their fumbled attempt at bugging my landline phone—I wanted to check with her. That's when I found out she'd left."

"And your charms didn't work on her replacement?"

"It's a guy." He cocked his head to one side and his lips curved into a half smile. "Didn't attempt to get friendly."

"How old?"

"Twenty something."

"Maybe I'll give him a shot."

"Don't tell me you're going to wear the same outfit you used to entice Zisk?" Sam said, raising an eyebrow.

"That's evening attire," she said with a smirk. "Tight jeans and a t-shirt will probably be enough for this guy."

Sam chuckled. "I'm sure that will do the trick."

"Somehow your SLI investigation and Aden's case are intertwined. I'll see what I can find out there tomorrow." Sidney grabbed a notebook from her briefcase and jotted down a few notes. "Maybe Aden can throw some light on this. I'm going to visit him."

"I thought I'd work on tracking down my client—check his house again, where he works. Even if it's Sunday, he might be catching up on something. And I know a few places where he likes to hang out."

"Client's name?"

Sam lowered his head. "Payton Russen."

Chapter 24

Stepping into the visitor's room at the county jail, Sidney felt the familiar signs: her breathing accelerated while her heart pounded rapidly. *How can the thought of seeing Aden excite me like this? It was just this morning that I woke up in Chas's loving arms.*

Sidney took a chair and stared at the door Aden would walk through. *I probably should have sent Sam to talk to Aden.* Yet, she felt she should be the one to tell him he hadn't cheated on Mara. Besides, she thought he'd tell her more than he would Sam. She tried to calm the desire for Aden that swirled through her body. Sidney closed her eyes and forced herself to recall being with Chas in the hotel Jacuzzi the night before.

The door squeaked open, snapping Sidney out of her reverie. She gasped when she glanced at Aden. He trudged toward her, eyes bloodshot and glassy, face pale and drawn. His shoulders sagged. A lump formed in Sidney's throat. Her body shifted from arousal to a strong sense of overwhelming grief for this man, dressed in a pair of orange coveralls with tousled hair and a stubble forming on his chin. She wondered how many days he had been like that.

Slowly, he lowered his body into the chair like an old man.

"How are you doing?" she asked in a gentle tone.

His head dropped to the counter. "Not well."

Sidney's eyes became moist. "Oh, Aden, I'm so sorry. Is there anything I can do?"

"Find the person that killed Mara." He swallowed hard, raised his head, and squinted. His eyes met Sidney's. "Looking at you, I almost feel like she's in this room with us. I still sense her every night. Inhale her sweet smell. But the last two nights, somehow her presence seems stronger. I actually feel her breathing next to me. When I wake up, she's gone." He ran his hands through his hair and then shook his head. "That's crazy, huh?"

"No. It's not," Sidney said, remembering her experience Friday night. "Aden, you never cheated on Mara."

His eyes opened wide. "Huh? What are you talking about?"

"Denver. The Hilton. Sam and I went there. A former hotel employee recognized you from a picture. She said you were intoxicated. She helped you to Kate's room per Kate's instructions. She also said you were in no condition to perform any sexual acts."

Aden sat quietly staring at Sidney. A shocked expression splashed across his ashen face. He stammered, "But...but...Mara, poor Mara. What I put her through."

"Aden, Mara knows."

"How?"

"Don't have any proof. But I positively know, she knows," Sidney said in a firm, unflinching tone. "Aden, you were set up that night. Sam and I made an uninvited visit to Victor's condo."

"You broke in?" he asked in a tone of disbelief.

"Sure did."

"Why?"

"Victor's name was mentioned when I visited Angelica Brimwell, and he's dating Deidre."

"You think Victor killed Mara? But why?"

"No stone is going to be left unturned. The murder weapon is still missing. I suspect it's been tossed, but I'm not going to stop looking for it," Sidney explained, opening her notebook and flipping through it. "In Victor's apartment we found a picture of you in bed with Kate. You were sound asleep."

"Clothes?" he asked, his bloodshot, dark eyes brimming with concern.

"Naked. Partially covered by the sheet." She gave him a faint smile. "It wasn't an x-rated Kodak moment if that's what you're worried about."

He sighed. "Thank God. The kids. The trial."

"The former hotel employee who helped you to Kate's room has agreed to testify on your behalf."

"Oh, Sidney, thank you," he said in an uplifted tone. "You have no idea how much that will mean to Mara's parents." His hands drummed on the edge of the counter. "Why would Kate take a picture like that and give it to Victor?"

"I was hoping you could tell me. I suspect Victor took the picture. A man helped the hotel employee take you to Kate's room. She identified him from a photo. It was Victor."

"Victor?" Aden looked confused. "You thinking blackmail? But I told Mara what I believed had happened. They couldn't use it."

"Maybe when it was taken, they expected to use it to blackmail you. You surprised them by confessing to Mara."

"Yeah, maybe, but I don't make much more money than Victor. Blackmail? What would he want from me?"

"That's the question," Sidney said, tapping her pen against her notebook. "The answer might shed light on the whole case. Were you aware of anything going on between Victor and Kate?"

"Sometimes they went out for a beer. It seemed like they were just friends. She didn't pester him at work."

"Like she did you?"

Aden nodded.

"So nothing romantic?"

He shook his head. "Not that I know of."

"And Deidre?"

"Victor kind of has a reputation of being a ladies man. He's ten years older than Deidre. Mara never liked Deidre dating him. But nothing Mara told Deidre prevented her from going out with the guy. Even when he brought a date to the Christmas party, Deidre couldn't be swayed from seeing him again."

Sidney glanced at her notes. "Deidre has a significant amount of wealth. How did she acquire that?"

Aden tilted his head and cocked an eyebrow. "How do you know she's loaded?"

"Her financial statements were in Victor's desk drawer."

"Geez," Aden said, rolling his eyes. "That's exactly why Mara thought Victor kept stringing Deidre along. A rich girl he could completely control."

Pressing the point, Sidney asked, "How did she become a rich girl?"

"She's an only child. About five years ago, her parents along with her mother's parents were killed in a plane crash. Her dad was the pilot. She inherited everything plus a continuous string of royalties from two of her grandfather's patents. Even if she spends every cent she now has, she'll have a considerable amount of money flowing in forever. But losing her parents and grandparents has been real hard on Deidre." He lowered his head. "Mara was always there for her. They were very close. Almost like sisters."

"How did she meet Victor?"

"At the office. She came there with Mara a few times. Mara regretted bringing her there, but she had no idea that Victor would latch onto her." He gripped his hands together. "You see, Victor normally likes his women a little older. There was a time I thought he had the hots for Angelica Brimwell."

"Angelica?"

"Yeah. Boy, the way he kept track of her at parties. I was surprised that he brought a date to the Christmas party."

"Did Marcus Brimwell notice?"

"Brimwell isn't a great host. During the two parties he throws a year, he's either hanging out in his den or chatting on his cell phone."

Sidney reviewed a page in her notebook. "There's quite an age gap between Brimwell and his wife. Has he been married before?"

"Yep. He married Angelica before I started working for him, so I never knew Jacqueline, his first wife. Even with the difference in their ages, Angelica and Brimwell used to seem like the perfect couple, always attentive to each other. She used to travel with him all the time. I think her heart condition has had a real toll on their marriage."

"What happened to his first wife—divorce?"

"No," Aden said, shaking his head. "She drowned in their swimming pool when he was out of town."

"How awful."

"He didn't mourn her long. Molly told me he married Angelica a couple of months after Jacqueline was buried."

Sidney jotted down that information. "Did he live in the same house with his first wife that he now shares with Angelica?"

Aden nodded. "Jacqueline inherited it from her grandfather. Brimwell inherited it from Jacqueline. He loves the place. I doubt he'd ever think about parting with it."

That answered a question that had been buzzing around in

Sidney's mind—how Brimwell could afford such a large mansion with servants. "Did he know Angelica before his wife died?"

"Aaah," Aden mumbled and slid further back in his seat. "Just rumors. This isn't going to tell us who killed Mara."

"Maybe not. But the more I know about your associates, it might help. Sometimes things that seem irrelevant become important in solving the crime. Jealousy is a strong motivator."

"Mara and Angelica were friends. Angelica was still healing from her heart operation. No way would she hurt Mara." He paused. "Jealousy. Now Kate, she's a person I can see harming someone, but she has an alibi. And since I know we never had a one-night stand, that rules out that motive."

Sidney scribbled in her notebook. "Why did Mara think Brimwell was cheating on Angelica?"

Aden cleared his throat, peered at the floor, and then said, "Things that go on between a wife and a husband are private. I don't feel comfortable talking about them."

"Aden, you're in jail for a crime you didn't commit. This is not the time or place to feel squeamish about telling me everything you know. I'm not going to broadcast anyone's extramarital affairs if it doesn't help free you."

He gazed at Sidney while she studied his face and patiently waited for him to respond. A minute later, he inhaled deeply. "Okay. I need to do this for Mara and my children. She'd never forgive me if I didn't do everything I could to get out of here and be a father again."

Sidney felt the weight of a hand on her shoulder and swung her head toward it. No one was there, but the sleeve of her blouse was crinkled as if a hand were resting on it. Sensing Mara by her side, she turned to Aden. "You know Mara well. She wants you to tell me everything you know, even if it seems trivial. So, why did Mara think Brimwell wasn't faithful?"

"The way Sam, Fowler's PI, looked at me when I told him something happened in the pool house, I think he thought it was between Mara and Brimwell, but that was only a little part of it."

Sidney tilted her head, recalling Sam telling her about the incident and agreeing with his assessment—that Brimwell had probably made a pass at Mara.

Aden continued. "Mara was on the ladies' side of the pool house. She had undressed to shower when she heard voices coming from the lounge. It's a room between the men's and women's sides. I've sometimes waited for Mara in there.

"She recognized Brimwell's voice but couldn't place the voice of the woman he was talking to. From the words she picked up, she knew it was an intimate conversation. Mara quietly wrapped a towel around herself and carefully peeked into the room. She saw Brimwell's back and the face of an attractive woman with long blonde hair. She watched as Brimwell embraced and kissed the stranger.

"Mara wanted to get out of there as soon as she could, so she hurried into the shower and hoped Brimwell hadn't realized she had seen him. But when she stepped out of the shower and wrapped her hair in a towel, she saw him in the doorway looking at her. She grabbed the towel from her head and held it in front of her body. He stared at her for a few more seconds and then turned around and left the pool house without saying a word. When Mara told me about his gawking, I wanted to confront him, but she persuaded me not to say a word—probably didn't want me to lose my job. Not that I would, but shouting at my boss at his place might not be a good idea. And the more I thought about it, Brimwell hadn't gone into the pool house to spy on Mara. It was for a rendezvous with another woman."

"Any idea who the woman was?"

"No. Mara thought the woman was wearing a uniform, like the catering company, but she wasn't sure until the woman appeared again at the Christmas party." Aden slowly shook his head. "What a party. First, Victor shows up with a date—not Deidre, and then Mara spots the woman. When I passed the closed den door on the way to the bathroom, I heard laughter coming from the other side. I didn't see that woman the rest of the evening. Mara thought Angelica knew because she noticed her staring often in the direction of the den."

"Poor Angelica. Here she's not well, and she has to deal with that in her house. Did all the guests suspect?"

"Doubt it. To tell you the truth, I wouldn't have thought anything about the laughter in Brimwell's den if Mara hadn't mentioned the woman to me. You see, sometimes during Brimwell's parties, he has a little one-on-one time with his employees. Just chatting. Nothing more. I've smoked a few cigars in his den with him." Aden squinted. "To think about it, maybe Victor knew. I noticed him whispering to Angelica a couple of times while they both looked in the direction of

Brimwell's den. He might have been consoling her. I just don't see how Brimwell's affair has a bearing on the case. So the guy cheats." Aden shifted in his chair. "Brimwell's pretty shrewd when it comes to money. He probably has a prenup with Angelica. Even if he suspected Mara knew and she was going to spill the beans to Angelica, that would have happened after the summer party. Mara never actually saw Brimwell and the woman together at the Christmas party. Some of the guys at work who've traveled with Brimwell, when Angelica wasn't along, have seen things. They think he's a womanizer. Brimwell always eyed Mara whenever he saw her. I hated it. People probably thought he was interested in her."

"Womanizer?" Sidney said, mulling it over. "Before Mara mentioned what went on in the pool house, you never saw it?"

"Brimwell and I have gone on some business trips together. He could've been busy picking up women after I'd gone to my room, but I never saw it nor do I care."

"Like I mentioned earlier," Sidney said while she wrote in her notebook, "the more information I know, the better. How did Victor's date act about seeing him with Angelica?"

"Victor's time with Angelica was brief. His date got most of his attention. The way she hung onto his every word and the time he spent with her out by the pool, I'd be surprised if she felt the least bit neglected," he said with an edge to his voice.

"You sound like you didn't like his date?"

"She clung to his arm at every opportunity, and she couldn't carry on a simple conversation. But my attitude was probably tarnished by the way Mara felt. I still don't understand why he would bring a date to a party when he knew Mara would tell her friend. What kind of a guy does that unless he planned to end his relationship with Deidre? But then took her out a few days later, so that must not have been his intention."

"Maybe originally it was. Then he somehow learned about Deidre's wealth. Does she live in a fancy place?"

"No. A nice two bedroom condo. Nothing that would give anyone the impression she was loaded."

Sidney jotted that down. "Let's move on. Have you ever heard of a company by the name of Stellar Land Investment, SLI?"

"That seems familiar." Aden stared at the counter and clasped his hands together. He looked up and said, "In Payton's den. I saw a document with that name on top. When he noticed me looking at it, he grabbed it and stuck it in his desk drawer."

"Did he comment about it?"

"Uh-uh. I recall the word contract on it. Since he was so quick at hiding it, I assumed he might be moonlighting. That's a no-no for Brimwell."

"Why?"

"Brimwell's view is that if we do engineering jobs on the side, it will cut into his business. All of his employees have signed an agreement stating they won't work on any engineering jobs that haven't been assigned by Brimwell. We can have other jobs, but they can't be engineering jobs."

"If Payton did an engineering job outside the company, would he be fired?"

Aden nodded. "Definitely. Pres would find himself gainfully unemployed. No room for negotiation."

"Pres?" Sidney asked, recalling the words Bernice had given her.

"Yeah. Mara called him that. A little inside joke. Payton's middle initial 'T' stands for Truman. If his contract with SLI was for engineering, I suspect it wasn't the first time he stepped over the line. Payton's always looking for some scheme to get rich."

Sidney noted the new clue. What Mara had told Bernice was starting to make sense to her. Pres, short, blond hair, all referred to Payton. *Could he be the perpetrator?*

"Time's up," said the guard standing at the back of the room.

"Yeah." Aden nodded toward the guard and eased out of his chair. "How's the search for the taxi driver going?"

"We're still looking," she said, folding her notepad.

"Hey, Sidney, thanks for everything you're doing." His sad eyes moved her.

"Aden, don't thank me until you're a free man. I hope that won't be long."

He didn't say a word. She watched him muster a smile, and then he turned toward the door and shuffled out. Pictures Sidney had seen of Aden and Mara flashed into her mind—the happy couple with bright smiles and glowing eyes. Now, Aden looked like a lost man. The love of his life was gone; his hope for being with his children again drained away with each passing day.

A tinge of despair rushed up Sidney's spine. She placed her elbows on the counter and cupped her chin in her hands. Her heart ached for Aden and Mara while her eyes shined with unshed tears.

Chapter 25

The sun was setting when Sidney reached her car in the county jail parking lot. After she was situated in the driver's seat, she pulled out her cell phone and called Sam. "Any luck finding Payton?"

"No. His car's still parked in his driveway. He didn't answer his door. Went to his office. No lights were on inside. Then headed to a bar and a health club—places he likes to hang out. No one claims they've seen him. His folks live out of town in a place with no cell phone coverage. Payton might've gone for a visit. Before I continue searching for him, I'm going to see if he shows up at work tomorrow. I *did* swing by Zisk's apartment building and managed to get a good snapshot of the guy that might be the taxi driver."

"Great," Sidney said, thinking she wasn't ready for another visit with Aden so soon. "Can you show Aden the picture tomorrow?"

"No problem. Anything else you want me to do tonight?"

"No. Go have a beer. Relax. Give me a call after you see Aden."

Sidney merged into traffic and drove toward Payton's house. Since he wasn't home, she decided it would be a good time to do a thorough search. Mara had given Bernice, the medium, the words "Pres," a nickname Mara used for Payton, and "safe." *Maybe there's something stored in there that will help solve the crime.*

She stopped across the street from the deserted looking house. Not even a speck of light shone. Payton's BMW was parked in the driveway. She climbed out of the Lexus and looked around the neighborhood. Satisfied there weren't any observers, she opened her trunk, snatched her duffle bag, and slung it over her shoulder. Her eyes darted back and forth as she approached the side of Payton's house. There, she slipped on a pair of latex gloves, hurried over the fence, and headed to the back door.

Sidney picked the lock and hurried inside, shutting the door behind her. She perked up her ears, expecting to hear an alarm as she flipped on her flashlight. No sound rang out. The only noise inside the house was the humming of the refrigerator motor. Stepping into the hallway, she noticed an alarm system panel on the wall with a steady green light in the corner of the unit. Still, she shined the flashlight on its monitor screen and verified the system had not been activated. Pausing for a minute, she wondered why Payton hadn't set it when he left the house. She briefly mulled over the various possibilities—some harmless and others dangerous. The harmless ones began to diminish as the image of Payton's car sitting in the driveway sprang into her mind. If he had been escorted out, she assumed the front door might be unlocked. She rushed to it and discovered it was locked and bolted. She swung the flashlight around the living room and didn't see any signs of a struggle.

Sidney stopped dwelling on the possibilities and headed up the stairs to the den. She went to the other side of the desk, placed her duffle bag on top of it, and then removed the picture that concealed the safe. Before taking out her stethoscope to crack it, she decided to try the combination she had acquired from Victor's condo. She reached in her duffle bag, dug out her notebook, and thumbed through it until she found the page she needed. Using those numbers, she began turning the knob on the safe.

She lowered the handle, and the door opened. Suddenly, a gust of air twirled around her, blowing her hair away from her face. A 9mm Luger lay on top of a stack of papers. A chill ran up her spine. The breeze continued while she yanked a plastic container out of her duffle bag. She carefully lifted the pistol, lowered it into the container, and placed it in her bag. The wind ceased and the air became still once more.

Sidney smiled. Mara had given her a sign. The weapon secured in her duffle bag must be the one that ended Mara's life. Yet, Sidney didn't have a clue why, and she wasn't certain Payton was the murderer. Victor had the combination. He could've planted the pistol there. Sidney thought about Payton's and Victor's relationship. *Did Payton just give Victor the combination, or had he acquired it by some other means?*

Regardless of whose fingerprints were on the gun, that wouldn't be enough proof for her they belonged to the killer, although, she hoped that piece of evidence would be enough to free Aden. A disturbing thought entered her mind. *Could Aden have touched the weapon?*

As a precaution, she called Sam. He picked up on the second ring. "Tomorrow morning when you talk to Aden, will you ask him if he's ever handled a 9mm Luger?"

"Will do. Anything else?"

"No, that's it." She disconnected and turned her attention back to the open safe. Searching for a motive, she lifted out a stack of papers along with a metal box. The top document was a contract between Payton and SLI. Skimming through it, Sidney noticed the various rates Payton would be paid for engineering services, but there didn't appear to be anything in the contract that Payton should have hidden from Sam. She laid it down on the desk, yanked her cell phone from her pocket, and took a picture of each page. The numbers 5 of 5 at the bottom of the signature page caught her attention. Knowing she had only taken three prior pictures, she counted the pages. Four. She scanned the numbers at the bottom of the pages. Number 4 was missing.

Sidney moved to the second document in the stack, another contract with SLI. It appeared to be identical to the first one except it referred to another property. She flipped through it and discovered it was also shy one page. *Strange.* Sidney only took a picture of the page that described the property and the signature page. Then she moved to the next contract. Like the other two, it also was missing a page.

She laid that contract out on the desk, raised her cell phone, and began snapping pictures.

A door slammed, echoing through the house.

Sidney flipped off her flashlight. With the dim light of the moon shining through a crack between the drape panels, she gathered up the documents and placed them back in the safe. Loud footsteps pounded against the wood floor a flight of stairs below her. She slowly pushed the safe door closed, carefully twisted the knob to a few numbers higher, and hung the painting over it without making a sound as light began shining through the doorway.

Sidney hunkered down, quietly slithered out of the room with her duffle bag, and made her way to the abutting bedroom as footfalls on the stairs reverberated through the hallway. After she unlocked the patio door, she no longer heard footsteps. Assuming Payton had gone into the den, she retrieved a small directional listening device Chas delivered the day before and then stuck earplugs into her ears. Pointing the device toward a wall shared with the den, she listened to a row of clicking sounds and wondered if he was opening his safe.

"Damn," an angry voice blurted out that didn't belong to Payton.

Sidney cocked her head to the side and moved the device across the wall, thinking perhaps two men had entered the house, though she had only heard one voice.

"It's me," a male said.

Sidney squinted as she tried to put a name to the voice, but nothing came to her.

"Nope...not here...why would he...not good...I'll search...yeah, sure."

A slamming sound, a thud, and shoveling of papers came through the listening device. When Sidney heard footsteps, she grabbed her duffle bag, silently opened the patio door, and slipped out. She took a rope out of her bag and draped it over the railing. Wanting to know the identity of the intruder, she hid in the shadows cast by a huge cottonwood tree and peered through a small opening in the drape at the bottom pane of the patio door. She saw two pant-clad legs wearing dark brown leather shoes enter the room. Sidney knew from that angle she would never be able to see the man's face. With her back pressed against the exterior wall, she rose to a standing position. Her eyes examined the closed glass door until she spotted a small opening in the center between the drawn drapes. She edged over to it and placed her eye over the spot. Inside the bedroom, a tall man with an athletic build and deep brown hair was rummaging through the top drawer of the chest. From what Sidney recalled when she had seen Victor through the slots in his closet door, she thought it might be him. She remembered listening to him on the phone while she was hiding at his condo. She closed her eyes and concentrated on the voice that had come from the den earlier but wasn't certain it belonged to Victor. Opening her eyes, she continued to stare at the man's back. She had planned to search the rest of Payton's house after checking out the den. Instead, she would watch and see if the intruder found anything interesting.

His cell phone buzzed, and he yanked it out of his pant pocket. "Hey," he answered, moving to the bed and sitting down. "No sign of him…I thought I saw a light upstairs and decided to surprise him… yeah, yesterday… his car hasn't budged since I marked the tire… Haven't got the foggiest…I'm still searching …he had to've snuck in here, got it, and left… can't figure out how he knew…he doesn't know I'm involved…no…sure…take him for a little drive…I'll let you know." The man stood up and tucked his cell phone into his pocket.

Sidney stayed vigilant next to the patio door and followed his every move. He continued looking through the chest, the nightstands, and under the bed. She finally saw his face when he turned around and gazed in the direction of the patio. Victor.

She carefully backed away and inched toward the rope while she took shallow breaths. Adrenaline spiked through her body. Footsteps approached the patio door. Anticipating it might fly open any second, Sidney gripped the rope, swung over the railing, and slid down in one quick motion. She no longer worried about being quiet. Her concern was fixed on getting away unseen. She yanked the rope free from the railing and headed to the corner of the house. The patio door snapped open. Sidney rushed to the fence and scrambled over it. Victor could make it to the front door and possibly see her license plate number before she had driven out of sight. Sidney charged across the street and moved into the shadows until she reached a vantage point where she could see her car and the front of Payton's house. She ducked behind a nearby bush and focused on the house.

Within a few seconds, Victor charged out the front door and sprinted up to the street. His head swung back and forth while he looked up and down the pavement. He stared at a blue Toyota RAV driving past him and then trudged along the sidewalk, glancing around the neighbors' houses, while Sidney remained well-concealed. Ten minutes later, he went back into Payton's house.

Even though Sidney had the urge to head to her car and drive away, she didn't want to take a chance that he might spot her through Payton's front windows. She waited patiently until she saw Victor step out of the house, lock the door, and stride to a white Porsche parked two houses away from Payton's. Besides the combination to the safe, Sidney wondered if Payton knew Victor had a key to his home.

When the Porsche was out of sight, she eased out of the hiding spot and hurried to her car.

Chapter 26

The following morning, Sidney drove to Fowler's office to fill him in on the status of the investigation. Before she entered the building, she chatted with Sam. He told her that Aden swore he had never touched a 9mm Luger.

As Sidney walked into the law firm lobby, Phyllis said, "Good morning, Sidney. Did you have a nice weekend?"

"Busy."

"He's expecting you. Just go on back."

Sidney approached Fowler's office. Suddenly, his loud, angry voice came through the doorway.

Phyllis rushed past her, slipped around her desk, and sank down in her chair. "He's been like that all morning," she whispered.

Sidney stayed by his secretary's desk until she heard him slam down the receiver. Poking her head around his open door, she noticed his nostril's flaring and asked, "Everything okay?"

"Yeah. Baxter at the D.A.'s office claims we've been harassing Zisk, his witness." He waved his hand at the chair on the other side of his desk and motioned for Sidney to sit down. "Have you or Sam even talked to the man recently?" he asked, anger still evident in his tone.

"I haven't. Sam's been looking for the real taxi driver and got a picture of a guy that matches Aden's description of the driver. The guy lives in the same building as Zisk. Maybe Zisk spotted him there and started feeling uneasy about his lies. How did the search go for the house Zisk described in his deposition?"

"Just like we suspected. That house does exist on Aden's street. It's located at 7614, not Aden's 6714. How was your trip to Denver?"

"Good." She pulled out her notepad. "A prior hotel employee named Teri Crane helped Kate and Victor take drunk Aden to Kate's room."

Fowler's eyebrows furrowed. "No one-night stand?"

"That's how it appears. Aden only believes he had a one-night stand with Kate because he woke up in her bed. Teri will testify he was in no condition for any sexual activity," she said and then continued to brief him on everything she had learned from Teri. She reached into her briefcase, took out the copy of the invoice showing the listing for a broken chair, and handed it to Fowler.

"Of course, the prosecution can claim that Aden and Kate still had an affair even though they didn't have sex that night."

"That's exactly how I suspect they'll play it."

"I won't add Teri Crane to our witness list until after Kate has been interviewed. Let's see if she lies about that night."

Sidney reached again into her briefcase and dug out the plastic container with the Luger inside. She had no intention of telling Fowler that she acquired it in an illegal search by breaking into Payton's house. Also, she knew Payton would not be stupid enough to admit it had been stolen from his safe. Feeling very certain no one would dispute how she claimed it came into her possession and recalling the vegetation around Aden's neighborhood, she began her lie. "After Sam and I got back from Denver, I spent the rest of the weekend searching for the weapon around Aden's place. I found this tucked against the trunk of a pine tree under low lying branches."

Fowler tilted his head and cocked his brow. "How could everyone have missed it? His yard and his neighbors' have been searched by the police and a team I sent there."

Sidney detected he might be suspicious but betrayed no indication of her guilt. "I had to crawl on my stomach to get under those branches. Got a couple of scratches." She pointed to some scrapes on her arm that she had suffered hustling over a fence the night before.

"Instead of sending my runner over to the police department, I'm going to deliver this item myself," Fowler said in a pleased tone. "Maybe Aden will be freed before the day ends." He cast his eyes on the weapon, tapped the edge of his desk, and shook his head.

"They've built a case against him without a weapon. I doubt they'd let him go that easily."

Sidney nodded. "Yeah. If they're going to stick with the affair scenario as the motive, they could claim he hired the trigger man. Uncovering the real motive might be the only way to free Aden. Sam and I are working on it." She ran her fingertips along the arms of her chair and mulled over how the police might react to the weapon. *Is there any possibility they might search for another suspect?* Her cell phone chirped. She pulled it out of her purse and looked at the caller ID. "It's Sam," she said and then answered it. "Can I call you back in fifteen minutes?"

"Sure," he said.

Sidney pushed the end button. "The two rock samples I brought you...did either one of them match the orange substance from Aden's front yard?"

"The first rock came from the same quarry. Where did you get it?"

"At Brimwell's house."

"Brimwell's house?" he asked, narrowing his eyes.

"Uh-huh."

Fowler latched onto a corner of the plastic bag and raised it into the air. "Let's see if this is the murder weapon. Have you run this by Aden? There's no possibility his fingerprints might be on it?"

"He doesn't know a gun has been found, but he swears he's never handled a Luger."

Fowler bobbed his head. "Good. Let's see whose fingerprints are on it and go from there."

The image of Victor searching Payton's house, the picture of Aden found in Victor's condo, the break-in at Sam's office, and the SLI contracts bounced around in Sidney's head. "I don't want to wait for the results, so I'm going to keep working on the case. I have a couple of leads I want to follow up."

"Anything else you want to share?"

"Not yet," she said, thinking about Payton. *Did he show up at work today, or had he become another victim?*

Sidney sat in her car and skimmed over her notes while she figured out her next move. She called Sam back. After a quick greeting, she asked, "What did Aden say about the picture?"

"It's the guy that drove the taxi. Now, we have to figure a way to get him to talk."

"Are you in your office?"

"Yeah."

"I ran into some interesting information yesterday. I'll be there in twenty to fill you in."

"I'll put on a pot of coffee."

Driving toward Sam's office, she pondered if she should tell him the truth about where she found the weapon or stick to the same story she gave Fowler. Turning onto his street, she spotted a dark gray Suburban with a tag hanging from its rearview mirror parked a half block from Sam's office. Going past it, she glanced at the driver through her passenger window. He had a long slender face that sported a close-clipped beard and mustache. From his height in the seat, Sidney assumed he was tall. An occupant sat in the passenger seat. She didn't get a good look at his features but saw he had medium brown hair. She still couldn't come up with a logical reason why SLI didn't try to be inconspicuous.

Strolling through Sam's door with a duffle bag over her shoulder, she said, "They're outside again."

"I know." Sam poured coffee in two mugs. "They followed me last night to a friend's house and to and from the county jail this morning." He handed her a mug. "Someone is paying big bucks for twenty-four-hour surveillance."

"Can't figure it out." She dropped the duffle bag to the floor and sat down on the couch.

"Me either." Sam took a large gulp of coffee and then placed the mug on the desk. "Never had this kind of attention before."

"I visited Payton's house last night," Sidney said between sips.

Sam shook his head. "Another illegal search?"

Sidney gave him a faint smile and nodded. "Broke into his safe."

"Oh, you've got to be kidding," he said, grinning.

"Had to be done," she justified. "Used the combination I got from Victor's."

Sam squinted. "Really? You never mentioned you found a combination."

"I found a series of numbers hidden in his desk and wrote them down. Didn't know for sure they were a combination until I tried them out."

"Victor had Payton's combination?"

"Yep. Along with a key to his house."

"Didn't realize they were such great buds. Payton's name appearing often in Victor's appointment book surprised me. When I questioned him about Aden's case, he acted like his only buddy at work was Aden, his best friend."

"It's possible that Payton didn't give the key or combo to Victor."

"That just crossed my mind. What did you discover through your snooping?"

"Ran into a gun tucked away in his safe."

Sam's eyes shot wide open. "What a find. Was that the reason you wanted to know if Aden had handled a Luger?"

"Exactly."

"You snatched it?"

"Sure did. Fowler has it. I told him I found it hidden under a pine tree close to Aden's house."

"He bought it?"

"He seemed a little torn between being skeptical and being a little excited at the same time. Excitement won out. He's taking the weapon to the police station today."

"If that's the murder weapon, then we're done. Aden will be off the hook." Sam shrugged and slightly shook his head. "Payton, the killer? Aden's friend. He's always a little jittery, but a killer?"

"When I was busying myself at Payton's, Victor showed up. He used a key to get in. Assuming it was Payton, I locked the safe and ducked into the bedroom. He headed straight to the den. I heard him opening the safe. Then he made a phone call. That was when I realized it wasn't Payton in the den. Victor complained to someone on his cell phone that something was missing. It sounded like he thought Payton might have taken it."

"The gun."

"Probably, but I can't be certain. The SLI contracts were also in the safe, and each one was missing a page. I didn't hear him flipping pages, but maybe he was talking about the missing pages."

"Contracts?" Sam asked, his eyes narrowing. "More than one?"

"Yep." Sidney nodded. "Four."

"Payton mentioned he'd done business with SLI before and always got paid. I must admit I doubted it. After all, if they paid him before on other jobs, why aren't they paying him now? Did he do a shitty job?"

"Maybe if we locate the missing pages, we can figure it out."

"You thinking it might be something illegal?"

"That certainly ran through my mind. That's the only thing that makes sense. I took pictures of the other pages." Sidney unzipped her duffle bag and pulled out her printed copies. "Here." She handed them to Sam. "I made two copies. Payton's engineering services and fees are spelled out in these documents. That's the type of work Brimwell doesn't allow his employees to do on the side. The missing page has to have something on it that he doesn't want anyone seeing, including his friends." She rose to her feet, picked up the coffee carafe, and filled their mugs.

Sam scanned the pages. "What do you want me to do with them?"

"Read them with a fine-toothed comb like I'm planning on doing later. See if anything appears strange about them besides the missing pages."

Sam nodded. "Got it. You still planning to visit SLI today?"

Sidney ran her finger around the rim of her mug. "Yeah. You said the new receptionist was a guy twenty-something. Did you catch a name?"

"Nope."

"Your place is closer to SLI than my hotel. Is it okay if I change here?" she asked, gesturing toward her duffle bag.

"Sure. The door at the back of my office leads to the stairs. I'd go with you, but with those goons hanging around outside, I don't want them getting any ideas if they notice no one is in the office."

"It might take me awhile to look more than ten years younger."

"Ten years? Naw. You don't need to go that young. The guy's at least twenty-two."

Sidney hoisted her duffle bag strap onto her shoulder. "Twenty-two-year-olds generally go for chicks younger."

An hour later, Sidney, dressed in a pair of tight navy-blue jeans, a low-cut pink silk blouse, and wearing five-inch stilettos and a short, curly, light brown wig with blond streaks, sauntered back into Sam's office. As he looked up, she smiled and fluttered her false eyelashes at him.

"Wow!" he muttered as his eyes lit up. "You certainly are skilled with disguises. Had I not known you were the same woman that strolled into my office earlier, I never would've guessed who you were. That new receptionist is going to be eating out of your hands."

Sidney's cheeks reddened. "So you think this getup will catch his attention?"

"He's gay if it doesn't work." Sam leaned back in his chair and tapped his index finger against his lower lip. "What reason for being in SLI's office are you going to give?"

"Looking for a job." She bounced her eyebrows and gave him a coy smile. "Think they'll hire me?"

"Absolutely."

She took a device the size of a cell phone from her duffle bag and handed it to Sam. "This is a receiver. In case I run into a problem, I'm wearing a bug. Push the 'on' button and you can hear everything being said around me if you're within a two-mile radius. Farther away than that, push the button marked 'L.' A map will appear showing my location."

Sam studied the gadget for a minute, pushing various buttons. "Cool."

"I can't have your surveillance crew seeing me leave here like this. Can you go for a ride and draw them away? I'll set your alarm and lock up your office when I leave."

Chapter 27

Not wanting anyone at SLI to see her car, Sidney parked two blocks away from their office and trudged along the sidewalk in her five-inch heels. By the time she reached the office, her feet ached, and she told herself she needed to wear pumps more often so she could handle them better.

SLI's foyer had an upscale décor with floor-to-ceiling windows that faced the street and were covered with electrical, vertical blinds that moved according to the glare of the sun. A sleek, black leather couch and matching chair stood against one wall behind a chrome and glass coffee table. In the center of the room, a square-faced, twenty-something guy sat by a white marble counter. A long hallway ran next to it.

The receptionist had a lean body and thick brown hair. A light blue shirt with the sleeves rolled up revealed suntanned arms. He looked up when a small bell rang announcing someone was entering the building. His eyes lit up when he saw her approaching him. "May I help you?" he asked politely and rose to his six-foot-two height.

"Yeah. Maybe," Sidney said, resting her forearms on the counter and bending slightly toward him to make sure her low-cut sweater didn't go unnoticed. "My mom walks by here every day on her way to the bus stop. Someone at the bus stop told her that the gal that used to be your receptionist quit. Mom thought you might be looking for a new one. And I sure could use a job close to where I live."

"Miss…" he began.

Sidney interrupted. "Call me Diana."

The telephone rang. The guy held up his index finger and mouthed, "One minute," and then lifted up the receiver and pushed a button on the telephone console. "Mr. Smorick's office. May I help you?…He should be in shortly." He snagged a pencil lying by a pad of pink forms and wrote on the top one. "I'll give him your message as soon as he comes into the office."

Trying to read what was written on the pink sheet, Sidney cocked her head. She saw the name Victor on it but didn't have enough time to pick up anything else before the receptionist replaced the receiver, picked up the form, and laid it on the ledge of the counter closest to the hallway.

"Okay, Diana," he said with a smile. "I'm the receptionist."

She popped her eyes wide open like she had never heard of a guy being a receptionist. "Really? But you're a guy."

"You got that right. I'll…" He stopped when the bell above the door chimed. His eyes moved toward it.

Sidney turned and saw a tall man in his early fifties step into the lobby. He sported a square jaw, a pair of wire-rimmed glasses perched on his nose, and a pinstriped, navy-blue suit.

A stern expression defined the stranger's face. He briefly eyed Sidney, then looked at the receptionist. "Kyle."

"Dad," Kyle said.

"What have I told you about friends coming here?" he said in a harsh tone.

"But Dad…"

"My office." The new arrival picked up the message and headed down the hallway.

"I'll be right back," Kyle said, his cheeks a little flushed.

As Kyle trotted after his father, Sidney felt pleased how well she had disguised herself. From Mr. Smorick's reaction, she figured she looked around Kyle's age. While she waited, she mulled over the new possibility of finding out information about SLI—Kyle was Mr. Smorick's son. She suspected it was Randolph Smorick, the man who signed Payton's SLI contracts and the same man who supposedly had left town.

"Hey, sorry about that," Kyle said, stepping behind the counter. "My dad didn't realize we weren't friends."

Sidney gave him a seductive smile. "Well, we could become friends."

"Sure." He returned her smile and placed his hands on the counter. "Before my dad came, I was going to tell you that my job here will open up in a couple of months when I go back to school."

"Great." She tilted her head, raised her hand, and trailed her fingers over his hands. "Can we meet later and talk about it?"

He pursed his lips in a thoughtful expression, and then stared at the floor. Sidney wondered if he had a girlfriend and she had made him feel uncomfortable. She withdrew her hand from his. "Kyle, I'm not asking you out on a date or anything. Just to talk so you can tell me what it's like working here. We could go for a Coke."

"No, no. That's not it." He raised his chin and looked at Sidney. "Listen, my dad didn't believe me when I told him we weren't friends. My folks are having a barbeque Friday night. My mom would really like me to bring a date. Could you pretend to be my girlfriend for one night?"

"Yeah." Sidney suddenly felt a little awkward about leading on this innocent kid who didn't have anything to do with the case. To help set the record straight, she added, "That really might help me get the job here."

A tinge of disappointment flashed across Kyle's face. "Yeah, it probably will," he said, sounding rejected.

"What time, and do I need to dress up for the barbeque?"

"Six-thirty. Jeans are okay. Where do you want me to pick you up?"

"After I lost my last job, I had to move back home to my mom's. We don't always get along. It'll be easier if I meet ya here. Will that be okay?"

A buzzer sounded on Kyle's desk phone. He swung his head toward it. "It's Dad. Gotta go. Meeting here's fine. See you Friday." He turned and hurried toward his dad's office.

Sidney walked at a brisk pace back to her car, but not so fast that she would attract attention. She hopped into the front seat, lowered her head, and removed the wig. She swung her head back and forth to shake out her hair and then ran her fingers through it until it flowed down to her shoulders.

When she was about three miles away from SLI, she stopped at the side of the road and called Sam.

"How'd it go?"

"Got a date for Friday night," she said with a smirk.

"With the receptionist?" he asked, sounding puzzled.

"Yeah. He's Smorick's son."

"Randolph Smorick?"

"I never heard the first name, but I'm assuming it's the same guy. Smorick isn't exactly a popular name."

"Judy said he left town."

"Maybe she thought he did. Did you ever check out the addresses she gave—drive by or anything?"

"No," he said in a sheepish voice. "She seemed so forthright. I didn't doubt for a minute she wasn't telling the truth."

"Maybe he left for a while."

"Could be. I'll check and see if he's still living in the same place. Where are you going on this hot date?"

"To a barbeque at his parents' house. It'll give me a chance to snoop around. It isn't until Friday. I want to search around the office before then."

"I'm in. They visited my place enough. It's time to reciprocate."

"Hey, is Payton at work?"

"Nope. But he called me this morning. His sister had a baby last week. He flew out of town to see the kid. He'll be back tomorrow morning. I told him about the break-in at my office. He seems pretty upset about it. I'm picking him up at the airport. Could we switch cars for a couple of hours tomorrow? Don't want my little surveillance squad following me to the airport."

"No problem." Sidney cringed at the thought of driving Sam's old truck and then proceeded to tell him someone with the name Victor called to talk to Smorick.

"You thinking the caller was Victor Grenshaw?"

"That thought did bounce into my head."

"When are you going to pay an evening visit to SLI?"

"After you have a chance to chat with Payton. Since SLI now knows his identity, he might give you some valuable information."

"Good point.

"Judy, SLI's prior receptionist…what's her last name? And where did she use to live?"

"Fuller. I've already tried finding her."

"I'm going to give it a shot."

"Okay, let me get her prior address." Sam flipped pages in his notebook until he found the entry. "Got it," he said and then gave it to her.

"Thanks. Call me if Smorick lives at the same place Judy mentioned."

"Will do. Anything else you want me to work on today?"

"See if you can figure out where the real taxi driver hangs out."

"With the gun, do you think we still need him?"

"The gun might not turn out to be the murder weapon, so we need to be prepared."

Chapter 28

Sidney stepped back into her suite at the Hyatt and saw Jean knitting away while her eyes were glued to the television screen.

Hearing the door close, Jean looked at Sidney and said, "This has got to be the best job I've ever had. I'm working on my third sweater. Are you sure you want me to continue staying here with you?"

"Yes. Chas is still worried my chest pains could return," Sidney said, thinking it could happen if she couldn't find the killer and clear Aden. She doubted Mara would set her free before she accomplished that task.

"Okay." The corner of Jean's mouth curved up. "Can't complain for getting paid to make Christmas presents."

"How many sweaters do you need?"

"Eight."

"Well, then, I'll leave you to it." Sidney went into her bedroom, and Jean's attention turned back to her television program.

Sidney sat at the desk. She had moved it into her bedroom from the main living area so she could work late at night without disturbing Jean. She dug her cell phone out of her purse and called Chas.

"Hi, Babe," he answered. "Did the gun set Aden free?"

"I gave it to Fowler this morning. I haven't heard the results yet. Since the police force here was ready to lynch him without finding the weapon—and on what I would call skimpy evidence—I'm not going to hold my breath that the weapon will get him out of jail." She sighed. "Unless, of course, he points it at them. That might do the trick."

"Do I detect bitterness in your tone?"

"Me?" she said, attempting to sound surprised by his allegation. Sidney heard commotion on his end of the line and Chas's muffled voice telling someone that he'd be right there.

"Hey, Babe, I need to get to a meeting, and I'm sure you didn't call me to discuss the merits of the police department there, so what's up?"

"Can you have one of your paralegals—the one who's an expert with research—find Judy Fuller?"

"The woman you mentioned that used to work for SLI?"

"Yeah. That's her. I've got the address where she used to live if that will help."

"What is it?" he asked, and then Sidney gave it to him. "I don't like you this far away from me, so I'll get Susan on it first thing in the morning."

Sidney glanced at her watch and realized from the time difference it was after 6 p.m. in New York. "You're working late."

"Well, there isn't any reason for me to rush home with you in California. I'll call you later, and we can chat more."

After Sidney clicked off, she pulled out her notepad and the contracts. She read through them again and jotted down additional notes, hoping she'd run across something she'd missed earlier.

While she was still concentrating on the documents, her cell phone rang. Grabbing it, her eyes dropped to the caller ID, and she wondered if it could be the answer she'd been waiting for.

"Hello, Greg." Forcing her voice to remain calm, she asked, "Any news on the pistol?"

"Yes, but it's unofficial." Disappointment radiated in Fowler's tone.

Sidney bit her bottom lip, knowing from his tone that he wasn't going to tell her what she wanted to hear.

Fowler continued. "I had to call in a favor to get it, so it has to be kept hush-hush until the police department makes an official statement. And who knows when that will be."

"Was it the murder weapon?" Sidney held her breath.

"Yes."

She exhaled. "Fingerprints?"

"Brimwell's…Aden's boss."

Sidney had been certain that Payton's fingerprints would be on the gun. Definitely not Brimwell's. Puzzled by the result, her eyes narrowed, and she scratched her forehead. "Marcus Brimwell?" She sounded skeptical.

"Yes. And his were the only prints on it. The brownish-orange substance could have come from a rock at his place and been picked up on a shoe."

Sidney wondered if Brimwell had some kind of a record. "Did they already have a set of his fingerprints?"

"They were in the database since his company has government contracts. Everyone that works there has fingerprints in the database." Fowler paused and inhaled deeply. "Apparently, the Luger belongs to Brimwell. A motive? Mara suspected he was having an affair a year ago. Silencing her over that doesn't make sense at all, especially since Brimwell has a prenup with his current wife."

That statement took Sidney by surprise. "Prenup? How do you know that?"

"Sidney, I shouldn't have mentioned it. It slipped out since I've been trying to figure out what Brimwell could've had against Mara."

Sidney guessed Fowler knew about the prenup through one of his associates, and since that was a breach of confidentially, she decided not to push him about it. "Mara was friends with his wife. Maybe there's something there." She replayed through her mind everything she could recall about her conversation with Angelica. Besides the woman mentioning Mara getting upset with Victor at the Christmas party, nothing else stood out in Sidney's head. "Do you know what the police will do about this new-found evidence?"

"No, but it's clear they're not planning to release Aden, or it would have already happened. Brimwell's out of town. He won't be home until Wednesday. According to my contact, they aren't going to do anything until they've had a chance to talk to him."

"His fingerprints are on the murder weapon. And they're just going to wait until he gets back into town?"

"That's what I understand."

"Do you think there is any hope that they might open the investigation again and postpone the trial?"

"We can always hope, but I doubt they'll open the investigation. Some twist will be put on the weapon—Aden wore gloves and snatched it when he was there at the Christmas party—something like that. Brimwell's a pretty wealthy man. They won't go down the road claiming his employee, Aden, hired him to shoot Mara."

"It appears the only way Aden will be a free man again is if we can deliver the evidence, the motive, *and* the murderer."

"Not necessarily," Fowler said. "Their motive is based on an untrue assumption—the love triangle and his supposed affair with Kate. If the jurors believe that affair never happened, he could be acquitted."

"True, but I don't want his fate to rest in the hands of twelve people. I'm determined to solve this case before it goes to trial," Sidney said in a tone that amplified she meant business.

"Aden is one lucky man to have you on his side. It's late. This has been a long day. I need to get out of here and have a drink. You might think about doing the same."

"That's exactly what I'm going to do. Thanks for letting me know the results."

"Wish it had been better news."

"Me too," Sidney said and then disconnected. She sat quietly and stared at the documents on the desk while she tried to understand why the murder weapon didn't appear to have caused anyone at the police department to snap into action. A few minutes later, she stood, walked into the main room, and opened a bottle of Merlot.

Sidney sipped on her third glass of wine and called Chas. She told him she didn't want to talk about the investigation. It didn't take Chas long to get her laughing about the time they first met in a courtroom. She marched up to the stand and was questioned by the Assistant DA, Chas. He had a hard time waiting for the case to be over so he could ask her out. The tension of the day vanished as they chatted and laughed about their honeymoon. Sidney longed to be in his arms. Her phone beeped, indicating she had another call. She briefly moved her phone away from her ear and glimpsed at her screen. Their walk down memory lane ended when she said, "Honey, Bernice is calling me."

"You better talk to her. Maybe she'll give you something besides words this time," Chas said over the airwaves. "Babe, talk to you sometime tomorrow. Hopefully, by then Susan will have located something about Judy Fuller. I love you."

"I love you, too." She clicked off and glanced at the clock on her nightstand. It read 9:36 p.m. Since it was after midnight in Florida, she punched in Bernice's number, wondering if she had been awakened again.

"Hi, Sidney," Bernice answered. "Mara's bugging me. I did a late reading this evening for a loyal customer, and Mara wouldn't let me finish it." She sighed. "Has something happened today?"

Sidney filled Bernice in about the murder weapon being found. "The police know the fingerprints on it don't belong to Aden, but they haven't released any information about whose prints are on it," she said, keeping the identity confidential like she had promised Fowler.

The phone went silent.

"Bernice, you still there?"

"Yeah. I've been trying to make sense of the message Mara gave me…Brimwell…is a guy by that name a suspect?"

"Why?"

"Mara kept repeating, 'Brimwell. Not him.'"

"I understand her comment." Sidney's eyes darted around the room, wondering if Mara was somehow listening. "Anything else?"

"She showed me a row of file cabinets, a shoebox, and a woman's face all bandaged. This was the first time she showed me images. She's coming through stronger."

Envisioning the bandaged face, an uneasy feeling vibrated through Sidney's body, and she brushed her hand over her cheek. "These images—have they already occurred, or are they something that might happen?"

"They've happened. In a reading, the bandaged face could be interpreted as someone that has been in an accident or had an operation. Given it's the face, it might even be elective plastic surgery. Would any of that fit anyone involved with the case?"

The faces of everyone she had met since she started the case ran through her mind. "Boy, not that I know off."

"Something important must be in the files and a shoebox, or Mara wouldn't have continued showing me those images over and over again."

"It gives me some other things to look for. Thanks for letting me know."

Bernice sighed. "Mara probably wouldn't let me sleep tonight if I didn't call you. I sure hope her husband gets out of the joint soon."

"So do I."

Chapter 29

A harsh buzzing sound woke Sidney with a start. She grabbed her Glock from under her pillow, sat straight up in pitch-blackness, and then realized the noise came from the nightstand clock. Clicking off the alarm, she saw it was 6:00 a.m. and wondered why she had set it. Then she remembered—her car. Sam wanted to pick up Payton in her car, and his plane was scheduled to land in two hours.

Shortly after 7:20 a.m., Sidney, dressed in jeans and a baggy shirt, strolled into Sam's office, dreading driving around in his old truck.

Sam had a newspaper stretched out in his hands and a coffee mug on the coffee table. "Want a cup?" he offered, raising his mug.

"No, thanks. I already drank a whole pot this morning." She placed her keys on the table, plopped her duffle bag on the floor, and sat down next to Sam. "Do you know if anyone working for Brimwell has ever been in some kind of accident that affected his or her face, or maybe had some facial surgery?"

"No. Why?"

Sidney hesitated telling Sam about Bernice, but at the same time, she wanted his help in solving the crime. "I have a friend who's a medium."

"A person that talks to the dead?"

Sidney nodded. "Without going into all the details, I talked to her last night, and she said that Mara..."

Sam rolled his eyes and cocked an eyebrow.

Sidney went on. "…showed her the image of a bandaged face."

"You believe in that kind of stuff?" Sam said, folding the newspaper.

"I'm starting to. She mentioned some other things that have proved to be accurate."

"Like what?" he said, his voice full of skepticism.

"I'm not going to go into that now," she replied, irritated by Sam's demeanor. "Anyway, when you pick up Payton, can you ask him if anyone at Brimwell's has had some facial surgery?"

"Yeah, but I'm not going to mention the ghost appearing."

Sidney pressed her lips together and shook her head. "Good. I don't want you to."

"Glad we're on the same page." Sam stood, dug a set of keys out of his pocket, and handed them to Sidney. "My truck's parked on the side of the building." He gazed at her for a minute. "Your hair. If they notice the driver has long hair, they won't follow you."

"Got it covered." She unzipped her duffle bag, plucked out a cap and a large jacket. She twirled her hair, put the cap over it, and tucked in a few loose strands. She slipped on the jacket. "The Suburban isn't parked close, so this should work," she said, waving her hand over her outfit.

"It will. There's a side window in my office next to where I parked." He led her to it, pushed it open, and Sidney quickly climbed out. "I'll call after I drop Payton off at his office."

Sidney spotted the dark gray Suburban two cars behind her when she stopped at a red light. Thinking about the shoebox Bernice mentioned, she decided to check out Payton's house again, but first she needed to lose the tail.

Darting in and out of traffic, she was surprised how well Sam's truck handled. Sidney executed a left turn, followed by a sharp right. Then she sped through a narrow alleyway and flipped a left turn onto a quiet street. She took a right at the next intersection and moved swiftly up and down several heavily-travelled roads. Hoping she had lost the tail, she made a skidding turn to the right to check if somehow the Suburban had managed to keep up with her. When she couldn't see any sign of it, she careened down another alleyway, pulled into a small parking spot, and turned off the engine. She rummaged through her duffle bag until she located a tracking device detector. Sidney got out of the vehicle and swept the device over the frame and wheels. Satisfied, she climbed back into the driver's seat and turned the key in the ignition. The truck shimmied as its engine thundered back to life.

Sidney parked a few doors away from Payton's house. She walked at a leisurely pace along the sidewalk and kept glancing around, checking out the deserted street. She figured most of the neighbors were at work and the children were either in summer school or playing computer games.

When she passed the far corner of Payton's place, she jogged over his lawn to the fence. She threw her bag over and quickly followed it. A moment later, she had picked the lock and pushed open the back door. A loud, unexpected, beeping sound echoed through the house. She rushed to the alarm monitor and swiftly disarmed it.

Sidney stared at the alarm system and wondered who had set it. Payton hadn't been home since she had been there Sunday night. *Did Victor set it? But why?*

As she went up the flight of stairs, Payton's landline started ringing. She stepped into Payton's office, and stood quietly while she waited for the answering machine on his desk to click on. When it did, she stared at the floor, rubbed her hands together, and listened to the message she didn't want to hear—Payton's security calling about his alarm going off. Sidney knew she had disarmed it within a minute and couldn't figure out why it would be set so it wouldn't give the homeowner an opportunity to turn it off before the system contacted the security company. She anticipated it would only take five to ten minutes before someone showed up.

Sidney rushed into the closet in the bedroom and began searching through shoeboxes stacked on the shelf. The first box held sewing items—needles, threads, and buttons. The second box was filled with drugstore envelopes containing pictures and negatives. Miscellaneous items were in the third and fourth box. No shoes. Her face lit up like she had struck gold when she opened the lid on the last box and saw folded documents. She spread them out on the carpet, and thumbed through them. Realizing they were reports he had written in college, she sighed with disappointment and put them back in the box. *Why did he keep this stuff?*

The doorbell buzzed.

She doubted the security guard would attempt to enter the house, but she *did* expect the person to walk around the house and check windows and locks. Replacing the shoebox on the shelf, the edge of something behind a golf bag caught her eye. She dropped to her knees and crawled toward the dark object. It was another shoebox. Sidney gripped it and yanked it into the light. Her hand slightly jerked while she raised the lid. Inside, a journal rested on top of some folded sheets.

The sound of a door swinging open startled her. She backed out of the closet and eased the door shut. Grabbing her duffle bag, she charged to the other side of the bed and hunkered down.

The pounding sound of someone barreling up the stairwell reverberated through the house. Then came the noise of a chair squeaking, drawers slamming, and shuffling of papers in the den. A few minutes later, footfalls descended the stairs and voices drifted up the stairwell.

Taking a deep breath, Sidney inched back to the closet, opened the door, and scooted inside. Reluctantly, she replaced the lid on the shoebox and pushed the box back into its hiding place. Planning an escape route, she peered out the closet and looked at the patio door. She figured the security guards could still be outside checking the house for signs of a break-in and decided not to go that route. She crept to the hallway door, poked her head out, and then without making a noise, she inched her way to the closed door across the hall. Carefully, she turned the doorknob and peered inside. The room was a sparsely furnished bedroom. She stepped through the doorway, slowly closed the door, and lowered herself to the floor on the far side of the bed, a place she wouldn't be spotted if someone looked into the room. With her ears on full alert, she opened her duffle bag and took out the directional mike. She flipped it on and pushed one of the earbuds in place.

"...finish." A male voice came through the receiver.

"You sure you didn't set it," Sam said. His voice Sidney knew well.

"Positive. I thought about it on the way to the airport, but I didn't want to tell the taxi driver to turn around."

A loud cracking noise rumbled through the mike, followed by a squeaking sound. "Mr. Russen, the back door and all the windows are locked. We don't see any signs of a break-in. Do you want us to look around inside?" a man said.

"No. I'll take it from here," Payton said, and then a door shut. "I need to grab that folder and get to work."

"We're not through talking about the problem," Sam said.

"I know. Thanks for picking me up."

"No sweat. I'll see you after work."

Sidney listened to the sound of a door opening and closing again. She wondered if Sam had noticed his truck parked down the street.

Footfalls ascended the steps and then pounded down the carpet-covered hallway. Next came the creaking sound of a door opening and the rustling of papers. "Got 'em....I'll take them to work," Payton said.

She heard more rustling of papers, a door closing, and footsteps moving along the hallway and hurrying down the stairs. Sidney sat up when the clicking sound of a key turning in the lock came through the earbud. Intensely listening, she quietly waited for a few minutes until she was sure no one else was in the house.

Stuffing the receiver and earbuds into her duffle bag, she rose to her feet and cautiously moved to Payton's bedroom and opened his closet door. Her shoulders sagged and her chin dropped as she stared at an empty, open shoebox on the floor in front of her. She shook her head, thinking about how close she had been to the contents before they were snatched away. A deep sigh escaped her lungs. Feeling frustrated, she left Payton's house.

Sidney stopped a mile from Sam's office and hid her hair again under the cap. The Suburban was back in the spot it had been earlier when she arrived at Sam's office. Her car was nowhere in sight. She turned into the alleyway that abutted Sam's office to make her way to his window.

As she climbed out of the truck, Sam poked his head out of the open window. "What took you so long?" He smiled. "It wasn't that detour you made to Payton's house, was it?"

"I figured you probably saw your truck," she said, approaching the window. "Did Payton?"

"Doubt it. His attention was focused on the security vehicle parked in front of his house. Didn't you get the alarm disarmed in time?"

She lifted her leg over the window ledge, ducked her head, and moved into Sam's office. "I had it off in about fifteen seconds. It must have been set without giving any leeway for anyone to turn it off."

"Yep. That's how Payton sets it when he goes out of town. He figures it's safer that way, and then he just has to give the code when the security company calls. Payton claims he forgot to set it. Did it go off when you were there Sunday night?"

"Nope. I got out of there before Victor. He must have set it. Any thoughts on why he might've done that?"

"He has Payton's safe combination, a key to his house, and probably the security code. You said he was looking for something. If he's in cahoots with SLI, he knows we're snooping around."

"Good observation. He set it so we couldn't spend much time there." She paused. "At the time, I thought Victor was just searching for the gun. Now, I'm not sure."

A puzzled expression crossed Sam's face. "Why? Did you find something else?"

"A shoebox with a journal in it along with some folded pages. When I heard you and Payton in the house, I stuck the box back and hid in another room in case Payton headed to his bedroom.

"After you left, he emptied the box and made a call telling someone that he had the stuff and he was taking it with him to work."

"Maybe the missing pages of the contracts," Sam speculated.

"That's what I'm thinking. I only needed this much time," she said, raising her hand and holding her thumb and index finger an inch apart, "and I could've snapped a picture of the pages."

"I'm putting on a pot of coffee since it's too early to start drinking," he said, walking toward the door that led to the staircase. "Want a cup?"

"Sounds good."

"Mind staying down here alone while it brews?"

"No problem." Sidney sank down on the couch. "I can keep a watchful eye for the goons. By the way, where's my car?"

"At a parking garage a few blocks away."

Within ten minutes, Sam, carrying a pot full of coffee and two mugs, was back in his office. He filled the mugs and grabbed packets of sugar, artificial cream, and plastic spoons out of a desk drawer and laid them on the table. Then he plopped down in the corner of the couch.

"Thanks." Sidney stirred sugar into her mug.

Sam took a big swig. "It feels like it should be late afternoon, not late morning."

"You got that right," Sidney said, feeling a little drowsy from a restless night, waking up early, and her adventure at Payton's place. She sipped the coffee, hoping it would spark her energy. "How did Payton react when you told him about the break-in at your office?"

"Nervous. He fidgeted with his fingers, his watch, and his cell phone all the way to his house. And when he saw the security vehicle, his face turned stark white. He held his breath until one of the security guards explained the situation. I had the impression he thought they were there for another reason, almost like they were cops, not security guards. As soon as he opened the front door, he sprinted upstairs."

"Checking his safe?"

"That's what I thought, but he wasn't gone long enough to open it. Probably just a quick look to see if his den was still intact."

"Did you ask him if anyone at Brimwell's had a facial operation or problem of some sort?"

"Yeah. He couldn't think of anyone. No one's ever gone to the office with a bandaged face. He did mention Kate. He thought she was pretty vain, and she'd be the type to have a little work done."

"How old is Kate?"

"I've only seen pictures of her. Since she started there right after she graduated, I'd figured mid-twenties, maybe younger. According to Payton, she's in her mid-thirties."

"Interesting," Sidney commented, recalling she had also assumed Kate was younger. "Given her age, I can't imagine she would've had major work done—nothing that would require most of her face to be bandaged."

"Maybe a nose job?"

Sidney raised her brow. "Mmm-hmm. That's a possibility." Emptying her mug, she sensed they were barking up the wrong tree focusing on Kate.

Sam held up the coffee pot. "Want another?"

She nodded and then the image of a bandaged face bounced around in her head. "Plastic surgery," Sidney said, thinking out loud. Instantly, she felt a hand patting her on the shoulder and swung her head in that direction. No one was there. She was on the right track. "Do you think any of the guys you've talked to at Brimwell's would consider having plastic surgery?"

Sam chuckled. Then he noticed the serious expression on Sidney's face. "You're kidding, right?"

She shook her head. "No."

"Sid, the only guy I know who has ever had plastic surgery, had it after he sustained a serious burn on his cheek. Guys just don't go in for that kind of thing unless they've been in an accident." He gulped his coffee. "Movie stars, maybe."

"Okay, how about any of the women you've talked to regarding Aden's case?"

Sam scratched his chin, and his eyes dropped to the table. "Doubt it. Molly's a nice-looking woman, but she looks her age. Deidre strikes me as being too young. However, she does have great boobs," he said with a smile, raising his head and gazing at Sidney. "Do boob jobs count?"

Sidney rolled her eyes. "Never heard of anyone having a bandaged face for a boob job."

"Good point."

"I understand Angelica is quite the looker," Sam said, leaning back in the couch. "You've seen her. Any possibility there?"

"Angelica?" Sidney felt a tap on her shoulder again. Squinting, she wondered what that meant. *Could Brimwell's wife be involved?*

"Hey, Sid," Sam said, touching her arm. "You okay?"

Snapping out of her deep thoughts, she sighed and said, "Sorry, about that. I was just thinking about her. How old do you think she is?"

"Even if I haven't seen her, someone—can't remember who—said she was fifty-three or four. Around there." Sam raked his fingers through his hair. "I don't even know why someone mentioned that." He tapped his fingertips on the side of his head. "Maybe it's in the notes that were stolen." Sam lowered his hands and rested them on his lap. "At the time, I probably figured it wasn't important. Do you think it is now?"

"Don't know, but I *do* know that she looks younger than fifty. I would've put her in her early forties."

"Plastic surgery?"

"With her heart problems, I can't imagine she'd go in for elective surgery. She just might age well." Sidney made a mental note to ask Aden more about Angelica's health condition and then moved on. "At Payton's house, I overhead he was going to see you after work. Why?"

"We both know he's holding out. I told him I'd drop him as a client unless he came clean. He almost panicked, so he's coming here to discuss it."

"Do you expect him to spill anything—like what's on the missing page of the contracts?"

"Nope. He doesn't know we've seen and read the other pages. I'm curious how he's going to skirt around not telling me everything." He slid farther back in his seat and leaned on the armrest. "What's our next plan of action?"

"Visiting the SLI office tonight," Sidney said, thinking about the image Bernice received from Mara—the file cabinets.

Sam raised an eyebrow and gave her a crooked smile. "Another break-in, officer?"

"Yep." She stood up. "It could be a late night, so I'm going...." Her cell phone buzzed. She reached in her pocket, pulled it out, and gazed at the ID. "I better take this. Might be important." She pushed a button on her phone. "Hi, honey."

Sam looked out the window and tapped his fingers on the armrest.

"SLI's prior receptionist moved to Riverside, California," Chas said.

"Judy Fuller is that close?" Sidney cocked her brow.

That got Sam's attention. He twirled around and gazed at her.

"Yes," Chas said. "It took Susan less than fifteen minutes to locate the woman. Anything new on the case?"

"Honey, I'm in Sam's office. I'll call you later."

"Don't forget how much I love you."

A warm smile crossed Sidney's face. "I won't, and I love you too." She put away her phone and then stared at Sam. "Judy Fuller is in Riverside, California. Did you even look for her?"

"Well," Sam said with a sheepish expression and lowered his eyes.

"Why not? Payton was paying you."

"He wasn't paying me to find her. What he wanted was contact information for the local guys that signed the contract." He drummed his fingers on the armrest. "That's a pretty lame reason to hire an investigator. I didn't even want the job."

"So you just strung him along without doing anything?"

"Not exactly. I talked to Judy. According to her, the two guys who signed the contract were out of the country. Then she was called away from her desk. I went back the next day and she was gone. The kid, your Friday night date, won't tell me anything. I've already told you that, and I went to Judy's apartment. She'd moved."

"But you also told me you couldn't find her."

"Yeah, I exaggerated." He shrugged his shoulders. "It happens."

Sidney shook her head in frustration. "Here I thought something unpleasant might've happened to her."

"What can I say?"

"Since you obviously made an impression on her before, tomorrow you're going with me to Riverside," she said emphatically. Her eyes bored into his. "And you're not going to charge anyone for your time. Understood?"

Sam hesitated as he thought about all the times he had worked for Fowler. "Understood," he uttered, not wanting to take a chance of not being considered for future jobs with Fowler. "But now that it seems there's a connection between SLI and Aden's case, I think that might be the reason Payton hired me."

"Why?"

"Every time I see him, he drills me about how the investigation is going. I figured it was because Payton and Aden were buddies. Now, I'm not sure."

"Have you told him much?"

"No. Just stuff he already knows—like the taxi cab driver. Aden told him Zisk wasn't the right guy. We've chatted about that."

"Nothing about our trip to Denver?"

"Nope. I've only talked to him about the taxi driver. I should probably tell him to find another investigator when he gets here."

"Not so fast," Sidney said with her elbow on the arm of the couch and her hands clasped together. "Let's see what he has to say about SLI first."

Sam nodded. "Is your husband also a policeman?"

"No," she said with a pleasant expression. "He's with the D.A.'s office."

Sam grinned. "Well then, maybe he can help get us out of jail if we get caught at SLI."

"Mmmmh. Committing a crime—I'd never hear the end of it.

Fowler will be the guy we call." She picked up her duffle bag. "Can you tell me how to get to my car?"

Chapter 30

At 8:15 p.m., Sidney returned to Sam's office, spotting the SLI watchdogs on her way.

"Did you get anything from Payton?" she asked as soon as she walked through his door and saw Sam sitting on the couch reading a stack of papers.

"He gave me this." Sam held up a copy of the contract Payton had with SLI.

"Does it have the missing page?"

"Naw. He claimed the page numbering was off on the document, but the whole contract was there. I was just about to tell him I wanted to sever our relationship when an idea popped into my head."

"What?"

"This afternoon I went to the address Judy had given me to Smorick's place—where he supposedly moved from. Got out of my truck to find out who lives there. Didn't want to ring that doorbell. Went next door, pretending I was looking for the Smorick family. The woman that answered the door told me they were her neighbors. The family's still there. I wonder why Judy lied to me."

Sidney tilted her head and furrowed her brows in a confused expression. "What does that have to do with keeping Payton as a client?"

"I didn't give him Smorick's address. I thought I'd wait 'til Friday to give it to him."

Sidney cocked her head. "Friday evening?" she said, understanding his motive.

"Yep. When you're on your big date enjoying a barbecue with the family and friends, it might be interesting if Payton makes an appearance there."

"You planning on hanging around outside?" she said with a lopsided smile.

He gave her a mischievous smile and replied, "Wouldn't miss it." Then Sam moved on to that evening's adventure. "What time do you want to hit SLI?"

"Now, but we need to lose your buddies driving the Suburban before heading there."

"They're still with us," Sam said, staring out the back window of Sidney's Lexus.

"They might not be clever, but they certainly know how to handle a car." She executed a sharp right turn. "Time to get serious." She revved the engine, skidded around a bend, and peeled into heavy traffic. She darted between cars as horns erupted around them. Sidney blew through a red light, almost clipping a car.

"They stopped at the light," Sam said with his eyes fixed on the side mirror.

Sidney made several sharp turns to get out of their pursuers' line of sight. Then she barreled down an alleyway, spinning up gravel and dust, tires squealing as the car passed a slow-moving vehicle. Swerving back onto a road, she steered to the left lane and maneuvered onto the freeway entrance ramp. Darting between cars, she kept glancing at her rearview mirror until she felt confident she had lost the gray Suburban. Sidney moved to the far right lane, went with the flow of traffic, and left the freeway at the next exit.

As she backtracked to the SLI office, Sam said, "Great driving. Did they teach you that at the police academy?"

"No. That's something you have to pick up on the street. Besides your friends who like to keep an eye on you, do you know if SLI has a whole fleet of Chevy Suburbans?" she asked, wondering if one or more was stored in SLI's parking lot or if that would present another problem.

"I've never seen any Suburbans in their parking lot. This local office only has eight employees. Can't imagine they'd have a fleet."

Sidney went by the SLI building and glanced at the windows. It appeared to be pitch black inside. Still, she drove around the structure and looked for cars in their lot. Satisfied that no employees were in the office, she said, "I'm going to park a block away."

Sidney turned off the road and parked in a spot away from the street lights. After she flung her duffle bag over her shoulder, she walked with Sam toward the SLI building and wondered why Smorick didn't use the door off the parking lot when he entered the building. "The few times you were at SLI, did you ever see any employees coming or going through the back door?"

"Yeah. Once I hung out in their parking lot, thinking I could spot management leaving. You know, the guys that dress a cut above their employees and drive nice cars? I watched the employees leave and didn't see one person who met that criteria. The following day, I waited at the front door. Still, no one stood out."

"Smorick wore a suit when I saw him."

"No suits the days I hung around."

Sidney guessed it had only been a day or two since Sam had begun to take a serious look at Payton's situation. At the same time, she knew Payton hadn't been forthright with him, so she wasn't too irritated. Reaching the edge of the building, she stopped, looked around for anyone who might see them, and then headed to the back door. There, she opened her duffle bag, dug out two pairs of latex gloves, two ski masks, and two mini flashlights, and gave Sam his share of the items. Once the ski mask hid her face and gloves covered her hands, she went to work with her lock picks.

Seconds later, she pushed the door open. Loud beeping from an alarm system rang out. Neither one of them could see a blinking red light. Sam rushed to the lobby, and Sidney attempted to open the doors along the hallway only to discover they were all locked. "Shit!" she said as the beeping continued.

"It's here!" Sam yelled.

Sidney hurried to the front of the building and found Sam ducked down behind the counter busy dismantling the system. Within a few seconds, the beeping ended.

"Strange place to put this." Sam straightened up.

Sidney reached in her duffle bag and pulled out her new, cutting-edge laser device, a gadget the size of a cell phone, and pushed a button in the center of it. A soft blue beam appeared. With the large front windows, she knew anyone driving by could easily spot the light and quickly swept it along the ceiling and walls. She caught Sam staring at her out of the corner of her eye. "Looking for cameras and other security devices that aren't attached to the system you disabled." The steady stream of light remained blue, indicating no bugs or cameras were detected.

She swung around and headed down the hall with the beam glowing in front of her, searching for hidden security devices. "Clear," Sidney said, turning off the detector. "Let's get started picking the inside door locks and looking for file cabinets."

Recalling that Smorick's office was a distance from the lobby, she began with the door closest to the back exit. She discovered the room was impeccably decorated. A huge, sleek, dark walnut desk dominated the space. A black leather couch with chrome legs and a matching chair stood in the corner along with a chrome-and-glass coffee table. Impressionist paintings hung on the walls. Sidney had no doubt the office belonged to Smorick. Standing in the hall, she saw a walnut credenza with file drawers behind the desk, but there were no file cabinets. She closed the door and moved onto the next lock.

"Found the file room," Sam announced, pointing his flashlight at Sidney.

Sidney came to him and shined the blue beam detector into a long, narrow room. A copy machine and shredder stood on one side. A row of four-drawer dark gray, metal files lined the other wall. She flipped off the device, dropped it into her duffle bag, and stepped through the doorway. Sidney pushed her ski mask up to her hairline and pointed her flashlight toward the cabinets. "I didn't expect this many."

Sam removed his mask and laid it on top of the file cabinet closest to the door. He gripped the handle on the top drawer. "Are we looking for anything else besides Payton contracts?"

"Let's find those contracts first, and then we'll go from there."

"Damn," Sam said, tugging on the handle. "They're locked." He pulled his picks out of his shirt pocket and pushed one into the lock.

Thumbing through the third drawer of another cabinet, Sidney came to an abrupt halt. Three manila file folders with the name Brimwell on the tabs were in front of her. She took them out, laid them across the open drawer, and looked inside. The top one contained a contract. Her eyes narrowed. The contract was between

Marcus Brimwell and SLI. She scanned the document and discovered that SLI was purchasing some land for Brimwell. The title to the property would be vested in the name of SLI. Sidney wanted to study the contract further, but not in the SLI office. She plucked a small digital camera from her duffle bag and snapped a picture of each page.

"You found the contracts?" Sam asked, kneeling on the floor and flipping through the files in a bottom drawer.

"Not Payton's. Brimwell's."

Sam cocked his brow. "Brimwell?"

Sidney nodded. "Uh-huh. I guess Payton isn't the only one that did business with SLI." She opened the second folder. It contained real estate contracts. Glancing through them, she saw they were purchase agreements for parcels of land in Brazil between SLI and various sellers. She took pictures of the documents and then opened the last folder. It contained sales contracts that looked like they were for the same parcels of land as in the prior folder, but on each one, the sales price appeared to be appreciably larger than the purchase price. After snapping an image of every page, Sidney put the three folders back into the file drawer.

Two hours later, Sidney and Sam had finished going through all the file cabinets. "The Payton contracts are either merged in with other contracts, or they're not here," Sam said, resetting the lock with his picks on the last cabinet.

"I've run across a lot of contract folders. They're all clearly marked. I doubt Payton's are concealed in any folder in this room. Maybe in Smorick's credenza?" Sidney speculated, lowering her ski mask over her face and heading down the hallway.

Slipping on his ski mask, Sam stepped out of the room. He locked the door behind him and followed Sidney.

She pulled the detector out of her bag, pushed it on, and as soon as she pointed it into Smorick's office, the stream of blue light turned a bright orange color and the device hummed softly. "This room has an additional security system." Keeping the beam of light shining into the room, her eyes darted around the corners looking for cameras. Not spotting any, she remained in the hall and closed the door. "I didn't see any cameras, but that doesn't mean there aren't any." She checked her watch. "It's almost 2:00 a.m. I need some additional equipment before we locate and tackle this security system. We'll come back tomorrow night after we've had a chance to visit with Judy."

Chapter 31

The next morning, Sidney and Sam met at a coffee shop. His truck was parked in a visible spot near the entrance. Her Lexus was a short jaunt away. They sat in a booth by the window and enjoyed breakfast while they occasionally glanced at SLI's Suburban parked across the street.

"Maybe we should invite them to have breakfast with us next time," Sidney said, raising her coffee cup.

A faint smile crossed Sam's face. "Good idea. It might help strengthen our ties to them. Almost finished?"

Sidney dabbed her mouth with her napkin and then nodded.

"See you in a few." Sam stood and walked toward the restrooms.

A few minutes later, a tall man with medium brown hair, similar to Sam's, climbed into the booth opposite Sidney.

"Thanks for doing this. My husband has me followed everywhere I go," she said, tilting her head and looking out the window toward the Suburban.

"No problem," the stranger replied.

Sidney slid off the bench and headed toward the restrooms. She exited the back door and found Sam standing in the alleyway smoking. "Good match."

"Yeah. In a minute, a slender woman with long blonde hair like yours will be joining him. They'll chat, drink coffee, and stay for lunch while our boys in the Suburban keep a watchful eye."

Two hours later, Sidney stopped in a visitor-designated parking spot in front of the building that housed Judy Fuller's new place of employment, a mortgage company in Riverside, California. "You know her," Sidney said to Sam. "See if she can take a break and talk to us."

"I'll give it my best shot." Sam opened the car door. "I might have a better chance if she thinks I'm alone. I noticed a café on the corner. If I come out with her, meet us there."

"Okay, turn on the charm." She watched Sam enter the two-story office building. While she waited, she read through the copy of the Brimwell contract acquired the previous night.

Within twenty minutes, Sam came out of the building's swinging doors alone and climbed into the Lexus.

"Did you get a chance to talk to her?" Sidney asked.

"She was working at the receptionist desk. Not excited to see me. It took some persuading, but I convinced her to meet me at the café on the corner for lunch. Her lunch break is at 12:30." He looked at his watch. "In twelve minutes. She's not anxious to talk about SLI. I better talk to her alone, or we might scare her off."

"Maybe I can sit at a nearby table," Sidney suggested. "Let's check out the layout of the café."

The café was called Ed's Eatery. Windows lined the two walls that faced the intersection. The other walls were decorated with pictures of cars from the sixties. Booths stood against the windows and along the back wall. Tables with red-and-white plaid tablecloths were scattered throughout the center of the space. Patrons seated themselves.

Since the establishment was close to where Judy worked, Sam and Sidney decided not to walk in together. Sidney pulled a mini-microphone out of her duffle bag and handed it to Sam. She put the receiver in her purse.

Sam strolled into Ed's and headed to an empty booth on the back wall.

A minute later, Sidney entered and spotted Sam scanning the menu. She moved to an unoccupied table twenty feet away from him and sat down. She reached in her purse for her earbuds and stuck one in her ear. Sidney picked up the menu, propped between the salt shaker and the napkin holder, as she kept the corner of her eye on Sam's booth.

Wanting to test the mike, Sam said, "Can you hear me?"

Sidney slightly nodded without looking up from her menu.

At 12:35 p.m., Sam stood up and motioned toward the door. A five-foot-four, slightly overweight woman with a round, attractive face and shoulder-length, light brown hair walked toward Sam's booth. She was dressed professionally in a nicely tailored navy-blue skirt, a soft light blue blouse, and two-inch heels.

Sidney ordered a salad while she listened to Sam and Judy chatting about Judy's new job and placing their lunch order. Sam kept the conversation light until they were almost finished eating.

"I tried to find you in San Diego after you left SLI, but you'd moved out of your apartment without a forwarding address. Why?"

"I *did* leave a forwarding address with the apartment manager. He wouldn't give it to you?"

"No. Claimed you moved out without leaving one." Sam drank a long swallow of his iced tea. "The last time I talked with you at SLI, you didn't mention anything about going to Riverside. Was there a special reason you left in a hurry?"

"Aaaah, my mom was sick. I had to come here to help out," she said with a quivering voice as she stared at her plate.

Sam reached across the table and placed his hand on hers. "Judy, you can tell me. I know something isn't right about SLI operations, but I can't seem to get past the new receptionist."

"Kyle. Smorick's kid."

"Is that the guy that took your place?"

"Yeah. When I told Smorick about my mom, he let me go without giving a two-week notice. I only trained Kyle a couple of days. During the first week after I left, he called me often when he didn't know how to handle something."

Sam patted Judy's arm. "Is your mom really sick?"

Judy lowered her hands into her lap and clasped them together. "She's sick."

"Well…she obviously doesn't need twenty-four-hour care or you wouldn't be able to work. Was she the only reason you left SLI?"

Without answering, Judy's eyes dropped again to her empty plate.

"Judy, would you rather talk after work?"

"Maybe." She sipped her water. "There's something I want to talk to you about, but you have to promise me you'll never tell anyone you heard it from me."

"I promise."

"What about your client, the guy SLI hasn't paid? Will you tell him you talked to me?"

"Judy, he doesn't know I tracked you to Riverside. He's only interested in getting paid by SLI. Is this about him?"

She shook her head and fidgeted with her napkin as her gaze scanned the cafe. "No. It's not all about him."

"You want to talk here or someplace else?"

"Not here, and I need to get back to work. I'm living with my mom, so I don't want to talk there. Across the street," she said pointing at the window, "and around the next corner is a small park. Can you meet me there shortly after five?"

"Sure can."

"Thanks for lunch." Judy stood and headed out the door.

Sidney watched Judy walk along the sidewalk until she could no longer be seen through the windows. Without glancing at Sam, Sidney paid her check and left the café.

The park didn't cover more than about 8,000 square feet. A row of bushes surrounded it, and shade trees were strategically placed throughout the small area. A fountain stood in the center with water spouts rising and dropping around a brass figurine of an angel.

At 5:00 p.m., the park was almost deserted with only a group of six people milling around the fountain. Sam sat down on a bench under a tree where he could easily spot Judy when she arrived.

Sidney moved her car closer to the meeting place, attached the receiver to her car speakers, and listened to muffled voices a short distance from Sam. She took a notebook and pen out of her briefcase and stared through the windshield, observing Judy moving toward the park on the sidewalk.

After Sam and Judy exchanged greetings, he asked, "Is this spot okay?"

Easing down on the bench, Judy swung her head around and eyed the people by the fountain. "This will work." She tucked her hair behind her ears. "I don't know what to do. Maybe I should go to the police. Since you're an investigator and you told me you sometimes work for lawyers, I thought you could tell me if I'm trouble if I don't do anything. Or maybe I should see a lawyer." She placed her hands in her lap and rubbed them together. "I just don't know."

Sam slid closer to her and touched her arm. "Why don't you start at the beginning, and then we'll go from there."

"I didn't leave SLI because my mom was sick. She does have lupus, but that's not the reason." She fidgeted with her bracelet. "Sam, do you know what SLI does?"

Sam tilted his head, and his eyes slightly narrowed. "It's an investment company that buys and sells vacant land, hopefully at a profit. Right?"

"Yes, but..."

"But what?"

"There's more to it. They buy and sell land in various countries when they learn a road, waterway, bridge, or some kind of development is planned that will need that property."

"With inside information?"

Judy nodded. "SLI has contacts with various people who can provide that information, and they pay for it. Their investors supply the funds and reap the benefits when the property is resold."

"Did you know all the time you worked for SLI that what they were doing was illegal?"

Judy exhaled an unsteady breath. "No. At first it appeared they speculated in land purchases based on population growth and other criteria. I've read their annual reports showing the return on the land investment. Nothing struck me as not being above board. Then about two years ago, a large check came across my desk payable to a high-ranking government official. I never would've seen it, but it didn't have a complete address on the envelope—the city and state were missing. SLI has fewer than fifty investors. I knew he wasn't one of them, but it showed as an investment return on the stub. His name wasn't in the computer system. I couldn't re-address it and send it out, so I went to Mr. Smorick.

"He grabbed the check and said he'd take care of it. It bugged me that the guy wasn't in our system. I couldn't let it go." She massaged her temple. "They might not have inside information for all their deals, but they've got it for some. The contracts for those people are kept in Smorick's office."

"Contracts?" Sam said, bewildered. He couldn't comprehend why anyone would want to leave a trail of their illegal acts. "He writes up a contract to obtain inside information?"

"I couldn't find anything in the file room with that official's name on it. Smorick keeps files in his credenza and at his house."

"His house?"

"Yeah. I saw him taking files out of his credenza and putting them in a box. I thought he intended to shred them, but he left the building with them. I've been to his house for company parties. He has a big den. I assume that's where he took them, but I could be wrong."

"How do you know any of the files he keeps have contracts in them?"

"When Smorick steps out of the office, he normally locks his door. One day when he went with a colleague to lunch, he forgot to do it. I hurried in there, thumbed through his credenza, and found three folders with the official's name on it along with a project number. I took one to my desk. I didn't want to take a chance of being caught in Smorick's office if someone came into the building. The language in the contract was vague; it only mentioned consulting services. In the file was a handwritten page that stated exactly the type of information the government official would provide. That contract was for the site of a highway expansion. I made a few notes so I could check it out. You know, I had a hunch it was inside information since the guy was paid so much, but I wanted to make sure.

"I spent that evening at the library going over newspapers. There wasn't any mention of that expansion until two months after the contract had been signed." She lowered her head and stared at the ground.

Sam sat quietly for a minute and then asked, "Did you notice if there were contract files in there for Payton Russen?"

"There might have been. I was in a hurry. I only looked for a folder with that particular official's name on it. When I put it back, I was too afraid to stay in Smorick's office and look through other folders."

"You discovered this two years ago?"

"Uh-huh."

"Why did it take you two years to leave the company?"

"Well...I liked my job. I was paid well. And even if they were doing something illegal, I never would've known about it if I hadn't snooped around. You know, the stuff I dealt with at work was legal. I never got involved with those contracts. No one told me to do anything illegal."

"Then why did you leave? What changed your mind?"

"Even if they were doing something wrong, Payton was the first guy who came in there complaining about not getting paid. Smorick and Gamboa wouldn't talk to him. They claimed he was a nut case and had never worked on any project for SLI. They told me to call our security company if he came in again. I did. While Payton was hanging around in the foyer, two men from the security company marched into the building and escorted him out. Never saw him after that."

"SLI doesn't have their own security people?"

She shook her head. "No."

"Does SLI have company cars?"

"No. Why?"

"I thought I saw a vehicle with SLI on the side doors."

"SLI has offices at various places around the world. There are two in the United States, one in the east, and one in San Diego. Maybe the other U.S. office has company cars."

"Getting back to Payton. Why did you decide to talk to me?"

"You came in with the signature page of a contract when both Smorick and Gamboa were in South America."

"You told me they'd both moved out of the country, not just gone on a business trip."

"Yeah, I'm sorry about that. Since they'd been so adamant that there wasn't a contract, you caught me off guard. I gave you the addresses."

Sam cocked his head. "So the Russen contract was the reason you left?"

"No. It was when Gamboa and Smorick returned from their business trip. Without saying your name, I told them an investigator had been in asking about payment for Russen's contract. That day I stayed late since I came in late—had a doctor's appointment. I heard loud voices coming from behind Smorick's closed door. I was curious about what was going on and went down the hall and listened. Smorick shouted something about it was the wrong site, we don't pay for bad information, something like that. Then I could only hear muffled voices, so I started heading back to the foyer when a man yelled, 'A woman is dead because of that damn bridge site.'"

"Who yelled it?"

"I think it was Gamboa, but I can't be sure."

"Did you hear anything else?"

"No. After that, I hustled back to my desk. Even though I knew the company was doing something illegal, I didn't think anyone would get hurt. That was when I decided to leave." Her hands shook, and she gulped. "Am I in trouble since I didn't go to the police or do anything?"

Sam patted her arm. "No. You'd need some type of proof about SLI's illegal acts before you could take it to the cops. By any chance, did you copy the contract and Smorick's handwritten note?"

Judy shook her head.

"And like you said, you wouldn't have known about it if you hadn't been snooping."

"What about the woman?"

"You only heard about her because you were eavesdropping. Again, you have no proof that statement was said. If you went to the cops about it, Gamboa and Smorick would deny it."

"Gamboa moved out of the country. I only gave a two-day notice. He was gone before I left."

Sam took Judy's hand. "You look like you could use a drink. Is there a bar close by?"

"Well, it's about time," Sidney huffed, putting away the receiver as Sam climbed into the Lexus. "Your drink turned into dinner, and then you offered to drive Judy home. How were you planning to pull that off?"

Sam gave her a sheepish smile.

"Were you expecting me to stand on some street corner waiting for my car to return?"

He slightly shook his head back and forth. "Feeling bad you didn't get to walk the streets of downtown Riverside while I took her home?"

"Sure," she said in an irritated tone. "You just don't know how lucky you are that Judy had driven to work today instead of taking a bus."

"It's getting late."

"Tell me about it." Sidney started the engine and merged into the traffic.

"Judy gave us some valuable information. I couldn't just leave her at a bus stop." Sam studied Sidney's face. "You didn't sit in the car all the time I was gone?"

"No. I enjoyed a great meal at a nearby fast-food place, wrote some additional notes, and talked to my husband while you were out on your date."

"I kept the bug on so you'd know how things were going."

"Glad you did." Sidney drove up the ramp to the Interstate. She sighed, realizing Sam probably handled Judy appropriately. Still, she felt annoyed that she had to wait over four hours for him. "Were the pool games necessary?"

"She was uptight after spilling her guts about SLI. Thought that might help her relax, but I had no idea she was a pool shark."

Sidney smiled. "That was funny. You probably thought it would be an easy game."

"I did. I had to work hard to win one of three." Sam reclined the back of his seat and leaned against the cool leather. "You still want to hit SLI tonight?"

"No. I figured after you downed at least three beers and a couple of mixed drinks, you wouldn't be up to prowling around. We'll meet in your office tomorrow morning and go over where we are. Take a nap. I'll wake you when we reach your place."

Chapter 32

Wearing only his pajama bottoms, Sam opened his office door for Sidney and handed her a filled coffee mug. He explained that a friend had called after he got back the prior night and wanted to get together.

While Sidney waited for Sam to shower and dress, she sipped coffee and thought about SLI, wondering why Brimwell's contract hadn't been put in Smorick's credenza. Instead, it was among the company's other files, a place where it could easily be found.

The sound of high heels clicking on the stairs brought her out of her reverie. Her eyes darted toward Sam's inner office door. An attractive blonde in her mid-thirties came through the doorway. The woman glanced at Sidney, smiled, and exited the main door.

With an amused expression on her face, Sidney realized why Sam wasn't ready for their 9:30 a.m. meeting. Then she took a folder and a notepad out of her briefcase and read over the notes she had made during Sam's meeting with Judy in the park.

Ten minutes later, heavy footfalls pounded down the stairs. "Sorry, I slept in," Sam said, pulling up a chair on the other side of the coffee table.

"I understand," Sidney said, her eyebrows bouncing.

A coy smile flashed on Sam's face. "What's the game plan for today?"

"Well, now we know that the bridge site—I'm assuming it's the one in Brazil, the one Aden was working on—has something to do with Mara's death."

"You thinking what I am? Aden was the intended victim?"

Sidney nodded. "No one knew Mara would be there. The murderer probably went in the backyard to hide until Aden got home. Mara probably startled the perpetrator. He panicked. She died."

"You sure it was a guy?"

"I wouldn't rule out that it could be a woman. But Payton, Brimwell, and Victor appear to be involved with both the bridge site and SLI. We haven't run across anything indicating a woman might have played a role, at least not yet. I'm curious about the dark gray Suburban."

"Judy said they didn't have any company cars. That Suburban started tailing me right after my first visit to SLI's office."

"Ever check out the license plate?"

"No. With the sign on the vehicle, thought it was a moot point. Got the plate number. Just need to call my DMV contact. You still want to visit SLI tonight?"

"Did you find out where the real taxi driver hangs out?" she asked without answering his question.

"Yep. A pool hall with a huge bar that stretches almost the length of the building."

"Since I'll be tied up with my date tomorrow night," Sidney said, referring to the barbeque with Kyle Smorick, "I thought I'd work on the taxi driver tonight."

"You as good at pool as Judy?"

Sidney rolled her eyes. She hadn't played for years but used to be able to hold her own. "Doubt it."

"The cops didn't let Aden go after they found out his fingerprints weren't on the murder weapon. Why waste your time on the taxi driver? The only damn thing that's going to get him out of the joint is if we can point the cops to the murderer and give them enough evidence to make it stick."

"Whether or not a taxi driver heard a gunshot might not make a difference, but it'll support Aden's recollection of that evening. Also, there's a slim chance the driver might've seen something." Flipping through her notepad and knowing Sam was also working on other investigations, Sidney asked, "Are you available to work for Fowler the rest of the day and this evening?"

Sam ran his fingers through his hair. "Can always use the bucks.

But got something else lined up around seven. It should only take a couple of hours."

"Do you know if the taxi driver stays late at the pool hall?"

"Only followed him there once. He got there around nine…stayed until midnight. The bartender and some other guys called him by his name, Cesar. Figured he's a regular, but he might not go there every night."

"Did you try to talk to Cesar?"

"Sure did. He speaks with a heavy Spanish accent—broken English. Kept saying, 'Me no drive taxi.'"

"I'll go shortly after nine. When you finish with your other investigation, go to the pool hall parking lot and text me. If I don't respond within five minutes, you'll know Cesar is there. Then you can pay him a visit and ask him about driving the taxi again in front of me. That'll help me stir the conversation that way."

Sam's head bobbed up and down. "Got it. What about during the day?"

"Follow Brimwell. I'll tail Victor."

"They're probably both at the office working."

"Yeah. If they stay put until five, it'll turn out to be a long, boring day." Sidney jotted down the planned activities in her notepad.

"What about Payton?"

"I'm going to put a tracking device on his vehicle. If he leaves, we'll know where he goes. Since Smorick is avoiding him, I want to focus on Brimwell and Victor first. Hey, do you know what types of cars those guys drive?"

"Victor, a white Porsche Boxster. Brimwell, a silver Mercedes sedan."

After spotting Victor's car in the Brimwell Engineering parking lot, Sidney stopped next to the curb between two cars on the other side of the street. From that vantage point, she had a clear view of the front of Brimwell's building and the white Porsche. Glancing around, she couldn't see Sam's truck, Brimwell's Mercedes, or Payton's BMW anywhere within her line of sight.

Sidney leaned over the seat, lifted up her duffle bag, and began assembling the needed equipment. She laid the directional mike, binoculars, and her laptop computer on the front passenger seat.

With a tracking device clutched in her hand, she slipped out of the Lexus and walked at a brisk pace down the street until she was past the Brimwell building. She scanned the area, searching for people outside the buildings. Two men were standing and puffing on cigarettes near a construction site across the street. She continued strolling along the sidewalk and stopped when she could no longer see the smokers. Then she doubled back and sighed in relief, seeing the spot that had been occupied by the two men was empty. Only parked cars lined the street. No people were in sight.

Sidney moved stealthily into Brimwell's parking lot at the side of the building, ducked down behind the white Porsche, and stuck the tracking device under the wheel well. She inched her way to the rear of the building, looped around it to the other side, and headed to her car.

After she was situated in the driver's seat, she plugged the digital mike receiver cord into the cigarette lighter to juice up the battery. Then she pushed a CD into the Lexus's sound system, leaned back, and listened to the music while she maintained her vigil outside the building.

Twenty minutes later, Payton's BMW pulled into Brimwell's parking lot. She checked her watch and assumed he was returning from lunch.

Sidney sat up straight when both Payton and Victor climbed out of the BMW. She turned off the car's sound system, grabbed the mike, flipped on the switch, and pointed it toward the two men as they walked to the entrance.

"…it," Payton said.

"Now, Payton…" Victor said in an angry tone.

"Yeah…yeah…I'll do it."

"Today?"

"Yeah, sure," Payton said, entering the building.

Sidney kept the mike directed at the building, but several voices blended together. What she was able to catch sounded like Molly asking them about the restaurant where they ate. Sidney lowered the mike and turned on the music again. Sitting in a car and waiting for someone to make a move was the part of surveillance she hated. Though, she knew it was a requirement in the line of work she had chosen.

Her cell phone buzzed. Sidney fished it out of her purse and glanced at the caller I.D. "Where are you?"

"Brimwell's out of town. He'll be back sometime this evening," Sam said, ignoring her question.

"How do you know that?"

"Called Molly. Told her I wanted to talk to him. She filled me in. Got the name of the registered owner of the dark gray Suburban. Been trying to do some research on her."

Sidney squinted. "Her? Who owns it?"

"Marsha Eddington, a ninety-year-old woman who hasn't had a driver's license for over ten years. Haven't been able to find where she lives. The street address on the car's registration turned out to be an empty lot. The title and registration were sent to a P.O. box."

"Where's the P.O. box?"

"At a private company called Mail Stop. Can't get info about who rented the box."

"Address and box number?" Sidney scribbled it down while Sam rattled it off. "Were you able to find out if any of our suspects have relatives with that last name?"

"Been working on that angle. Nothing's popped up yet."

"Did she sign the car documents?"

"Shaky, jagged signature. Looked like it belonged to an elderly senior citizen. One document was notarized." Sidney heard him shuffle a few pages, and then he continued. "The Suburban's two years old. Doubt Mrs. Eddington went car hunting. It was purchased from a private party. I'm heading to the last owner's address. He might not remember the name of the person that paid him for the car, or it might have been an alias. I've got pictures of Smorick, Victor, Kate, and Brimwell on my cell. I'm betting it's one of them."

"How did you get a picture of Smorick?"

"Couldn't tail Brimwell today. I hung around outside SLI while I researched the owner of the Suburban. Around noon, three guys came out of the building. Two wore suits. Assuming one was Smorick, I snapped pictures of all of them. Hey, you know what he looks like. Can I send you those pictures?"

"Sure."

"Give me a second to pull off the road and text them to you."

Within two minutes, Sidney had the pictures and called Sam. "Smorick is the guy with the wire-rimmed glasses. When I was at SLI, I didn't see the other two men." She noticed Victor stepping out of the Brimwell building. "Gotta go." She clicked off.

Victor slid into his Porsche and drove out of the parking lot. Keeping a safe distance behind him, Sidney followed the blip displayed on her computer. A half an hour later, Victor turned onto a street with houses hidden behind solid walls and locked gates, a neighborhood Sidney recognized. He was going to Brimwell's house. She expected Brimwell had arrived home early from his business trip and wanted to talk to Victor. At the same time, she wondered why Brimwell didn't go to the office and chat with Victor there. The blip on her computer screen stopped. She parked behind a tree over two hundred feet beyond Brimwell's gate, a place where her car wouldn't be seen when Victor left.

There, she opened her trunk, took out her backpack, and checked the contents. Then she put the digital mike in it. Next, she changed into a pair of athletic shoes, tied her hair into a ponytail, and put her cell phone on vibrate.

She locked the Lexus, went to Brimwell's cobblestone wall and, in order to remain hidden from passing cars, slipped behind a cluster of trees. Sidney scanned the wall for cameras and spotted only one. It was aimed at the gate. She lowered her backpack and pulled out a rope. She attached a hook to it and flung it over the corner of the stone wall. She tugged on the rope until the hook caught something on the other side and then climbed over the wall. Sidney couldn't recall hearing or seeing any dogs when visiting Angelica, yet she still remained motionless for a few minutes and listened for movement in the foliage.

Satisfied no hounds were in the yard and shielded by large bushes and trees, she crept toward the house. When she was close to the structure but still concealed from anyone who might be looking out a window, she slipped off her backpack, got out the directional mike, and stuck an earbud in her ear. Switching on the device, she caught a glimpse of someone standing on the front porch. She sank down on her knees, peered out through a small opening between two bushes, and aimed the mike.

"... not sooner," she heard a familiar female voice say.

"No," Victor replied. "I didn't even dare call you with that cop and investigator snooping around. We're so close I don't want to take a chance of screwing up now."

"You're sure they found everything?"

"I'll know more later. Meet me at the same place?"

"Marcus will be home around nine. Can we meet at six-thirty or is that too early?"

"That works."

Sidney watched Victor and Angelica, arm-in-arm, step down the porch stairs. When they reached his car, Angelica wrapped her arms around Victor's neck and said, "I love you so much."

"Just hang in there, sweetheart." He embraced and kissed her.

Sidney stared at them as Victor held Angelica tight against his body. She felt dumbfounded. Those two together wasn't a relationship that had even crossed her mind. She had briefly talked about Victor and Deidre with Angelica. The woman hadn't given off the smallest indication that she knew Victor more than any of Brimwell's employees. Suddenly, she recalled Aden telling her there was a time that Victor had been attracted to Angelica. Victor brought a date to the Christmas party. *Was that a cover-up, or did that happen before Victor and Angelica's relationship began? And the guy's still dating Deidre. What's going on?*

As Sidney mulled over the various possibilities, Victor drove out the driveway. She tucked the mike in her backpack and crept away from the house to the corner of the stone wall. Her rope dangled from a tall tree next to it. She yanked the hook out of the tree trunk and put it along with the rope in her backpack, flung it over her shoulder, scurried up the tree, and jumped to the stone wall. She slid down the other side and sprinted to her car.

Chapter 33

Sidney followed the blip on her computer monitor and ended up at the Brimwell building. She parked across the street in the spot she had vacated two hours earlier, reached in her duffle bag and took out another tracking device. Following the same maneuvers she used when she had attached a device to Victor's car, she expertly put one on Payton's BMW.

When Sidney opened the Lexus's driver's door, her cell phone vibrated. She sank down into the seat, looked at the caller's name, and pushed the talk button. "Find out anything?"

"This case is getting stranger by the minute," Sam said.

"Tell me about it," Sidney replied, thinking about Victor and Angelica.

"The man thought the name of the guy who bought his car was Jim something, but he wasn't sure. He didn't have a copy of the bill of sale."

"Jim?"

"Yeah. Since we don't have any Jims on our radar yet, I showed him a few pictures on my cell phone. None of them sparked a memory. He began describing the guy—five-foot-seven or eight, blond hair, thick glasses. Payton popped into my head. I brought up his picture on my phone. He bought the car."

Sidney shook her head. "Strange is right. How did you happen to have a picture of him?"

"Take a picture of all my clients. Too many have lied to me about who they are. I met Payton at Brimwell's building and knew who he was, but I still like having photos. It's become an ingrained policy that I don't break. How you getting along with Victor?"

"He's having an affair with Angelica."

The line went silent.

"You still there, Sam?"

"Yeah. With Angelica's heart condition, she wasn't even on my radar as a potential player in this case. You sure?"

"Followed Victor to Brimwell's house. Saw them hugging and kissing."

"That guy gets around. He's spreading himself pretty thin between Kate, Deidre, and now Angelica. Mmmmh. Must be a full time job keeping those ladies satisfied." Sam chuckled.

"Well, Kate lives in Denver. She can't demand too much of his time. When Brimwell's in town, I doubt he has much access to Angelica. Probably the one he has to keep entertained the most is Deidre, and she's left for a while to be with her dying aunt." Sidney tucked a few loose strands of hair behind her ear. "Getting back to Angelica. She's going to meet Victor someplace at six-thirty. He mentioned to her that they needed to be careful because an investigator and cop were snooping around. Any idea how they know about us?"

"No. Payton visits Aden often. Maybe he told him and Payton told Victor."

"Possibly. Victor and Payton went to lunch together. I overheard Victor telling Payton he wanted him to do something today. Didn't catch what it was. Payton said he'd do it. I put a tracking device on his car."

"Remember, I've got an appointment at seven. Want me to tail him before then?"

"Yeah, since I'll be following Victor." Sidney paused and skimmed through her notes. "I've been thinking about the medium's vision of a bandaged face and wondering if Angelica really has a heart condition. Could she have been hospitalized for another reason?"

"A facelift?"

"She looks awfully good for being in her early fifties."

"Her operation didn't slow Brimwell down from going out of town. Maybe that's why."

"I want to ask Aden some questions about Angelica's health problems next time I see him."

"Before you do that, let me see if I can find out what doctor treated her and at which hospital," Sam said. "I have a friend that works for a medical association that owes me a few favors."

"That would be a good start. Medical conditions are confidential, but we'd at least know if the doctor is a heart specialist. Do you have a laptop with a tracking system on it?"

"Nope. I have a receiver I use, but it only works with a certain type of tracking device."

"Okay, I'll…"

Sam interrupted her. "Payton's calling. I better take it. Call you back." He hang up.

Within fifteen minutes, Sidney's cell phone vibrated. She glanced at the caller ID and answered, "What did he have to say for himself?"

"He claims SLI paid him," Sam said. "He no longer needs my services."

"Do you think they threatened him or something?"

"He sounded nervous and jittery, but he sounds like that often. I just went outside to check on the gray Suburban. It's nowhere in sight."

"We're missing a huge piece of this puzzle. Payton buys the Suburban. He has it titled and registered under a woman's name. Hires you to help get him paid by SLI. He sets up a surveillance on you using that vehicle after having SLI's emblem painted on the doors."

"Yeah. He even went so far as having bugs planted in my place, having two guys rough me up for the name of the person that hired me. Paying for twenty-four hour surveillance. Can't imagine Payton would spend that type of dough." Sam rubbed his jaw. "Someone else is footing the bill, but who? And why?"

"Did you mention to Payton you were being tailed by SLI?"

"Nope. I'm leaving now for Brimwell's office. Want to be there when Payton gets off work."

Sidney disconnected and thought about the Suburban. *Could Payton have been coerced into purchasing the car? Is Marsha Eddington related to him? Could he be completely unaware that it was being used to tail Sam?* She placed a call to Chas and left a voice message asking if he could have Susan try to locate an address for Marsha Eddington and proceeded to give all the information she knew about the woman.

A little while later, Sam drove by Sidney's Lexus, and she watched his truck turn at a corner and vanish out of sight. She wondered if he had parked someplace that gave him a view of Brimwell's building's entrance, or if he expected her to call him when Payton stepped out of the door. Pulling out her cell phone, she caught a glimpse of a figure ducking down in the parking lot. Her eyes focused in that direction, and she spotted a man's arm, clad in a light blue, rolled-up sleeve, sticking out from behind Payton's car. Sam was dressed in a light blue shirt. Sidney smiled. The BMW now had two tracking devices.

Shortly after 5:00 p.m., the Brimwell employees began to pile out the door and go to their cars. Payton was among them, but not Victor. When the BMW had been gone for about five minutes, Sam's truck again drove by Sidney's Lexus.

Minutes ticked away while Sidney kept her eyes peeled on the entrance, expecting Victor to emerge. The employees of other companies, who had parked their cars along the street, climbed into their vehicles and left. Within a half an hour, the Lexus sat alone on the edge of the road. She started the engine and drove a block, turned down a side street and flipped a u-ey. A hundred feet away from the intersection, Sidney cut to the curb. She brought up the tracking program on her computer and waited for the blip to move.

Around six o'clock, the blip budged. Victor's Porsche zoomed past her on the main road. She merged into traffic and followed the blip to a hotel near the center of town. Sidney entered the hotel's parking terrace and drove around the parking levels until she found Victor's car. She pulled into a parking space two aisles away from the Porsche.

On the way to the elevator, she looked through his car windows and saw a stack of folders in the back seat. She stared at the top folder that had "Brimwell" printed on the tab, and under it was the word "Project" with small numbers next to it. She couldn't make out the digits. The folder underneath it had a label that started with the letters "Ru." The other tabs were hidden from view in the ruffled stack.

Sidney walked out of the elevator into the lobby, took an empty nine-by-twelve envelope out of her backpack, and headed toward the woman standing behind the check-in desk. "I need to deliver this to Mr. Victor Grenshaw. Could you give me his room number?" Sidney said, waving the envelope in the air.

"We don't give out that information without the permission of our guests. Let me call him," the clerk said, searching for his room number on her computer screen. "I'm afraid we don't have a registered guest by that name."

"It might be under the name of Angelica Brimwell."

"Let me check." The clerk looked at her computer screen again. "No, sorry."

Sidney doubted the hotel would allow anyone to register without providing a credit card. "How about Payton Russen?"

"Yes," the woman said in an uplifted tone. "Oh, but it doesn't show there is more than one guest registered for that room."

"Oh, dear, Mr. Grenshaw must be staying at another hotel. I'll give this," Sidney said, raising the envelope, "to him tomorrow. Thanks for your help."

Sidney headed into the restroom, took a baseball cap out of her duffle bag, and placed it on her head, tucking her hair under the rim. She dug out a pair of mirrored sunglasses and slipped them on. Looking at her image in the mirror, she wished she could've better disguised her appearance, but she wasn't prepared with the right makeup. Still, she thought Angelica or Victor wouldn't immediately recognize her. She had never met Victor. Yet, she wouldn't rule out the possibility that he could have seen a photo of her since he had mentioned an investigator and a cop were hanging around.

Sidney went back into the lobby and sank down into a cushioned chair that faced the bank of six elevators—four went to the guest rooms and two went to the parking terrace. Based on the discussion she overheard between Angelica and Victor, she figured their romantic get-together couldn't last past eight in order for Angelica to make it home before Brimwell arrived. She speculated about Brimwell's servants. *Would any of them spill the beans to him?* Sidney felt certain that Lewis was completely loyal to Angelica by the way he doted over her.

She picked up the newspaper lying on the table next to her and began to read it, keeping her face well hidden behind it. Though she had slightly camouflaged her appearance, she didn't want to give anyone the opportunity to study her features.

Every time the elevator bell rang, she peeked over the top edge of the paper and observed the people exiting. At 7:48 p.m., Sidney saw Angelica stepping out of a guest elevator and pushing a button by the parking elevators.

Sidney had a list of the cars Brimwell owned but didn't know which one Angelica drove. Deciding it was time to find out, she stood, shouldered her duffle bag, and held the newspaper casually in front of her chin and mouth. Then, she walked at a brisk pace toward Angelica. The parking elevator doors opened. She followed Angelica inside and edged around her into the back corner. Sidney got off on the same level as Angelica. Angelica stopped at a black Saab and climbed into the driver's seat.

Moving to the next aisle, Sidney noticed Angelica raising a cell phone to her ear. When she was out of Angelica's line of sight, she ducked down between two parked cars, yanked the directional mike out of her duffle bag, and pushed in the earplug. Hunkering near the cement floor, she crept toward Angelica's car and pointed the mike in that direction. Sidney heard numerous voices through the ear piece. Inching closer, she managed to hone in on Angelica's voice.

"…Possibly…No, he's clueless…I know. Whenever I turn around, it seems like she's right there. We can't talk there anymore. I wish I could fire her, but she's been with Marcus too long…He's getting anxious… No…Dumb. What an idiot…shooting the wrong person…Vic doesn't have any idea why the fingerprints didn't work…"

Fingerprints? Could she be talking about the fingerprints on the gun? If so, how did she learn the police have the gun?

Angelica went on. "His guy saw them enter the building and heard they found the Brimwell contract." She snickered. "Sometime tonight… Honey, I've got to get going if I'm going to beat Marcus home. See you in a little while." The engine of the Saab blared.

While Sidney wondered about the identity of the person on the other end of Angelica's phone call, she put away the mike, peered over the hood of the car parked by her, and saw the Saab moving toward the exit ramp.

Chapter 34

After Sidney ate a quick bite with Jean, she changed into the outfit she had worn for her meeting with Zisk—black fishnet tights, short red-leather skirt, low-cut blouse, and five-inch stilettos. She put the finishing touches on her heavily made-up face. Then Sidney headed to the pool hall where Cesar Ortega, the guy who drove Aden home April 20, hung out.

Just past 9:30 p.m., she sashayed up to the bar completely aware that her entrance into the place had not gone unnoticed. The noise of balls being struck by cues ended, and almost every guy had his eyes focused on her.

"Sweetheart, what can I getcha?" a burly bartender asked.

Sidney scooted onto a barstool and smiled. "A daiquiri." As the pool games resumed, she twirled around in the seat and scoped the place, looking for Cesar. She spotted him at the pool table closest to the bar while the empty barstools next to her became immediately occupied.

"Hey, baby, do you play pool?" a bald, overweight man with tattoos running up his arms asked.

Sidney turned to face him. "Ssh-ure," she said in her role-playing drawl.

"Here you go, sweetheart," the bartender said, sitting her drink down on the bar.

A tall, lean, clean-shaven man sitting on her other side inched closer to her and said, "I've never seen you in here before."

"Wantta play?" the bald man asked, talking over the lean man.

Then his eyes bore into the other guy.

"Okay, Buck," the lean man said, raising his hands to his shoulders with his palms toward the bald man in a surrendering gesture. The man picked up his beer and strode to the pool tables.

"I wanna watch for a few mins," Sidney said between sips of her daiquiri. "'Til I finis dis." She tapped on her glass. Holding it in her hand, she swung her stool around and watched Cesar hit a ball into a pocket. The bald man's hot, cigarette-laden breath skimmed her arm. Ignoring him hovering over her, she continued following Cesar's game. He was playing against another Hispanic guy who was a few inches taller than Cesar and at least fifty pounds heavier. Cesar missed his next shot, stood up straight, and glanced at her. Their eyes met. She gave him a seductive smile, making sure Buck didn't see her. Then she turned and faced Buck. "Why donna we play 'em?" she said, pointing at Cesar and his friend.

"You think they're good?"

Sidney curled her lips and shrugged.

"We can do whatever you want, baby," Buck said, standing up. He sauntered toward Cesar and his buddy and spoke to them quietly. Then he motioned to Sidney. "Come on, baby."

Sidney put the strap of her purse over her shoulder, picked up her drink, and went to the pool table.

"This is Cesar," Buck said, nodding toward him, "and Miguel. What's your name, baby?"

"Deedee," she said with a coy smile. Sidney moved to the counter on the far side of the table and sat her glass down. A ringing sound drifted from inside her purse. She plucked out her cell phone, glimpsed at the caller ID, and then turned it off. She dropped her phone back into her handbag and placed it on the counter.

Buck handed her a cue. "Is that about the size you use?"

She ran her finger along the end of it. "Uh-huh," Sidney mumbled, picking up the blue chalk and rubbing it onto the tip of the cue.

"You wanna break?" Buck asked her.

"No, you."

Buck lined up the white ball, bent down, and struck it. The balls bounced off of each other and spread across the table. One rolled into a pocket. "We're stripes," he announced. He managed to sink another striped ball but failed to get the next one into a pocket.

Cesar sank a green ball just as Sam trudged through the door and headed straight toward him.

"Wha ya wan?" Cesar said in broken English.

"I want to talk to you about the night you drove Aden Uzelac in a taxi to his house."

Cesar fidgeted with his pool stick. "Mister, I no drive no cab."

Sam put his hand on Cesar's shoulder and glared at him. "Tell the truth. The guy's in jail because you won't come clean."

Cesar knocked Sam's hand away. "Gettaway. Me know nothin'!"

Miguel stepped closer to Sam. "You. Go," he said as Buck moved to the other side of Sam.

Sam's gaze drifted between Buck, Cesar, and Miguel. He raised his hand and wiggled his index finger at Cesar. "You haven't seen the last of me." Then he turned on his heels and strode out of the pool hall.

"He talkin' about the guy that shot his wife?" Buck asked Cesar.

Cesar nodded.

"You know something about that?"

Cesar shook his head.

Buck's eyes lowered to his empty beer glass on the counter. He grabbed it and looked at Sidney. "Need another?" he asked, referring to her daiquiri.

"Not yet." She took a sip and saw Buck head to the bar.

Miguel asked Cesar in Spanish, "Why didn't you tell Buck that you drove that cab?"

"He might ask more questions," Cesar replied in Spanish.

"Like..." Miguel abruptly stopped when Buck returned, carrying a beer bottle.

Being fluent in Spanish, Sidney wanted to hear more and figured with Buck lingering near her, she wouldn't have an opportunity to get Cesar alone. She gulped down the rest of her drink and raised her glass toward Buck. "Mind?"

"Sure, baby." He took the empty glass.

When Buck was out of earshot, Miguel asked Cesar in Spanish, "You see something at that guy's house?"

"Heard the gunshot and someone running through the bushes. I was afraid the shooter might fire again. I backed out of that driveway so fast I almost hit a sports car parked across the street."

"You don't want to help the guy in jail?"

"Can't," Cesar said just as Buck handed Sidney another daiquiri.

"Cesar, get going." Buck tilted his head toward the pool table. "Finish your turn."

Cesar positioned himself for another shot, hit the cue ball, and sank a solid-colored ball. He attempted to get in another one. It missed the pocket by a fraction of an inch.

"Your turn, baby," Buck said with a smile.

Sidney swayed her hips as she moseyed up to the pool table. She slowly raised her stick, leaned over the edge of the table, and sensed Buck's eyes staring at her bottom. Gazing at the balls, she contemplated if she should try to get one in or completely miss a pocket and continue playing the role of being not very bright. Sidney's ego screamed to let the skilled woman hidden inside her out, especially since she doubted that any more information was forthcoming from Cesar. She aimed the pool stick, pulled it back, and sent the cue ball bouncing against the far side of the pool table. It struck two striped balls. They rolled into pockets.

"Good shot, baby," Buck said, disbelief evident in his tone. "Keep 'em coming."

Sidney sank another ball, and then felt the long day of tailing Victor, Angelica, and preparing herself to meet Cesar catching up with her. She decided it was time to get back to the Hyatt. Sidney pointed the pool stick at the cue ball and hit it. A striped ball teetered next to a pocket, but refused to drop into it.

Buck swigged his beer. "Too bad."

Sidney leaned her cue against the counter and picked up her purse. "Need to go to the little girls' room," she said, sashaying toward the restroom sign. The ladies' door opened up to the main room. Suspecting Buck might be keeping an eye on her, she couldn't make a quick dart to the hallway next to the men's room.

In the restroom, she breathed a sigh of relief when she saw a window ajar above the corner stall. She walked into it, locked the door, and climbed up on the toilet seat. The bathroom door squeaked open. Two women entered, chattering and laughing. Sidney quickly dropped down to the floor so her legs could be seen under the stall door. She waited patiently while the women used the facilities and talked non-stop about a guy playing pool with a floozy. Both women seemed interested in the man. One mentioned muscular, tattooed arms. Sidney guessed they were talking about Buck. Compared to the other guys she had seen in the place, he definitely had the best build and was handsome in a rugged way.

As soon as the women left, Sidney hustled onto the toilet seat, pushed the window completely open, and gripped the metal frame. She raised herself through the opening and dropped to the ground in the unlit alley. While she scanned the area, a silhouette came around the edge of the building and strode toward her.

Chapter 35

Sidney's hand flew to the sheath secured on her thigh. She wrapped her fingers around the knife's handle and focused her attention on the dark figure.

"Knew you had to come out that way," Sam said, partially hidden in the shadow cast by the building.

Sidney expelled a long, slow, calming breath and released the knife's handle. "Sam, you startled me." She smoothed down her skirt, making sure the sheath was well concealed. "We need to get moving. It took me a while to get out of the restroom. Someone's going to come looking for me soon." She headed toward the street.

"No, other way." Sam pointed toward the back of the structure. "My truck's behind the next building. I'll drop you off at your car."

The following morning Sidney arrived at Sam's office thirty minutes past their prearranged meeting time. "Sorry I'm late," she said, checking his baseboards.

Sam peeked over the top of a newspaper he held. "No problem."

Sidney bent down next to the edge of the couch and looked behind it.

He folded the newspaper and laid it on the coffee table. "You lookin' for something?"

"Yeah. An outlet."

"Behind the plant stand," Sam said, pointing toward it.

Sidney took a two-by-two inch gadget out of her duffle bag and plugged it in.

Watching her, Sam asked, "What's that for?"

"It blocks out our voices if someone is using any type of electronic equipment to eavesdrop."

Sam stood and gazed at the plugged-in device. "Cool. Sometimes I could use one of those."

"It does have a downside. When it's plugged in you can't talk on a cell phone, use a cordless phone, or anything that sends signals through the airwaves."

"There aren't any bugs in here. I check every day. So why do we need it?"

"They—Victor and Angelica—know we went to SLI and saw Brimwell's folder."

He winced at the thought. "How?" Then Sam noticed Sidney eyeing the coffee pot and the extra cup on the low table. "Help yourself."

Sidney picked up the coffee pot and filled the empty mug. "I think whoever is keeping track of us might be using a directional mike."

"The Suburban guys?"

"No, not those guys." She cocked her head. "Well, I guess it could be one of them, but not in the Suburban. We surveyed the area before we entered SLI's building. We would've spotted it."

"How do you know someone saw us?"

"Angelica. When she finished her rendezvous with Victor, she chatted on her cell phone while she sat in her Saab. She told whoever was on the other end of the line that Vic's guy saw some people break into the building, and he heard the intruders talking about the Brimwell contract they found." Sidney took a drink of her coffee. "You think she might have been talking about someone else besides us?"

Sam shook his head and flopped down on the couch. "Nope." He ran his fingers through his hair. "I'm thinking set up. That contract should've been in Smorick's office or at his home, not in plain sight among the company's legal business folders."

That was what Sidney had originally thought. Yet, the more she had mulled it over, she began to doubt that SLI needed to conceal it. "Not necessarily. It was just a contract to buy and sell property in Brazil."

"Yeah, but yesterday while I was waiting for Payton to leave

Brimwell's office, I called Molly. She told me where they were going to build a bridge in Brazil. She wants to visit the site. Brimwell told her he'd take her with him when he went to get the first phase started. Molly's pretty excited about it. Anyway, she emailed me a couple of pages about the project. And to my surprise," he said in a sarcastic tone, "the parcels that Brimwell directed SLI to buy cover that site."

"Still, as far as SLI was concerned, they weren't doing anything illegal. They had no reason to hide the contract."

Sam cupped his hands behind his head and leaned back. "We've been set up. The phony SLI surveillance. The break-in at my office. Payton's SLI investigation files were taken, but so was the stuff I had about Aden's case." He shook his head. "We were led right to the SLI office. We knew Brimwell Engineering had been working on a site for a bridge in Brazil. Running across those files at SLI, we thought the reason Brimwell wanted SLI to buy up that land and not put his name on any of the deeds had to do with Brimwell's plan to propose that site for the bridge. Talk about inside info. Someone wants to sock it to Brimwell. Probably hoping he'll end up behind bars in Brazil."

"Agreed." Sidney poured coffee, refilling both mugs. "Why would Angelica want to ruin her husband?" She stirred sugar in her coffee as she gathered her thoughts. "Let's assume Brimwell is thinking about a divorce. He no longer takes Angelica with him on trips, and it sounds like he's interested in a woman who works for a catering company, or maybe that's just a role she plays to give her and Brimwell a little time together. Who knows?" Sidney shrugged her shoulders.

"My person that works for the medical association came through. There's no record of Angelica Brimwell being in any Southern California hospital."

"Huh?" Sidney squinted. "Could she have used another name? But why?"

"No," Sam said with a crooked smile, shaking his head.

"Okay, Sam. What gives?"

"Apparently, facelifts are performed in doctor's offices or clinics. Not hospitals. Angelica Brimwell's name appeared in a patients' database. Over the past few years, she has seen Dr. Lawrence Grant, a plastic surgeon, numerous times. Grant is highly acclaimed in his profession for facelifts."

Sidney wrinkled her nose and pressed her lips together. "The bandaged face. Angelica?"

"At least now I understand why Brimwell didn't worry about hanging around when she was supposedly in the hospital. I used to think he was a callous guy—leaving town when his wife was having heart surgery."

"Heart condition? Why would she want people to believe that?"

"Sympathy?"

"Or so no one would suspect she could be involved in any crime," Sidney said, tapping her fingertips together. "Angelica also mentioned during her cell phone call that the wrong person had been shot. She knows who the killer is. But I'm sure she won't willingly divulge it." She cocked an eyebrow. "Torture has crossed my mind."

"Bruises, lacerations, a few broken bones? That might work. Give it a shot," Sam said, scratching his chin.

"We've already broken a few laws. Can't break that one."

"Any idea who Angelica was talking to?"

"I suspect Lewis, her butler."

"Huh?" Sam asked, furrowing his brows in confusion.

"Have you seen her butler?"

Sam shook his head. "Nope."

"He's tall, muscular, good-looking."

"So he looks like me," Sam said without a hint of humor on his face.

Sidney smiled. "Sure, Sam, but he's a little younger—late thirties. You two could pass as twins if there wasn't the age difference."

"I guess I'll just have to wait for him to catch up." Sam stretched out his long legs in front of the couch. "If Lewis was the guy on the other end of the line, why didn't she wait until she got home?"

"Apparently another servant is keeping an eye on Angelica. She wants to fire the gal, but Brimwell wouldn't approve."

"She said that to the person on the other end of the line?"

Sidney nodded.

"How many servants do they have?"

"When I was at Brimwell's house, I saw Lewis, and Angelica mentioned what a great cook they had." Sidney grabbed her notepad out of her briefcase. "Let me see if I wrote down her name." She flipped through the pages. "Here it is. Thelma." She laid her notepad on the table and lifted up her mug. "Where did Payton go after he got off work?"

"Home. Maybe when you heard Payton and Victor talking, the thing Victor wanted Payton to do was fire me."

"Could be. Every time I've seen Payton, he always seems like a high-strung, nervous person. Is he always like that?"

"Yep," Sam nodded. "The guy can't seem to relax. It could be whatever is going on, he's in too deep, and he fears the law will catch up with him."

"Let's have a meeting with him tomorrow and see if we can't get him to crack."

"You want me to arrange that?"

"No. A surprise visit would be better. We don't want to give him a chance to prepare. I'm going to search Smorick's den this evening."

"You think your new boyfriend will let you out of his sight that long?" Sam said, referring to Kyle, Smorick's twenty-two-year-old son.

"You busy tonight?"

"No. You want me to hang around Smorick's house?"

"Yeah. If the college kid keeps tabs on me, you can check out the den. We'll have to play it by ear...see how the party goes."

"Anything else you want me to work on today?"

"Several things." Sidney looked through her notepad. "I know you got Judy's phone number when you were out on that date." Sidney noticed Sam rolling his eyes. "Ask her if she can remember the name Brimwell among SLI's customers."

"You thinking those folders were planted?"

"Anything is possible. I'd just like some verification. Also, when you're chatting with Judy, find out if SLI acts as the middle man on purchase and sales transactions like the Brimwell/SLI agreement."

"Yeah, that does seem a little unusual for them. Based on their annual report, the company purchases and sells property, distributing a portion of the profits to their investors, not just one person. But I didn't read the whole report. Guess they could have different types of agreements."

Sidney flipped to the next page in her notepad. "You and Brimwell's secretary, Molly, seem to be great buds. Can you get something from her with Brimwell's signature on it?"

Sam nodded. "If you're planning to compare his signature to the one on the contract, you'll have to get Fowler to come up with an expert that can do that."

"I can get that taken care of. After you've chatted with Judy and Molly, you get to visit a rest home."

Sam's eyes narrowed. "Huh?"

"I was late this morning because I was on the phone with my husband. He had a paralegal do some research on Marsha Eddington, the elderly ninety-year-old who owns the Suburban." Sidney took a folder out of her briefcase and handed it to Sam. "She lives in a rest home in San Diego. The address is in the folder. Hopefully, she still has a clear mind. Find out who approached her about signing the car papers. Along with your other pictures, do you have one of Angelica?"

"Nope. I should probably pay her a visit first. It'll give me a chance to check out my twin," he said with a sly smile.

"You'll need to make an appointment or you won't get through the gate."

"Maybe I'll ask her about her husband's business. If she's trying to hang him, she'll snap at the opportunity to paint a dark cloud over his head."

Sidney's eyebrows bounced. "Good point."

Chapter 36

At the pool hall, Sidney had overheard Cesar telling Miguel there'd been a sports car in front of the house across the street from Aden's the night Mara died. She guessed it was Victor's Porsche. Though she hadn't ruled anyone out yet as the potential perpetrator, he was her prime suspect. Planning to ask Aden's neighbors about the car, Sidney drove up the well-manicured neighborhood and parked close to Aden's driveway.

She headed to the house on the other side of the street and rang the doorbell. The sound of chimes came from inside the house but no movement. Sidney pushed the button again and still no footsteps echoed on the other side of the door. She walked along the path at the side of the house and looked over a locked gate. Not seeing anyone, she went to the next house.

Trudging up the concrete driveway, she heard a dog barking. As a precaution, she slipped her hand in her briefcase, felt the can of mace, and held it in her palm without pulling it out.

She stepped closer to the front door. The dog inside barked louder and faster. Before she had a chance to ring the bell, the door cracked open. A short, heavyset woman squeezed around a growling Doberman Pinscher and nudged her way onto the porch.

"Bart, quiet," the woman said to her pet. The dog ignored her command and continued barking and howling. Aden's neighbor closed the door behind her. "May I help you?"

"I'm an investigator," Sidney said, "doing some follow-up work on the Aden Uzelac case."

The woman briefly closed her eyes and shook her head. "That poor family. All the neighbors liked them. Cute kids. Loving parents. We've talked about them often. No one around here can figure out what went wrong. We had no idea they were having problems. Just goes to show you how sometimes you really don't know your neighbors."

"Mrs.?"

"Mrs. Williams."

"Mrs. Williams. I'm an investigator for Gregory Fowler, Mr. Uzelac's attorney. We don't believe Mr. Uzelac committed the crime."

Williams's mouth fell open, and she squinted. "You don't?"

"No."

"The police talked to all of us. They seemed like they had a solid case. Has something new been discovered?"

Sidney didn't plan on revealing any more to Mrs. Williams than she felt absolutely necessary. "We've gathered some facts, but at this time I'm not at liberty to divulge the information."

"Really?" Mrs. Williams said, lifting an eyebrow. "Why are you here?"

"The night of the shooting someone saw a sports car parked along your street." Sidney nodded toward the road. "Do any of your neighbors own a sports car?"

"No, but Gil, he lives next door," she said, pointing to the house Sidney had just left. "He complained about one blocking part of his driveway when he came home. He went inside to write a note to put on the windshield. When he came out, the car was gone. The wheels of that sports car tore up the edge of his grass along with a couple of sprinkler heads. Gil was pretty mad. When our whole street was lined with police cars, and we were all outside wondering what was going on, Gil asked my husband and a few of the other neighbors if the car belonged to one of our visitors."

"What's Gil's last name?" Sidney asked, holding her pen above her notepad.

"Kender."

Sidney wrote down the name. "Do you know what type of sports car it was?"

Williams nodded. "A red Corvette."

Feeling disappointed it wasn't a white Porsche like Victor's car,

Sidney asked, "Do you remember anything else unusual about that night?"

"No. Ralph, my husband, claims he heard the gunshot. The police asked us about it. Ralph thought it came from the direction of Aden's house, but he wasn't sure."

Sidney had to find the owner of the Corvette. That person might have heard or seen something, maybe even been involved in the crime. "Do you know if anyone mentioned the Corvette to the police?"

"We didn't. Gil might have."

"Does Gil live alone?"

"No, but his wife is gone a lot on business trips."

"Do you know about what time he gets home from work?"

"Around three."

"Thank you for your time." Sidney turned to leave.

"I sure hope you're right about Aden," Williams said. "He was always such a good neighbor."

Sidney climbed into her car, looked at her watch and saw it was almost two. She decided to wait for Gil, the neighbor, to get home. Recalling Cesar saying he heard someone running through the bushes, she wanted to determine if it was possible that the runner could have made the sprint unseen. She also wanted to check out the crime scene again. Sidney retrieved a pair of latex gloves from the trunk of her car and then strolled toward Aden's back yard while her eyes swept over the foliage. Noticing the ends of some of the limbs had been snapped off, she stepped between two bushes for a closer examination. The bare bark had turned a yellowish-brown, indicating they weren't fresh breaks. From where she stood, she was only partially visible from the driveway. Sidney surmised that in the dark she would be completely hidden from any vehicle pulling into Aden's driveway. She swung around and made her way to the road by following the path laid out by the severed twigs. Standing at the edge of the asphalt, she was even with the driveway that belonged to Gil Kender across the street. She headed to the other side of the pavement and knelt down to inspect the front of Kender's lawn where the Corvette had been spotted the night of Mara's murder. The green grass was perfect. No sign of any indentation remained. Two sprinkler heads appeared newer than the others.

Just as Sidney rose to her feet, a dark blue Jaguar swung onto the driveway. A middle-aged, husky man climbed out of the vehicle. "Can I help you with something?" he asked, gazing at Sidney.

She walked closer to him. "I'm doing some follow-up investigation on the Aden Uzelac case."

"You a cop?"

"No. I work for Mr. Uzelac's lawyer."

"I like the guy. Any chance he might get off?"

"We're trying to prove that he's innocent."

"Tell you the truth, I never thought he plugged his wife. Don't believe anything I've read in the papers. So what can I do for you?"

"The night of the shooting, I understand a red Corvette was parked in front of your house."

"Yeah. Tore up the edge of my lawn along with two sprinkler heads. Part of that red monster stuck into my driveway. I had to maneuver my car to get around it. Whoever was driving that beast was a real jerk. Went in the house to write a note. When I came out, the Corvette was speeding away. What a creep."

"Can you recall about what time that was?"

"Yep. Looked at the clock in my kitchen when I wrote the note. Exactly 8:34 p.m. That must've been when the jerk climbed into his car. Shortly after, sirens came racing this way. Two police cruisers and an ambulance stopped in front of Aden's house. Neighbors poured out of their doors. Asked all of them if they knew who owned the Corvette. No one did."

"Did you mention the Corvette to the police?"

"Sure did. The detective that came around asking questions...I told him about it. He wrote something down."

Sidney had read over the case files and wondered why the sports car wasn't included in any of the police reports. "Was there anything odd about the Corvette—a dent, a sticker on the bumper, something hanging from the rearview mirror?"

Gil shook his head. "Nothing like that, but I got part of the license plate number as it raced away."

"Can you give it to me?"

"Yep. Got it inside." He spun around on his heels and headed into his house. A minute later, he returned with a sheet of paper. "Here," he said, handing it to Sidney.

She reached into her briefcase for a pen and notepad. "Let me write it down."

"No need. Keep that. I wrote it down a few times in case I see that red beast. In fact, when I see one in a parking lot or on the street, I look to see if it has a California plate that begins with 5FM," he said, pointing to the paper he had given Sidney.

She glanced at Gil's note: 5FM and a 6. "Do you know where the six is placed in the number?"

"It's either the third or second number from the end. I'm missing the alpha after the M and two numbers."

She held up the sheet. "Did you give a copy of this to the detective?"

Gil nodded. "Don't know if he tried to find the owner."

"The night Mrs. Uzelac died, did you hear a gunshot or see Mr. Uzelac being dropped off?"

"A taxi turned into his driveway when I went inside, you know, to write the note to put on the Corvette's windshield." He tapped his fingertips on the side of his face. "I'm deaf in one ear and wear a hearing aid in the other. It was making a squealing sound. Took it out…changed batteries. Never heard a gunshot. Can't hear anything when I'm changing batteries."

"Thanks for the number. Will you give me a call if you spot the Corvette anywhere?" She handed him a plain, white business card with only her name and phone number on it.

"Yeah," he said, studying the card. "Aden's a nice fella. Sure hope you can get him out of the joint."

"So do I."

Chapter 37

When Sidney was getting ready for her date with Kyle, Sam called. "Hey. Anything new?"

"Yep," he said. "Mrs. Eddington, the old lady at the rest home, happens to be Victor Grenshaw's aunt. Nothing like keeping it close to home."

"Strange. That didn't show up in the research my husband's paralegal did."

"Well, technically, she's not his aunt—just plays that role."

"Huh?"

"The woman shared an apartment with Victor's aunt. His aunt died. Mrs. Eddington moved into the rest home. Somewhere along the line, he started calling her an aunt and she calls him a nephew."

"She told you all that."

"Nope. Got it from one of the staff."

Sidney figured Sam must have turned on his charm again since that was a lot of information to divulge about the woman. "Getting back to the 'aunt,' did she know she owned a car?"

"Nope. Can't remember signing anything."

"Was it her signature on the title?"

"Yep. She seems confused. Wants to see her car."

"She'll have to ask Victor for a ride."

"Not likely. Can't remember his name. Doubt she'll remember about the car tomorrow."

"Dementia?"

"That's the diagnosis."

"Too bad. Did she recognize his picture?"

"Not at first. Three of the pictures seemed familiar to her. If it weren't for the staff member narrowing it down, going to the rest home wouldn't have been a productive trip."

"Mrs. Eddington most likely didn't have the capacity to enter into a contract. Putting that issue aside, she only purchased a car. That's not illegal."

"Coercion? Victor? Someone used that vehicle to get around, spy on us, and bug and break into my office," Sam said in a raised tone.

"Besides Victor being the woman's unrelated nephew, do you have any proof he was connected to the break-in or to the guys who drove that car?"

Sam took a deep breath and slowly exhaled. "Good point."

"Did you get to visit with Angelica?"

"Yeah. She painted Brimwell as a wonderful man...loving husband. Not what I expected."

"Clever girl," Sidney commented. "She's not going to let the cat out of the bag. Did you see the butler?"

"Yep. Caught him eyeing Angelica several times during the twenty minutes I was there, but he knows how to play the role—formal, polite, and no emotion showing on his face."

"Did you get a chance to see Thelma?"

"No, but I've managed to get her cell phone number."

"How did you pull that off?"

"Connections. Brimwells only have two full-time servants— Thelma and Lewis. Lewis has only been with them for about eighteen months."

"What happened to the prior butler?"

"Sergio Brennon. He quit. He'd been with Brimwell for over twenty years. I'm in the process of tracking him down."

"Do you know Lewis's last name?"

"Watford. Got someone checking where he worked before he joined the Brimwell household. What time do you want me at Smorick's house?"

"Seven."

Sidney expertly applied makeup and fixed her hair to make herself look ten years younger. Then she squeezed into a pair of tight black jeans, slipped a three-quarter-sleeve white peasant blouse over her head, and strapped on a pair of four-inch platform heels.

As she strolled out of her bedroom, Jean looked up from her knitting, smiled, and said, "High school or college?"

"College." Sidney grinned. "But don't worry. I haven't registered for any classes yet."

"Yet?"

"Well, if I don't solve this case soon, I want options on the table."

"In that outfit, you're going to turn the head of every college guy...and those older."

"That's the plan." She grabbed her oversized purse and slung it over her shoulder.

Sidney parked a block from SLI and leisurely walked to the office, stopping occasionally and glancing around, searching for cars or people who might be tailing her. After listening to Angelica's conversation the night before, she didn't want to take a chance of having anyone follow her to Smorick's. Satisfied, she opened SLI's door.

Kyle eyed her, an anxious expression on his face even though she was only five minutes late. "Hey," he said, walking toward her. "Did you take the bus to get here?"

"No. I walked. My mom only lives a few blocks away."

"That's right. I remember you saying that." He locked the front door. "My car's out back." He set the alarm. It slowly peeped while he guided her through the hallway and out the back door. After checking to make sure that door was securely locked, he led her to a new, shiny, yellow Mustang.

"Nice car," Sidney said, climbing into the passenger seat.

Kyle started the engine. "Got it last year for my birthday."

While they drove, Kyle talked about the other cars he had owned. The Mustang was his fourth car. Sidney doubted Kyle had bought any of them.

Kyle turned onto a street in an upper-class neighborhood. Cars lined both sides of the pavement near the Smorick house. Sidney scanned the area, searching for Sam's truck. It was nowhere in sight, but she knew he wouldn't park in a place where it could be easily spotted.

Taking Sidney's hand, Kyle headed to the walkway that ran along the side of the house. The sounds of laughter, chit-chatting, and music flowed from the back yard.

Sidney looked at the people milling around the swimming pool and immediately understood why Kyle wanted a date. The average age of the guests was somewhere between fifty and fifty-five. Kyle was by far the youngest one there. "Do you have any siblings?"

"A sister. She's in Oregon visiting a friend." Kyle moved through the crowd, still clutching Sidney's hand. He stopped behind a slender, petite woman with short, brown hair. "Mom." The woman turned around. "Mom, this is Diana."

Mrs. Smorick's eyes glowed. She placed her hand on Sidney's arm. "Diana, I'm so happy we finally get to meet. Kyle has told me so many nice things about you."

"I'm glad he invited me," Sidney said, beaming at Kyle and wondering what he could have possibly told his mother about her.

"You kids planning to jump in the pool?" Mrs. Smorick said, glancing at Sidney's oversized bag.

"No, Mom."

"Well, then, take Diana in the house and find her someplace where she can put her purse. I'm sure she doesn't want to haul it around all evening."

As Kyle led Sidney to the patio door, Mr. Smorick stepped out of the house. "Dad, this is Diana."

Smorick patted his son's shoulder as she felt him studying her closely. "Hello, Diana. Kyle mentioned you'd like to work for SLI."

She gave him a pleasant smile, her eyes sparkling. "Oh, I would."

"Come see me next week. I'm sure we can work something out."

"Oh, thank you, Mr. Smorick."

A short, plump, bald man walked toward them. "Randolph."

"Stan," Smorick said, turning his attention to the bald man and holding his hand out to shake.

Kyle and Sidney headed through the patio doorway into a large family room. On one side, a large television hung from the wall with a sectional couch and low table in front of the screen. A bar lined with stools and a pool table stood on the other side of the room. A few guests occupied the space. Some were seated on the couch and a couple leaned against the bar chatting away.

"What would you like to drink?" Kyle asked, scooting around the bar.

"A beer," Sidney said, recalling that was her beverage of choice when she was in college. She watched Kyle pull two bottles out of a fridge, screw off the caps, and hand her one.

"Hey, thanks for talking to your dad about hiring me."

"No problem. Drop your purse anywhere in here. It'll be safe. Mom and Dad don't have friends that snatch things."

"Before I dump it, can I use your bathroom?"

"Down the hall." Kyle gestured with his hand toward an opening in the far wall. "Second door on the right. If it's occupied, go farther down the hall and you'll run into another one."

Sidney placed her beer bottle on the bar and headed into the hallway. She noticed a double door with one door ajar. After glancing over her shoulder, she peeked into the room. It was the den. She ducked inside and nudged the door with her elbow, leaving it just slightly open—not wide enough for anyone to look inside but large enough where she could hear anyone approaching. As she intensely listened for footsteps, she crept to the window, grabbed the bottom of her blouse, and wrapped her hand in it. Using her covered hand, Sidney unlatched the double-paned windows.

With that task completed, she checked out the room. Behind a modern, oak desk, a built-in credenza ran the length of the wall. A light tan leather couch with short, chrome legs stood by the opposite wall. Next to it, a blue upholstered wingback chair and a hassock filled that corner of the room.

Sidney moved closer to the credenza and had the urge to start searching the drawers for Payton's contract when she heard heavy footsteps pounding against the tile floor and men chatting.

She rushed to the wingback chair and crouched down behind it just as the den door flew open.

"Here it is," a man with a deep voice said. "No matter how hard I try, I keep forgetting it everywhere."

"Know what you mean, Milt," another man said. "Left mine in the club's restroom. Nearly had a heart attack until I found it."

"All my numbers, appointments...," the deep-voiced man began, and then his voice trailed off as the two men wandered back into the hallway.

Sidney peered around the edge of the chair to make sure the coast was clear before she stood. The men had left the door wide open. With her feet barely making any noise, she scurried out of the room and came face-to-face with a sixty-year-old, gray-haired woman searching for the bathroom. "It's the second door to the right," Sidney said, pointing down the hallway.

After Sidney saw the woman enter the bathroom, she closed the den door and hurried to the other bathroom farther down the hall. She locked the door, dug out her cell phone, and called Sam. "I'm not going to be able to get into Smorick's credenza without being missed."

"Do you know where his den is in the house?" Sam asked.

"The first room east of the front door. I might be able to keep a lookout from the hallway, but I'm not sure. I've unlatched the two windows that lead to the front yard. The interior door can be locked."

"I'll lock it when I get inside. Any security system that I need to worry about?"

"Not sure, but with this place swarming with guests, I suspect everything is turned off. Oh, on second thought, maybe you shouldn't lock the door. I wasn't able to check out the wiring. That could activate an alarm system in the room."

"I'll work on some other way to secure the door."

"Call when you're finished." Sidney disconnected and stuck her cell phone in her pant pocket. She straightened her hair, applied more lipstick, and then went back to her date.

Kyle was playing pool with one of the male guests, an average-sized man with a round face in his mid-forties. "Did you have a problem finding it?" he asked her.

"No, but I couldn't find my lipstick in here," she said, motioning toward her large handbag.

"That's understandable," the round-faced man said.

"Walt, this is Diana. Diana, Walt," Kyle said, lining up his cue stick for his next shot.

"Glad to meet you," Walt said, giving Sidney a smile.

Returning the smile, she wondered how much the round-faced man knew about Smorick and SLI. *Does he know about the illegal part of the business?* While the two guys finished the game, she mulled over how many of the guests were in Smorick's inner circle and either knew or suspected the illegal transactions.

Kyle won the game. Walt went to join the other guests outside.

"Boy, you're good," Sidney said.

"You play pool?" Kyle asked.

She nodded. "Yeah."

"Want to play? Or eat?"

She moved closer to Kyle. "A lot of strangers make me feel self-conscious," she said in a voice just above a whisper. "Could we eat in here and then have a game?"

"Sure." He cocked his brow. "Most of my parents' friends are pretty boring. I figured we'd hang around in here anyway. Last time they had one of their parties, a couple of my buddies came. We swam. It seemed like every single one of their friends sat around the pool staring at us. We couldn't even talk without being overheard. Anyway, food. There's ribs, hamburgers, and chicken. Do you want me to get you something, or do you want to go with me?"

"Would you mind getting me a hamburger?"

"All the trimmings?"

"All, except for onions."

While Kyle was getting the food, Sidney grabbed a pool stick, practiced a few shots, and kept an eye on the entrance to the hallway. Each time someone went that direction, she picked up the blue chalk and ran it over the tip of the stick as she inched closer to the hallway with her ears on full alert.

An idea snapped into her head. She rushed to the other side of the bar, took a glass off of the shelf, and poured her beer into it.

"You don't like drinking out of a bottle?" Kyle said, carrying two plates, each filled with a hamburger and a stack of fries.

"I like glasses better." She glanced at the plates. "Fries?"

"Yeah. Dad doesn't think a hamburger tastes right without fries, so he had a fryer installed next to the barbeque pit."

Sidney came around the bar, sat on the bar stool next to Kyle, and picked up a fry and took a bite. "Mmm. Good. I think your dad's right."

When they finished eating, Kyle racked the balls as Sidney anxiously waited for her phone to vibrate. Glancing out the patio door, she noticed that most of the guests were through eating, and their plates were being gathered by a woman dressed in a black dress with a white apron over it. It appeared that the Smoricks had hired help for the party.

While she struck the cue ball, out of the corner of her eye, she saw Smorick and Walt walking toward the patio door. Her striped ball rolled into the pocket. She quickly lined up another shot and deliberately missed.

"You can't rush it," Kyle said, stepping up to the pool table.

Smorick and Walt strolled through the game room. Sidney picked up her glass, backed into Smorick, and spilled the beer on his pant leg with some of it splattering on her jeans. She gasped. "Geez, Mr. Smorick, I'm sorry," she said, her voice quivering. Playing the role of an upset college student, she plastered a petrified expression on her face, swallowed hard and took a deep breath.

"Diana, it's okay," Smorick said in a soft tone. Sidney was surprised that his voice lacked any trace of irritation. "It will just take me a minute to change." His eyes dropped to her jeans. "But I'm afraid we don't have any extra jeans in the house your size."

Her hand brushed her pant leg. "It's only a few drops. They'll dry soon."

"Walt, I'll be right back," Smorick said, and then he headed to the hallway.

"Who's winning?" Walt asked.

"He is," Sidney said, fidgeting with her hands.

"Hey, you need another beer," Kyle said, taking Sidney's empty glass.

"Thanks. Mind if I sit out the rest of the game?" She slid onto a bar stool.

"No." Kyle placed a filled glass on the bar in front of Sidney. "You okay?"

"Yeah. Just a little worried about your dad. He won't hate me for ruining his pants, will he?"

"Nah. No big deal. He's cool." His attention turned to Walt, "You wanna play?"

"I'll rack 'em," Walt said, picking up the wooden rack.

As Walt sank the first ball, Sidney's cell phone vibrated. She plucked it out of her pocket, glanced at the screen, and smiled to herself when she saw the caller was Sam. Sidney turned it off and slipped it back into her pocket.

Shortly after 11 p.m., Kyle drove Sidney back to the SLI building. "You sure you don't want me to take you to your mom's place?"

"No. I can guarantee you she'll be peering out the window, watching for me to come home. Then she'll ask questions like she always does. It's better if she doesn't know I had a date."

"Okay," he said with a tinge of disappointment in his tone. They both got out of the Mustang. He looped around the hood of the car and stood by her.

"Thanks for this evening. I really had a good time. Do you think your dad will still hire me after I drenched him in beer?"

"Yeah. A little beer doesn't bother him."

"A little?" she asked, tilting her head and wrinkling her nose.

Kyle put his arm around her shoulder and attempted to pull her closer. She raised her hands, preventing him from hugging her. "Kyle, I really like you, but I just broke up with my boyfriend. I'm not ready for this yet."

He dropped his hands to his side. "Got it. See you Monday." He moved around the Mustang and climbed into the driver's seat.

"See ya," Sidney said, though she never planned on seeing him again.

She waved to Kyle and watched him drive away and then checked her phone messages. Clicking on the icon, there were two text messages from Sam and four voice messages—one from Chas and three from Bernice. With her cell phone pressed against her ear, she walked along the deserted sidewalk toward her car and listened. Bernice's messages were all the same. "I need to talk to you. Give me a call."

Chas's message was a follow-up to Bernice's. "Babe, Bernice has been trying to reach you. She sounds like it's urgent. I suspect you're still on your date," he said with a slight chuckle. "Call me when you get back to the hotel, even if it's the wee hours in the morning New York time."

Sidney smiled and put away the phone, thinking of all the times she had called Chas in the wee hours of the morning since there was a three-hour time difference. She reached the intersection where her Lexus was parked around the corner. Turning to go down that street, she heard and saw a group of five rowdy young men outside an apartment complex entrance.

"Hey, baby, wanna party?" one yelled, strutting toward her.

Chapter 38

After playing the role of a college kid all evening, Sidney felt completely drained and longed to stretch out in her bed. Running into a group of hooligans who had downed too much beer certainly wasn't anything she wanted to deal with. She doubted she could make it to her car without having some type of confrontation.

Listening to the guys hooting and making lewd remarks about her, she continued at a brisk pace toward her Lexus, which was parked a building away from them.

Two of them were only a few feet away from her when Sam's truck barreled up the street. He slammed on his brakes. Tires squealed and skidded into the gutter next to Sidney.

Sam pushed the passenger door open. She jumped into the seat and pulled the door shut.

The men stopped in their tracks as Sam plowed out of his parking spot and executed a right turn at the intersection. "It's Friday night," he said, giving her a quick glance. "A party night. Bound to run into punks like that with booze filling their bellies."

"I could've handled those two, even though I didn't feel like taking them on. Thanks for coming to my rescue. Did you have any problem getting into Smorick's den?"

"Nope. With all the cars parked out front, it was easy to come and go, completely hidden from anyone driving along the street." He briefly looked at her. "How was your date?"

"Great. It won't be long before Kyle and I will be going steady."

"Tell him you were married?"

"Never came up. Find the contracts?"

"Yep. I have pictures of page four, the contract page we were missing, along with handwritten notes that were in each file. The contract only mentions consulting. The notes spell it out." Sam moved over to the side of the road and parked. "Payton was paid twice by SLI for giving locations for two bridge sites—one in Argentina and another in Mexico. He didn't get paid for the Brazil site because he gave SLI the wrong location. SLI lost money on the deal. They had purchased some of the land before they realized it was the wrong site."

"Did they purchase the land before or after the Brimwell contract?"

"After."

"SLI should've figured that Brimwell's contract was for the land parcels applicable to the bridge site."

"Someone didn't put two-and-two together. Otherwise, they never would've started buying up the land based on Payton's information." Sam pulled his cigarette package out of his shirt pocket. "Mind?" he asked, holding it up.

The inside of Sam's truck already reeked of stale cigarette smoke. "Not if you roll down your window and blow the smoke outside."

"Got it." He lit a cigarette, took a long drag, and exhaled out of his open window. "I talked to Judy. She recalled a customer named Brimwell and seeing his name on Smorick's appointment schedule. Brimwell never personally came to any of the appointments. He sent a representative—a tall, good-looking fellow with a short-clipped beard."

"Victor?"

"That's who I'm thinking. I texted Judy the picture. She hasn't gotten back to me yet. She said that SLI does transactions like the one described in the Brimwell contract. They have the know-how on acquiring and selling property in various countries. The customer has to put down a large deposit up front. SLI's fee starts at twenty percent. Then it depends on how the title is held. If it's in SLI's name or one of their subsidiaries, they also receive twenty-five percent of the resale profit."

"That's a money maker." Sidney rubbed her forehead. "Subsidiaries?"

"Yeah. Don't recall seeing them mentioned in the annual report I thumbed through at the SLI office. Never got the names. Do you think we need them?"

"Doubt it. But whenever I think I know what's going on, another twist pops up."

"Well, if we run into a company name we don't recognize, I'll check with Judy." Sam took another deep drag on his cigarette.

Sidney drummed her fingers on the passenger door armrest. "Boy, I can't remember the initial dollar amount in the Brimwell contract. Can you?"

"After I chatted with Judy, I looked it up. Four-hundred-thousand bucks."

"Let's say the man claiming to be Brimwell's representative was Victor. Where would he come up with that much money?"

"Angelica?"

"Siphoning off so much of Brimwell's liquid assets could send up a red flag." A thought popped into Sidney's head. "Deidre?"

"You saw her financial statements at Victor's. That would explain why he's still dating Mara's best friend."

"I looked at some of the parcels in SLI's purchase contracts and found a resale match with an appreciable higher price. Shouldn't whoever put up the money have received at least part of it back by now?"

"I did the same thing with the purchase and resale contracts you sent me, but there were a few parcels that didn't have a match. SLI probably hasn't resold all of them yet. The Brimwell contract settlement date is either when all the parcels have been sold or six months after its execution, whichever comes first."

"What happens if all of the parcels haven't been resold by then?"

"The title to those parcels will go to a person designated by Brimwell. Also, I laid out the map with all the parcels stated in Brimwell's contract and checked them against the parcels SLI had purchased. There are a few gaps. It doesn't look like SLI has acquired all the parcels."

"Maybe some people wouldn't sell. I need to read that contract again. But the bottom line is that Brimwell's representative hasn't received any of the money back yet. Right?"

"That's how it reads."

"I'll work on trying to find out if Deidre made a significant withdrawal out of an account around…what's the contract date?"

"March twenty-second."

Sidney squinted. "March twenty-second? That was before Aden returned from Brazil. I wonder if that's important."

"Could be. It depends if Aden…" Sam was interrupted by the chirping of Sidney's phone and watched her take it out of her purse. "…talked to Brimwell about the sites while he was there."

She looked at the caller ID and saw Bernice's name. "This woman has been trying to reach me all evening. She's in a different time zone. I better take it."

"Go ahead." Sam lifted another cigarette out of his package and lit it.

"Hey," Sidney answered. "What's up?"

"Didn't you get any of my messages?" Bernice asked, sounding annoyed.

"I did, but I'm on the road right now. Can I call you in about an hour?"

"It's three in the morning here. I need some sleep. I'll make it quick."

"Okay."

"Mara messed up my late appointment last night. At first I tried to ignore her, but the images she kept throwing at me made it impossible. I had to reschedule my appointment. Even that was almost impossible as the visions kept bouncing around in the room. Some were only fragments. I called my psychic friend, Trudy, to see if she could help me figure it out. Remember me telling you about her?"

"Yeah."

"Trudy sensed Mara's spirit hovering around my living room when she stepped through the front door. She managed to communicate a little with Mara and got more complete pictures. We both got the images of a woman being held under water, another woman trapped under some scaffolding or something like that, and a bandaged face, like I got before. Trudy also got a male figure lying in a bed under covers, men storming through a door, a pistol with the name 'Browning' on it, and she heard gunshots." Bernice sighed. "Finally, my head isn't pounding anymore."

"What does it all mean?"

"I think the visions I saw have already happened. The additional ones Trudy put together haven't happened yet. Her intuition is telling her that someone is planning to kill a man with a Browning pistol while he's sleeping."

"Any idea when this is supposed to happen?" Sidney asked, mulling over who the intended victim might be.

"No, but it's probably soon since Mara wouldn't give me any peace until I told you about the images."

"Let me know if you hear from her again."

"I can't avoid it. Now, maybe I can get some sleep," Bernice said, yawning.

Sidney clicked off, dropped the phone into her purse, and then scribbled a note about the images.

"Your medium?" Sam asked, raising a brow.

She nodded and said, "Where were we?"

"Talking about the date on Brimwell's contract."

"We know Payton was in Brazil with Aden. He would've known how things were going." Sidney shrugged her shoulders. "I guess it's time for me to visit Aden again," she said, already dreading it. Sidney loved her husband but couldn't stop the desire for Aden that surged through her body whenever she saw him. Just having that sensation made her feel like she was being unfaithful to Chas.

"I also chatted with Molly," Sam said, leaning back in the driver's seat and resting his hands on the steering wheel. "She emailed me a document with Brimwell's signature on it. I'll text it to you. Will that work to compare the signatures?"

She bobbed her head. "I noticed two text messages from you. What's in the other one?"

"Page four of Payton's contract."

Sidney cupped her face in her hands and briefly closed her eyes. "I feel beat. Can you take me to my car?"

"Yep." Sam turned the key in the ignition and pushed on the accelerator. He merged into the traffic. "If it weren't for Judy hearing Smorick say that a woman died because of a bridge site, we probably wouldn't even be looking at the people who work for SLI. The Brimwell contract was filed with their other contracts. No effort to conceal it."

"Everyone I talked to at the party was very pleasant. Smorick seems like a real good family man. The company is obviously involved with some illegal transactions, but I'm having a hard time seeing how they might have played a role in Mara's death."

"Maybe we'll discover something when we quiz Payton." Sam eased into a parking spot behind Sidney's Lexus. "They're still there," he said, motioning toward the hooligans hanging out in front of the apartment building. "A couple of ladies have joined them."

Sidney looked at the two women dressed in short, tight skirts, sleeveless tops, and spiked heels. They were laughing and flirting with the guys. "With those gals keeping them occupied, they won't pay any attention to me."

"Don't count on it. Hey, you want to meet me downtown tomorrow morning to have coffee with Thelma?"

"Thelma? Brimwell's cook?"

"Yeah. Called her right after I visited Smorick's den. I suspect someone was listening in on her conversation. She kept calling me by another name—Warren. Sound familiar?"

Sidney shook her head. "No. It could be someone she talks to often or just a made-up name to throw off the eavesdropper."

"Thelma seemed anxious to talk about the Brimwell household. She has a dentist appointment tomorrow at eight. Wants to meet in the medical building's coffee shop around eight forty-five. Figures she'll be through by then."

"I wonder who'll be making breakfast for the Brimwells?"

"Lewis?"

"Doubt it."

"Maybe they have to fend for themselves when she's gone. I left a message on Sergio Brennon's, the prior butler's, answering machine. Haven't heard from him yet."

"Thelma can probably fill us in on why Brennon left."

Chapter 39

Sidney parked in the medical building parking terrace and headed inside. As she walked through the foyer, she saw Sam, looking a little groggy, near the coffee shop entrance. "Rough night?"

A faint smile crossed his lips. "Rough? Naw."

They strolled into the seat-yourself place with windows lining half of one wall. A long counter stood on the other side, and tables were scattered around in front of it. They selected one near the back of the room, away from the door and windows. They didn't want to take a chance their interviewee would make a mad dash for the door if they pried too deeply.

A waitress, carrying a coffee pot and two menus, hurried over to their table. "Coffee?" she asked.

"Yes," Sidney and Sam replied in unison.

"Any idea what Thelma looks like?" Sidney said, stirring sugar into her cup.

Sam shook his head. "Glad there aren't many folks in here. She may be nervous. Don't want to scare her off before she even gets started. Told her I'd probably be coming with a colleague. No other table has two people at it. Thelma's been with Brimwell for over twenty years. Suspect she's middle-aged. Perhaps a little chunky from being around food all day." His eyes moved to the entrance.

Inside the doorway, a woman in her late fifties stood with her head moving back and forth, as if she were searching for someone. She wore a loose-fitting, cotton dress and had thick chestnut-brown hair highlighted with gray streaks.

"That's probably our gal." Sam rose to his feet and walked toward the middle-aged woman. He greeted Thelma and escorted her back to the table. After introducing her to Sidney, he motioned toward the waitress and ordered Thelma a cup of coffee along with a toasted bagel.

They chatted about the weather until the food arrived. Then, Sam started in on the questions without wasting any time. "Just for background, how long have you worked for the Brimwells?"

"Are you recording this?" Thelma asked, her brow wrinkling and her gaze sweeping around the room.

"No," Sam replied, squinting. "Why?"

"I just wanted to be sure. That's how Sergio was forced to quit."

"What was recorded?" Sidney wanted to know.

"Well," Thelma said hesitantly. "It's not my place to say. Sergio might tell you. Do you have his number?"

"No," Sidney said, though she knew Sam had it, but she didn't know how he had acquired it. She lifted up her pen and scribbled down the number as Thelma rattled it off. "Did he give his notice to Mrs. Brimwell or Mr. Brimwell?"

"Angelica. She recorded Sergio. Mr. Brimwell was out of town." Thelma looked at Sam and narrowed her eyes. "You told me you wanted to talk about the Brimwells. Is it about Sergio instead?"

Sam shook his head. "No."

"Is there something I should know about?"

"We're investigators looking into the murder of Mara Uzelac," Sam explained.

"That poor family. Marcus, I mean Mr. Brimwell, is real worried about Mr. Uzelac. You know, he works for Mr. Brimwell."

"Yes, we know," Sam said. "Mrs. Brimwell isn't concerned about Mr. Uzelac?"

Thelma stared at the table and shook her head. "That woman only worries about herself. She knows the right way to act around people. You'd be amazed at the things she says when she doesn't think anyone is listening."

Sidney put down her coffee cup. "Like what?"

"After sweet Mara visited her, she laughed with Lewis. Saying things like how dumb and gullible Mara was since she fell for Angelica's story about her heart condition. Once Lewis made a big mistake by saying how gorgeous Mara was. Angelica tore into him and said something like that's what plastic surgery can do for a simple gal. Mara was naturally beautiful. She didn't need that. Not like Angelica. She's had everything tucked, tightened, and lifted. You probably can't find any part of that woman's body she hasn't had fixed."

Sam tented his fingers. "Was her plastic surgery the reason she stopped traveling with Mr. Brimwell?"

"No. Marcus, aaah, Mr. Brimwell..." Thelma began.

Sam leaned toward Thelma and patted her forearm. "You're not at work. It's okay to call Mr. Brimwell Marcus in front of us."

She smiled. "That's what I call him when we don't have company. Angelica got mad about it, but Marcus set her straight. About two years ago, when Angelica was having a facelift..."

Sidney suddenly felt a poke in her shoulder and turned that direction. No one was there.

Thelma went on. "Marcus discovered she was having an affair." She shook her head. "The guy sent her flowers after her surgery."

"Stupid," Sidney scoffed while the image Mara had sent to Bernice of a bandaged face lingered in her head. Without dwelling on it any further, the shoulder nudge had convinced her it represented Angelica.

"Not really. You see, Angelica had told the guy she was separated from Marcus."

Sam waited for the waitress to fill their coffee cups and then said, "Know who the guy was?"

"Philip something. Angelica doesn't see him anymore. She's had a lot of affairs—several before Philip. I wanted to tell Marcus about them, but it wasn't my place."

"So the Philip affair is the reason Brimwell no longer has his wife accompany him on trips?" Sidney asked.

Thelma nodded.

Sidney continued. "I've been led to believe that Mr. Brimwell has an eye for the ladies. Is that true?"

"That sounds like Marcus has a lot of women in his life. That's not true. There's only one. Well...besides Angelica. He used to be a faithful husband until two years ago. He never cheated on Jacqueline, his first wife." Her eyes drooped, and a sad expression crept across her face. "If only I hadn't gone to visit my brother that day, Jacqueline would probably still be alive. I still think about her often.

She was a great swimmer. I can't figure out how she drowned in that swimming pool."

Sidney wanted to ask Thelma why she thought it would have made a difference if she'd been there. *Did she sit by the pool when Jacqueline swam?* As she began to open her mouth, another one of Bernice's visions flashed into her mind—a woman being held under water. "How long ago was that?"

"Nine years."

Sidney jotted down a note. "Did Mr. Brimwell know Angelica before Jacqueline died?"

Thelma glared at Sidney, her eyes boring into Sidney's. "You're not suggesting that Marcus had anything to do with Jacqueline's death? I can guarantee you he didn't," she snapped, her voice an octave higher. "He went to pieces. He visits her grave at least once a month."

"No. No. I wasn't thinking about Mr. Brimwell. I was wondering about Angelica."

Thelma's eyes popped wide open. "Angelica?" She pressed her lips together and tilted her head. "They were members of the same fitness club and became friends. Angelica had been to the house a few times with her husband."

"Husband?" Sidney asked. "Angelica was married when Jacqueline died?"

"Yes, but not for long. She married Marcus five months later. Marcus was real lonely. Angelica took advantage of that. She came to see him almost every evening. Brought cute little presents. Took him to dinner," Thelma said in a sarcastic tone.

"Her husband go along with them to dinner?" Sam asked.

Thelma shook her head. "No. They separated a few weeks after Jacqueline died. That woman wanted Marcus. She wasn't about ready to let a husband stand in her way."

Sidney wondered if Thelma had feelings for Brimwell and that was clouding her view of Angelica and making her seem more callous than she actually was. "Thelma, are you married?"

"I have been. My husband died in Vietnam. He left me with a beautiful daughter. Now I have two grandchildren." Her face glowed with pride. "If you want to know if I have a special man in my life, I do. Sergio. So you see it was just as hard on me as it was on Sergio when he had to quit. Our time together is now limited to a couple of nights a week, but that isn't the reason I wanted to talk about the Brimwells. It's because I fear for Marcus's life."

Sidney and Sam gaped at each other. "What?" Sidney said, crinkling her eyes.

"I think Angelica is planning to kill Marcus. I've tried to talk to him about it, but he's not buying it. He doesn't believe she's capable of being that vicious."

"Why do you believe he's in danger?" Sidney asked.

"From overhearing Angelica on the phone. She knows who killed Mara. It wasn't Aden. But I don't have any evidence or anything I can take to the police. It would come down to her word against mine."

"Did you hear who it was?" Sidney asked.

Thelma shook her head. "No. She had someone plant one of Marcus's guns in a safe." She paused and rubbed her hands together. "The police can't find the gun used by Mara's killer. Maybe it's Marcus's. The police talked to him recently about the case, but he's pretty closed mouth about it. I don't understand why."

Sidney wondered when the police would release that information to the public since Marcus's gun was indeed the murder weapon. Yet, since Fowler had told her that confidentially, she couldn't divulge it to Thelma.

Sam scratched his chin. "Even if Angelica knows who murdered Mara...doesn't mean she's going to gun down Brimwell."

"Well...one day I heard her talking to Lewis, her lover, the guy who took Sergio's job. She told him it wouldn't be long before they didn't need to worry about Marcus. They'd have the whole house to themselves and wouldn't have to sneak around."

"Maybe she wants to divorce him, and she thinks she'll get the house in the settlement," Sam said.

"Not a chance," Thelma said. "Marcus and Angelica have a prenup. The only way she'd ever get that house is over his dead body. And Marcus is going to divorce *her*. Not the other way around."

"Has Marcus filed for divorce?" Sam sounded dubious.

"Not yet. He won't until after the Aden trial. You see, some of his employees will be testifying, and he doesn't want to deal with anything else right now. He no longer sleeps in the same bedroom with Angelica."

"He doesn't?" Sidney wanted to acquire more information from

Thelma.

"No. Marcus moved out of that room a couple of months ago. Angelica acts like they're going to patch up their relationship, being extra nice to him and trying to cuddle when they're watching television…stuff like that."

"Since he continued to sleep with her after he discovered the affair, do you know why he stopped?" Sidney asked.

Thelma shook her head. "No. I'm curious, but that isn't the sort of question you would ask your boss."

"You mentioned there was another woman in Mr. Brimwell's life."

"Yes. Elizabeth Heller. Such a nice person. She owns a catering company. She and her husband got together often with Jacqueline and Marcus."

"What happened to her husband?"

Thelma briefly closed her eyes again and rubbed her forehead. "Terrible accident. He died with his father and brother in a plane crash. It was his brother's plane. They were going on a fishing trip to Alaska. Left three widows and five kids. Terrible."

"How long ago?" Sidney asked.

"Oh, my. Maybe five years."

"After Brimwell married Angelica, did they ever get together with Elizabeth and her husband?"

"Just a few social occasions, but Marcus always insists that Elizabeth's company do the catering whenever a big event is happening at his house. I help with some of the cooking. Elizabeth sure knows how to handle a big crowd."

"When did Marcus start seeing her on a personal basis?"

"A couple of years ago right after he learned about Angelica's affair. I think he knew about some of the men who came before Philip, but that was the one he couldn't get past, or maybe he didn't want to. Anyway, Elizabeth is just as worried about Marcus as I am." She glanced at her wrist watch and then stood up. "I've got to get back and start making lunch."

"We really appreciate you talking to us," Sidney said.

"I sure hope what I've told you helps. I think if you find Mara's killer, Marcus will be safe."

Sam rose from his chair. "We're doing our best." He got a business card out of his breast pocket. "Call if you hear anything else that concerns you." He handed Thelma the card.

"I will. Marcus just doesn't want to believe he married an evil woman," Thelma said and headed to the exit.

"That certainly was interesting," Sam said, sinking back down in his chair. "Did you get that all down?"

"Yeah. I noticed how you didn't even pull out a notepad."

He tapped his temple. "Keeping it all in here. Want another cup of coffee?"

"Sure do."

After the waitress filled their cups, Sam asked Sidney, "What time do you want to go to Payton's?"

"Why don't you give him a call? Not to tell him we're coming. Ask about your bill to see if you can find out if he has any plans for this evening."

Sam nodded, took a gulp of his coffee, and called Payton. "Hello…Payton is that you?…Hello? Are you there?" Sam frowned, disconnected, and shrugged his shoulders. "Called Payton's landline. He prefers that when he's home. Someone picked up the receiver. Just heard heavy breathing and then nothing."

Chapter 40

Sidney pondered the possibilities of what might be going on at Payton's house.

Sam punched in another number. "Calling his cell phone."

After four rings, Payton answered. "Hey, Sam."

"Payton, I've been looking over your account. My hours don't add up to the whole retainer. You got a credit balance. Thought we'd get together, have a few beers, and I'd give it to you."

"Credit balance, huh? Here I thought I owed you money. I'm at my folks' house. My dad's gotten worse. He's not doing very well, but the doctor says he's stable. I'll be back in town late tomorrow night around ten-thirty. Want to get together Monday night?"

"Sorry, can't buddy. Got other plans. How about Tuesday night?"

"That works. Meet at Charlie's?" Payton asked, referring to a bar where he had met Sam previously.

"At eight?"

"See you there," Payton said and disconnected.

"He's out of town," Sam told Sidney and then filled her in about the conversation.

"You said you were busy so we could surprise him on Monday night. Right? It wasn't because you really had other plans?"

Sam gave her a coy smile. "Always got plans but willing to change them when I can make a few bucks."

Sidney returned his smile. "So who answered Payton's landline?" She glanced around the coffee shop and noticed the place was starting to fill up. "Let's talk in your office."

"I want to drive by Payton's house first. See if there's a familiar car in his driveway."

Sidney nodded and checked her watch. "Call if you see anything interesting. Otherwise, I'll meet you at two at your office."

Since Sidney's early morning call to Chas was brief, she went back to her Hyatt suite and called him.

"What did Bernice say?" Chas asked.

After filling him in, she said, "Hey, if I send you two signatures, can you have someone analyze them to see if the same guy wrote both of them?"

"Sure, but not until Monday. Babe, I'm getting tired of sleeping alone."

"So am I. When I headed to San Diego, I thought it was going to be a simple 'who-done-it' kind of case. Not anymore."

"The case I've been trying will be going to the jury within a few days. Next weekend I'm coming out there again. Maybe you can find something I can do to help speed up your investigation."

"Oh, just remembered. Can you have someone check into Deidre Carlson's finances? I'm looking for a $400,000 withdrawal she might have made the latter part of March."

"I can do that. Has she become a suspect?"

"Not yet." Sidney told Chas everything she knew about Deidre and then said, "Enough shop talk."

"Agreed. Let's talk about that Jacuzzi in your bedroom."

An hour later, their call ended. Sidney felt refreshed, knowing Chas would be arriving at the San Diego airport in six days.

Like always, Sam had just finished brewing a pot of coffee when Sidney arrived. "That sure smells good," she said as Sam filled her cup.

Putting down the coffee carafe, Sam picked up a plate stacked with cookies and placed it on the short table.

Sidney eyed the cookie selection. "You expecting company?"

"No. A friend dropped them off."

Speculating if the friend could be the woman she ran into at Sam's place a few days earlier, she smiled. "Seeing the friend later?"

"Depends on our work schedule." Sam sat on the couch next to Sidney, took a sip of his coffee, and picked up a chocolate-chip cookie. "A white Porsche was parked in Payton's driveway."

"Victor. I wonder what he was doing there. And why did he answer the phone?"

"I figure he must have been expecting a call."

"What about his cell phone?" Sidney asked between bites on an almond cookie.

Sam shrugged. "Your guess is as good as mine. Judy called. She confirmed the guy in the picture I texted her was Brimwell's representative. Victor. That guy sure gets around."

"Does he ever—Angelica, Deidre, Kate, and now Brimwell's business partner."

"Business partner?"

She chewed and swallowed the rest of her cookie. "Thought I'd be kind. In reality, Victor's probably the exact opposite—a business adversary. I've been thinking about Sergio. He hasn't been with the Brimwell household for the past two years. He can probably give us some juicy tidbits about Angelica, but I doubt he can shed any light on who murdered Mara."

"We're on the same page. He hasn't returned my call. If he does, I'll put him on hold, stall him somehow, and turn on the recorder. He's still seeing Thelma. There's a slight possibility she told him something she didn't want to share with us."

"Good point. Fowler left me a message at the hotel yesterday. He wants me to go to his office Monday morning and fill him in on how we're progressing. I'm not going to reveal everything until we determine what has a bearing on Mara's death." Sidney pulled her notepad out of her briefcase and flipped to the page with a paperclip on it. "Thought I'd bring you up to speed on what I discovered yesterday—follow-up on what I overhead Cesar say in Spanish at the pool hall."

Sam nodded and filled their coffee mugs.

"Cesar Ortega, the actual cab driver, who is here illegally, heard a gunshot and someone running through the bushes when he dropped off Aden. He saw a sports car parked across the street. I doubt we'll ever be able to sway him to testify."

"Agreed." Sam grabbed another cookie.

"But if the sports car leads to a potential culprit, Aden's neighbor,

Gil Kender can testify it was there."

"The neighbor saw it?"

Sidney nodded. "None of the neighbors have a sports car. The driver parked on Kender's lawn. Ruined two sprinkler heads."

"Cops know about it?"

"According to Kender, he mentioned it, but it doesn't appear there was any follow-up. It's not in any of the police reports I've read. He even gave them part of the license plate number and the time it left—8:34 p.m. Even if the Corvette driver wasn't involved, he might have seen something."

"Corvette?"

"Yeah. I thought it might have turned out to be a white Porsche—Victor's car. Instead it was a red Corvette."

Sam leaned back into the sofa and scratched his chin. "Payton had one. He traded it in for a BMW sometime in May."

Sidney squinted in disbelief. "Payton?"

"Yeah, well," Sam mumbled, staring at the coffee table. "Victor has a key to his place and the combination to his safe. Maybe he borrowed Payton's car. Mara was killed on a Friday night. Payton's dad has been sick as long as I've known him. He goes to see him almost every weekend."

"He came home from Brazil before Aden. I'll check if he had an airline ticket for that weekend. Where do his parents live?"

"Seattle."

"Payton? He's Aden's buddy." Sam drummed his fingers on the armrest.

Sidney sat quietly and pondered the new information.

Sam took a gulp of his coffee. "Let's say they had a falling out, which I doubt. He visits Aden at least twice a week, and he wanted to kill the guy? Just don't see it. Payton would be pretty dumb to park right across the street. But if Victor did the crime and wanted it pinned on Payton, that would be the perfect place to park. The neighbor told the cops about it. Why didn't they follow-up on it?"

"Even though it's not mentioned in the police report, there's a slim possibility they did and ruled out the driver from any connection to the crime."

"You have part of the license plate number?"

Sidney nodded and looked at her notepad. "5FM and a 6. It's either the third or second number from the end. Kender, the neighbor, wasn't sure."

"I'll contact my friend at DMV on Monday. Find out Payton's old license plate numbers. If none of the digits match, maybe she can track down the owner. There can't be that many Corvettes in San Diego with license plates beginning with 5FM."

Sidney rubbed her hands together. "Why did someone want to kill Aden?" She stood and paced around the room. "It's got to have something to do with the Brazilian bridge site. We need proof and a motive. Maybe we can force Payton to shed some light on it Monday night."

"Want my two cents?"

"Sure."

"I think it centers around Angelica."

Sidney felt a poke in her right shoulder and knew no one was behind her. Assuming Mara was telling her that Sam was on the right track, she rubbed her shoulder. "Angelica? How?"

"Don't know yet. You heard her on her cell phone. She knows the shooter. Why hasn't she stepped forward? From everything Thelma told us about her, Angelica isn't likely to protect anyone unless it's for her benefit."

"I need to visit Aden and ask him about the date he informed Brimwell about the best of the three sites. And then, I don't want to work on this case until tomorrow."

"Giving me tonight and Sunday off?"

"Tonight. Maybe tomorrow. It depends what Aden has to say." Sidney picked up another cookie. "Your friend deserves some company after baking you all these cookies."

A mischievous smile crossed his face. "Couldn't agree more."

"I'll call you tomorrow morning, and we can discuss our game plan."

"Don't make it too early."

Chapter 41

While she sat and waited on the visitor's side of the partition in the county jail, Sidney glanced over the questions she planned to ask.

Aden stepped into the room with a guard at his side. As usual, Sidney's breathing accelerated, and her pulse raced, but not as intensely as it had before. The urge to knock down the panel, run into his arms, and smoother him with kisses had become more manageable. The tingly sensation inside her wouldn't relent, but she felt a little relieved that she had made some progress in conquering Mara's takeover of her emotions. Inhaling deeply, Sidney held firmly onto the edge of the counter and watched Aden, his face pale and his eyes dull, lower himself into the chair.

"Having any luck?" he asked in a forlorn tone.

"Well, if you're asking if we've found the killer, we haven't yet, but we're getting closer," Sidney said, though she doubted that was the truth. A few suspects had surfaced, but they still lacked the evidence needed to determine the guilty party. Gazing at Aden, she saw the faraway, lost look in his eyes. She wanted to wrap her arms around him to comfort him, not to satisfy the yearning for him that still boiled inside her. "How are you doing?"

"Mara's folks were here earlier. They're always so positive that it won't be long before I get out. They wanted to bring the kids, but I can't stand seeing them and not being able to give them a hug." He swallowed hard, his lips trembled, and his eyes became moist. "If it weren't for sensing Mara close to me every night, I'd go crazy in here."

"Aden, we're going to get you out," Sidney said with a firm voice. "Are you up to answering some questions?"

Staring at the floor, he nodded and wiped his eyes with his fingertips.

"When did you give Brimwell the best location for the bridge in Brazil?"

A confused expression splashed on his face. "What does that have to do with Mara's murder?"

"We've run into some documents that indicated several people were interested in that site, so we're trying to determine if it's significant to this case."

"Well, Payton sure was hot under the collar because he couldn't sway me into agreeing with the site he'd picked, but Payton would never hurt Mara."

"Would he hurt you?"

"He comes and sees me all the time. If you think Payton's involved, you're barking up the wrong tree."

"Payton wasn't the only one interested in the site selection."

"Who else?"

"We're trying to figure that out," Sidney said, not wanting to tell him about Brimwell's contract until Chas had verified Brimwell's signature. "Getting back to my question, when did you give Brimwell the best location for the bridge?"

"Not until I was in jail. I talked to him a few times when I was in Brazil, but I wasn't finished gathering data at that point. I didn't even tell him how the report was coming." He stroked his chin. "Thinking about it, he didn't even ask. We mainly talked about a bridge underway in Switzerland."

"So he came to see you in jail, and that was when you told him?" Sidney asked, scrawling down notes.

"That wasn't exactly how it went."

She looked up at him. "What do you mean?"

"Well, the report was in my luggage, still unpacked from my trip since I'd returned. The Brazilian officials needed to know before May first which site Brimwell Engineering had selected. Mara's dad had a key to our house. I had him go there to get the report. He couldn't find the printed copy or the files with all the supporting documents in my luggage. My laptop was in my carry-on bag, and the report was on it along with scanned copies of the documents.

"Thomas, Mara's dad, tried to find it on the computer so he could print out another copy. He couldn't see it among my documents, so he took my computer to Brimwell Engineering. Marcus wasn't in. Thomas knows Payton. He had him look for it. Payton found the file. All the supporting documents were in it, but the report was missing.

"The following day Marcus came to see me, and we discussed the Brazilian site."

"Do you recall the date?"

He shook his head. "No." Aden looked down and tapped his fingertips together. "I'd guess I'd been in here three or four days...Must have been around April twenty-fourth."

"Was that the first time Brimwell came to see you here?"

"Yeah. He was out of town when I was arrested. Maybe he just got home that day. I can't remember. When he's not travelling, he normally stops by on Sundays."

"Did any of your co-workers know which site you were selecting?"

"I don't select a site. Marcus does. Based on all the tests we ran and the economics, I ranked the three sites. He selected the one with the best ranking, the one that was on top of my list. The same one I would have picked if I had to make the choice. Payton and Vic both came to Brazil at different times to help out. They saw the results of the tests. They're engineers, so they knew which site was coming out on top. Like I said earlier, Payton wasn't happy about it. He even wanted me to change some of the results."

"Do you know why?"

"His cousin owns land that's part of one of the other sites. He wanted to help the guy out. There wasn't any development around two of the sites. The only way his cousin probably could get a good price for his land would be if that site were selected."

"Did the one that ranked the highest have development around it?"

"No. Only a couple of shacks that people lived in." Aden scratched his chin. "Come to think of it, a woman who lived in one of them died." His brow creased, and he stared at Sidney. "You think her husband might have killed Mara to get even?"

"Was it your fault the woman died?" Sidney asked, trying to absorb this new revelation.

"No, but her husband sure didn't agree."

"How did she die?"

"We'd erected some scaffolding on the side of a cliff to get ore samples. One morning when we went to the site, the scaffolding was spread over the ground, and the woman, surrounded by a puddle of blood, was lying under several pieces."

Bernice's image of a woman trapped under scaffolding sprang into Sidney's mind, along with what Judy had heard Smorick say: "A woman died because of that bridge site." *Was he referring to this local woman or Mara? If it was the former, was Mara trying to tell her Smorick had no connection with her death?*

Aden continued. "I don't know how it happened. We'd been using that scaffolding for several days. It'd been set up in accordance with standard procedures. Some of the locals believed the woman had been with a group of people who were stealing the metal piping."

"Was some of it missing?"

He nodded. "Yeah, almost half of it."

"Why did her husband blame you?"

"It had been erected per my instructions. I was the one in charge."

"After the incident, did you have any problems with him or other people that knew her?"

"No, but someone killed Mara. And that woman's husband called me every derogatory name I knew in Spanish. He also shouted a few I'd never heard before."

"You said they lived in a shack. How would he get the money and means to come to the United States to gun down your wife? How would he even know where you lived?"

Aden's shoulders sagged, and his chin dropped. "He wouldn't." He sighed. "I guess I'm just searching for something that might make a little sense."

"As far as you know, do any of your colleagues own guns?" Sidney asked, thinking about the vision of the Browning pistol.

"The murder weapon. Do you think it'll ever be found?"

"Yes," Sidney replied without giving him any indication that it had already been located.

"Guns," Aden said, tapping his lower lip. "Marcus has a whole collection. He keeps them in his gun safe. Vic goes target shooting sometimes, so he must have a gun. I don't know if it's a rifle or a pistol. Payton doesn't own one. Some of the other people who work there might have weapons, but we've never talked about it."

"How about Kate?"

"Yeah. I told the cops she had a pistol. She brought it to work one day to show it to Payton…or maybe Vic. Molly came unglued. When she was a kid, one of her neighbors killed himself with a gun. She had gone with his daughter and a bunch of kids into the house. They found him in a pool of blood on the kitchen floor. Molly can't stand to be around any weapons. That day, she stormed into Marcus's office and demanded that he tell Kate to take her dangerous toy home. Never saw Molly so mad—probably neither had Marcus. He marched out of his office and told Kate weapons weren't allowed in the building."

"Do you know if it was a 9mm?"

Aden nodded. "A Browning. She was busy showing it to everyone in the office before Marcus stopped her. She acted real proud of it. Claimed she hits the bull's-eye all the time. The cops have already ruled Kate out as a suspect. They believe I committed the crime and are determined to see me pay for it. They're not even considering any other possibilities."

"Aden, you're innocent. We'll find the culprit and get you vindicated. It's just taking a little longer than we hoped. But we're not giving up. I won't leave California until you're a free man."

He raised his chin and a hint of a smile crossed his lips. "You have no idea how much it means to me that you're on my side."

Seeing his face light up and his eyes fixed on her, an unexplainable warmth streamed through Sidney's body, and she felt blood rushing into her cheeks. Across from her sat a stranger, a stranger who, through some unnatural force, she knew intimately. Even her rational side couldn't prevent her from blushing like a school girl, knowing he was glad to have her in his corner.

Chapter 42

Monday morning, Sidney was having breakfast with Jean when her cell phone chirped. She saw Sam's name on the screen, looked at Jean, and said, "I better take this," and then pushed the answer button on her phone. "Sam, I'm in a restaurant. Can I call you back in an hour or can't this wait?"

"It's important, but not urgent. An hour or two won't make any difference. Call me when you get back to your room."

While Sidney finished eating, a tall waiter with crew-cut medium-brown hair accidently dropped a fork off his tray. It slid next to Sidney's foot. He bent down to retrieve it. As the waiter rose to his feet, Sidney sensed there was something familiar about the man but couldn't recall seeing him in the restaurant before. Sipping her coffee, she kept an eye on the waiter and tried to remember where she had seen him.

Returning to the suite, Sidney went into her room and pushed Sam's number into her cell phone. "Okay, I'm all ears."

"Thelma called in a dither. She had Sunday off. When she came home around midnight, she overheard Angelica on a phone call. She doubted Angelica knew she was in the house. Normally, Thelma stays away until six Monday morning. As soon as Angelica got off the phone, Thelma called, waking me up. Afraid my notes are a little sloppy."

"You took notes?" Sidney said in disbelief.

"Mental notes."

"She called you shortly after midnight. You didn't call me until almost nine, so it must not be very important."

"It is, but it could wait until later. Didn't want to wake you up. Still, I thought you'd want to know earlier than our three o'clock meeting."

"Go on. What did Thelma hear Angelica say on the phone?"

"Angelica mentioned the word gun. Something like, 'Did you have any problem getting the gun from her?' Then Angelica giggled and said, 'She sleeps with it under the mattress.' Apparently, Angelica moved out of the kitchen and into the hallway while she was still on the phone. Her voice became a little muffled from where Thelma stood, but she did pick up a few words of the conversation, 'Tomorrow night…we can use it then.' Thelma told me Brimwell is out of town. He's due home sometime tonight. She didn't know when."

"Where is he?"

"San Francisco."

"Thelma believes Angelica is going to shoot him when he gets home?"

"That's the drift of it. She expects me to protect Brimwell somehow. How am I supposed to do that without staying at his place?"

"Let's think about this. Thelma heard 'tomorrow night' and then later she heard 'we can use it then.' Based on that, they might not be connected. Also, if they are connected, Angelica isn't going to be the one pulling the trigger. She's too clever for that. I suspect the shooter would either be Victor or Lewis. There has to be a plan where they think they can get away with it."

"Yeah. Molly books all of Brimwell's business travel. I thought I'd give her a call after I talked to you. She probably knows when he'll be arriving."

"I'm sure you'll find a way to sweet talk her into giving you that information. Was Lewis at home when Angelica was on the phone?"

"Yep, his car was there, but apparently the boy likes his sleep. Since he was nowhere in sight and the house was quiet except for Angelica's voice, Thelma thought he'd already gone to bed. So, unless Angelica has another admirer that we don't know about, the person on the other end of the line was probably Victor."

"Kate owns a pistol—a Browning."

"Aden tell you that?"

"Yes, and it sounded like it was one of her treasured possessions. Maybe Kate, the woman Aden supposedly had an affair with," she said in a sarcastic tone, "came here for the weekend, or Victor went to see her in Denver."

"He was in town Saturday morning. At least, his car was parked in Payton's driveway."

"He might've been busy planting more evidence there." She pursed her lips and squinted as she collected her thoughts. "Why doesn't Thelma just call Brimwell and tell him what she overheard?"

"I tried to talk her into doing that, but she's attempted to warn him before about Angelica. She doubts he'll listen to her."

"If we only knew how the pieces fit together and had some supporting evidence, we could go to the local authorities and let them handle it. From what you read in Victor's appointment book, we know he gets together with Kate often. He might've flown to Denver Saturday afternoon. If Angelica was talking to him, the gun could be at his place."

"Another illegal search, Detective Langston?" he said in a joking tone.

"Got any other way of finding out?"

"Nope."

"After we've checked Victor's place, let's do a quick search of Payton's and see if there's something new in his safe. I'll pick you up in a couple of hours," Sidney said, hoping Chas would call with the information she wanted before she left.

Sam slid into Sidney's car and said, "Brimwell's plane lands at 10:10 p.m. That'll give us plenty of time to question Payton before I head out to Brimwell's place."

"Will you be a late-night visitor?" Sidney asked as she drove toward Victor's condo.

"Thelma called again. Still upset. To get her to calm down, I told her I'd come by around eleven. That'll probably be fifteen…twenty minutes before Brimwell gets home. She wants me to sneak in through the back door."

"How are you going to get through the gate?"

"Call her. She'll push the release button, opening it from inside the house."

Sidney wondered whether or not she should go with Sam and decided to hold off on making a decision until after they had questioned Payton. She didn't want anything to happen to Brimwell, but at the same time, her focus was on freeing Aden. Based on all the circumstantial evidence she had uncovered, she assumed Brimwell's situation was tied to Aden's. She suspected it had something to do with the date on the Brimwell contract but needed a motive and proof.

When they were close to Victor's condo, Sidney and Sam began surveying the cars parked along the street, looking for his Porsche in case he hadn't gone to work. They continued searching for it as Sidney turned into the building's parking lot. The Porsche was nowhere in sight. She stopped in a stall with the hood of the car facing toward the exit.

As they climbed out of the Lexus, Sidney noticed a man with curly, auburn hair walking away from the condo building at a brisk pace. She quickly sank back down into the driver's seat and squinted at the man several hundred feet away, trying to capture his features. "Stay," she said, gesturing to Sam to get back into the car.

"What?" he asked, closing the car door behind him.

Pointing toward the curly-haired man, she said, "Over there. Is that Lewis?"

"Can't tell. He has to drive right past us to get out of the parking lot."

The curly-haired man moved between several rows of parked cars until they no longer could spot him from inside the Lexus. Staring through the windshield, they waited for him to leave. A cream-colored Corolla with a brunette behind the wheel drove past them followed by a silver Mazda driven by a bald man. A few minutes later, a dark blue Scion pulled into the exit driveway with a curly-haired driver.

"The hair looks right. But only seeing the back of his head, I can't tell if that's Lewis," Sidney commented.

"Got the license plate number. I'll make a call," Sam said, pushing buttons on his cell phone and easing out of the Lexus.

Assuming he didn't want her to hear the name of his contact, she remained in the vehicle until he lowered his cell phone.

"Any luck?" she asked, stepping onto the asphalt.

"While I was chatting with my contact," Sam said, "I asked about the license plate number Payton had on his Corvette. It was 5FMA368."

"That works with the neighbor's numbers. So it was his car parked across the street from Aden's house when Mara was shot. And the dark blue Scion?"

"Registered to Lewis Watford, Angelica's butler. What do you suppose he was doing at Vic's condo?"

"Getting the gun?" Sidney speculated.

"That's exactly what I was thinking. Victor's fingerprints will be all over it. Still want to check out his place?"

Sidney nodded, and they strode to the building. After she briefly disabled the key pad, they entered the structure and took the elevator to the third floor. Since Sidney had picked Victor's lock the time before, Sam insisted on doing it.

Sidney headed to Victor's bedroom and started searching while Sam began in the den. As she looked through boxes on the shelf in Victor's closet, her cell phone rang. She dug it out of her pocket and looked at the caller ID. "Hi, Honey," she answered.

"Got your answers. I'll start with the Brimwell contract. That is his signature. Since you still don't know who shot Mara, I decided to have Susan do some additional research on Marcus Brimwell. That man has plenty of money. He doesn't ever need to work."

"Yeah, like you," Sidney said, referring to Chas's trust fund.

"Exactly. I work because I want to and enjoy what I'm doing. I suspect that's the same reason Brimwell works. Why would he risk going to prison by making extra money he doesn't need? I had the signature page analyzed. Bottom line, it's been cut and pasted by an expert. Had the font next to his name not been slightly different from the rest of the document, it probably never would've been discovered."

"It's Brimwell's signature, but he didn't sign the contract." Sidney took her notepad out of her backpack and jotted it down.

"Moving on. Deidre Carlson made a withdrawal of four hundred thousand from one of her accounts on March nineteenth. She also made another withdrawal of two hundred thousand on May tenth."

"I wonder what the second withdrawal was all about."

"Maybe her boyfriend needed a few extra bucks. Last thing you wanted to know was if Payton Russen was out of town on April twentieth. He flew home from Brazil on April twelfth. After that, there were no airline tickets issued in the name of Payton Russen until May fourth when he flew to Seattle. He still could've driven out of San Diego. Any more questions?"

"No. That's it for now."

"This morning I ran into your boss, Captain Barstow. He mentioned that the Feds had been inquiring about you."

"Huh?"

"That was close to my response. He seemed to be concerned that you might have applied for a job with the FBI. I assured him that wasn't true."

All the open cases Sidney had been working on before her chest pains ran through her mind. "Boy, I can't think of one case I was working on where the feds would be involved. Oh...oh, there might be one," she said as a murder case drifted into her head. Her partner had speculated whether the prime suspect was involved with a murder in another state since the MO seemed to match. "Did they discuss any cases with him?"

"No. And they didn't ask about any of your co-workers."

"Strange. I think I'll check in with the captain tomorrow. Just to touch base. Maybe he'll tell me more about it then."

"I need to get back in the courtroom to listen to the defendant's closing arguments."

"You're through?"

"With this case. A colleague will stand in for me when the verdict is delivered. I need to finish the paperwork, and then I'll catch a red eye. I should be there tomorrow morning around eight. Babe, I need to go. Love you."

A tinge of excitement bubbled up through her body as Sidney could almost feel his touch. She couldn't imagine being away from Chas for two months—the length of time Aden and Mara would have been separated had she not met with a terrible fate. "Love you, too," she said and disconnected. With a smile on her face, she continued searching Victor's bedroom.

"Hey, got something," Sam said, gazing at a letter in his hand.

Sidney hurried through the hallway and stepped into the den.

"A letter from Angelica to Victor," he said, waving it in the air. "In summary, it says she wants him to stop bothering her since she's a married woman." He raised the envelope. "It's postmarked Saturday."

"Mmmm," Sidney muttered. "Victor wouldn't have received that letter before he went to work. That might be the reason for Lewis's visit. Was it in plain sight?"

"Nope. Taped underneath the bottom desk drawer. Now I can guess Angelica's plan for eliminating Brimwell—the jealous lover. Do you want to keep looking for the gun?"

"Yes, but I doubt we'll find it." She squinted and stared at the letter. "If it's that simple, what role did the Brimwell contract play?"

"Not a clue," Sam said, shaking his head.

Sidney wondered if the contract had been a ploy to divert Victor from uncovering Angelica's true plan. "Smokescreen?"

"Possibly. What should I do with the letter?"

"Snap a picture of it and the envelope, and then put it back where you found it. I want to check Payton's safe before he gets home from work. Let's only look another fifteen minutes for the pistol and then go to Payton's place."

Chapter 43

At 3:30 p.m., Sidney turned onto Payton's street. She parked a half a block away from his house in case they decided to do a more thorough search after they reviewed the contents of the safe.

Walking along the deserted sidewalk, Sidney and Sam scanned the cars lining the curb on both sides of the street. Nothing appeared out of the ordinary. They quickly headed to the backyard. Sidney was surprised when Sam opened the gate. "Each time I've been here, that's always been locked."

Sam gave her a puzzled look. "Besides the time I was with you, how many other times have you been an uninvited guest?"

"A few." A grin splashed on her face, recalling the first visit, the time she ended up being stuck in the bathroom while Sam used the facility.

"What's so funny?"

"A private joke."

Sam cocked a brow and slipped on a pair of latex gloves. Reaching the back door, he gripped the doorknob and turned it. "Mmmh. He forgot to lock it." He stepped inside with Sidney right behind him.

"No beeping alarm."

"Payton only sets it when he goes out of town."

They headed to the den. Sidney lowered the picture concealing the safe, took the combination out of her pocket, and opened it. Inside lay a thin nine-by-twelve inch envelope and Payton's passport. "His SLI contracts are gone. What do you suppose he did with them?"

"Probably burned 'em," Sam said, staring into the almost-empty safe. "That's what I would've done if I discovered the pistol'd been taken." He scratched his chin. "We know Victor's been here at least a couple of times when Payton was out of town."

"Payton might not've even known the pistol was in his safe. It's possible the contracts weren't removed by him." Sidney stuck her fingers into the large envelope and lifted out a picture. Her eyes opened wider as she studied the picture of Aden and Kate in an old brass bed in a room painted bright orange with a small striped red, orange, and yellow rug hanging over the bed. Aden's and Kate's pose seemed identical to the picture she had discovered in Victor's apartment.

Sam had moved closer to her and looked over her shoulder at the photo. "Different place. Maybe Aden hasn't been truthful about his relationship with Kate. Married men lie about affairs all the time."

"Look at the way Aden's body is positioned." Sidney slid her gloved fingertip over his image. "His eyes are closed and his pose appears to be the same as in the other picture. Hold this." She gave it to Sam and then pulled out her cell phone, brought up the prior picture, and showed it to him.

"Uh-huh. Identical. Photoshopped. But why?"

Sidney placed the picture on Payton's desk and took a snap shot of it. "Maybe Payton can answer that question." Putting the photo back in the envelope, she looked at the clock on the wall. "It's after 4:30. It's early for dinner, but let's grab a quick bite, head back here, and wait for Payton to show up. I don't want to take a chance he'll leave before we get an opportunity to question him."

"Good idea. With something going on at Brimwell's house later, it could be a long night."

Sidney and Sam returned to Payton's street with hamburgers, fries, and soft drinks. She parked a few houses away from Payton's in a spot where they had a clear view of his driveway and front door. When she had eaten her last fry, she asked, "Shouldn't he be home by this time?"

"Yep. He should be here."

"My laptop's in the trunk. The tracking device might still be on his car." Sidney got the computer out of her duffle bag. After she was settled back behind the steering wheel, she booted it up and found the program she needed. She set it down on the column between the seats, and they both looked at the blips on the screen. "The yellow one is Payton's. The green one is tracking Victor's vehicle."

The green blip traveled on a road on the opposite side of town. The yellow dot was stationary a few blocks from where they were parked.

"There's a grocery store in that general vicinity and the bar he likes to frequent," Sam said. "He's probably shopping or having a drink."

"If that dot doesn't move in thirty minutes, we'll head over there." She leaned over Sam, opened her glove compartment, and took out a recorder smaller than a cell phone. "We need evidence." She attached it under her blouse. "He might say something we can use."

Eighteen minutes later, the yellow blip made a U-turn and moved toward Payton's house. Within five minutes, the BMW pulled into Payton's driveway. Sam and Sidney watched Payton unload groceries from his trunk.

"I hope we don't have company," Sam said, pointing toward Victor's green blip. "He's a distance away. It looks like he's heading toward us. I'd say thirty minutes and he could be at Payton's door."

"He's too far away to be sure he's coming here. Just in case, we'll skip the pleasantries with Payton and dig right in to asking questions. It's time to find out the truth about the SLI contracts. Since Payton believes you're his buddy, I'll take the lead and play bad cop, and you can be good cop."

"That fits," he said with a smile. "I'm always the nice guy."

Sidney rolled her eyes. "Sure you are, Sam."

They gave Payton a few minutes to put away his groceries. She turned on the recorder, and then they briskly walked to his house and rang the bell.

Payton opened the door. His eyes darted between Sidney and Sam. "I thought we were meeting tomorrow night," he said, looking at Sam.

"This is on another matter." Sam pushed the door wide open and stepped inside without being invited by Payton. Sidney followed on his heels.

"Hey, what's going on?" Payton asked.

"We need to talk." Sidney grabbed his arm and led him into the dining room. Pushing him down, she forced him to sit on a wooden, upholstered chair while Sam closed the door and locked it.

Sidney and Sam yanked out two other chairs and placed them right in front of Payton, sitting down on them.

Payton squirmed under their steady gaze. "What's this all about?"

Her eyes bore into his. "Payton, we've been investigating Mara's murder, and we know what you've done. We have proof," she began, referring to his SLI contracts.

His hands flew up to his head and wrapped around his forehead. "Oh, God! I knew I couldn't get away with it!" Payton's voice cracked. "Victor thought I would, but I knew someone would find out the truth." He lowered his head with his hands cradling it, and tears sprang into his eyes. "Honest, I didn't mean to. She shouldn't have been home!"

Sidney and Sam shared a quick glance at each other. That was a confession she hadn't anticipated. Going along with his statement, she asked, "Why did you allow your best friend to suffer for your action?"

"It's Vic's fault. I believed him. But when I saw Aden in jail..." Payton's lips quivered. "Vic lied." His hands trembled as he brushed away the tears. "How could I tell Aden I'd killed his wife? How could I do that?"

"Why is it Vic's fault?"

Payton swallowed hard, breathed deeply, and adjusted himself on the chair. "He told me that Aden was going to let Brimwell know about the deal I made to make some extra money."

"The SLI contract?"

"Yeah, that was part of it," he stammered. He raised his head. With tears streaming down his checks, his moist eyes fixed on Sam's face. "Sam, you know about my contract."

"Only know what you told me. Not the part where you were going to be paid to tell SLI the location of the Brazilian bridge site before it was released to the public. You screwed up. Gave SLI the wrong site. They forked over money without any return."

"It wasn't just SLI that lost money. I put up every dollar I could raise to buy up some of that land."

"Before the testing had been done? Why?" Sidney asked, thinking Payton would have had the inside track on the bridge site if he had just waited.

"The preliminary tests I ran showed that was the best site, but

Aden thought more testing was needed. He wouldn't go to Brimwell with my results. I messed up by mentioning it to Vic."

"What proof did Vic give you that led you to believe Aden planned to expose you?"

"He told me he found a copy of my contract in Aden's desk drawer in his den and another one in his drawer at work."

"How did he claim he found it?"

"Deidre was watching the kids while Mara went to the hospital to visit a friend who had just had a baby. Deidre had left her cell phone at Vic's place. He took it to her. While he was there, he needed to write something down. He went into the den to get a pencil. There wasn't one lying on the desk, so he opened the top drawer and spotted my contract."

"Had you told him about SLI?"

"Well." He hesitated. "Well…yeah, since I sank all my money into the Brazilian site, I wanted a partner when another site needed to be picked."

"When was that?"

"Before I went to Brazil."

"And when did he tell you your contract was in Aden's drawer?"

"Around the middle of March."

"Payton, Aden was your best friend. Was that all it took for Vic to convince you that he would turn you in?"

Payton shook his head. "No. Vic found a file Aden had put together about me when he was in Brazil. He copied it, and showed it to me as soon as he got back in San Diego."

"You were in San Diego when he showed it to you?"

"Yeah. I came home from Brazil because my dad was having an operation. I flew back there the next day."

"The date?"

"Either March thirty-first or April first. Vic thought I should confront Aden. Get him to change his mind about which site was the best."

"By swinging a pistol in his face?"

"And a picture of him and Kate. Aden had lied to Mara when he said it was only a one-night stand in Denver. Here he acted all upset like he was afraid she'd leave him. Then he has Kate visit him in Brazil. She slept with him in the same motel where I was staying."

"Picture?" Sidney said, knowing he was talking about the one in his safe. "Who took it?"

"Kate. She set it up to prove to me that Aden and her had a thing going."

"Why did she need to prove that to you?"

"Aden wouldn't talk to her on the phone if I was with him. Acted like he couldn't stand her. I thought I was helping Aden out when I told her to leave him alone. That's when she told me they still had a thing going and she'd prove it."

"How did Vic know about that?"

"Kate confided in him. She couldn't understand how Aden could be her lover one night and then act like he hated her the next day."

"So Vic thought you could use the picture to blackmail Aden into changing the ranking on the various sites?"

"Well, yeah. Even if Aden wanted to keep Kate on the side, I didn't think he wanted another scene with Mara. She would've left him."

"You certainly took care of that," Sidney said, her voice dripping with sarcasm.

"I didn't mean it. She wasn't supposed to be there!"

"And if Aden didn't agree to your demand, the plan was to shoot him. Is that why you brought along the gun?"

"Victor suggested that I should bring it for my own protection if Aden decided to get aggressive." He cradled his head in his hands again. "I don't know why I believed him. Aden doesn't knock people around. He gets mad and yells, but he never punches anyone."

"Why aren't your fingerprints on the gun?"

Payton's brow furrowed. "You took the gun from my safe? I thought Vic had taken it."

"Let's say we ran into it and turned it over to the police."

"Vic wanted me to wear gloves and told me Aden's prints were on it. He said he had taken Aden target shooting. I stuck it in my safe so it wouldn't be found."

"If you hid it to protect Aden, why didn't you wipe it clean?"

"I was going to when I remembered how Aden didn't even want to touch Kate's pistol when she brought it to work—not to use, just to show Vic and me. So I decided I'd talk to Aden about guns first— you know, I'd start by asking if the gun had been found. After he told me it was still missing, he said he hadn't even shot a gun since he was sixteen." He squinted as he looked at Sidney. "If things looked hairy for Aden during the trial, I was going to turn it in. Since the police have the gun, why hasn't Aden been released?"

Sidney shrugged. "Let's get back to your plan. Had Aden agreed to changing the report, no one would have gotten hurt. You would have made some money when your parcels were purchased by the Brazilian government, and you would have also been paid by SLI. Is that how it was supposed to go down?"

"That was the plan, but now I don't know if that's what Vic wanted. A few days after Aden was arrested, he told me that Aden never would've changed his mind about the site since Brimwell had a contract with SLI and an agreement with Aden. Since Vic had been filling me with lies, I insisted on seeing them. The contract covered the land needed for the best site in Aden's report. In the agreement, Aden would get twenty-five-percent of the profit. I recognized both Brimwell's and Aden's signatures."

"Have you got a copy of the contract and the agreement?"

"No, but then I knew for sure Aden wasn't going to have me arrested when he was doing the same thing."

Sam broke his silence and asked Payton, "Why did you hire me?"

"That was Vic's idea, so I could keep track of how the case was going."

Sidney continued questioning Payton. "Did you ever ask Vic why he was looking out for you?"

"He didn't like the way Mara treated him because he was dating her friend, and then when he found out that Aden was scheming against me, we became better friends. And friends help each other out. That's the lie he gave me."

"Where was he the night Mara was shot?"

"Close by in case I needed help convincing Aden."

"So he was going to shoot Aden?"

"Going to Aden's house that night, I believed no one was going to get shot."

"Why did Vic want you to bring a loaded gun if it was never intended to be used?"

"It wasn't supposed to be loaded! Just seeing it should have been enough to scare Aden."

"If you didn't think it was loaded, why did you aim it at Mara and shoot?"

His body trembled and tears flowed again. "God...God...I don't know."

Sidney gave him a minute to compose himself, and then she said, "Go on with the plan. If Aden didn't listen to you and change his mind, what was supposed to happen?"

"I was going to point the gun at him, handcuff his hands behind a chair and tie his feet together. Vic claimed he had some more things that might help change Aden's mind—he wouldn't tell me what they were. He wanted Aden restrained before he talked to him. So after I tied him up, I would call Vic and he'd come."

"How close was he?"

"A block away."

"And you were going to stay there while he talked to Aden?"

"No. Vic didn't want me to hear what he had on Aden. I'd head out and Vic would come to my house later."

"What about the gun?"

"Vic wanted me to leave it at the house."

"He told you it had Aden's fingerprints on it."

"Yeah, that's why I wore gloves."

"Did you ask him what the importance of the fingerprints were?"

"Yeah. He him-hawed about it, but finally said it had been used in a crime. He wouldn't tell me anything else about it. I figured that was one of the ways he was going to get Aden to change his mind, and that was probably why he wanted Aden tied up so he wouldn't try grabbing the pistol."

"A crime Aden hadn't committed. You didn't see anything wrong with that?"

"Well, yeah, but I didn't want to go to jail."

Sam touched Sidney's arm, letting her know he wanted to ask some questions. She gave him a nod. Sam began. "Payton, what about the Suburban with SLI on the side that kept track of me? Why did you do that?"

"Oh," he sighed. "You know about that too. Vic wanted to steer you to SLI. I bought the Suburban, but he did everything else."

Sidney heard a small creak. The back door was being opened. Without drawing attention to herself, she pushed her chair back so she could clearly see the kitchen doorway and still be facing Payton. While Payton was answering Sam's questions, she raised the bottom of the back of her blouse and retrieved her Glock from the holster. Keeping it hidden in her lap, she wrapped her hand around the handle, prepared for an intruder who might emerge from the kitchen any minute.

"Hiring twenty-four hour surveillance can be pretty expensive. Even good friends wouldn't want to pay out that type of dough," Sam said. "How did he explain that?"

"Deidre has lots of money. Vic wanted to buy Brimwell Engineering. He had approached Brimwell about it, but Brimwell didn't want to sell. Then Vic found out about the Brimwell contract and wanted you to find it at SLI. He thought Brimwell would get thrown into the clinker when it was discovered." His shoulders sagged, and he shook his head. "I don't know if any of that's true."

"Did he ever mention Angelica Brimwell to you?" Sidney asked. She kept her eyes on him, but stayed on full alert with her ears focused for any unusual sounds coming from the kitchen.

"No. Why would he say anything about her? She doesn't have anything to do with this. Oh…would she get Brimwell Engineering if Brimwell went to jail?"

"Probably, but I don't know," Sidney said. "Have we covered the whole plan?"

"Yeah. That's it."

"Ready to turn yourself in?" Sidney asked.

"No. And you're not a cop. There isn't any way you can make me do anything."

"But I can," came a baritone voice from the kitchen.

Chapter 44

Sidney drew her pistol and pointed it toward the kitchen doorway. Four men stepped into the dining room. Two wore police uniforms. The other two were dressed in suits. One was Walt, the man she had played pool with at the house belonging to Randolph Smorick, an SLI executive. The other was the familiar waiter at the Hyatt hotel.

Walt held up an FBI badge. "Mrs. Langston, you can put away your weapon now."

Surprised that he knew her name, Sidney slipped the Glock back into its holster.

A police officer walked up to Payton and said, "Payton Russen, you are under arrest for the murder of Mara Uzelac." He read Payton his Miranda rights.

Sidney rose to her feet as the FBI agent came closer to her. "Care to let us know how you became involved in this case? We could've used your assistance earlier."

Walt nodded toward the police officers. "I'll explain after they take Russen away." He gazed at Sidney, studying her. The corners of his mouth eased into a crooked smile. "You look a little older than last time I saw you."

Thinking about the night she had to look twenty-two for her date with Smorick's son, Kyle, she returned his smile. "And you look a little more honest than last time I saw you."

With a puzzled expression on Sam's face, he went and stood next to Sidney.

She assumed Sam couldn't figure out when they had crossed paths with the FBI agent, so she whispered to him, "He attended Smorick's barbeque."

Sam's brow rose, and he nodded.

Walt's eyes followed the officers while they escorted Payton out the door. After they stepped over the threshold, his attention turned to Sidney and Sam. "I'd talk to you at headquarters but can't spend the time getting there. Take a seat, and I'll briefly fill you two in."

Sidney and Sam sank down on the couch. Walt sat in the upholstered chair opposite them while the other FBI agent closed the front door and remained next to it. Based on the man's stiff posture, it appeared he had taken on the task of guarding the door to make sure no one entered during the briefing.

Sidney swung her head toward the man standing by the door, the guy who had been disguised as a waiter at the hotel. "You put a listening devise on me earlier. Didn't you?"

"Yes," he said with a hint of a smile crossing his lips. "It wasn't the first time."

"How long have you been keeping track of us?"

"Since you two broke into SLI's office," Walt replied.

"That covers a lot of territory," Sam commented. "Why didn't you step up sooner?"

"You two were doing such a good job, we thought we'd stay in the wings and see what you turned up about SLI."

"Is the FBI investigating their illegal activity?" Sidney asked.

"Yes. We've been working on that case for over a year."

Cocking her head, Sidney's gaze drifted between the two FBI agents and landed on Walt. "Is that why one of your colleagues questioned my boss about me?"

"Yes. We were impressed with your credentials. But being away from your job for two months on sick leave…and then suddenly flying to California?"

"I was on sick leave when I discovered my friend, Aden, needed my assistance."

"We know that's the story you've been giving everyone. We don't need to know more," he said in a tone that left Sidney without doubt that he had heard from someone the real reason she had become involved with Aden's case.

"You're looking for the politicians who have provided SLI with information," Sidney said.

Walt's eyes fixed on her. He rested his elbows on the arms of the chair and clasped his hands together. "We're investigating that company. Let's leave it at that."

"You mentioned briefing us," Sam said. "If it's not about SLI, then what?"

"Victor Grenshaw."

Sidney tapped her fingertips together. "What's the connection?"

"That's what we're working on. Grenshaw has been at the SLI office on three occasions. As we all know, he claimed to be Brimwell's representative on a land deal he wanted SLI to handle. We also know Brimwell didn't sign that contact. Grenshaw set up various accounts to handle the flow of money needed to finalize the investment."

"Deidre Carlson's money," Sidney remarked.

"We've traced it to her, but we're convinced she had no idea he planned to use it for an illegal activity. Based on additional information we've recently acquired, Angelica Brimwell is involved, but we lack admissible evidence."

Sidney suspected they had tapped phones without going through proper channels. She smiled to herself, thinking she wasn't the only one with a badge who had worked outside the law in San Diego.

Walt continued. "We've listened to enough of your conversations to know that you both, along with Thelma Jones, believe Angelica Brimwell plans to kill her husband. We would rather have her and Grenshaw arrested for that crime than anything concerning SLI."

"Why is that?" Sam asked.

"We're not ready to move on SLI. We don't want any red flags raised prematurely."

Sidney tucked a loose strand of hair behind her ear. "Does that have anything to do with why Marcus Brimwell wasn't detained when the police discovered his fingerprints on the pistol that killed Mara Uzelac?"

"Marcus Brimwell had an engagement that evening. It's been checked out. Someone else had to be the shooter. The detectives handling the case weren't convinced it wasn't Aden Uzelac."

Aware of protocol regarding ongoing investigations, Sidney tapped her fingertips on the armrest and said, "You wouldn't be discussing any of this with us if you didn't want our help in some way. What would you like us to do?"

"We knew about Payton Russen's contracts with SLI and the contract Grenshaw initiated under the name of Marcus Brimwell. We did not suspect they had a bearing on Mara Uzelac's murder until you made a late night visit to SLI's office. That was when we stepped up surveillance on Victor Grenshaw and discovered Angelica Brimwell's involvement. It appeared they were working on a scheme where Marcus Brimwell would serve some time behind bars. Today, you uncovered a letter that contradicts the conversations we heard between the two."

"Can you explain why they wanted Aden dead?" she asked, suspecting it was about the date on the Brimwell contract but wanted confirmation.

"Assuming they managed to get Marcus Brimwell indicted over the SLI contract, they couldn't have Aden Uzelac around to testify on Marcus Brimwell's behalf. You pinned it. The contract date."

Sam scratched his chin. "Brimwell's loaded. He's got plenty of dough. Even without Aden's testimony, it would be hard to say the guy wanted a bigger piece of the action on that bridge and risked everything for more bucks."

"His wealth wouldn't sway the jury that he's innocent," Walt said. "In fact, it could have the opposite effect—greed."

"They failed to kill Aden," Sidney said. "How did they plan to prevent him from testifying?"

"Their plans go back to December. Since Brimwell respected all of Uzelac's opinions and Uzelac was considered second in charge at the office, they wanted something on him. Grenshaw and Angelica Brimwell knew how devoted he was to his wife. In January, they set up the Kate affair. Uzelac blew their plans when he confessed to Mara."

The image of Aden suffering in jail flashed into Sidney's mind. Anger boiled up inside her. She kept her face immobile, stared at the agents, and said, "The police claim his affair was the motive for the shooting. Since you knew the truth, why didn't you come forward?"

"We only learned about the fabricated affair recently," Walt justified. "Moving along, they revised their plan and started working on another way to keep Aden silent. From what we've been able to piece together—and Russen confirmed part of it today—he was to restrain Uzelac at gunpoint. Grenshaw would kill him and leave Brimwell's 9mm Luger at the crime scene along with a few torn sections of the SLI contract and the agreement."

"You said earlier that Marcus Brimwell had an alibi that night," Sidney commented.

"Yes, but Grenshaw and Angelica Brimwell believed he was at the office alone."

Sam stretched his long legs out in front of him and crossed his ankles. "Well, Payton blew that scheme for them. What was their next move?"

"Grenshaw suspected that one of you would come up with evidence that would free Uzelac. If you didn't, he'd be the Good Samaritan, step forward and say Uzelac never had an affair with Kate Morrison. He had been recording some of the conversations he had with her. Before Grenshaw turned over the tapes, they would've been doctored up.

"While you were investigating Mara's murder, he pointed you to SLI, wanting you to uncover the contract between Brimwell and SLI. That's why he had Russen buy the Suburban and place SLI signs on each side. He arranged for the surveillance and the theft at Jordan's office." Walt nodded toward Sam.

"Well, it worked," Sam said.

Sidney leaned forward in her seat. "With Aden free, they were going to make another attempt on his life?"

"Yes. We lack details."

"Angelica wants Marcus dead, not imprisoned," Sam said. "Knocking off Aden wouldn't help her there."

"She needs someone to take the fall for killing Marcus Brimwell. We've heard enough to know the plot is an elaborate smokescreen to ring in Grenshaw. Angelica Brimwell wanted him to believe they were conspiring together against Brimwell. She told him he could take her husband's place in the bedroom and at Brimwell Engineering."

A look of disdain flashed on Sidney's face. "The plan to kill Aden was just to convince Victor Grenshaw they were working together?"

"That, and Aden saw Angelica Brimwell and Lewis Watford in a compromising position. She can't play the role of a grieving widow when she has a witness who could testify otherwise."

Sidney slowly nodded, wondering why Aden had never mentioned that to her. "She spelled out in the letter that Victor was after her, but she was a married woman. It would be a 'he-said-she-said' thing.

Aden could tip the scales, but so could Thelma, Brimwell's cook. Is she safe?"

"No. In fact, we doubt Grenshaw is. His fingerprints are on the Browning retrieved from his condo today. Angelica Brimwell and Grenshaw have never discussed killing Marcus Brimwell."

"You think Victor would have qualms about it? He wouldn't have hesitated to shoot Aden. So why would he suddenly develop a conscience about Brimwell?"

"We don't know yet how it's going to play out. Angelica Brimwell and Watford live in the same house. We didn't hear their initial discussions about the whole scheme. What Grenshaw anticipates he'll get when Marcus Brimwell goes to prison, he could've more easily obtained if they'd killed Brimwell without going down the road they took. Adding extra layers to the crime helps camouflage Angelica Brimwell's role in her husband's death."

"If Victor is somehow shot in the crossfire, all the better for Angelica," Sidney remarked. "Lewis might make sure that happens. He'll probably be the one to take care of Aden when he gets out. Oh, will he be released tonight?"

"The local authorities aren't going to release him until tomorrow morning."

"Will Aden be told Payton's been arrested for Mara's murder?"

"No. That information won't be released to anyone until we give the word."

Sidney hated the idea that Aden would be spending another night behind bars. At the same time, she didn't want him in harm's way. If the news spread about Payton's arrest, it was bound to hit the ears of Victor and Angelica.

"Okay," Sam said. "It sounds like you guys know what's going down. How can we help?"

"By doing what you were already going to do," Walt said. "Go to Brimwell's house and have Thelma Jones let you in."

"You want someone on the inside," Sidney said. "How many are you going to have on the outside?"

"Six."

"All FBI?"

"No. Two will be from the San Diego Police Department."

"Does Marcus Brimwell know?"

"Yes. Not all of Mrs. Jones warnings fell on deaf ears, and a friend of Brimwell's urged him to take precautions after she received an untraceable, threatening letter a couple of months ago."

"What did it say?" Sam asked.

"Confidential."

"Was the friend Elizabeth Heller?" Sidney asked.

"Confidential," he said as a ghost of a smile crossed his lips.

"That's when Marcus Brimwell moved out of the bedroom he'd shared with Angelica," Sidney said. "Did you fill him in then?"

"No. I'm not going to go into details. Let's just say he knows now. He wants justice, so he's agreed to cooperate. He'll be well protected. We'd like both of you to concentrate on Jones and possibly Grenshaw if it appears he's in danger."

"No problem," Sidney said. "Grenshaw can't turn on Angelica if he's dead."

Sam nodded. "Yeah. He'll sing like a canary when he learns he was just a patsy in her game.

The other FBI agent walked over to Walt. "Sir, it's getting to be that time."

Chapter 45

At 10:35 p.m., Sidney's Lexus stopped next to Brimwell's gate. Sam pulled out his cell phone and called Thelma. "We're here....Who?...Yeah." Slipping his phone back into his pocket, he said, "Turn off your headlights. Angelica has company. Victor."

The gate swung open, and Sidney rolled up the driveway with six men following on foot. By the time she had parked at the side of the house, hidden in the shadows, the men had dissipated into the foliage and couldn't be spotted anywhere. "Where's Victor's car?"

Sam shrugged. "Our FBI buddies hear everything we say. They know he's here."

Sidney opened her trunk and grabbed her duffle bag and then moved with Sam around the corner of the building to the back door.

Thelma stood in the open doorway. "Victor and Angelica are in the living room. I'm not sure where Lewis is."

As they stepped over the threshold, Sam asked Thelma, "Do we need to whisper?"

"No. Not in the kitchen. They can't hear us in the living room."

"Anything new?" Sam asked.

"After Victor arrived, I heard his loud voice. Something to do with a missing gun. Then it sounded like Angelica was trying to calm him down. From a few of Victor's words I picked up, I think he's going to be leaving soon. He probably doesn't want to be here, or at least not in the house, when Marcus gets home. Maybe if the gun they want to use is missing, nothing will happen tonight."

"We'll stick around just in case," he said, patting Thelma's shoulder. "Can you give us a layout of the house?"

"Through that door," Thelma said, pointing at a closed door that swung on hinges, "is the pantry. All the dishes, silverware, and serving pieces are kept in there. The door on the other side of the pantry leads to the dining room. Across the foyer is the living room. The library is behind it. You can enter the library through the living room and the hallway off the foyer. It's a wide foyer with a spiral staircase running on one side. Past the stairwell, the hallway divides in two directions. Going straight takes you to the pool and turning left leads to a one-story wing that has a workout room and a bedroom. Upstairs are five bedrooms."

"Where does Brimwell sleep?" Sidney asked.

"Upstairs. The master bedroom is at the end on your right. Marcus used to sleep there with Angelica. When he moved out, he took the bedroom at the other end of the hall. Those two bedrooms have balconies that overlook the pool."

"Where do those doors go?" Sam asked, making a sweeping gesture toward two doors on the opposite side of the kitchen.

Thelma pointed to the one tucked into the corner. "That one goes to the patio surrounding the pool, and my room is through the other one. It's more than a bedroom. I also have a sitting room and a bathroom."

Sam's eyes fixed on the door. "If someone wants to enter your space, do they have to go through the kitchen?"

Thelma nodded. "Yes."

"What time did Victor get here?" Sidney asked.

"Around nine-thirty."

Sidney lowered her bag to the floor, took out her directional mike, and aimed it toward the living room.

Thelma directed her index finger at the gadget. "What's that?"

"A listening device," Sam explained. "Will Lewis come in here to get anything?"

"Not at this hour. Angelica has already told me I could retire for the evening. The only person who might wander into the kitchen would be Marcus." She smiled. "He still sometimes likes cookies and milk before he goes to bed."

An indistinct but loud, angry male voice drifted into the kitchen. Sidney slipped on an earbud to listen to the argument.

"Why don't you go in there," Sam said, motioning toward

Thelma's door. "We'll make sure nothing happens to Mr. Brimwell."

"But...but... I want to stay here. Marcus might need me," Thelma said, her face full of concern for the man who was her employer and friend.

It took Sam a few minutes to convince Thelma she should leave the protection of Brimwell to Sidney and him.

When Thelma was safe behind the closed door, Sam asked, "What's going on?"

"Victor's a little ticked off. He thinks we broke into his condo and stole Kate's gun. From the pounding of feet, it sounds like he's pacing. Oh..." She stopped talking when another voice came through the earbud.

"Mrs. Brimwell?" Lewis said.

"Yes, Lewis," Angelica replied.

"Mr. Brimwell should be home soon."

"I better get out of here," Victor said.

The sound of pounding feet came again through the digital mike, followed by whispers. The voices were too soft for Sidney to pick up any words.

A loud, crashing sound erupted from the living room, like a piece of furniture had tipped over and landed on a hard-surfaced floor.

Thelma poked her head out her door. "What was that?"

Sam raised his hand in a stop motion. "Stay inside," he ordered.

Reluctantly, she closed the door.

The banging of furniture, metal scraping the floor, and creaking noises flowed from the direction of the living room.

"He looks dead," Lewis's voice sprang through the mike.

"He's not. Remember the plan. Have you got him?" Angelica said, followed by the unmistakable sound of something heavy—probably a body—being dragged along the floor.

Sidney turned toward Sam. "Victor has either been knocked out or maybe drugged. Angelica could've slipped a knock-out drug in his drink."

"Yeah, whatta sap. Fell for the wrong gal. She led him by the nose every step of the way. Angelica and Lewis—wouldn't be surprised if he's also being used—will keep Victor out of the way until the deed is done and then blame him. From the game plan Victor's been working on, the next victim should be Aden, not Brimwell. Getting Kate's gun now makes sense to me. She'd be accused of Aden's murder—jilted lover scenario."

"The Feds are taking care of Brimwell. If we're going to protect Victor, we need to get closer." Sidney slowly swung open the kitchen door to the pantry. With Sam right behind her, she crept into the dining room.

Angelica's voice blurted through the mike. "Let me make sure she's not in the kitchen." Shuffling feet moving along the floor became louder.

Sidney ducked down on the far side of the table. Sam edged back into the kitchen and hid at the end of a row of cabinets near the back door, a vantage point where he could clearly keep a watchful eye on Thelma's door.

Angelica walked through the dining room, opened the pantry door, and stepped across the floor. She pushed the kitchen door open and peered inside. Letting the door swing closed behind her, she headed back into the living room. "She's called it a day. But I know as soon as she hears a gunshot, she'll come bursting out of her room."

"Baby, you think of everything," Lewis said, followed by smooching sounds.

Sidney listened intensely to heavy breathing and wild gasps while Sam inched back into the dining room and moved quietly around the table. They stealthily worked their way toward the open, oversized dining room door and ducked into the corner, out of sight from anyone walking by. Even though they couldn't see Angelica and Lewis, they were close enough to them that Sidney no longer needed the directional mike. She removed the earbud and slid the equipment on the floor.

"The bullets?" Angelica asked.

"Not a one in his room," Lewis said.

"You left his gun, right?"

"Yeah, baby, I followed all your instructions. Marcus's other gun is right here, ready to take care of Victor after he shoots Marcus and Thelma." Lewis chuckled.

Now Sidney and Sam knew their scheme—Angelica and Lewis planned on framing the unconscious Victor for the killings before they killed him. Sidney wondered if Lewis would survive after that deed had been accomplished.

"Honey," Angelica said, "Marcus will be walking through that door any minute. Keep Victor company until I come for you."

"Got it," Lewis said, and heavy footsteps strode away on the hardwood floor.

Sam and Sidney caught a glimpse of him through the crack by the hinges as he trudged down the foyer. After a door snapped shut, a soft clicking sound came from the living room, a familiar sound they had both heard before.

"Huh?" Sam whispered, cocking an eyebrow, knowing Angelica had just slipped a magazine in a pistol.

"No survivors," Sidney commented.

The front door creaked open.

"Hi, Honey, how was your trip?" Angelica asked in a sweet tone.

"Fine," Brimwell said. "I thought you'd be in bed by now."

"I wanted to spend some time with you when you got home."

"Angelica, let's not do this tonight," Brimwell said, sounding exasperated. "I'm worn out. I'm hitting the sack." His footfalls pounded up the stairs, echoing through the house.

A minute later, Angelica hurried through the foyer and turned down the left hallway. Muffled voices came from that direction. She stepped back into the foyer with Lewis by her side.

"I'll wait until there isn't any light coming from under his door," Lewis whispered as he moved to the stairwell.

"Then it's time," Angelica said softly. "I'll be right up."

Darkness descended around Sidney and Sam as lights were flipped off. They heard footsteps going up stairs. Then the house became silent. The only sounds Sidney could still hear were the pounding of her heart and Sam's breathing. Beams of light streamed from outside through the edges of the drapes, illuminating part of the house.

Concealed in the shadows, Sidney and Sam padded quietly into the foyer. Hearing movement at the top of the stairs, they pushed their backs against the wall with their hands resting on the handles of their weapons.

Sidney focused on the two dark figures standing in the upstairs hallway and watched them go in opposite directions.

The clicking sound of a key turning in a lock and a door being forced open drifted down the stairs.

Sam darted around her. She grabbed his arm. "Remember your promise," she mouthed, referring to the promise they made to let the FBI handle the Brimwell attack.

A gunshot rang out. That promise was forgotten as Sidney and Sam drew their pistols, bolted up the steps and turned toward Brimwell's bedroom.

"FBI. Put down the weapon!" a man shouted from inside Brimwell's bedroom.

Sidney spotted Angelica coming out of the master bedroom and racing down the stairs. Knowing Angelica was armed and Victor was lying unconscious in some room, she said, "I'll get her," and charged after Angelica with Sam on her tail.

At the same time, the pantry door flew open, and Thelma rushed through the dining room. Sam swung around, quickly holstered his weapon, and grabbed her. "Go back to your room."

"But Brimwell."

"He's okay," Sam said, hoping he was right as he led her away.

Sidney tackled Angelica and pinned her against the floor.

"Get off me!" Angelica huffed while she squirmed.

Sidney ran her hand down the woman's body until she felt the handle of a pistol in Angelica's skirt pocket, yanked out the weapon, and tossed it farther down the foyer.

Angelica shouted, "Lewis shot my husband! He'll be after me next!"

"Angelica, save it. We've heard the plot."

"You tapped my phone? That's illegal."

Sidney rose to her feet and aimed her Glock at Angelica.

A police officer stepped through the front door. Angelica leaped to her feet, ran to him, and gripped his arm. "Thank God you're here." She pointed toward Sidney. "That woman," she said, her voice trembling. "That woman and my butler shot my husband."

Sidney rolled her eyes and shook her head. "Angelica, he knows. Save your drama for the courtroom."

Angelica's eyes darted to the officer's face. "How dare you break into my house like this?"

Ignoring Angelica's remarks, the policeman began reciting her Miranda warning as he slapped handcuffs on her wrists.

Sam stepped out into the foyer through the dining room doorway. "You okay?" he asked Sidney.

Sidney straightened her blouse and brushed off her slacks. "Yeah," she said with her eyes fixed on the handle of Angelica's weapon. It was covered with a transparent, plastic material. She pulled a bag out of her pocket and carefully put the weapon in it.

"How's Thelma?"

"Brimwell's talking to her. The FBI got him outside before this all went down."

"That's what I expected, but sometimes things go wrong. Where did the bullet end up?"

"Killed a sleeping dummy," Sam said with a smile.

Lewis's hands were handcuffed behind his back, and he hung his head while two officers escorted him down the stairs. Walt, the FBI agent in charge, along with one of his men trotted behind them.

"Where's Victor?" Walt asked as the officers led Lewis to a patrol car.

"Haven't had a chance to search for him yet," Sidney said. "Do you know if he was knocked out or drugged?"

"Drugged," Walt replied without hesitation. "Angelica has a close doctor friend, and we saw her slip it into Victor's drink."

Sidney assumed they had planted a camera somewhere in the living room and felt irritated they hadn't shared that information with her. "Saw?"

"We managed to plant a camera in the living room yesterday."

"And you didn't think it was important to share that with us?" Sidney said with an edge to her voice.

"Oversight," Walt said.

Sidney didn't believe that for a minute but saw no point in arguing with the FBI agent.

"Since you could see everything happening on the main floor, why are we here?" Sam asked.

"We only had enough time to plant one camera without being spotted. We didn't have eyes everywhere."

"How are you going to keep SLI out of this after you arrest Victor?" Sidney asked.

"Leave it to us," Walt replied, moving past Sidney with an FBI agent in tow.

Chapter 46

Sidney picked up Chas at the airport and then drove to the county jail. Aden was due to be released at 10:00 a.m., and she sensed she needed to be there. She had shared with Chas how she felt whenever she saw Aden and knew Chas worried about how she might react when there weren't bars or panels separating them.

"Babe, you've done your job. Do you really think this is necessary?"

She squeezed his thigh. "Chas, something inside me is saying I have to do this. I can't explain it. Maybe it's Mara. I don't know." Sidney glanced at his features lined with concern. She hated causing him any grief. He had been her rock through the whole situation starting with her chest pains, helping her solve the crime by giving her data, and providing her with a nurse, Jean, to watch over her if the pain returned. She felt torn between driving straight to the hotel or continuing on to the jail, but she couldn't shake the feeling she had to go see Aden regardless of Chas's anxiety.

Shortly before 10:00 a.m., Sidney parked in a stall 100 feet from the jail exit and gazed around. "I thought I'd see Aden's family."

"He didn't want his children to visit him while he was locked up," Chas said, "so he won't want them to see him leaving jail."

They got out of the Lexus. Sidney looped around the vehicle and stood next to Chas by the passenger door.

"You're not going in?"

"No. I'm going to say good-bye to him after he's been set free."

They waited in silence as their eyes focused on the exit. She felt her stomach churning and a tinge of fear that Mara's desires for Aden might emerge in her body when she saw him. Sidney forced herself to rein in those unwelcome thoughts and maintain a solemn expression on her face.

Fifteen minutes later, the door opened. Fowler and Aden stepped out into the parking lot.

Relieved that seeing him hadn't sparked Mara's emotions, Sidney said, "I'll be back soon." Strolling away from Chas, she saw a look of anxiety creep across his face.

As she moved closer to Aden, she expected a surge of emotions. Nothing happened. She was free from all the feelings that had dominated her each time she had seen Aden in the past. She sighed and then greeted the two men.

"Sidney, thank you," Aden said. His face still looked drawn, his eyes lacked luster, and his breathing seemed forced.

"Your kids are going to be so happy to see you," she said with a smile, wishing she could somehow cheer him up just a little.

"They wanted to come, but I need a few hours of freedom to rejuvenate before I see them."

A strange sensation suddenly surged through her body. She lost control of her arms and they wrapped around Aden's neck. Her head bent back and her mind went blank. Gazing at his face, an unnatural voice sprang from her throat. "Adie. My dear Adie. I can't wait a lifetime to be with you again. I'm coming back to you. I won't look the same, but you'll know it's me by the way I walk and brush my hair away from my face. My eyes will glow when I see your face. I won't know you, so you'll have to court me all over again. When you no longer feel me lying next to you in bed, it'll be time for you to look for me. I'll be strolling on the beach. The same place we met the first time. Oh, Adie, find me." Sidney pulled Aden's head down and kissed him passionately.

"Hey, hey, Sidney," Fowler said, standing behind her, blocking Chas's view of her caressing Aden. "Your husband."

Something snapped in her. She blinked and found herself staring into Aden's eyes with her arms wrapped around him. Sidney dropped her arms to her side and backed away from him. "What...what happened?" she asked as she tried to compose herself.

"You...you," Fowler stammered. "You talked to Aden. Are you okay?"

A sense of peace flowed through her. She inhaled deeply. "I couldn't be better." Then she noticed tears streaming down Aden's cheeks. She patted his arm. "Aden, you're free. Life will be good again someday."

The corners of his mouth curved up. "I know," he said, wiping his face with the back of his hand. "It's going to be hard waiting." He reached out and took both of Sidney's hands in his. "Sidney, I will always be grateful to you."

"Goodbye, Aden," she said and then turned and hurried to Chas.

He folded her into his arms and smothered her lips with his. She raised her chin, met his glowing blue eyes, and hummed their favorite tune.

He squeezed her tightly. "I got you, Babe," said the man she would love forever.

THE END

ABOUT THE AUTHOR

Inge-Lise Goss was born in Denmark, raised in Utah, and graduated from the University of Utah, magna cum laude. She is a certified public accountant and worked in that field for more than twenty years.

Goss lives in the foothills of Red Rock Canyon with her husband and their dog, Bran. She spends most of her time in her den writing stories. There, with her muse by her side, her imagination has no boundaries, and her dreams come alive. When she's not pounding away on the keyboard, she can be found reading, rowing, or trying to perfect her golf game, which she fears is a lost cause.

www.Inge-LiseGoss.com

www.ingramcontent.com/pod-product-compliance
Lightning Source LLC
Chambersburg PA
CBHW071256170626
46809CB00001B/242